FIVE TRIBES

ALSO BY BRIAN NELSON

The Last Sword Maker

FIVE TRIBES

BRIAN NELSON

BLACK STONE PUBLISHING

Published in 2022 by Blackstone Publishing
Cover and book design by Sean M. Thomas
Map by Amy Craig
Cover art by Josh Newton

Printed in the United States of America
Originally published in hardcover by Blackstone Publishing in 2021

First paperback edition: 2022
ISBN 979-8-200-83422-8
Fiction / Thrillers / Technological

Version 1

CIP data for this book is available
from the Library of Congress

Blackstone Publishing
31 Mistletoe Rd.
Ashland, OR 97520

www.BlackstonePublishing.com

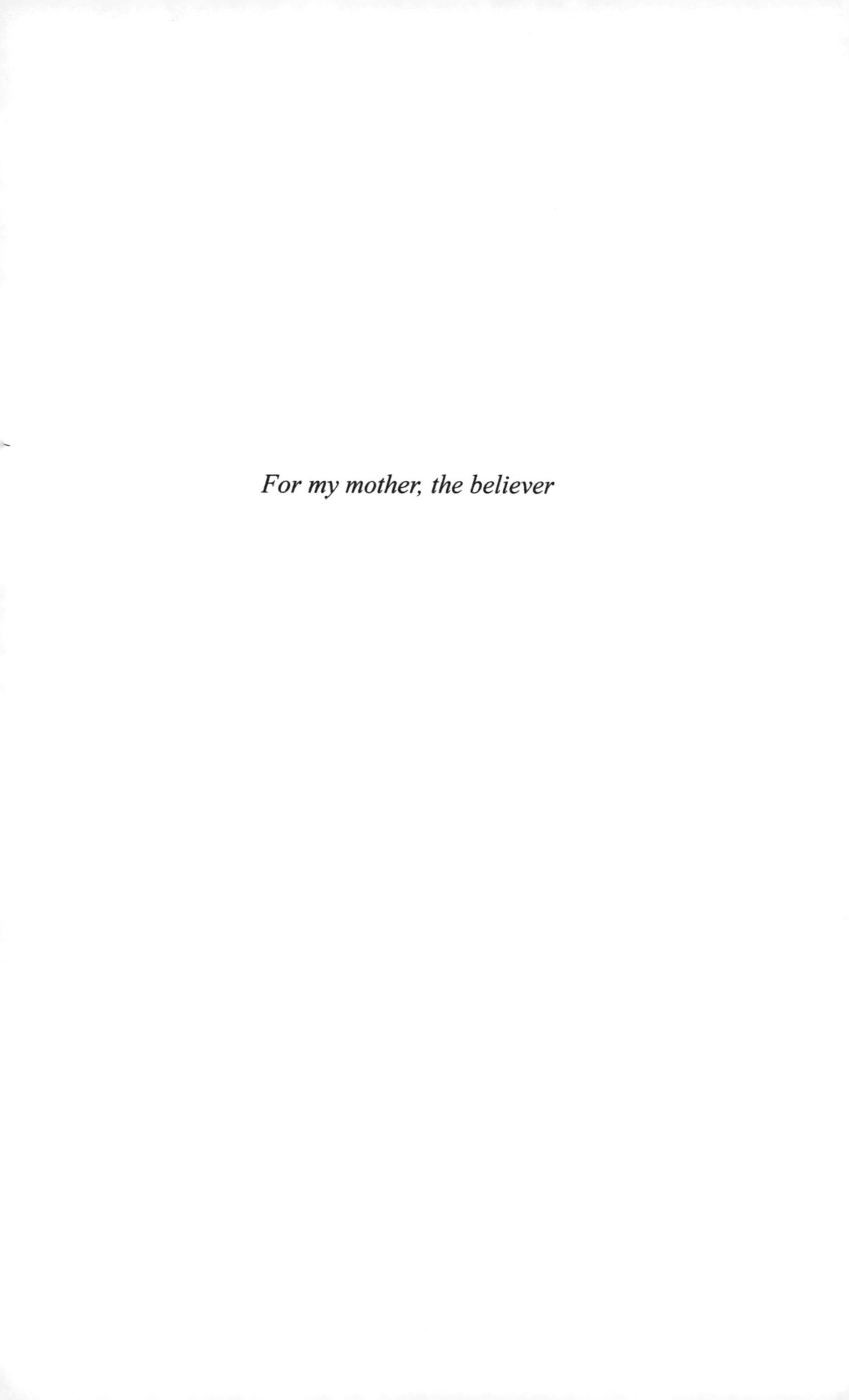

For my mother, the believer

First Freedom and then Glory—when that fails,
Wealth, vice, corruption.

—Lord Byron,
Childe Harold's Pilgrimage, Canto IV

The New York Times

NEW YORK, OCTOBER 17, 2026

TURMOIL IN CHINA

Protests Continue as Wave of Democracy Sweeps Globe

by R. N. Feldman

BEIJING—Protests and violence continued in China for the third straight week, with large-scale demonstrations spreading to more than a dozen cities. Tens of millions of Chinese citizens took to the streets again yesterday, demanding that the government meet a long list of demands including an end to government corruption, better environmental safeguards, release of political prisoners, and free elections.

The scope of the protests appears to be causing major rifts in China's leadership, with President Zhao being conspicuously absent in recent days, and there are persistent rumors of a shakeup within the politburo.

China's mounting crisis is being called a "perfect storm" by some experts, who say that many of the nation's problems have been building for decades. But others point to the recent wave of similar changes across the globe. "On almost every continent—from South America to Africa, from Asia to Europe—we are seeing major shifts away from authoritarianism and toward democracy," said Thomas Williams, former UN Ambassador. Williams cited recent regime changes in countries such as Cuba, Guinea-Bissau, Laos, and Venezuela as evidence of a “revolutionary transformation” of the geopolitical landscape.

“Some of these changes are coming from surprises at the ballot box,” Williams said. “Others from mass protests and strikes, some from armed rebellion, and still others from unexpected circumstances, such as the sudden death of Venezuelan President Muñoz.”

Professor Katherine Li of the Harvard Kennedy School agreed that when taken as a whole the changes amount to a fourth wave of democratization. “The tectonic plates are still shifting,” she said. “But if democracy really is taking hold in these countries, then this will be bigger than the fall of the Berlin Wall and will likely be remembered as a moment when the whole face of the globe was dramatically reshaped.”

PROLOGUE

GOD IS AMERICAN

"Nearly all men can stand adversity, but if you want to test a man's character, give him power."

—Robert Ingersoll

As Vice Admiral James Curtiss set the newspaper down on his desk that morning, he realized that he had become one of the most powerful men in the world. The evidence was right in front of him, spread out in black and white.

. . . A revolutionary transformation of the geopolitical landscape.

And the best part about it: nobody had a clue.

Yet he still wondered if they had gone into Venezuela too quickly. The left-wing media had cried foul, of course, saying it was a conspiracy, a black op by the CIA. But then again, they would have said that even if it weren't true.

Ironically, this time it was.

The important thing was that there was no evidence. The autopsy of the dead president showed nothing more than common pneumonia, and the subsequent election results had been perfectly clean.

Still, he had to admit the op had been rushed and sloppy. And that was Curtiss's own fault. He had told the Joint Chiefs they needed one more practice run, one more time to get the kinks out of the new technology before they took on China. But that was only part of the reason. The truth was Curtiss had wanted Muñoz . . . bad. Because Muñoz was the worst sort of third-world despot—arrogant, fanatical, and incompetent. He had run his oil-rich country into the ground, was responsible for mass starvation and the needless deaths of hundreds of thousands of his own people. But there was one particular fact that had sped Curtiss's hand: Muñoz's incompetence led to daily blackouts that killed dozens of patients in the nation's hospitals every day. When the power went out, the older patients on respirators and the infants in incubators died in a senseless and completely avoidable daily purge. Yet his intel told him that the lights at the presidential palace always stayed on.

Curtiss couldn't let that lie. He knew he should. As a soldier, it wasn't his business to decide what was right or wrong. His job was to stay focused on what was best for America. But the thought of those senseless deaths had gnawed at him, so he used his influence to push the mission timeline. And that wasn't all. Curtiss made sure that the "pneumonia" that killed Muñoz did so painfully slowly, giving him the terrifying feeling of perpetual drowning. Curtiss had ordered a nanosite transmitter and microphone put in Muñoz's bedroom. The sound of the man's suffering gave Curtiss nothing but deep satisfaction.

Curtiss knew that most people wouldn't understand that, but to him it was a simple fact of life: some people needed to die. He just happened to be fortunate enough to be one of the few who got to decide who should remain among us and who should not. By a mixture of dedication, sacrifice, sweat, and luck, he had arrived at a critical moment in history—as the wielder of a technology that most people could only perceive as magic.

One thing's for certain, Curtiss thought, *global politics has never been quite so interesting.*

Within the past four months, he and the Joint Chiefs had accomplished things that were unthinkable just a year ago. They had fixed many of America's disastrous foreign policy mistakes from the previous thirty years as well as undermined half a dozen international scumbags in the process. After so many years of witnessing America's decline on the world stage, they now had the technology to turn things around. The world was their oyster once more. Or, as his boss Admiral Garrett had said after the Cuba operation, "It looks like God is American again."

And they were just getting started.

Once a new government was installed in China, Curtiss would move on to the Middle East, perhaps do a little tweaking in central Europe, then move on to the last domino, the great bear. The thought literally made his mouth water. Purging Russia of its kleptocratic system of oligarchs and former KGB agents—the ones who had yanked the country back into a totalitarian dictatorship just at the moment she was casting off the yoke of seventy years of Soviet rule—well, taking care of them would be the crowning achievement of his career.

Once that was done, Curtiss could finally retire knowing that he had done good, that he had made the world a freer, more open, more democratic place. That was what mattered to him. It would mean that all the terrible things he had done in his long career in the name of keeping America safe would have been worth it.

God is American again.

That wasn't quite true, of course, but it was okay because the most powerful technology in the world was.

★★★

At that moment Curtiss's personal iSheet rang. One glance told him it was the call he'd been waiting for. It was from the USS *Gerald R. Ford* strike group, presently off the coast of Angola.

The man on the other end of the line was one of the most valuable members of Curtiss's team, which was saying something. As the leader of the Naval Research Lab, Curtiss had over three thousand military scientists and computer engineers on his staff. But in the last eighteen months, this man, Eric Hill, only twenty-seven years old, had been responsible for some of their biggest breakthroughs. No one understood the new science as well as he did.

Curtiss answered the call.

"How's carrier life treating you?"

"Better than I'd expected. The food is surprisingly good, and I'm staying in shape. Although jogging eight miles a day on a treadmill is mind-numbingly boring."

"Shit, you've got it good," he said. "My first cruise was on a Cyclone class patrol boat, it was only fifty-two meters long—zero privacy, no gym, awful food. It was pure hell." Curtiss laughed at the memory. "So what have you got?"

"Not much. The logging camp in Botswana was

deserted. We flew two drone flights over the area but we couldn't ascertain where they'd gone."

Curtiss cursed under his breath. "Anything else?"

"Yes, some good news. Satellite intel found two other mining operations. One in Botswana and one in Namibia. We are currently underway and should be in position to fly over the Botswana camp by noon tomorrow."

Curtiss nodded. "I know it's a painstaking job. But each camp you knock off your list puts you closer to finding him."

"I know. Don't worry, our morale is high. We are all committed to this, especially me. It's the least I can do." Curtiss thought back to Hill's harrowing mission to China. Just six months ago he'd been involved in a secret operation to infiltrate and sabotage China's rival weapons program. What Hill was doing now would tie up the final loose end from that mission.

"Okay, keep me posted," Curtiss said. "I know you can get this done."

"Yes, Admiral, I will, and thank you."

Curtiss hung up. They had been searching for two weeks but still nothing.

Despite all the amazing advances they'd made in the past eighteen months, when it came to this—finding one man—they were reduced to twentieth-century technology, satellite reconnaissance and drones.

Perhaps we haven't made so much progress after all.

All in good time, he reassured himself. The technology would be able to handle a job like this soon enough.

That was the beauty of the new science, which was really the merging of three sciences—genetic engineering, artificial intelligence, and nanotechnology. It was versatile. Insanely versatile, in fact. Why? Because it was alive and could evolve. The same technology that could grow into a synthetic virus to kill a dictator could also make a fighter jet both lighter and stronger, could protect a soldier from gunfire, and could make a young man want to protest against his government.

In theory there was nothing it couldn't do.

And that was why the Africa mission was so important. It appeared simple—rescue a single man from a Chinese prison camp—but in many ways it was going to be the most audacious mission of all. For the first time they were going to use the new technology in almost every facet of the operation, from the aircraft that delivered the rescue team to their armor and camouflage. It would be their first taste of what he suspected all combat operations would be like in the twenty-first century.

PART ONE
THE RAID

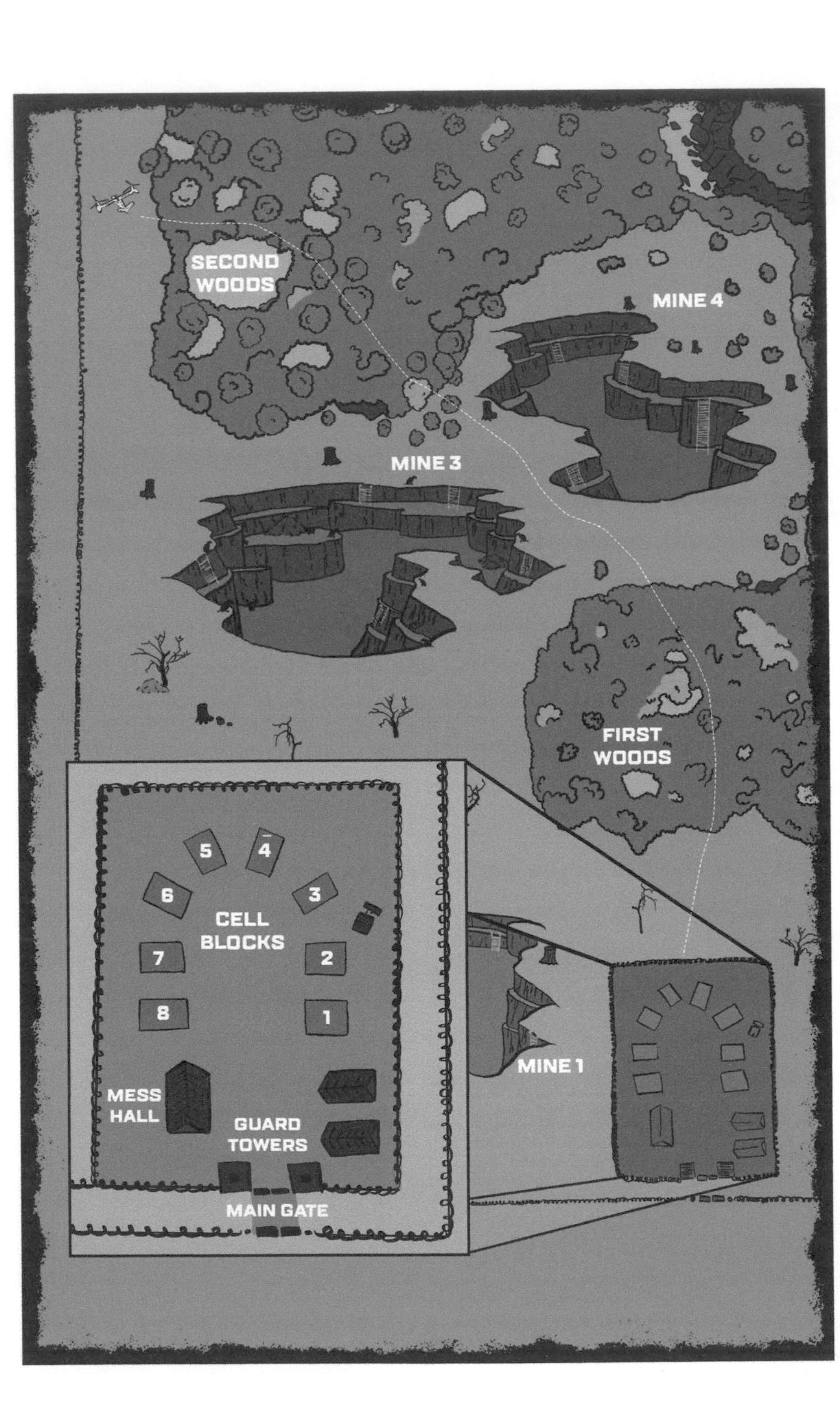
SECOND WOODS
MINE 4
MINE 3
FIRST WOODS
5
4
6
3
CELL BLOCKS
7
2
8
1
MINE 1
MESS HALL
GUARD TOWERS
MAIN GATE

CHAPTER ONE

THE VOICE IN THE DARKNESS

October 19, 2026
Somewhere near the Namibia-Angola border, Africa

Xiao-ping stood in three feet of muddy water with seven other men as a Caterpillar excavator lowered a two-thousand-pound concrete cylinder into the flooded mining pit. He and his fellow prisoners had to guide the massive tube into the grooves of a second, submerged cylinder. Once in place, the water could be pumped out, allowing the workers to enter the shaft and dig deeper for gold.

Xiao-ping wiped the sweat from his brow. It was only eight thirty in the morning and already the hot African sun was baking his skin and keeping the water around him as warm as a bath. This was Mine Three and, like the two others, it was a huge gash in the middle of the emerald jungle, an open canyon of orange mud and water that stretched five hundred meters long and fifty meters wide. Hundreds of wet, mud-smeared Chinese men worked the pit, passing baskets of earth up the steep slopes. Ropes and wooden ladders rose haphazardly from all sides, and in his ears was the incessant rattle and sputter of a dozen Honda generators straining to suck up the water from the bottom of the pits.

Xiao-ping suddenly coughed, a violent fit that wracked his whole body. When it had passed he looked around nervously. *Please just be a cold!*

Tuberculosis ran rampant in the camp. Thousands of men working in close proximity and sleeping together in large cells where they were packed so tightly that everyone had to lie on their sides. It was the perfect breeding ground for TB. As he worked, the sound of other men coughing was constant in his ears. If it were true, this would be Xiao-ping's third infection since being sentenced to the laogai—China's "Reform through Labor" program. Each infection was harder to beat because the TB became drug resistant. It was a bitter truth: most inmates didn't survive their third infection. If he didn't get proper treatment soon, he was going to die.

He coughed again. *Just a cold*, he told himself.

He looked up and watched as the huge cylinder was slowly lowered into the water. The men used their bodies to guide it into place while one man gave hand signals to the excavator operator. Xiao-ping had done this many times and had learned to use his thighs and forearms—never his hands and fingers—to guide the cylinder.

Suddenly he heard a creaking sound followed by a loud ping. A piece of broken chain zipped by his head, and he jumped back reflexively. There was an enormous splash as the cylinder crashed down. Men screamed. When his eyes cleared, he saw a horrible sight. The young Mongolian man next to him was holding up a hand with no fingers, only a thumb, the blood bubbling out of the four stumps like water out of a drinking fountain. The young man stared at it and began to weep. Not for the pain, but for what it meant. He knew his life was over. Losing the ability to work in the laogai meant there was no need to keep you alive.

On the far side of the cylinder another man was still trapped. Xiao-ping rushed to him and saw that it was his friend, Nur Zakir, a Uyghur imprisoned for his religious beliefs. The cylinder had caught his wrist and yanked him down until his face was just above the waterline. "Xiao-ping, please!" The man panted, "It hurts." Xiao-ping felt under the water and ran his hand down Nur's arm to the wrist before he met the concrete.

"Get a new chain," he called. A search was made, but there were none to be found. A runner was sent to Mine Number Two. They waited ten, then fifteen minutes. All the while Nur was gasping and screaming in pain. But the runner never returned.

Xiao-ping climbed out of the pit and went to the foreman—a dangerous decision as this was considered an "illegal movement." Xiao-ping had once been a lawyer, and while the laogai had drained much of his spirit, he still had moments where he felt he had to fight back . . . as best as he could.

"Please, sir, can we do something to help him? We have the sledgehammers, we can break the cylinder apart."

The foreman glanced at the cylinder and shook his head. "Then I'll have a useless prisoner *and* a broken cylinder."

Xiao-ping returned to the pit and rallied the other men. They wrapped the broken length of chain around the top of the cylinder and heaved. If they could just tip it enough to get the man's hand out . . . but it was useless. He looked up at the foreman, hoping that he would take action, but the man just stood there smoking a cigarette.

"Please help me," Nur kept muttering. "Please . . ."

"I'm sorry," Xiao-ping said. "It's just too heavy." Nur continued to moan for a time, but after an hour the shock began to take its toll. He began to shiver and speak nonsensically, mumbling about his childhood in Uyghur. Then his face turned an ashen grey and he grew quiet.

The foreman ordered the rest of them out of the pit, and the daily work continued around the trapped man.

Xiao-ping was sent to work the sluice box. At dinner he learned that Nur had died before they could remove the cylinder.

That night, Xiao-ping lay awake in his cell, listening to the sixty-four other men around him snore and cough. The death of yet another friend weighed on him and he was overcome by a feeling of helplessness. He had no power to help his friend, no power to change his fate, and little chance of ever going home.

He coughed again, lightly. Once. Twice. Then he was wracked by a long fit.

That's not a cold, said a voice in his head. *You can't deny it any longer.*

He gave a long sigh and coughed again.

If you want to live, you're going to need a full regimen of antibiotics. Easier said than done. The guards gave them the antibiotics until they stopped coughing, then they gave them to someone else.

Just face the truth: You're never going to get better.

You're never going back to China. You are never going to see Lili again.

It was a dangerous thing to accept defeat. If he gave up all hope, he would just die quicker. He'd seen it hundreds of times in the other inmates.

He needed to hold on to something, to believe. And the thing that kept him alive was the memory of Lili. But it had been so long since he had heard from her—four years. Her last letter had arrived just before his transfer to Africa. How precious it was to him, just to hold something in his hands that she had held in hers. *I love you and will wait the rest of my life for you if I have to.* He could still see the words on the page and tried to hold on to them as if they had just been written, but a part of him had grown cynical. *You're a fool to keep believing she's waiting,* the voice said. *You know she's moved on by now. After all, she has no idea you're even alive. And there are so many eligible bachelors in China. Certainly someone has come along . . . and . . .*

He tried not to think about it, yet it was the thing he thought about the most. *You never could give her a child,* the voice in his head said, *so why wouldn't she find a man who could give her what you couldn't?*

He was wracked by another fit of coughing. When it finally stopped, he felt a mass of tissue and phlegm in his mouth. Spitting it into his hand he saw that it was marbled with blood.

The next morning, three new prisoners arrived at the mining camp. This was big news, and the other prisoners began whispering and gossiping about them.

"One of the guards told me they were from the mainland."

"He's lying to you! They came from the copper laogai."

"No, it was timber," another prisoner said. "And they tried to mutiny. That's why they've been beaten." This seemed to make the most sense to Xiao-ping. He had heard rumors about unrest in some of the other camps, perhaps inspired by the protests in China. The new men had bruises on their faces and arms, and they refused to speak to anyone. Clearly they had been threatened and were scared.

And they weren't the only ones who were afraid. Xiao-ping could tell that the managers were nervous: they doubled the guards and gave them orders to crack down on the smallest infractions. By lunch time, three inmates had been disciplined with cattle prods for gossiping.

For the next three days, the newcomers were kept apart from everyone else, but slowly they were integrated into the camp and began to talk.

One of them was a short and frail man who wore thick plastic glasses that he was always pushing up his nose. Despite the glasses, he always seemed to be squinting, as if he couldn't quite make out what he was seeing. At dinner one night he sat next to Xiao-ping. He said his name was Zhang Yong and he admitted that he was a hopeless worker. "At the timber laogai, I crashed two trucks. They put me in solitary confinement for two weeks. The first day back I cut down a tree, and it landed on another truck."

Xiao-ping knew that Yong was the type of man who would die quickly in the mines if he wasn't careful. A person who was clumsy by nature never lasted long, and there was little anyone could do to help them. But for some reason, perhaps because of his cough and the inevitability of his death, Xiao-ping decided to take Yong under his wing. Over the next few days, he taught him how to protect his skin from the sun, how to prevent foot rot by rubbing rotten fruit on his skin, and, most importantly, telling him who in the camp he could trust and who would betray him.

It was soon apparent that it was a miracle that Yong had lasted this long. He had an amazing capacity for breaking everything he touched. The guards noticed too and began to kick him and slap him for the most minor transgressions like spilling his soup in the mess or breaking a shovel.

It also didn't take long for the "Corpse Squad" to single him out. Their leader, Suen Peng, began to taunt Yong. "Don't worry, we will take good care of you," he snickered.

One of the most sadistic ways the guards toyed with the prisoners was by pitting them against each other. Those who spied on or tortured other prisoners for the guards were rewarded with extra rations and little bottles of liquor. The Corpse Squad was a group of prisoners responsible for disposing of dead bodies, a job that terrified the guards because they were so afraid of catching one of the many diseases that ran rampant in the camps. Since the calories from extra rations could mean the difference between life and death, the Corpse Squad often grew impatient if people were not dying fast enough. At first they targeted those who were taken to the infirmary, but eventually they began suffocating people in their sleep. The unspoken rule was that they couldn't touch a man who was meeting their quota in the mines. But a chronic underperformer, like Yong, was fair game.

One night after dinner, Peng and his friends cornered Yong between two of the cellblocks. They began smacking him and pushing him around. When he tried to run, they pinned him to the ground.

"Help! Please somebody," Yong cried. A guard in the watchtower looked down at them but did nothing.

"See? They don't care," Peng said. "You belong to us now."

"Should we break his leg or just suffocate him?" one of the inmates asked.

That's when Xiao-ping shoved Peng to the ground.

"Leave him alone!" He tried to strike a menacing pose but a sudden coughing fit doubled him over.

Peng stood and smiled. "You don't sound so good, Xiao-ping. Maybe you should check into the infirmary." His friends chuckled.

Xiao-ping got control of himself and raised his fists. Peng circled around him calmly, then rushed forward as if to strike him, stopping at the last second. Xiao-ping flinched and cowered, and Peng laughed at him. But then Xiao-ping noticed Peng looking over his shoulder to the guard tower. The guard was now watching them closely. While Yong was prey for the corpse squad, Xiao-ping was not. He was a good worker and always made quota.

"Fine," Peng said, addressing Xiao-ping, but loud enough so the guard could hear. "We can wait. But sooner or later, you're both going in the pit." He and the other men left.

Xiao-ping helped Yong to his feet. Wet mud made his clothes stick to his skin. "Thank you," he said. "But what did they mean by the pit?"

"Do you ever hear the hyenas going wild at night?"

Yong nodded.

"The pit is an old mine at the far end of the camp where they put the dead. The hyenas can smell the bodies, but they can't get through the fence. That's why they go wild."

"I don't want to go there," Yong said.

Xiao-ping wrapped his arm around Yong's shoulder and led him back toward their cellblock. "Me either," he said.

The next day he and Yong were on top of the sluice bucket, using a high-powered hose on tons and tons of earth. No one could hear them over the rush of the water. Xiao-ping took the chance to ask about the mutiny. Yong looked around furtively, nodded slowly, then began to tell the story.

"It started early in the morning," Yong began. "Six or seven prisoners attacked the guards with chainsaws. That was the signal for the other prisoners to rise up. I don't think I'll ever get it out of my head, the men cutting into the guards, the sound of it   The fighting probably only lasted a half hour, but it felt like forever."

"How many escaped?"

"At least forty. Some fled into the woods, others stole trucks and got away. But many died. Some of the guards were ready and were merciless."

"And what happened to you? Did they catch you?"

Yong hung his head in shame. "I was too afraid to fight or run. I just lay on the ground playing dead. I know you think I'm a coward. But you have to understand how terrified I was."

"It's okay," Xiao-ping said, "I'm not judging you."

The story gave Xiao-ping much to think about. Such a mutiny would be much harder here than in a timber camp, where the inmates had access to "weapons" like chainsaws and were constantly moved around. Here, the entire mining site—seven square kilometers—had ten-foot fences topped with razor wire surrounding it. Inside was the prison compound, which also had eight-foot fences, razor wire, and guard posts. Any attempt of mutiny here felt like suicide.

"And what news from home?"

"Just rumors. They say the Central Committee is pushing to end the laogai, but of course the business conglomerates are opposed—they need the free labor. Many prisoners think now is the best chance we'll get. Better to risk death once in escaping, than risk death every day as a slave."

Xiao-ping nodded slowly. Would he try to escape if there were a mutiny? He thought back to his life as a human rights lawyer. Once upon a time he had been a leader who could rally people and inspire them to action. But that was twelve years ago, another lifetime, and he no longer thought of fighting or justice anymore, only survival. And what about Lili? The guards were always warning them that if they escaped, their families in China would suffer the consequences. But now, with the upheaval in China, the mutineers were betting that there would be no retribution. But what if reform didn't last? What then? Xiao-ping realized it was a risk he couldn't take. The more he thought about it, the more he realized there was little he could do. He had to hope reform would come to China . . . and quickly.

Over the next three days something strange began to happen: Xiao-ping began to feel better. His cough came less frequently, and he felt stronger. It didn't make sense, but his body was beating the TB. He thought that perhaps it was a reward for helping Yong. Good karma. Whatever the reason, he was getting stronger and with that strength came something he hadn't felt in years.

Hope.

★★★

It was fifteen days after Yong arrived that he heard the voice.

"Xiao-ping!" the voice said. "Xiao-ping! Wake up!" He opened his eyes and sat up. Everyone around him was fast asleep. He looked into the gloom for the man who had spoken to him . . . in English. He heard three men snoring. Nearby a man coughed. He lay down again. "I'm dreaming," he muttered and lay his head down.

"No, you're not dreaming," the voice said. "This is going to sound strange, but I've placed a microphone in your ear. I can see you and hear you, too."

He sat up again and looked around. He put his finger to one ear, then both ears. "I'm starting to lose my mind," he whispered.

"No, you're not."

"But how?"

"Never mind, it's complicated. But I'm going to get you out of there."

"That's impossible. There's no way to get out."

He heard a kind-hearted laugh. "You'll see."

"Who are you?"

"I'm a friend of Lili's. She's safe in America. Mei is with her."

This has to be a dream, he thought. But it wasn't a bad dream. Perhaps he'd play along. "Prove it," he said.

He heard the friendly laugh again. "Let's see. Your wife

never shuts up, and Mei can eat her weight in butter-pecan ice cream."

Xiao-ping felt a rush of emotion and tears began to stream down his face. It was not so much the man's words, but his relaxed tone that told him that he was telling the truth. It was an undeniable proof of intimacy and it triggered a wellspring of emotions. Suddenly those twelve lost years—more than a quarter of his life—rushed up inside him. Lili had not forgotten him. The love was still there. And Mei, who had only been a bubble on his sister-in-law's belly, was now a girl, a girl with a personality, with likes and hates, charms and faults and a favorite ice cream. And perhaps the most powerful feeling of all was relief. They were safe, safe in a place the party couldn't reach them. For several minutes he sobbed for the lost years.

The voice waited then eventually spoke. "It's going to be all right. Trust me. We have been trying to find you for months. The hard part is over. Can you tell me how you're feeling?"

"I have TB. It's the third time."

"I know," the voice said, "but that's under control now."

"How do you know?"

"I started you on an antibiotic seven days ago. I'm also treating you for your intestinal parasites and I've been putting extra calories in your stomach to build up your strength."

"I'm sorry, but none of this makes sense."

"I know it's confusing, but I work with some very advanced technology. I have the ability to get inside your body if I wish. I can do this . . . and many other things. I hope you take the fact that you are feeling better as proof."

Xiao-ping nodded. He couldn't deny how much stronger he felt.

"Do you believe me?"

"I suppose."

"Well, you are going to have to start trusting me. The guards typically wake you at 6:00 a.m. That's fifteen minutes from now. But in ten minutes things are going to start happening. And when they do, I need you to do exactly as I say. In fact, I'm going to ask you to do some things that might seem very dangerous. But don't be afraid; I'll make sure the guards don't hurt you."

"This is all happening so fast. Can I think about it?"

"I know I'm asking a lot. Perhaps this will help." He heard a click in his ear, as if a phone had been connected.

"Panda bear?"

The tears came again to Xiao-ping's eyes. "Lili? How? Where are you?"

"I'm safe. Don't worry. We are waiting for you. I just need you to be brave a little longer. We are going to get you out. Just do as my friend says."

He nodded to himself, still overwhelmed by his emotions. "I'll try."

"Just think, twenty-four hours from now, we'll be together again."

"Is it really possible?" Xiao-ping said.

"Yes," she said.

"The thought of that will give me all the strength I need."

CHAPTER TWO

THE JUICE

November 4, 2026
Namibia

Seven miles from the Chinese mining camp and forty feet off the ground, Eric Hill sat in back of a Bell V-280 Valor, a tilt-rotor aircraft that was half helicopter, half plane. The body of the Valor looked like a Black Hawk helicopter, broad and squat, but instead of a single rotor on top, it had a fixed wing. At the end of each wing was a Rolls-Royce turboshaft engine and propeller that could tilt up or forward. The hybridization meant that the aircraft was much faster and had a longer range than a conventional helicopter.

Eric was sitting in a specially designed control chamber at the back of the cabin called "the egg." It was from here that Eric could do his very specialized work.

He pulled up the camera in cellblock eight where two hundred prisoners were still sleeping. That was about to change. He checked the time. Yes, in exactly five minutes.

Days before, he had programmed the nanosites to set up tiny cameras throughout the prison compound. The lenses were smaller than a nickel and ethereal—there was distance between the nanosite bundles so they were invisible to the eye. You could pass your hand through one and it would dissolve like a swarm of gnats, only to reorganize a second later.

He opened the commlink to the USS *Gerald Ford*. "This is Zulu Five One, we are ready and in position."

He immediately heard the Captain's response. "This is Viper One Nine to all elements. We are go here for Operation Devil's Island, repeat, go for Devil's Island."

Each team leader reported in, acknowledging the order.

"Roger," Eric said, "I'm going to juice them up."

In the cockpit Major Dave Winfred kept the Valor in a low holding pattern over dense jungle, watching as his rotor wash stirred the treetops below him. It was still dark, but his night vision let him see the trees as a lime-green ocean stretching out in every direction. There was a sliver of a moon, a waning crescent, approaching the horizon. Across the night sky he could see a slow armada of stratocumulus clouds drifting in from the ocean. It was the perfect time for night ops, as the low moonlight enhanced their tactical advantage of being able to see in the dark.

Winfred had to admit he'd been skeptical three months ago when he'd gotten the call from Special Operations Command that he was needed at the Asymmetrical Warfare Center at Fort A.P. Hill in Virginia. Winfred was a Night Stalker with the 160th out of Fort Campbell, Kentucky, home to many of the best helicopter and Valor pilots in the country. Even in that distinguished company, Winfred was considered a cut above the rest. Between Iraq, Afghanistan, and Syria, he had been flying in combat zones for almost fifteen years. Not surprisingly, he had come to expect to be given the most interesting missions and the very best toys. Truth be told, it felt a bit beneath his experience and pay grade to waste his time helping some egghead scientist try to refit a perfectly good Valor, then fly it around the hills of Virginia.

His first hint that this might not be a total ass suck was when he'd landed at Fort A.P. Hill and saw Master Chief Sawyer out on the tarmac. The old SEAL had given a sly grin and said, "Ah, my favorite taxi driver."

"Well, if it isn't Methuselah himself," Winfred said. "I must be getting close to my retirement date if you're here."

"That date has come and gone for me. They're just trying to kill me off now."

Winfred laughed, and the two embraced. "So what's this all about?"

"Well, I'm not at liberty to discuss that. But I certainly hope I'm there when they tell you, because I imagine the look on your face will be a lot like if you discovered you were shitting gold bricks."

"That bad, huh?"

Sawyer only smiled.

It was at that moment that Winfred saw a young civilian approaching them. He was tall and looked like he had been an athlete once. He had thick black hair and a handsome but boyish face. Winfred thought he detected a slight limp in his walk. But it was when Winfred got a look at his eyes that he got the strongest impression. There was an intensity there that he'd seen only rarely, one he associated with the ability to notice, absorb, and process things at a faster rate than most. He'd seen it every now and then in young pilots, the ones that turned out to be good. *Probably CIA*, Winfred thought, *maybe DARPA*.

"Just one minute, Dave," Sawyer said and went to meet the man.

Winfred watched them and his curiosity grew. He knew how much Sawyer disdained the Agency, civilian contractors, or anyone who meddled in the military but had never worn a uniform. Sawyer was old school to the core, and he didn't hold his tongue about it either. He'd tell you how McNamara and the Whiz Kids had lost Vietnam and that the problem with the military today was how quickly good soldiers left to get better pay as defense contractors or PMCs. To Sawyer they were little better than traitors.

Winfred expected Sawyer to flash him a knowing smirk. This guy couldn't be more than thirty. What could he possibly know that would be of any interest to a man like Sawyer? But there was no smirk, no rolling of the eyes, none of that. It was clear Sawyer not only respected the young man but genuinely liked him. Winfred felt a touch of jealousy. A new kid had been invited into the clubhouse and no one had bothered to tell him.

The young man turned to him, smiled, and came closer.

"Major Winfred," he extended his hand. "I'm Eric Hill. I'm very glad you've come. Sawyer says you're the best and that's what we need."

"So it's his fault I'm here," Winfred said.

Sawyer raised his hands in mock surprise. "I would *never* say you were the best."

Hill laughed. "I'm sorry to keep you in the dark on the mission details, but I'm sure you'll find it very interesting.

In the meantime, if there's anything you need, either for yourself, your crew, or your Valor, you let me know and I'll get it for you."

"Thank you," Winfred said with as much professional courtesy as he could muster.

With a smile and nod Hill left.

When he was out of earshot, Winfred turned to Sawyer. "Is it me or does that guy think he owns the place?"

"In a way he does."

"Who is he?"

"Just wait and see . . . and don't forget what I said about the gold brick."

It had only taken Winfred a week to become a believer. It was the day he watched the body armor tests. The bullets had somehow been dissolved in the air. It was surreal watching one man unload an M4 on another man without leaving a scratch. Winfred had stood there, jaw agape. Sawyer had been beside him and gently put a finger on his chin to close his mouth. "Told ya," he said.

Winfred gave a breathy laugh. "I'm feeling something heavy in my undies."

Then they had gone to work on the Valors. Honestly, Winfred didn't completely understand it, but the basic idea was that they were taking concepts from biology and applying them to weapons. They had treated a decommissioned bird with these invisible machines, then punched holes in it with a .50 cal. Winfred had watched in amazement as the holes in the metal had grown over, like a wound healing itself. You could actually see it happening. When he'd inspected the circuitry and fluid hoses, those too had grown back together. And that wasn't all. His Valor now ran as quiet as a diesel truck, was as stable as a Chinook, and felt as nimble as an Apache. He felt like he could take on an F-35 in it.

He didn't *need to know* how it worked, but he was, naturally, intensely curious. So one afternoon, he sat down with Hill in the mess hall determined to get some answers. At first the scientist was evasive.

"I'm essentially a thief." Hill said. "I've stolen a technology that's been around for billions of years and made it work for me."

Winfred scowled. "What's that supposed to mean?"

Hill paused for a moment, and Winfred was afraid he was about to say "that's classified," but instead Hill took a different route. "Let me try to give you a demonstration," he handed Winfred a baby carrot. "Eat this."

"What?"

"Go on. Eat it. I'm going to make you healthier and smarter."

Winfred bit into the carrot with a loud crack. "Now what?"

Hill laughed. "Well, now things are starting to get interesting. At this moment billions of superfast operations are happening in your body—inside your mouth, your brain, your stomach—so many things, in fact, that it's difficult to imagine them all. But let's try to break it down. You already know that a carrot contains lots of minerals like potassium, niacin, and manganese, as well as vitamin C. But did you ever wonder how your body gets all that good stuff where it needs to go? How does the potassium get to your muscles? How does the niacin get to your skin and neurons? How does the manganese get to your brain?"

Winfred shrugged.

"The answer is that your body is full of microscopic machines—biologists call them enzymes and proteins, but I call them machines. They're an invisible workforce that keeps you alive, working every day and night, and they are very, *very* fast."

"How fast?"

"Every second a single enzyme can do close to a million operations."

"Bullshit," Winfred said, and he began to laugh. "Nothing in my body moves that fast."

"Sure it does. The proof is already in your stomach. An enzyme in your saliva called amylase digests about thirty percent of all the starch you eat before you even swallow it. In the time it took you to chew and swallow that carrot, billions of complex operations occurred inside your mouth. That's also what you saw today on the test range when you watched the aircraft 'heal.' Those nanosites were doing close to fifty million operations per second.

"That's why I say I'm a thief. I've just copied what nature does in order to make my own microscopic workforce. We don't call them enzymes, we call them nanosites. And ours are actually better than anything in nature."

"Better?"

"Yes, because life on earth is based on the protein model. Once our DNA began using protein as a building material in some primordial pool, it couldn't switch to steel or copper, which is why our bodies need just the right conditions to survive. But nanosites are made out of what is essentially diamond. They're very tough and they don't stop working when it gets too hot or too cold. Is it starting to make sense?"

Winfred nodded.

"Good, but that's only the nanotechnology part. There are two other parts: replication and AI. We've used advances in genetic engineering to allow the nanosites to make copies of themselves. Then we use AI to guide them."

"It sounds like you are saying they're alive."

"According to most people's definition of the word, they are."

"Fuckin' A."

Hill laughed. "When you create a large swarm of nanosites or a combination of swarms with different programs, there isn't a whole lot that you *can't* do. A camera, a radio transmitter, a synthetic virus, body armor . . . There's really no limit."

Hill told him they'd soon make a new generation of aircraft that were manufactured by swarms—lighter, stronger, and all but invisible—but there wasn't time right now to do all the designing and testing (and no way this Congress would pass a defense bill to make them) so they were using a proven airframe, the Valor, and enhancing it.

Winfred was beginning to understand why Sawyer held Hill in such high regard. He was smart, for sure, but he was also driven. Hill was trying to think of every contingency they might confront in battle and find a solution for it. That was the type of egghead you wanted on your side, because his answers could save your life. In fact, Winfred noticed that Hill behaved like someone who had actually been in combat. Because, as he well knew, an experience like that changes you forever. And, like a veteran, it seemed personal to him. Especially when it came to China.

Winfred asked Sawyer about it.

"Let's just say that Hill is essentially a former POW."

That's when it clicked for Winfred. Hill had a score to settle.

Now Winfred was on his first mission with the new team, hovering over the African jungle. This was the real deal.

So far everything was going as planned. The only thing that worried him was a report they'd gotten this morning that the *Liaoning*, one of China's two aircraft carriers, had arrived in the area, most likely because they were curious about what the Americans were doing here. He hoped it was nothing, but if the captain of the *Liaoning* figured out they were messing with the mining camp, it could get ugly.

Winfred pushed the thought out of his mind. His only job right now was to keep his holding pattern. Seven miles was close enough to the mining camp to provide an uninterrupted connection between Hill, the operators on the ground, and all of Hill's little toys, but too far away for anyone to see them.

Hill had wanted to stay on the Valor that delivered the SEALs to the landing zone, just five hundred meters from the prison camp, but Captain Everett vetoed that idea. Hill was just too valuable to the navy. Winfred was amazed Everett had let the scientist off the carrier at all. It was only Hill's insistence that he had to have perfect communication with the swarms that had persuaded the captain.

In the back of the Valor, Eric swiveled between three separate workstations arranged in a tight semicircle. One held a real-time map of the compound, with his swarms overlaid like bubbles, the second was filled with smaller images—the footage from each of the nanosites cameras—and the last screen held his code and command prompts for controlling each swarm.

He expanded the camera for Cellblock Eight. He'd been monitoring the camp for weeks, learning the routines, listening to the guards, understanding how the whole operation worked. A laogai camp, he discovered, held few real criminals. Most were serving time for political reasons. Many were intellectuals—professors and lawyers and scientists, those who were often quickest to criticize China's one-party rule. Others were religious prisoners—Christians, Tibetans, Muslims, Falun Gong. There were, of course, real criminals, too. But in the laogai there was no distinction between the gravity of a crime, so political prisoners, drug users, and sex workers often served the same sentences as murderers and rapists.

Cellblock eight was where they kept the troublemakers. The Lifers. Those who the party deemed beyond rehabilitation.

Three days ago, Hill had inserted nanosites clusters into all of the men's brains. Now, on his command, they entered each man's hypothalamus and induced a rapid increase in vasopressin, oxytocin, and corticotropin-releasing factor (CRF). This caused a chain reaction in each brain. The pituitary responded by releasing adrenocorticotropic hormone (ACTH), which, in turn, caused the adrenal glands to flood the inmates' systems with corticosteroids. Instantly, their blood pressure surged, and their heart rates climbed. They woke with goosebumps as their skin constricted in order to send more blood to the major muscle groups. Their nonessential systems (like digestion and immune) shut down and they could no longer focus on small details; their brains were now wired to focus only on a potential threat.

Mok Enlai sat up with a start, suddenly filled with a strange rage. His eyes were wide, his mouth dry. He looked down at his trembling hands.

Around him, the other inmates were suddenly awake and on their feet. They felt it, too. Some began shouting.

"We've had enough!"

"I can't take it anymore."

"Open the door!"

Four guards came to the metal cell and told them to be quiet. They held up their electric batons and threatened to shock them through the bars. "Get back! All of you!"

But the inmates didn't back down.

"Let us out! Let us out!" They chanted.

Enlai was struck by an overpowering claustrophobia. The smell of sweat and urine and dried mud that he lived with every day was suddenly unbearable. He had to get away from it! He surged toward the door with the mass of inmates.

The leader of the guards, Lieutenant Hee, gave an order and, in unison, the soldiers drove their electrified batons though the bars. Nothing happened. There were no shouts of pain, no one fell. Some of the prisoners snatched the batons from the guards, and one guard who resisted was pulled up to the bars and his neck was quickly broken.

The inmates surged again and somehow the weight of their bodies knocked the metal door open. There was no snap of the lock or bending of metal; it was as if the U-shaped bike lock that held the door had simply disappeared.

Enlai saw the confidence in the guards' eyes disappear—replaced by shock and fear. They turned to flee but only made it a few steps before the prisoners were on them, clawing, tearing, literally trying to rip the men apart. Enlai grabbed one and forced him down, a moment later he was gripping the man's hair and smashing his face into the cement over and over. Never in his life had he felt such rage, such an overwhelming need to hurt. His veins were full of jet fuel, his muscles tight as steel. The sense of release he felt at letting it out, at hearing the thud of the man's skull hitting the ground until he finally heard the bone crack, was pure elation, a deep orgasmic release.

He heard other guards screaming in pain, underneath the angry curses of the convicts. He heard one guard plead, "My eyes, no, not my eyes!" The prisoners were showing no mercy. In the past, guards had often used the electric batons to sodomize the prisoners. Now the guards were being paid back in kind.

More guards arrived, some with electric batons, others with AK-47 rifles, unaware that neither would help them. Nine guards with batons fell on the prisoners, giving a battle cry and swinging down in unison. Once again the batons didn't work, and only a few blows fell before the guards were consumed by the mob.

The second wave held back, holding their rifles, ready on the firing line. "Get back in your cells or we'll kill all of you!" There was a moment of hesitation among the convicts. Enlai was now in front, ready to charge the riflemen.

"Fire!"

He heard the firing pins click metal on metal, but nothing

happened. The convicts rushed forward. Enlai reached the guard named Gou first, but others soon joined him. Gou was one of the most sadistic guards, the inventor of the Corpse Squad, and he often led the torture of the prisoners. Five or six of them kicked and stomped on him, then they clawed at his face and groin. When Enlai stood up, his hands and forearms were splattered with blood. At his feet was one of the Kalashnikov rifles. He inspected it and rechambered a round. The other men had moved on, leaving Gou on the ground, moaning, spitting up blood, both arms and legs clearly broken. Enlai pointed the rifle at his chest and pulled the trigger. The rifle jumped in his hands, sending three rounds into Gou's body.

"Get the rifles," Enlai called. "Get them! They will work for you!"

CHAPTER THREE

DRAWN LINES

Five hours earlier
The Pentagon, Ring B, Washington, DC

"I can't believe this," General Walden's face was pink with rage. "It's treasonous! A major event concerning global security and you intentionally hide it from me?"

Curtiss knew he had to choose his next words carefully. "I reported the facts to my commanding officer," he said. "It was not in my purview to inform anyone else, unless I was so ordered."

That had been the decision of CNO Michael Garrett, who was also sitting in the room. Walden glanced at the big man, then back at Curtiss. It was clear to Curtiss where Walden preferred to focus his ire.

"And did you brief Carlson?"

General Ellis Carlson was the outgoing chairman of the Joint Chiefs.

Curtiss looked to Garrett, and Garrett nodded.

"Yes," Curtiss replied.

"And the president?"

Again the glance and the nod.

"Yes."

Walden shook his head in disbelief. "I'm the vice chairman of the Joint Chiefs."

"Yes, sir," Curtiss said. "And I understand your recent promotion is the reason why we're here."

Curtiss hated kowtowing to a prick like Walden. But he knew he had to be diplomatic. This was a very delicate situation. Yes, Walden was an asshole and a liar and ladder-climbing bureaucrat. But he had just been given a lot of power. If the briefing went badly . . . no, it was going to go badly. That was inevitable. It was just a matter of how badly.

The real problem was that it didn't matter how diplomatic Curtiss was *now*, because he and Walden had a long history of being at odds, and for most of that history Curtiss had gotten away with openly displaying his scorn for Walden. That had worked out fine because Curtiss had always outranked Walden and had more powerful friends.

Not anymore. The tide was changing. The outgoing head of the Joint Chiefs had been a sailor, like Curtiss, but the new chairman was not. He was an aviator, just like General Charlie "Chip" Walden.

For Curtiss it felt like a bad dream. Within the armed forces, he couldn't think of anyone who was more different from him. Where Curtiss was a combat veteran, Walden was a career bureaucrat. Where Curtiss hated politics, Walden was a master of the game and knew how to squeeze every bit of nectar—every travel voucher, per diem expense, and Disney World discount—out of the DOD. He was the kind of rear-echelon pogue who would fly to Kuwait for three days every month—on the taxpayer's dime—so he could qualify for combat pay. He'd briefly been a B-52 pilot, but by 9/11 he was already a full-time pencil pusher and had spent the Iraq, Afghanistan, and Syrian Wars at the Pentagon.

Even in appearance they were strikingly different. Curtiss was Native American, short and with a crooked nose. Walden, although the same age, still looked like he belonged on a recruitment poster—tall, blond hair, a square jaw, and striking green eyes.

Curtiss had known Chip long enough to know that he always played it safe, never exposing himself or showing initiative unless he was certain of victory. In real war, that was a luxury you rarely had. Sometimes you had to enter a house not knowing what was inside; not knowing if you were outgunned. It was a problem that the air force rarely had to deal with. In fact, Walden was extremely proud of the fact that he'd never lost an airman in combat. But to Curtiss, he was missing the point.

His opinion of Chip had been solidified during the Battle of Abu Hamam in Syria, when he and Chip were both in Joint Operations Command. One hundred thirty-five marines were pinned down near the central market by roughly two hundred fifty Syrian soldiers. That was bad enough, but things went from bad to ugly fast. A battalion of five hundred Syrian soldiers with Russian "advisers" were heading up the road to encircle the town. Curtiss had ordered Walden to strike the battalion while they were exposed on the road. But Walden had already deployed all his available drones on other missions. In order to strike he'd have to use manned aircraft—F-35s and F-16s out of Cyprus. Suspecting the Russians had given the Syrians surface-to-air missiles, Walden had stalled, making excuses about fuel and armaments. When Curtiss confronted him—knowing full well the fuel and armaments were there—Walden changed tactics and said he'd need to send in wild weasels before authorizing a full strike against the battalion.

For Curtiss it was unconscionable. One hundred thirty-five marines needed air support, but Walden wouldn't give it to him because he didn't want his career tarnished by the death of even one pilot. And Curtiss knew it had nothing to do with the pilots themselves—who were fully aware of the risks they took—and everything to do with Walden's career.

In the end, Curtiss had gotten the F-35s from the USS *Stennis* in the Mediterranean, but it had taken an additional half hour, and in that time fourteen Marines were killed.

In the aftermath of the operation, Curtiss had pushed to have Walden court-martialed. It hadn't stuck, but Walden never forgot how Curtiss had tried to blemish his sparkling record.

Now Walden was looking across the table at Curtiss with the same contempt that Curtiss had always shown him.

"Well, *Vice* Admiral," Walden said. "Why don't you tell me everything? And no more of this 'need to know' bullshit."

Curtiss sighed inwardly, then gave a slight bow to his assistant.

The wall-mounted iSheet came alive, showing drone footage of a parched, windswept landscape. In the center of the screen was a huge traffic circle, with roads coming off it like spokes on a wheel. "This is the site of the incident," Curtiss began. "Only fifteen people have seen this footage. Unfortunately, the drone did not capture what actually happened, only the aftermath."

Curtiss had seen the images hundreds of times, but it

still amazed him. Four destroyed Z-10 attack helicopters were visible at various points in the distance, all of them ablaze and sending long plumes of black smoke into the sky. Near the center of the frame were four huge military transport trucks—three clustered together and a fourth tossed two hundred yards from the others like a child's toy, crumpled at the end of a long trail of debris.

"Good Lord," Walden muttered, leaning forward on the edge of his chair, his contempt for Curtiss replaced by amazement at what he was seeing.

The drone's camera zoomed in near the cluster of military trucks. Here the ground was littered with at least fifty bodies, most in Chinese army uniforms. Many were bloodied, and the resolution on the camera was so good you could make out bones that protruded from skin and clothing.

Curtiss continued: "Eyewitness accounts confirmed that this destruction was accomplished within a matter of seconds. That is: the downing of four Z-10 attack helicopters; the killing of fifty-three Chinese soldiers using weaponized nanosites that entered their bodies and killed them from the inside; lifting a nine-ton HG-17 military transport truck and depositing it one hundred ninety yards away, and neutralizing two American JDAM antipersonnel air-to-surface missiles."

"Such power!" Walden said. "And he did it all with his mind?"

Curtiss nodded.

"What have you learned about this . . . this man?"

"Almost nothing. The images we have of his face don't match anyone in the NSA's database."

Curtiss's assistant pulled up a blurry image of the man. He had sullen cheeks and a raised upper lip and thick black hair that rose haphazardly around his head. Curtiss found the face disturbing. There was something unnatural about the man. At least now he understood why.

"We are confident he has a way of disguising himself, which, considering his power, would be easy."

"But he saved your people?"

"Yes," Curtiss said.

"And he said that he got his power by using your technology . . . what was it called?"

"Forced Evolution," Curtiss said.

"Well, it doesn't look like you're running a very tight ship, Admiral. Someone in your organization must have leaked it to him."

"Or he hacked in," Curtiss said.

"Either way, it's inexcusable. You really screwed this one up. Now the question is, how do you intend to stop him?"

Finally, Admiral Garrett broke in. "Chip, the Joint Chiefs discussed this and we don't feel particularly inclined to pick a fight with an enemy we don't fully understand."

Walden shook his head then pointed at the screen. "Anyone who can do that either needs to be on our side or neutralized. So this is what we are going to do: We are going to find out *where* he is, then we are going to find out *what* he is, then, if necessary, we will destroy him."

Curtiss and Garrett shared a glance of skepticism.

"Sir, we need to be prepared for the possibility that killing him may not be possible," Curtiss said. "Eric Hill and our AI team estimated that he was eight to ten years ahead of us at the time of this encounter . . . and that was seven months ago. He told Hill that he can advance a decade in his own development every hour. If that's true, then by now the gap would be enormous."

"Well, if he got that far using your own technology, you'd better figure out a way to do what he did, because I have a real strong feeling that when push comes to shove, this guy is not going to be on our side."

There was a pause. Again, Garrett and Curtiss made eye contact. Curtiss closed his eyes for the briefest of seconds. This was the part he had been dreading the most. As much as he hated Walden, this was the type of news that you didn't wish on your worst enemy and, quite honestly, he felt sorry for the man.

Garrett shifted in his seat and leaned forward.

"Chip, there's more. And it's the real reason the Joint Chiefs kept you out of the loop."

Walden straightened in his seat, a look of cold resentment on his handsome face.

"There were six civilian casualties during the incident. They were innocent bystanders traveling nearby in their cars. We don't know why this man killed them—perhaps he didn't want any witnesses—but they were killed nevertheless."

Walden tilted his head to the side and eyed the CNO suspiciously. "What are you saying?"

"Look at the date, Chip."

Walden picked up the briefing. "Are you telling me . . . ?"

A look of shock and uncertainty flashed over his face, like a boxer who's been hit by a blow he didn't see coming. He shook his head, still trying to understand.

"You told me she died in a car crash!"

This was the moment Curtiss expected Walden to really explode, and for a moment he seemed like he would. He rose from his chair, fists clenched, neck muscles tights.

"You," he said, pointing his finger at Garrett. "You came

to my house and told me she died in a car crash. You lied to my face."

Garrett's visage remained hard. "The decision not to tell you was Ellis's," he said, "but he made it on my recommendation. I told him not to tell you, at least until we had a better idea of what we were up against."

"I had to fly to Beijing to identify her body. They had her in a fucking freezer at the embassy. Do you have any idea what that was like?"

Curtiss tried to imagine the scene, except with his own wife in place of Walden's. Even though Walden and his wife Jackie had been divorced for two years, it was no secret that Walden had hoped to win her back.

"I hope you can forgive me, Chip," Garrett said. "But the reason we didn't tell you still stands: You can't go using your power and influence to wage a personal vendetta. Now that you've been promoted, it's even more important."

Walden said nothing. The fight had gone out of him and he sat back, unsteadily, into his chair. "Murdered . . ." he whispered to himself. After a minute Garrett gave Curtiss a nod. The two men and their assistants began to collect their things, but before they left the room Curtiss spoke to Walden. "I'm sorry. I truly am."

Walden flinched and looked at Curtiss as if he were a complete stranger, an expression of confusion on his face. Then he seemed to remember himself.

"Go to hell, Curtiss."

CHAPTER FOUR

GHOSTS AND DEMONS

November 4, 2026
Namibia

Xiao-ping heard the shouting and screaming from across the compound. It was an alarming sound, the unbridled rage of so many desperate men, a roar that broke the jungle night. He watched as most of the guards in his cellblock ran in that direction.

"What's happening?" he whispered to the voice in his head.

"I'm creating a diversion."

He heard gunshots and his heart rate jumped.

In the Valor, Eric considered giving Xiao-ping a mild sedative but decided to wait. A little adrenaline at this point might be a good thing.

By now the noise was rousing the other prisoners. Within moments they were all awake, pushing and jostling at the bars in hopes of getting a glimpse of what was going on.

"It's happening!" someone said.

"The mutiny!"

One of the mine managers ran by, wearing overalls and a yellow hardhat. When he saw the remaining guards, he called to them. "What are you standing there for? Get down to number eight!" The guards obeyed.

The voice in Xiao-ping's ear spoke again. "Move to the back of the cell. I'm going to open the door."

"What? How?"

The Kryptonite lock that had held the door fell to the floor in pieces, and the door swung slowly open with a creak.

The prisoners at the front hesitated, peeking out to make sure no one was watching. But almost immediately the prisoners in the back pushed them out in a flood.

"Wait a moment," the voice said. "Let them all go."

Most of the men made for the front gate, others hatched a quick plan to use one of the bulldozers to ram through the perimeter fence, still others made for cellblock eight to join the fight.

A moment later Xiao-ping looked up and realized he was alone in the cell. He stared at the open door, still not sure if he was dreaming or not. There it was. Freedom. After all these years.

"What do we do now?" said a voice in Chinese. But it was not Xiao-ping or the stranger's voice.

Xiao-ping turned to find Yong standing just behind him, as silent as snow. As soon as he saw the man, Xiao-ping knew he couldn't leave him.

"Tell him to join the others," the voice said.

"No, we have to take him with us."

"*Nǐ zài gēn shéi shuōhuà?*" Yong asked. *Who are you talking to?*

"My mission is to get you home. You and *only* you."

"You don't understand. He won't survive. Another month in the camp and he'll die."

"We don't have time to talk about this. You need to move now."

"Not without Yong."

Eric knew he could do nothing but agree. He had to get Xiao-ping out fast. There were too many moving pieces, and a delay could be fatal not only to Xiao-ping, but to the other operatives now on the ground.

"Okay, okay, just get moving."

Eric quickly relayed the change through the command net. *Sawyer is not going to be happy about this.*

Outside was pandemonium. Everywhere Xiao-ping looked, the brutal battle was being fought. While some of the prisoners had rifles, much of the fighting was primal hand-to-hand combat. Many guards had been overwhelmed, but dozens were still fighting, using their batons as clubs.

About twenty enraged prisoners had captured the warden and put a rope around his neck. They were dragging him to the top of one of the guard towers, while some of the guards appeared to be mounting a counterattack. The bulldozer had been successfully captured and was making its way toward the first perimeter fence. Three men sat on its hood, one with an AK-47 taking wild shots at the guards.

The voice came again. "Make for the fence on the northeast corner, between cellblocks four and five. Then wait there."

Xiao-ping knew that getting out would be difficult.

There were eight cellblocks in the compound, arranged in the shape of a horseshoe. At the bottom of the horseshoe was the mess hall, the officers' and managers' quarters, and a small shack that served as the infirmary, plus two wooden guard towers on either side of the main gate. The prison compound area was surrounded by an eight-foot-high fence, but the entire compound itself was set inside a seven-square kilometer rectangle that was also surrounded by a ten-foot tall fence topped with loops of razor wire.

Xiao-ping turned to Yong. "*Wǒmen zǒu ba!*" Let's go! They moved together, hunched over and trying to stay in the shadows. The locks of the other cells had by now been opened and men were streaming all around them, but no one seemed to notice them or care. As they emerged from the alley between cellblocks four and five, they found it deserted.

"There's no one here," Xiao-ping said to the voice.

Just as the words were out of his mouth, he saw the walls on both sides of him begin to move. He jumped back with fright, and Yong let out a yelp of surprise. It was like seeing a shimmering mirage, as if a man had just emerged from the cinder block wall. But not a man, a ghost of a man, a specter that could change color as needed to reflect the things behind it. Only when it moved could he see it and then only barely.

The first ghost spoke, "Xiao-ping. I'm Sawyer. This is Patel," he motioned to the other ghost. "Does your friend speak English?"

"No," he said.

"Then I'll need you to explain everything I tell you to him." Sawyer handed him a lightweight windbreaker.

"First, put this on. In a moment you'll be just like us."

It was true, as soon as the jacket was over his shoulders he felt a sudden coldness all over his body then he was a ghost, too. He looked at his arm and saw only the copper colored mud that covered the ground. It gave him a slight dizziness. One function of the eyes is to help the inner ear maintain balance, and without the visual confirmation, his brain was confused as to exactly where he was in space, and he pitched forward like a drunk. Sawyer steadied him. "Just wait a minute and you'll get used to it.

"Unfortunately, we don't have one for your friend. Please explain to him that it is *imperative* that he stays as close to the rest of us as possible. He doesn't have protection like we do and if he moves more than five feet away from us, he will be vulnerable." Xiao-ping did his best to explain it to Yong, who still couldn't believe his eyes.

Suen Peng had been a prisoner in cellblock eight when the rage had overcome his mind. But his rage had taken a different form. Instead of a bloodlust to kill the guards, he wanted to kill the other prisoners. Peng was the leader of the Corpse Squad, so he had always known that if there were ever a mutiny, he would do his best to help the guards, because if the mutiny succeeded, he would surely be killed.

During the initial moments of the riot, he had played along, pretending his rage was directed at the guards, but once out in the open he hid between the treads of an excavator. He watched more guards being overwhelmed and killed, his panic rising. He had to think of a plan, for he knew that when all the guards were out of commission, they would come looking for him.

Just then another prisoner scrambled under the excavator, Peng turned on him, ready to pounce. Then he realized it was Keung, another member of the Corpse Squad. "*Guòlái zhèlǐ,*" he hissed. Come over here.

A plan began to take shape. Peng had seen how the guards' weapons had refused to work, yet had somehow fired when Enlai killed one of the guards. A thought came to him.

"The rifles," he hissed, "if we can get them, we might have a chance."

Keung pointed. Near the entrance of cellblock six lay a dead soldier, face down in the mud. It took Peng a moment to see the butt of the Kalashnikov sticking out of the mud. He ran for it, knelt down in the mud and rolled the soldier over. He scraped the mud from the barrel and trigger guard. At that very moment two prisoners came out of the door behind him. He pivoted on his knee and fired. Rat-tat-tat-tat-tat-tat. Bullets cut them down. Keung came and knelt beside him. Peng gave him the soldier's pistol.

The battle raged around them. The bulldozer had breached the first perimeter fence, and the warden was swinging from the guard post, his face purple, hands tearing at the noose, legs treading invisible water.

The battle was turning into a rout. Everywhere Peng looked, prisoners with rifles were shooting guards and prison officials. Those who didn't have guns were fighting hand-to-hand. Peng realized the only way for them to get more rifles was to kill the prisoners who had them. He motioned to Keung, and they took the long way around the mess hall where they were fewer lights, hoping to surprise the prisoners pushing toward the front gate. On their way they found Ju Long, another member of the Corpse Squad.

If they could each get a rifle, they might turn the tide of the battle.

"Viper One, this is Night Owl, I'm picking up something. Four bogeys coming in from the northwest." It was the voice of Master Sergeant Don Hendricks, the pilot of the Predator drone.

Suddenly Eric's audio feed was filled with chatter.

Sawyer: "Can you identify?"

Night Owl: "They're moving too fast to be choppers, but too slow for jets. Most likely Z-15 gunships . . . Black Widows."

Captain Everett: "They must be from the *Liaoning*. Either they detected you leaving, or someone there at the compound called for help."

Sawyer: "How long?"

Night Owl: "Less than two minutes."

Sawyer to Patel: "Let's get under those trees before they get here."

Night Owl to Captain Everett: "Permission to engage, sir."

Captain Everett: "Negative. Do not engage."

Back on board the USS *Gerald Ford*, Captain Everett had a difficult decision to make. The beauty of the new technology was that it was undetectable. No one could prove they had started the mutiny, and the Chinese would have no way of knowing the US was involved. But if his drone pilot shot down a Chinese gunship, that would change. There would be an investigation, and shrapnel from the Sting-ray missiles would be found. Besides, there was no way of knowing if the drone could take out all four of the gunships by itself. "Zulu Five One, is there any way you could help us out here?"

"I don't think so, sir," Eric replied. "The programming would take too much time."

Captain Everett would just have to hope that his team got back to the ship without being detected. But why had the gunships come? If it were just because of the mutiny, they would remain near the compound. But if they somehow knew that the USS *Gerald Ford* had two Valors and a drone in the area, they would be looking for them. "Proceed as planned," he said. "But, Night Owl, keep a lock on those gunships in case this gets ugly."

Xiao-ping heard an unearthly roar and looked up to see five strange aircraft crisscrossing overhead like huge bats silhouetted against the night sky. They were just suddenly there, on top of them, so low he could feel the rush of their spinning propellers. They were part plane, part helicopter, with two rotors on their short wings. Cries of alarm and fear went up from the prisoners.

The gunships opened fire on the camp. Orange tracer rounds arced out of their front cannons, ripping open the night, and cutting down dozens of men in seconds. The sound was deafening. One aircraft attacked the men fleeing through the front gate, killing some but forcing the others back into the compound. Another engaged the mutineers on the bulldozer. The gunship turned in a semicircle around it, firing the whole time. It was as if the nose of the aircraft was attached to the bulldozer by a long florescent orange string as it poured tracer rounds into metal and flesh and bone. Xiao-ping heard the *ping-ping-ping-ping* of the rounds as they smacked into the bulldozer's blade. The eight or nine men who had been on or around it were literally obliterated. The huge cannon rounds blowing them apart.

To Xiao-ping, it seemed like giant winged demons had risen from hell, from the very pits they were mining, to annihilate them.

CHAPTER FIVE

HIDE AND SEEK

Peng watched as the tide of battle suddenly reversed. Instead of fighting for his life, Peng and the Corpse Squad were now helping the guards and the gunships massacre the prisoners. He and his friends picked up more rifles from the dead prisoners and—thanks to the uncontrollable rage still running hot in their veins—began slaughtering the other prisoners. Peng shot one man in the back then turned. That's when he saw Yong, the pathetic little worm. He had somehow made it through the first perimeter fence and was heading for a thicket of trees. At this distance he was just a dark silhouette, but Peng recognized his profile. Peng called to his friends and pointed, then the three of them opened fire.

★★★

Sawyer heard the shots and knew they were aimed at them. When a bullet is coming at you, it makes a distinct sound, a hypersonic *t-chew*. He didn't panic, but it wasn't a sound he liked to hear. "Keep 'em moving," he said to Patel, then he quickly turned and knelt. He saw the three prisoners with rifles and shot one in the chest. The other two didn't react right away because they couldn't see him.

Then he heard Patel's voice. "No, wait!"

Sawyer turned to see the other prisoner, Yong, running wildly away . . . not toward the cover of the trees but perpendicular to it. It was the dumbest thing he could have done. The other gunman kept firing and even though they were poor shots, they managed to hit him before the three SEALs who were hiding in the woods cut them down.

Sawyer ran over and picked him up. He was moaning in Chinese as Sawyer carried him into the cover of the woods. Once concealed in the shadows, he set the man down. "Why couldn't you do what I told you?"

The man muttered something in Chinese.

"He says he's sorry," Xiao-ping said.

Specialist Loc, a medic, looked him over using a small pen light. The round had hit him in the left hip and exited out the right. Loc pull down the man's pants and saw that the bullet had gone through his buttocks. "I'm sure this hurts like hell but you're one lucky son-of-a-bitch. It's missed all the major arteries and your hip bones. You'll be fine." He stuffed some QuikClot packets into the wounds.

Yong grimaced and stiffened as Loc shoved the gauze in, then Loc gave him a shot of morphine. Yong panted and blew out air. "*Tā mā de*!" he cursed, but after a moment he blinked, surprised that the pain was already subsiding.

From the cockpit of his Z-15 Black Widow, Second Lieutenant Wen Fan saw three prisoners shooting at someone heading toward the woods. But then something very strange happened. All three of the prisoners with guns were cut down, but he couldn't tell from where. Were there gunmen in the trees? He banked over the woods to get a closer look but saw no one. When he glanced back, the dead man was somehow moving. He saw it for only a moment before his angle of flight cut off his line of sight, but the dead man seemed to be floating, as if an invisible force were carrying him. It happened so fast that he didn't believe his eyes. By the time he could bank to get a closer view, the man had disappeared into the woods.

Eric felt a sudden nausea when he realized that the prisoners were shooting each other. It was a scenario he never considered, and his lack of foresight now jeopardized the mission. He should have guessed that with the complicated social networks created in such a brutal place that there would be bitter vendettas. Now his friends were at risk because of his mistake.

It felt like things were about to unravel. First the Chinese gunships, now a wounded man. He hesitated. Should he try to find a way to down those gunships or should he just focus on getting the team back to the Valor safely? He decided on the latter. The Chinese pilots would have little reason to suspect that the US had a team on the ground, and if he could get everyone safely away, they would never know they had been there.

The problem was the wounded man. The team was still five hundred yards from the landing zone for EXFIL. There was protected tree cover where they were now and on the near side of the LZ, but in between was an open stretch of mud and dirt that ran between two of the mines. With their camouflage the SEALs and Xiao-ping could move through that open space without being detected, but the wounded man would give them all away.

It was a bitter lesson to learn on the battlefield: The technology only worked if everyone had it.

Eric's instinct was to simply leave Yong. He wasn't the mission, and his presence was putting everyone's life in danger. But Xiao-ping would not go easily if they tried to leave him, and that would jeopardize the mission, too. And there was one other reason—the ten weeks he had been imprisoned in China. How would he have felt if his friends had left him behind?

"Sawyer, take off your undershirt and put it on Yong. I should be able to reprogram it for camouflage."

Sawyer quickly complied.

Each of the SEALs had an armored T-shirt in addition to the outer shell that was both armored and camouflage. With the neural net cuing up his commands on the monitor, Eric took one-tenth of the nanosites from each of the SEALs' armor and reassigned them to Yong's shirt. "Just sit tight. I need a minute to copy the new program."

"Make it quick," Sawyer said. "The sun is coming up, which means it's going to be a lot easier to spot us in these woods."

Yong glanced back toward the prison camp. The gunfire had died down, and he only heard the occasional pop. The mutiny had failed. Yong could see that many of the prisoners had surrendered and were now lying face down in the mud. He saw a guard step up behind one of them and shoot him in the back of the head.

"Here, put this on." A soldier gave him a white cotton T-shirt. Once it was on, the man said, "This is going to feel a little weird." A moment later, Yong felt the strangest sensation, as if a coating of cold paint had suddenly been sucked to his skin by a powerful magnet—from the tips of his toes to the top of his head. It made him shiver all over. He looked down and found he was a ghost like the others.

Sawyer waited anxiously for Hill to finish his work. He hated sitting still; his instincts rebelled against it. "Duncan, as soon as we're ready, pick him up." He gestured to Yong.

Duncan nodded.

"You're good to go," Hill finally said.

Patel picked up Yong and raced under the trees toward the LZ. At the edge of the first woods Sawyer held up his fist and everyone stopped. He knew that the new camouflage was good, but it wasn't perfect. To run across open terrain with gunships overhead was dangerous.

Dawn was upon them, filling the world with a weak light. Sawyer pulled up his night-vision goggles. The landscape before them looked like heaven and hell had collided. In the foreground were three open-pit mines, gaping wounds in the skin of the Earth. In the half-light of the sunrise, the copper-colored mud looked like crimson blood. The rims of the pits were dotted with dead trees, earth-moving equipment, and trash. From the nearest pit came a stench of decay and rot that forced its way up his nose and into his brain. It was a smell that Sawyer instinctively recognized as death.

Yet beyond the mines was a scene of breathtaking beauty. Thick green woods dominated the hills around the mines, and the trees thinned into an open savannah. The first rays of morning lit the emerald and golden treetops with a warm light. Through that expanse of greens and golds, a wide, clear river meandered toward the foot of a distant sierra, the water twinkling and flashing with the light of the new sun.

They would have to run two hundred yards along the ridge between the two pits to reach the next patch of woods. Waiting for them on the far side was the Valor that would take them home.

Sawyer opened a channel to Night Owl. "Please give us the all clear."

"Hold tight, Papa Six Four."

A moment later one of the gunships came roaring over the treetops, banking hard. As soon as it was gone, they got the all clear. "Make it snappy."

"Go! Go! Go!" Sawyer told them.

They ran like hell. Patel was on point, Duncan carrying Yong in the middle. Sawyer took up the rear with Xiao-ping just in front of him.

Xiao-ping looked over his shoulder as he ran and saw in the distance the gunships swarming like giant dragonflies over the camp, occasionally opening fire.

It was slow going through the thick mud. He just couldn't get his body moving at full speed. He slipped once, but

Sawyer caught his arm and with incredible strength picked him up with one hand and kept him running.

Once in the far woods, two more ghost men appeared from the trees and silently escorted them down a wide trail. The morning sun was sending long shafts of gold light through the dusty air, and as the men ran through each beam, their ghost armor made it appear as if the light were passing through them. Watching the men move, the way they communicated with their hands, and the speed at which they worked was soothing to Xiao-ping. *Lili was right. Everything's going to be fine. Just believe.*

Five hundred yards to the east, Black Widow pilot Lieutenant Wen Fan did a slow sweep of the camp. The ground was strewn with at least a hundred bodies: prisoners, guards, and some of the mine managers. Many had been blown to bits by the Black Widow's massive chain gun. Some prisoners were being led back to their cells while others were being forced to lie on the ground. Fan figured the future wasn't bright for those on the ground.

With the fight all but over, his thoughts returned to the floating man. He knew that the USS *Gerald Ford* lay thirty miles off the coast. *Was it just a coincidence?* No, he didn't think so. What a discovery it would be to find evidence that the Americans were behind this. Was the floating man a clue? Even if it was just a trick of the darkness, the man had still managed to get into the woods.

He pushed on the control stick and the nose of the aircraft dipped as he headed north toward the small woods. He did a slow circle around the two-hectare copse of trees but saw nothing. Then he widened the search to the mines and the outer fence. Here the morning sun was brighter and he turned off his night optics. He swooped in close to one of the pits and saw that it was infested with vultures. Underneath were skeletons and rotting carcasses. It occurred to him that a clever man might hide in there and play dead, but he dismissed the idea. Any man who tried that would soon have the vultures pecking at him. He moved on.

Xiao-ping did his best to keep up with the others. Sawyer kept urging him on. "Just a little farther now." The trail through the woods sloped down then abruptly stopped. At the tree line, Patel extended a palm behind him. All the men stopped. Then he made a circular motion near his ear, and the men rallied around him.

From here Xiao-ping could see an open stretch where the trees had been cut down on either side of the perimeter fence. He didn't want to wait. Beyond that fence was freedom.

"Papa Six Four. We see you. You're clear to come aboard, but make it quick. There's a gunship snooping around the far end of the woods."

Aboard? Xiao-ping thought. *Aboard what?*

"Here," Sawyer said, "You'd better take my hand." Sawyer guided him forward, holding Xiao-ping's hand out in front of him. Suddenly he touched something metal.

"Step up . . . there you go."

Just as he extended his head forward, everything changed. It was like passing through a waterfall. On one side he saw nothing, on the other side he was inside an aircraft. He gaped at the soldiers inside. *How did they do that?*

A female soldier began speaking to him in Mandarin. “Hello, Xiao-ping, I’m Sergeant Kabat, assistant Crew Chief. Do you need anything?” Xiao-ping shook his head vacantly, still looking around in amazement. She guided him to a seat and buckled him in. “Have some water.” He took the proffered bottle robotically then watched as the other soldiers lay Yong face down on a gurney and strapped him in. He had assumed that the owner of the voice in his head would be in the aircraft, but he clearly wasn’t. “Where are you?” he said to the air.

“I’m in a different aircraft,” Eric replied. “Close, but not too close.”

In the cockpit of the Valor, Chief Warrant Officer Emilia Bailey was about to start the rotors when she got the call.

“Sit tight, Baker Five One, you are about to get company.”

On a normal mission, Bailey would keep the rotors spinning in order to lift off the moment the operators were on board. But the new technology required different procedures. The one flaw in the new camouflage was the rotors, which, when in motion, gave off a slight shimmer. To remain invisible they powered down in the LZ, and before they powered up, they had to be sure that the ninety seconds it required to take off would not be interrupted or they would be a sitting duck.

A second later she heard the Z-15, loud and flat. The air in the Valor grew tense.

"Let's pray they don't spot us," she said. She watched out the starboard window as the sleek gunship did a slow bank, its striped rotors spinning so fast it looked like they were ticking backward. As soon as it had disappeared over the tree line, Bailey requested permission to take off.

"Negative," Night Owl said, "he's coming back around."

"Shit!"

CHAPTER SIX

HOME FRONT

11:15 p.m., November 3, 2026
Washington, DC

While morning was breaking over Southern Africa, it was still the previous evening in Washington, DC.

A knock came on Jane Hunter's door.

She opened it to find her friend Hwe Lili standing there. The look of conflict on the woman's face told Jane that tonight was the night. She felt a fear that was oddly familiar, one that she hadn't felt in a very long time. It took her back to her childhood, whenever her father was deployed or she knew he was going on a particularly dangerous mission. But it was different now because for the first time it was not her father who was going to war, but the man she loved.

Jane opened her arms, and the woman fell into them. At Jane's touch, Lili immediately teared up. "I spoke to him, not twenty minutes ago. He sounded so scared."

Jane held the embrace, letting her friend get her emotions

out. This, too, brought up old memories, because as an army brat she'd learned all the etiquette for moments like this—how to treat one another, how to touch and hug, how to compose oneself—because they all knew someday they could be on the other side. "Try not to worry, okay? Remember they are all very good at what they do. Eric, Sawyer, Patel . . . they'll get him home."

"A part of me knows that, but I'm scared anyway. I'm scared he won't make it back, but I'm also scared of what happens if he does."

Jane pulled back and held the woman at arm's length. "What do you mean?"

"Jane, it's been twelve years since I last saw him. I know I still love him, but some people who are in that long, they're never the same. Even if he's okay physically, his mind . . ."

"Hey, hey, slow down, don't you think you're jumping the gun a bit? Let's get him home safe, then we'll worry about that."

Lili returned a faint-hearted smile and took a deep breath. "Okay."

"Besides," Jane said, "if he's made it twelve years, that means he's a survivor. I'm sure he'll find a way to make your marriage survive, too."

Lili fell into her arms again. "You're right. God, I'm just going crazy with the waiting."

"Come in . . . stay with me. We'll watch some mindless TV and be worried together."

"Oh, Jane, I'm so selfish. I wasn't thinking."

"It's okay. I get tunnel vision, too." Jane knew she could hardly be judgmental, especially considering that seven months ago Lili had risked her life to save Eric. When he and their friend Ryan Lee had been kidnapped and taken to

China, it was Lili and her twin sister Ying—both American spies embedded in the Chinese military—who had helped rescue them. Lili had already done so much (and lost much) for Eric: her twin sister had been killed during the escape.

The two women sat down on the sofa.

"Where's Mei?" Jane asked, referring to Lili's fourteen-year-old niece who had fled China with them.

"She's over at Curtiss's house."

"Really?"

Lili leaned in conspiratorially. "She's got a crush on the Admiral's son, Logan . . . says he's dreamy."

Jane laughed.

"Believe it or not," Lili continued, "the whole family has really taken her in. And between you and me, I think she feels safe over there. You know, the big house full of people, Curtiss's bodyguards and all that."

Jane nodded. After what the girl had been through, seeking out the safest place on base made sense. Yet Jane knew something about Curtiss that Lili didn't. During their escape from China, when it looked like Eric, Ryan, Mei, and Lili's sister might be recaptured by the Chinese, Curtiss had ordered a drone strike to kill them all. It was only because of the mysterious Inventor that they had lived. Jane would never forget what Curtiss had tried to do. It was proof of just how coldhearted he could be. He had been ready to kill four innocent people to make sure that there was no chance they could reveal state secrets to the enemy.

Jane wondered if Lili might feel different about Mei dating Curtiss's son if she knew the truth. Yet she also knew that now was not the time to bring up something like that . . . or was it? The meddlesome side of her personality couldn't help but probe a little.

"Do you trust Curtiss?"

Lil glanced away for a moment, her expression conflicted. "I've struggled with that question for a long time. When we were in China, we accepted that we were expendable and might never get out. But Curtiss didn't forget about us, and I owe the fact that I'm alive—and that Mei is alive—to him." She paused and Jane could see she was choosing her words. "I also know that he has ulterior motives."

Jane put her elbow on the back of the sofa and leaned closer. "Go on."

"Curtiss sees me as an asset to national security. Getting me out meant that he would gain all my expertise in weapons research to help him here, while simultaneously taking that expertise away from the enemy. In many ways, rescuing Xiao-ping is no different."

"What do you mean?"

Lili hesitated a moment. "I probably shouldn't be telling you this, but Curtiss's plan was to make me the new Director of Genetics. I was supposed to take Olex Velichko's place. But the DSS won't give me a security clearance while my husband is a prisoner of the enemy."

Jane raised her chin and opened her mouth. "Ah, so that's it." Now it was beginning to make more sense. The mission to Africa was not so much about saving a man's life as it was about advancing their weapons program.

Lili nodded. "I know he's a good man but sometimes I have dark thoughts. Sometimes I wonder—if Curtiss had a choice between rescuing Xiao-ping or simply killing him, what would he do? Either way, I'd get my clearance."

"No, no, that's going too far," Jane lied, knowing how astutely Lili had just judged Curtiss's character, for that was exactly his thinking during the escape from China. But she couldn't tell her that now. "Xiao-ping is going to be fine. You'll see. We have a tough few hours ahead of us, but then everything is going to be all right." She gave Lili another hug. "Come on, what do you want to watch?"

Soon the two women were huddled together under a blanket on the sofa watching a bad comedy, the cool blue light of the screen painting their faces. Jane laughed and smiled at each joke, but it was all an act to make Lili feel like everything was normal even though inside she was twisted up and nauseous.

She reminded herself that she was tough. That she could handle anything. *Don't worry*, she chided herself, *Eric's just in a support role, he won't even be in any danger*. But all the fear and anxiety she'd felt while he was in captivity in China flooded back into her mind. She swore that when he came back, she would never let him out of her sight again.

CHAPTER SEVEN

SEEING

Namibia

Lieutenant Fan glided slowly above the woods, trying to see through the tree cover. His aircraft did not have a chin bubble, so to see down he had to bank a little. The second perimeter fence cut through the western tip of the woods, but a no man's land had been cleared on either side of it to make escaping prisoners easier to spot.

He did another flyby but saw nothing. "Damn it, he must be in there." He looped around once more, slower this time, keeping his nose to the woods and hovering at twenty-five meters, low enough to look between the pillars of the trees for any glimpse of movement. That was when he noticed something odd. There was a dead tree that had fallen near the fence. Little was left of it but a long brown stump, half decayed.

If he held the gunship still, the trunk was straight, but

when he moved, it suddenly had a kink in it, like a reed in the water. At first he thought the refraction was caused by his Heads-Up Display (HUD), but when he turned so he was looking out the port window, he saw it again for the briefest of seconds. He pointed it out to his gunner.

"I don't see anything," he replied.

That's why you're the gunner and I'm the pilot, Fan thought. *There's something down there.*

On board the Valor, all eyes were glued on the menacing form of the Black Widow as it hovered lethally close. They stared at the long wand of the chain gun and the rocket pod clusters hanging under its wings.

"He sees us." Bailey said.

"No, he doesn't," Eric replied. "If he could see you, he would have fired by now. But he sees *something* . . . something he doesn't understand." Eric's aerial cameras were darting around the two aircraft, helping him decide what to do.

Everyone in the Valor held their breath. In the cabin, Sawyer got an idea. He slipped a three-foot metal tube from the weapons rack above his head and handed it to Patel. It was an AT4 Pansarskott, a single-shot anti-tank weapon. Patel, who was known for a decided lack of subtlety, often carried one into combat to blow holes in buildings. "Auxiliary points of ingress," he liked to say. He was also the best shot on the team. Patel took the weapon with a nod and knelt near the door. Curious, Sergeant Kabat stood behind the rocket to get a better look. Sawyer gently eased her to one side to prevent her from being killed by the blowback.

★★★

Staff Sergeant Bill Cantrell stood at the window of the Valor between the cockpit and the bay door looking through the sight of his .50 caliber machine gun, safety off, finger on the trigger. Cantrell could clearly see both the pilot and the gunner in the Z-15's two-tiered cockpit. The two men were talking, trying to figure something out.

"Permission to fire," he whispered into his microphone.

"Negative," Bailey said.

What are we waiting for? Cantrell thought. *Let's blow this fucker out of the sky before he can put two and two together.*

Truth be told, Cantrell was champing at the bit to take down the Black Widow. He'd been flying in Black Hawks, Chinooks, and Valors for almost twenty years. As the crew chief it was his job to know them inside and out—he could literally take any one of them apart and reassemble it. But Cantrell's knowledge of aircraft went far beyond that. He made it his business to learn as much as he could about any aircraft that flew in any military. To him, the Black Widow was an abomination—it embodied everything that disgusted him about not only the Chinese government, but also the United States government and its defense contractors. The Z-15 was an insulting combination of Chinese reverse engineering, Pentagon leaks, US government complacency, and contractor greed. Almost nothing in it was Chinese-made. Right down to the reverse engineered M242 Bushmaster chain gun mounted on its nose. *Oh, the irony*, Cantrell thought, *my crew and I are about to be blown to bits by an autocannon designed in the USA to keep Americans safe.*

Yet he had to admit the Black Widow was an effective killing machine. While the Valor was a multi-use aircraft, designed chiefly for getting troops in and out of the battlefield, the Black Widow was designed for attack—capable of supporting troops on the ground and destroying enemy tanks. It had a slim profile and carried only a pilot and gunner.

The cockpit and the engines of a Chinese Z-15 were well-armored too. In fact, they were specifically designed to take the impact of the very .50 caliber round he was ready to fire at it. But he suspected it had been tested with only a few .50 caliber rounds, not the thirty-three rounds per second at close range he was about to give them.

In the cockpit of the Z-15, Lieutenant Fan looked again at the log. It was like a mirage. Something had to be there . . . in the air between him and the ground. But how could he see it?

The sun was up, but in this small valley it was still dim enough. Yes. He reached up and pulled down his night-vision optics. He had to adjust the gain to eliminate the extra light, but when the optics adjusted he finally saw something.

Eric watched as the pilot lowered his night-vision goggles. At first, he was not worried. He had planned for this and knew that all the equipment and personnel in the aircraft were coated with nanosites that would be invisible to infrared. But the look of confusion on the pilot's face made him realize his mistake.

"He can see you! He can see you!"

It was Yong, the wounded man. The camouflage Eric had improvised for him did not have infrared protection.

Fan saw the torso of a man somehow floating in the air. It was so strange that he hesitated. *How could this . . .*

Cantrell opened fire, the .50 cal spewing hot metal like a fire hose, the illuminated rounds appearing out of thin air and smacking into the Z-15's armored plating. The gunship dipped its nose and tried to veer off, Fan still confused as to what was happening. "We have enemy contact, taking heavy fire."

Patel pulled the trigger on the Pansarskott. It sprang forth with a loud crack, like the sound of a tree split in a storm.

The Z-15's chain gun was just beginning to return fire when the AT4 warhead slammed into the rotor housing of the right propeller, knocking the blades clear off. The remaining bulk of the airframe slouched to the right and fell. Cantrell kept firing as it descended, watching as the pilot struggled vainly with the control stick.

Xiao-ping watched the explosion in amazement and felt the shock wave push against his face, followed by an acrid burn smell. One of the detached blades appeared to be coming straight at them, pitching at an angle like a giant rotary saw. "Ah, shit!" someone said. Xiao-ping ducked reflexively, but somehow it passed over them, cartwheeling into the woods, slicing though boughs, splintering tree trunks and creating a road of destruction.

"Nice shot, Patel!" Duncan said, patting him on the back.

Patel looked to Sawyer—his team leader—for his approval. The old SEAL mouthed the words, I love you.

"That's such bullshit, Patel," Cantrell said. "He was mine."

With great relief, Xiao-ping heard the engines come to life and the rotors begin to spin.

★★★

Suddenly the airwaves were alive with chatter.

Night Owl: "Tango Seven Seven, you need to get out of there ASAP. I have four more Z-15s heading your way."

Captain Everett: "Zulu Five One [Hill], what is the probability that the enemy will see the rotor glare?"

Eric: "It's high, sir. The armor will protect them against the chain guns, but it's untested against rockets and missiles. We never expected the camp to have air support."

Major Winfred: "Whiskey Nine Three requests permission to support Tango Seven Seven."

Captain Everett: "Negative, Whiskey Nine Three, you keep that cargo safe. Night Owl will handle this."

Everett realized the cat was out of the bag. The wreckage of the Black Widow would be littered with evidence indicating the US—the .50 cal shell casings and fragments of the AT4 Pansarskott. *This was supposed to be a quiet op,* he thought to himself. *If it got any louder, it was going to be live on CNN.*

"Night Owl, as soon you are convinced the enemy is in pursuit of Tango Seven Seven, you are weapons free."

"Roger that. I have eyes on all four bogies now."

CHAPTER EIGHT

COUNTDOWN

11:45 p.m.
Washington, DC

In less than twenty-four hours she was going to kill a man.

"Is everything in place?" she said into her phone, struggling to keep the anxiety out of her voice. As their leader, she knew she could not let her people sense her fear.

She was sitting on a park bench outside of the Smithsonian. Even though it was late, she'd been restless in the hotel and felt the need to be outside. Luckily it was a warm fall night.

"Yes, don't worry," came the man's reply. He had worked hard to get rid of his accent, but her trained ear still heard the faintish lilt to his *r*'s. "They put the furniture back yesterday and hung the paintings. Nobody suspects a thing."

She took a deep breath and tried to relax.

The man clearly perceived her anxiety: "Nothing's

going to go wrong," he said. "Remember, we've done this before."

She thought of reminding him that the previous victim had not been a high-level government official and the hit had not occurred in the heart of the nation's capital. But she didn't. Even though she knew their phones had the highest encryption, she dared not be so overt. "You know it's different," she said.

"Not for me."

She nodded slowly, acknowledging that he was right. He had done many things that were equally if not more audacious than this. At sixty-seven, he had survived one of the longest and bloodiest civil wars in history. He was a professional and a survivor, and that made her feel better.

The man added, "As I've always said, risk everything or gain nothing."

"Understood," she said. "Okay, let's go through it again. You'll get a final visual on the target, right?"

"That's right, then you'll have ninety seconds. No more."

"Got it," she replied. "Ninety seconds."

"Don't hesitate," he said.

"I won't," she said.

For a moment she considered herself from the outside looking in. An affluent, thirtysomething woman with curly, reddish brown hair, talking on her phone on a park bench. She knew no one would ever suspect that she was preparing an assassination because she still looked like the woman she used to be: the young college professor. Less than a year ago she'd been lecturing, holding office hours, and attending potluck dinners with fellow faculty—until she had discovered her true calling.

"Is there anything that we could be forgetting?" she asked. "Anything at all?"

There was a respectful silence as the man considered her question.

"We haven't missed a thing, *macushla*," he assured her. "You're going to make a big bang."

CHAPTER NINE

NIGHT OWL

Jacksonville Naval Air Station, Florida

Drone pilot Master Sergeant Don Hendricks (Night Owl) watched on his screen as the Valor lifted off, dipped its nose and headed west for the coast. From five thousand feet, its pace seemed painfully slow. It took only another thirty seconds for the other Chinese gunships to arrive at the site of their fallen comrade; the Valor now only a mile away.

They circled around the crash site like enraged wasps, dipping and darting to and fro. They looked in the woods, and one even opened fire. They couldn't figure out what had happened. *Good*, Hendricks thought, *each moment they waste gives us a better chance of getting away.*

He watched as one of the Black Widows came in low between the wreckage and the LZ. He appeared to be hovering just a few feet off the ground, turning slowly. Then he rose up quickly and headed directly after the fleeing Valor.

Hendricks lowered his altitude to three thousand feet and targeted the first Black Widow. As far as UAVs went, the Predator was a dinosaur, a relic from the War on Terror, a weapon system that had been replaced by bigger and more lethal drones in every branch of the service except the navy, who kept them because they were small enough and tough enough to use on aircraft carriers. But that smallness meant it had limited armaments. Its two hard points could carry either two Hellfire missiles or four Stingrays. Luckily, he was flying with the Stingrays, but he would have to make every shot count. What's more, he would have to fire the missiles as quickly as possible to keep the element of surprise. The Stingray was a "fire and forget" weapon. Once airborne the missile used a mixture of heat detection and a camera to zero in on its target.

He locked on the first Black Widow, waited for "tone," and fired. Then he did the same for the other three gunships. In less than fifteen seconds, he'd launched all four missiles. It was a drill he had practiced hundreds of times in a simulator, but never in real life.

Yet even before the last Stingray was away, the Z-15's started to react. Hendricks was surprised at how fast their radar picked up the missiles. The gunships broke formation and began to release countermeasures; streams of decoy flares rained down from both sides of each aircraft, like a sudden meteor shower across the African dawn.

As Hendricks had hoped, the flares were mostly positioned in the rear of the gunships and fell toward the ground. That's because they were designed to protect the aircraft from ground-to-air missiles. The fact that he was attacking from above meant the Stingrays were less likely to be confused by the decoys. The Chinese pilots began to realize this too. The first Black Widow tried to bank away at the last minute, but the missile struck just beneath the pilot, cracking open the cockpit. The gunship rolled completely over, and the still-spinning blades sucked it quickly to the earth.

The second missile rushed by its Black Widow, apparently confused by the heat of the decoys, then its searching camera locked on to the silhouette of the aircraft and it zoomed in, smacking hard against the tail boom. The gunship was knocked sideways by the concussion—there was a mist of oil in the air—but it flew on.

By the time the third missile was homing in on its gunship, the pilot had eight more seconds to react than the first pilot. He dropped rapidly while at the same time deploying the decoys, thus staying under them. The Stingray was fooled and detonated early.

The fourth pilot did the same and also eluded the Stingray.

Hendricks couldn't believe his bad luck. Only one in four!

But as he watched the remaining Black Widows, he noticed the tail boom of the second Z-15 was beginning to vibrate like a sounding fork. The pilot felt it too. He broke off and began looking for a place to land. Suddenly the entire tail boom broke away, sending the aircraft nose forward. The pilot attempted to rotate the engines to adjust but it was losing too much altitude, and soon crashed and exploded in the trees.

In the cockpit of one of the two remaining Black Widows, Lieutenant Cheung tried to make sense of it. "Blue Seven, come in? Yu, are you there? Cho, can you hear me?"

"We have to go and help them," his gunner said.

"No," he countered. "They're dead."

Saying it suddenly made it real and irrevocable.

Lieutenant Cheng steeled himself to the new reality: in the last five minutes, six of his friends had been killed by American treachery.

He now had only one thought: revenge.

Before the Stingray strike he had been pursuing a strange shimmer in the sky. It was gaining altitude, heading for the coast, trying to hide in the clouds. He had not been sure it was the enemy . . . until now.

"Red Nine to base," he said into his microphone. "We are under attack. Drone strike has taken out Red Four and Red Two. We are in pursuit of an odd shimmer in the sky, which we suspect is an American aircraft."

CHAPTER TEN

SHOT DOWN

Namibia

Captain Everett: "We need to get those last two gunships."

Winfred: "Whiskey Nine Three, respectfully request permission to assist."

Everett: "Negative, Whiskey Nine Three. I have four F-35s coming your way. ETA, seven minutes."

Winfred: "Yes, sir."

Then under his breath, ". . . Might as well be seven years."

Eric felt the heat of shame on his face. Everett was refusing to let them help because of him. *He* was the reason the mission might fail. Two Z-15s against a Valor was not a fair fight, but two Valors and the element of surprise might be enough . . . and definitely enough to last seven minutes.

Winfred was keeping them on a parallel course with Bailey as they headed for the *Gerald Ford*. Up and in the distance, Eric could see the two Black Widows as they closed on the fleeing Valor. Bailey was trying to get into the clouds, but Eric could tell she wasn't going to make it.

Then he got an idea. He acted on it as soon as the idea occurred to him, before thinking it through. With a flick of a switch, he turned off the ghost program.

Lieutenant Cheung saw the radar blip immediately. He turned his head to starboard for a visual. "American Valor, five o'clock, distance nine kilometers."

But he didn't turn the aircraft immediately. Instead he looked out at the shimmer of light. For a moment he considered holding the pursuit. But below him was a real target, something he could see, something he could destroy.

Eric: "Sir, we have a malfunction in the ghost program. I'm trying to reset it now."

Crew Chief Bob Hollis: "He can definitely see us."

At a distance of three miles the gunfire began.

Winfred: "Taking evasive action."

The Valor surged with renewed speed, rising, then dipping and weaving. Winfred headed south to pull the Black Widows away from Bailey and the others. Eric felt like his internal organs were being slammed to one side of his body, then tossed to the other. *Not exactly ideal working conditions.* But he was clearly seeing the enhancements to the airframe. It was far beyond anything he'd felt in training. Winfred was taking her to the limit. One moment he looked out and saw only sky, the next second, he was looking straight down at the green blur of the treetops.

For the first sixty seconds they held their own. The combination of Winfred's flying, their miniguns blazing out both sides, and the nanoarmor meant that they had taken no damage. But Eric knew the Chinese pilot would soon realize that the cannon rounds were having no effect, then he'd switch to the rockets. He could see the hard points on each wing for the unguided missiles as well as two larger rockets, one on each wing. These were likely laser guided and would mean trouble.

Eric: "I'm ready to reengage the ghost program."

Winfred: "On my mark. Three . . . two . . . one . . . now!"

Eric reengaged the program, and Winfred whipped the Valor to the side and let her drop in the hopes that he could get beneath the Black Widows so they would miss his rotor glare.

In his own cockpit Lieutenant Cheung's rage and frustration only grew as he fired away at the Valor. The American pilot was doing things with the aircraft that he didn't think possible—reverse S-turns, using the terrain then suddenly turning into the sun to blind him. He knew the very best US pilots were called Night Stalkers, and he suspected that this pilot must be one of those. But it wasn't just that. Somehow his gunner kept missing. He could see their tracer rounds heading straight toward the airframe, but then they seemed to disappear. He was also disappointed in his own aircraft. How could the bulky Valor compete with his sleek Z-15? It didn't make sense. The American shouldn't be able to break three hundred knots, but he was easily doing three forty, while Cheung's own turbines were screaming to keep up. *Enough! One Red Arrow rocket would end this.*

But just as he was positioning the laser on his target, the gunship disappeared. One second it was there, the next it was gone. He thought he saw something flash downward, then nothing.

"Tai, do you have him?"

"No, nothing."

An intense feeling of vulnerability came over him. A moment ago, he was the predator. Now he was the prey.

"Take evasive action!" He rose up and banked, his eyes straining to see something that had to be there but wasn't. Then he noticed something momentarily stir the leaves on one of the treetops. A moment later, he saw a strange glare, like the shimmer he had seen before. It was backtracking, heading northwest toward the coast. Trying to get away.

He pretended not to see it and kept the gunship flying away from it.

"I'm taking control of armaments," he told the gunner and he lined up the laser on the target, all the while keeping them flying the other way.

Major Winfred saw the K-19 Red Hawk launch and he tried to react, but at only nine hundred meters, he had just three seconds before the missile struck.

The swarm took the brunt of the impact, but it wasn't enough. The Valor was kicked sideways as bits of shrapnel ripped through the aircraft and its crew. The controls turned sluggish in Winfred's hands. He felt a hot burning sensation in his leg and heard men scream. He tried to close it out of his mind; they would all die if he couldn't keep the bird in the air.

"This is Whiskey Nine Three. We are hit. Say again, we are hit but she's holding together. I'm going to do my best to get her out."

He was losing oil and transmission fluid, but the Valor was designed to fly for a while with neither. He tried to accelerate; the airframe shuddered, but held firm. All along the fuselage, tens of trillions of nanosites were working to repair the damage. Patching holes, reconnecting wires, even pulling particles of the leaking fluids from the air and putting them where they belonged.

Lieutenant Cheung watched as the Red Hawk struck the Valor. It looked like it was going to hit it perfectly broadside. There was a muffled blast, much smaller than a Red Hawk should make. This was an antitank missile that had been redesigned for air-to-air use. It should have obliterated the Valor. But out of the explosion the Valor appeared once more, its incredible camouflage gone. Almost immediately it began to disappear again, in sections, like skin growing over muscles and bones. But one section, aft of the bay door where the missile struck, stayed visible, as if the skin could not grow there. Amazingly she was not only still airborne, she was picking up speed.

Eric had been thrown hard toward the bulkhead when the missile struck. His five-point harness held his body, but his neck whipped hard forward and he felt the vertebra pop. He was relieved to find his neck still moved. *Think! Find a way to take down those choppers!*

Then it came to him.

"Swarms two, four, and six, come to me."

He should have thought about this before. He didn't need a complicated program to take down the gunships, he only needed to disassemble them. And not even the whole aircraft. He pulled up a diagram of the gunship and outlined the tail boom. That was all he needed.

But the swarms had not responded to his command. *Shit!* How far away was he? Probably as much as forty miles now. He had lost the link. They couldn't hear him.

The fog of war was now on him, suffocating his thoughts, making him freeze. *Think! Do something.* There was only one swarm that was close enough to help.

He opened up a direct channel to Winfred, already knowing what Captain Everett would say to the idea. "Dave, it's Eric, I have an idea that can take out both Black Widows, but it will mean we lose our armor for about thirty seconds."

"Do it!" Winfred said. "I'll keep them off as best I can."

In less than a minute he had set up the crude program using an image of the Z-15. When he was ready, he called Winfred again.

"We are losing our protection . . . now."

God, I hope it works.

Bang! Bang! Bang!

At that moment he realized someone was pounding on the door to the egg, trying to get his attention. He had been so engrossed in his work, and the egg was almost soundproof, that he wasn't even sure how long the man had been pounding.

There was nothing more he could do with the swarms—either they would save them or they wouldn't—he unstrapped himself and opened the door to a horrific scene. The floor of the aircraft was slick with blood, and there was a strange mass of messy clothes in the corner. Moynihan, one of the crew chiefs, was stretched out on the floor, trying to reach for something outside of the aircraft . . . out the bay door. "Help me!" He commanded. But there was something not right about the man.

Oh, Jesus.

The bundle of bloody clothes was Moynihan's leg, blown off just above the knee. Blood was spewing from the wound, but the man stayed focused, reaching for the thing outside. At just that moment, the Valor tipped hard to the right. The severed leg slid across the floor and out the opposite door. As the aircraft righted itself, cannon fire swept through the cabin. Moynihan gave a guttural grunt and went still.

Eric strapped his harness to the rappel line and went to help him, but as he turned him over he realized he was dead, there was a gaping wound in his neck; the eyes were wide and rolled white.

"You! Get me that ammo feed!" It was the other crew chief, trying to work the minigun. Eric leaned out and saw what Moynihan had been trying to do—the ammunition feed tube for the minigun had broken off. Eric went to grab it, but his harness held him back. He unfastened it, gripped the rappel cable near the ceiling and grabbed the tube. Just as he handed it to the crew chief, he heard the copilot. "Here they come." Eric looked out and saw the Chinese gunships only three hundred yards away.

Suddenly, the closest Black Widow's tail boom disappeared. One moment it was there, the next it was gone. The gunship began to do somersaults then plummeted to the earth. "Yes!" he heard Winfred say.

But then the remaining Z-15 raked the side of the Valor with cannon fire once more. The aircraft dropped suddenly, and Eric felt a dizziness as the blood rushed to his head. There was a warning sound, a persistent alarm coming from the cockpit.

"Port engine hit."

"Oil pressure dropping," responded the copilot. "We are looking at a transmission fail."

The aircraft was listing to one side and losing altitude, but it was not in free fall. The treetops went by underneath them in a blur.

He looked out at the menacing form of the Black Widow.

Come on!

At that very instant, the nanosites attacked the Z-15's tail boom, but before they could finish their work, it fired its last Red Hawk missile. The missile came zooming at them even as the Black Widow began to spin and fall.

Eric knew they were dead. Without armor, the missile would annihilate them. He looked down at the jungle racing by just inches below their feet. There was a blinding flash. Something smacked him in the chest, and he fell backward into nothingness, the propeller wash momentarily flattening his uniform to his skin. He was overcome by the nausea of feeling nothing beneath him. Swimming in the air. Falling to earth.

Xiao-ping looked out from the door of his own aircraft as the Chinese gunships pursued the other Valor. It had been a deadly aerial dance, as the strange planes darted and swung about each other, the American aircraft disappearing then reappearing. Just as it looked like the Americans were finished, their aircraft smoking and listing, one of the Chinese gunships had suddenly fallen. A moment later, the second one did the same, but not before it had fired one more missile. Xiao-ping watched as someone fell from the American aircraft just at the moment of impact. There was flash of white, then the carcass of the plane slammed into the jungle.

The old soldier they called Sawyer was standing next to him. "Whiskey Nine Three, do you read? Zulu Five one, come in . . . Dave? Eric, can you hear me?" Then he slammed his fist against the bulkhead. "Eric Hill, come in!"

That was when Xiao-ping realized that the owner of the voice in his head had been in the crashed plane. Xiao-ping felt his stomach drop. Even though it had been only an hour ago that he had first heard the voice, he felt an incredible debt to the man who had rescued him.

A moment later Xiao-ping felt a cool mist on his face, a delicious sensation. The Valor had reached the clouds and was quickly consumed inside, now invisible to all eyes.

CHAPTER ELEVEN

MIA

11:54 p.m., November 4, 2026
Washington, DC

It was a quarter-mile walk from Admiral Curtiss's office to his bungalow along River Drive. Walking the distance alone each night was part of his daily routine, a way for him to decompress before he entered his home and changed from being a soldier to being a father and husband. But then he realized, there would be no need for such a transition tonight. Once again, he had stayed at work so late that everyone would likely be asleep when he arrived.

The officers' quarters sat in perfect symmetry along the street—nearly identical white clapboard houses with navy blue awnings on each porch. The lawns were neatly manicured with a single gas light at the bottom of each walkway. Curtiss mused that if you stood at the correct angle, the uniformity of it seemed to go on forever.

It was a crisp fall night, and there was a slight breeze

that rustled through the maple and poplar trees. Curtiss tried to get his mind off his work—and particularly the problem of Chip Walden—and focus on his home life.

His youngest son, River, had stayed home sick from school today, putting an extra burden on his wife, Evelyn. She would understandably grumpy about it in the morning. His eldest, Logan, was taking the SATs in a few weeks, and Curtiss was supposed to be helping him review his math. He'd have to make time for that tomorrow or he'd get an earful from Evelyn.

His phone rang.

He knew instantly who it was.

Another reason he was infuriated with Walden was because his "mandatory briefing" meant that he couldn't follow the African rescue op. He looked at the phone. As he suspected, it was Adams, his aide-de-camp.

"Curtiss."

"I'd better give you the good news first . . ."

Jane and Lili had finished their movie and were foraging through the refrigerator for food. Jane was opening up a carton of coconut milk when Lili's phone rang.

Jane felt a rush of adrenaline, and a shiver run down her back.

Please be good news. Please be good news.

Lili scrambled for the phone.

"Hello? Yes, yes, it's me. Yes, I'll wait." She flashed Jane a smile.

Jane exhaled with deep relief. *Thank God.*

"Panda Bear? Oh, God I can't believe it!" Lili squealed

with joy. Then she switched to Chinese, and Jane could not understand them. But she didn't care, she could feel the woman's happiness in any language.

Jane realized that for Lili and her family, a long hard struggle was finally over. Xiao-ping was the last piece of the puzzle. The last living member of their family to escape the Chinese and come home.

Jane heard Lili say the name "Eric" and she perked up. When she met Lili's gaze, she froze. The woman's face had suddenly gone pale.

For Jane it suddenly seemed as if the air had been drained of all its oxygen.

The coconut milk fell from her hand and hit the floor, its contents flowing out across the tile floor as the carton aspirated like a panting lung.

PART TWO
TRIBAL FORMATIONS

CHAPTER TWELVE

THE STORM

November 5, 2026
Naval Research Lab, Washington, DC

"I'm sorry, Jane," Sawyer said, "but I don't have much to tell you."

"How can that be? Is he alive or dead?"

"We don't know."

"How can you not know? I thought you were leading the rescue mission."

"Technically, I am, but we're stuck on the carrier."

"Oh, God, you mean he's still out there? He could be . . ." She felt her emotions welling up, but her anger quickly stifled her fear. "What the hell are you doing, Sawyer? What happened to 'never leave a man behind'?"

"The CSAR choppers were sent out before I reached the carrier. The problem is that the Chinese lost two aircraft just five hundred yards from our crash site. When our choppers saw theirs, somebody started shooting. It looked like it was going to be another clusterfuck, but luckily cooler heads prevailed, but the rescue mission had to be aborted.

"Then the Namibian government got involved and told both sides to stay the hell out of their airspace. Now the State Department's trying to get a solution. In the meantime, we're stuck here. I'm sorry. The only piece of good news is that we know the Chinese haven't gotten there either."

"Oh my God, Sawyer. You've got to go get him."

"There's more. A big storm is coming in. If we don't get clearance from the Namibians in the next few hours, Everett will have to suspend flight ops. The storm could last as long as twelve hours."

Jane pushed her palms into her eyes, feeling completely helpless. "Haven't you heard anything? No distress call? Nothing?"

"No. We were able to keep a drone over the area for a few hours. We could see the crash site pretty clearly, and there was no movement. But it's the region around the site that's the problem. The tree cover is thick in the spot where we think Eric would be."

"Why wouldn't he be at the crash site?"

"Because he fell out the starboard door a moment before the aircraft went down. I saw the footage from the drone myself. He must have fallen about twenty feet before hitting the forest canopy. If anybody survived the crash it would have been him."

Jane squeezed her eyes shut for a moment, trying to fight off the image of Eric lying wounded, with no one to help him.

"When are you going to get him?" It was part question, part directive.

"You know that if it were up to me, things would be different, right?"

She gave a long exhale. "Yeah," she said, "I know."

CHAPTER THIRTEEN

THE INFILTRATOR

November 5, 2026
Naval Research Lab, Washington DC

Vice Admiral James Curtiss looked at the dossier and scowled. *General Walden isn't wasting any time, is he? As if I don't have enough to worry about with the Namibian raid.*

It had been less than twelve hours since their briefing, and already the Assistant Joint Chief had launched the first volley. Curtiss could tell it was going to be a bitter fight. Oh, the irony. He had spent the last eighteen months battling (and eventually defeating) the Chinese in order to keep this technology safe . . . *to defend the Constitution against all enemies, foreign and domestic.* But now his biggest enemy was not a foreign power, but the very military institution that he had devoted his life to serve.

What a world.

He looked at the profile again.

- Top in her class at the Air Force Academy.
- A spotless record working in missile defense systems at NORAD.
- Four years at the NSA working on SIGINT.
- Seven years as a top AI researcher at Google.

Impeccable.

Perhaps I could dig something up from her high school . . . He stopped himself, realizing the length of his desperation.

There were several ironies here. Throughout his long career, Curtiss had encountered his share of fiefdoms within the DOD. Clusters of power or influence or laziness that were jealously guarded from the inside. Now he was on the other side of one of those fiefdoms. But his project was different. Here, for once, was a top-secret project that deserved protection, whose secrets had to be tightly guarded, kept to a wise few within the military and out of politics for as long as possible. This was not just for the good for the navy, it was the right thing for the whole country and, perhaps, all mankind.

But it was becoming increasingly difficult to keep this Pandora's box closed. If it could even still be considered closed.

Such is the nature of power, Curtiss thought. He finally had it. And now everyone with a star on his shoulder wanted to take it from him. He felt besieged by half the Pentagon, NSA, the CIA, and Homeland Security. Thank God Admiral Garrett had been able to hold them off. It was safer for everyone if the NRL kept control.

Now Walden threatened to mess the whole thing up. Walden never gambled unless he was sure he would win . . . and win smelling pretty. Which was why he had waited until *after* Curtiss had achieved replication before he set his sights on the Naval Research Lab. As soon as he began to understand what Curtiss had done and the power and influence it gave him, he had been trying every possible trick to get the NRL's secrets.

In Curtiss's hand was the most recent attempt.

Olivia Rosario, special envoy from the air force. "To be given full access to NRL facilities, personnel, and records, and integrated into the Artificial Intelligence team."

Special Envoy, Curtiss scoffed, *is that what they call spies these days?*

Curtiss intended to fight it, of course. The problem was that Walden had picked well. Rosario was one of the best in her field, a top AI researcher at Google who had, for some strange reason, left her seven-figure income and returned to the public sector. Why? Because she was dedicated to helping her country? Curtiss didn't think so. No, there was only one good reason: there was something here she couldn't get there. And he knew what it was.

Forced Evolution.

It was the key to everything, the single most important innovation that had gotten them to replication. And it was Eric Hill's brainchild—an idea that was both simple and ingenious. He had realized that they could use the principles of natural selection to make dramatic leaps forward in their engineering processes. While human evolution was measured in thousands of years, the evolution of their nanosites could be measured in milliseconds, even nanoseconds. Just as bacteria could quickly evolve a resistance to an antibiotic over successive generations, their swarms could be forced to evolve into any tool or instrument they needed.

It was the one idea that had allowed them to defeat the Chinese, and its applications were endless.

That's why Rosario was here. He knew it.

CHAPTER FOURTEEN

BOOTS ON THE GROUND

November 5, 2026
Namibia

Master Chief Nathan Sawyer moved through the night jungle toward the downed Valor. He led his team cautiously. All their intel told them that they were alone and the first ones here, but he wasn't taking any chances. The last thing they needed was another run-in with the Chinese.

He'd had to pull out all the stops to convince Captain Everett to let him and his team off the *Ford*. After the botched raid, the man was afraid of losing his command. He'd told Sawyer flatly that he couldn't afford any more bad news. Sawyer had assured him they could use the cover of the receding storm to make a clean insertion.

The storm had been a nasty one, and the rain was still pouring down around them. The sound of it filled his ears as it smacked off the wide leaves of the tropical forest. Yet despite the rain and the night, his visibility was excellent and not a drop of water touched him, thanks to the Venger armor and optics that filtered out the rain and turned night into day. Enhanced by AI, it was often difficult to tell it wasn't daytime; only when he turned his head upward and saw the stars did he remember.

As he parted the foliage, the hulk of the ruined Valor appeared in front of him like the carcass of a prehistoric beast. The nose of the aircraft had slammed into the ground so hard it had snapped the fuselage in half, leaving the cargo area and wing upside down on the other side of the cockpit. The way the jungle had swallowed up the plane, with vines and tree limbs draped over the wings and rotors, made her look like she'd been sitting there for years.

"Patel and Duncan, you keep a perimeter watch. Loc, you go ahead." The medic and his assistant sprinted for the downed bird, eager to find any survivors.

Sawyer headed northeast, following the path the Valor had been on when she was hit. One hundred and fifty yards on, he found a scattering of broken tree branches on the forest floor. He looked up. Sure enough, he could see where Hill had crashed through the canopy. He saw several cracked limbs including one as thick as his thigh that still clung to the tree by a long strip of bark. *Must have hurt like hell*, he thought. *But where's the body?* He began searching the area, but there was no sign of Hill. He thought of Jane, waiting for him to bring her man home . . . dead or alive.

He stopped. There, not four feet in front of him was a pair of boots, set perfectly upright as if left by the back door. A pair of socks lay neatly beside them. He rubbed his beard, examining them. Then he looked around once more.

Nothing.

He tapped on his mic. "Papa Six Four Actual to Tango Seven Seven."

"Go ahead, Papa Six Four." It was Bailey.

"Are we sure there are no bad guys in the area?"

"Affirmative. It's all clear."

He risked calling out. "Eric! Eric, it's me, Sawyer. Can you hear me?"

The only response was the pounding rain.

He circled the boots, looking for clues.

Nothing. He picked them up.

They were standard issue. They had to be Hill's. There were three inches of water in them, so they'd been there for most of the night.

"Eric! Eric Hill!"

No reply.

He called Loc on the radio. "Sit-rep."

"They're all dead. Probably on impact. The pilots were still strapped in. Did you find Hill?"

"I found where he landed, but he's not here. Do you see any sign that anyone else has been there?"

"No."

"Anything missing?"

"Negative, everything's where it should be."

"Do they have their boots on?"

"Say again."

"Winfred and the rest of the flight crew, do they still have their boots on?"

"Yeah, of course."

"Okay, over." He hailed Patel. "Give Loc a hand with the bodies, then set charges on both engines, the egg, and anything that's left of the cockpit. When you're done, come help me look for Hill."

"Roger."

Sawyer began searching the area more thoroughly and calling out to Eric, determined to figure out what had happened. Sawyer was an excellent hunter and tracker, so finding one wounded man should have been easy. But the storm had made things very difficult, wiping away any footprints or blood, and pounding down the foliage, jumbling any sign Hill might have left. The rain had also wiped out any heat signatures. The Venger optics could pick up a footprint hours after it had been made, but the cold rain had made everything uniform.

After a half hour of fruitless searching, he heard four quick blasts as Patel destroyed the remains of the Valor. A few minutes later he joined Sawyer. "Loc and Duncan are getting the bodies out. Any luck here?"

"Nothing!" He explained about the boots.

"So he falls forty feet through a tree, gets up, takes off his boots, and walks off into the jungle?" Patel asked.

"He couldn't have made it far. You don't fall like that without getting messed up. And he would have known that his best chance of rescue was remaining here. Maybe he was in shock."

Suddenly his radio came to life. "Tango Seven Seven to Papa Six Four." It was Bailey.

Sawyer tapped his mike. "This is Papa Six Four Actual, go ahead."

"We have three approaching aircraft. It looks like two Z-15s escorting a Harbin Z-9."

The Harbin was a typical CSAR bird. It looked like the Chinese were coming to collect their dead too.

"ETA?" Sawyer asked.

"About seven minutes."

Sawyer assessed the situation: This was bad news. He'd recovered the bodies of the crew and destroyed the Valor's advanced weapon technology. Most of the mission objectives were complete. Hill was the only missing piece. But he couldn't risk another confrontation with the Chinese. Not now. *Shit*! For a moment, Sawyer considered staying. Alone. He prided himself on his ability to survive anywhere, under any conditions. He could find Hill no matter where he was, if only he had more time. And time was of the essence. If Hill were still alive, he'd need medical attention fast. If only he could stay. But Captain Everett would never go for it.

He turned to Patel. "Time to go."

Patel sighed reluctantly.

"Eric!" Sawyer called as loud as he could over the pounding rain. "We will come back for you. I swear."

Three minutes later Sawyer was in the Valor, airborne, the black body bags of the four dead crew members on the floor in front of him. He looked out the window at the smoking wreckage of Winfred's Valor and the thick jungle where Eric Hill had to be . . . somewhere.

CHAPTER FIFTEEN

THE NEW ANARCHISTS

November 5, 2026
Washington, DC

The iSheet came to life in video mode. It was a night shot on a selfie stick, so the exposure was brightened and extra light was thrown on the subject—a pretty woman in her thirties, with curly reddish-brown hair under a baseball cap. The GPS locator identified their position as 38.891767 -77.008869, on the north lawn of the US Capitol building near Constitution Avenue. She was dressed casually in jeans, sneakers, a black North Face jacket, and the cap, similar to many of the tourists visiting the nation's capital. The only incongruity was that she was wearing sunglasses after dark.

"Start recording," the woman said.

A red light began to blink on the screen.

The woman began. "Directly behind me is the Russell Senate Office Building. There on the second floor"—the woman turned and pointed to a lit window—"is the office of Senator Nathanial Peck, a man who has been enriching himself with oil company profits for the last twenty-five years. His brother Anthony is a partner at Peck, Chase and Andrews, a PR firm that disseminates false information about climate change. In exchange for the lucrative contracts his brother receives, Senator Peck always votes in the interests of the oil lobby, which includes blocking efforts to clean up oil spills and supporting legislation that prohibits citizens from suing oil companies. Together, the two brothers receive over thirty-five million dollars every year to be lapdogs for Big Oil. But no longer."

At that instant, there was a blinding flash, and the Russell Senate Office Building exploded behind her. The woman was rocked forward by the blast, her hair blowing over her face.

With determined poise, she calmly removed her sunglasses, exposing lucid hazel eyes. "I am Riona Finley of the New Anarchists. This is what happens to elected officials who enrich themselves by poisoning the environment for the rest of us."

A fire alarm rang in the background, followed by the sound of approaching sirens.

"Eighty-two percent of Americans want better protection for the environment, yet year after year nothing changes. That is not democracy. So we are sending a message to America's leaders. You will be held accountable. Protect Mother Earth . . . or else.

"End recording."

★★★

Eight blocks away, FBI Special Agent Bartholomew "Bud" Brown was sitting in his office, bored out of his mind. He hadn't been assigned a case in months, and he knew he wasn't about to get one anytime soon. Especially not if the new assistant director, Anastasia Collins, had anything to say about it. Next month Bud would hit the FBI's mandatory retirement age of fifty-seven. While the limit was sometimes waived for "high value" agents, that would not be the case with him. And since he was unlikely to see any case to its conclusion in his last month, he was essentially off the roster. So here he sat, alone in his office, waiting for his inevitable retirement, mulling over cold cases that would never be solved. His own private hell.

He sighed, loosened his tie, and looked at the stack of manila folders on his desk. He leaned forward and was about to turn on his desktop computer (he was the only agent on the floor who still had one) when he caught a glimpse of himself in the dark screen. "Damn, you look like shit," he said aloud. The man he saw before him looked closer to seventy than sixty.

He could suddenly see how the thirty years of smoking had depleted the collagen and elastin in his skin. And his hair, well, it was just pathetic. Each morning he tried to rally the few remaining stands into a wispy comb over, but he suddenly realized how ridiculous it looked. Then there were the problems you couldn't see: the hypertension, the high cholesterol, the type II diabetes, his failing liver.

Suddenly he understood why the new assistant director had such little faith in him.

But she didn't understand that he'd been a good agent, once upon a time. Back in 1994 the FBI had recruited him from the Detroit Police Department because he'd been a prodigy, a homicide detective who got things done. And for the longest time, he'd felt it was true: he was built to solve crimes; built to reconstruct the past; built to play with time, to rewind the flight of bullets to their masters. Methodical. Analytical. Poised.

But while he was certainly built to solve crimes, he wasn't good for much else. He wasn't built to raise kids, not built to keep Carol in his life, and definitely not meant to interview next of kin—widows, widowers, orphans, parents—and stay sober afterward. It was the alcohol that had driven Carol away and, with her, the kids.

And that was the greatest tragedy: When the job ended next month, he had nowhere to go.

Suddenly there was a commotion outside his office, a dozen agents shouting, phones ringing, and the heavy footfalls of people running down the tile corridor. He went to his office door and flung it open.

The fourth floor was an open space, essentially thirty yards of desks. Brown looked out and saw Anastasia Collins standing on one of them, giving orders to the thirty or so agents assembled around her. On the far wall behind her was a chain of iSheets set to each of the major networks. Their scrolling marquees echoed one another: BREAKING NEWS: BOMBING ON CAPITOL HILL—TERRORISTS ATTACK US GOVERNMENT—SENATOR ASSASSINATED.

"We have a major terrorist attack on our doorstep," Collins was saying, "but I want everyone to keep cool. This is what you've been trained for. Now listen close: Thompson, call the director and brief him on what we know so far. Rivers and Wilson, you gather the best biometric team you can—find people with experience in arson and bombings—and have them ready to go. Edwards, you'll be our point of contact with Capitol Police. Contact Chief Kim and let him know we are ready to assist."

She paused for a moment, looking out at the agents. Her eyes fell on Brown. She considered him for a moment, then turned to another agent and began giving more orders. If Bud had had any questions about how Collins felt about his usefulness, they had just been answered. A part of him was fine with that. He didn't want to be part of an investigation that he'd never see closed. Yet another part of him felt the sting of the insult like a slap on the face—an insult that every agent on the floor had picked up on—and that made him want to prove her wrong.

Several of the networks were showing the video of the bombing. Bud recognized Riona Finley immediately. She was #7 on the FBI's most wanted, had killed three people in the last eighteen months: an oil company executive, an attorney, and a well-known blogger and climate change denier. But since those bombings had all taken place in Texas, the investigation had been on the shoulders of the local branch. Not anymore. Finley was now officially a national security threat.

"Vallarta!" Collins said, "Has anyone found Rogers? We need him ASAP."

Geoff Rogers was the top bomb tech at the bureau and a legend in the field. Before he'd joined the FBI he'd been an EOD guy in the marines—Explosive Ordnance Disposal. When 9/11 hit, he'd been called to active duty and spent six years trying to outthink ISIS and Taliban bombers. That experience had given him a sixth sense about tracking down terrorists.

"I can't get a hold of him," Vallarta said.

"I'm here!" came a bellowing voice, and Rogers emerged from around the elevator shaft. He was a big, barrel-chested man, with salt-and-pepper hair and a fat mustache that hadn't changed since the '90s. Rogers was from Bud's generation and a classmate from the academy. They had once been partners. In fact, Rogers's wife and Bud's ex were still close. Bud realized Rogers likely knew all about Bud's miseries. And while Rogers was also fifty-seven, he'd gotten his waiver because he was so valuable to the FBI.

"My apologies, Assistant Director," Rogers said and came close to her and whispered to her. Bud could see her shaking her head.

Rogers leaned in again, trying to persuade her of something.

Now Collins voice was full of annoyance: "Whatever it is, just say it."

Rogers nodded, stood up straight. "The director has reassigned me to the National Security Branch and has asked me to lead the investigation. Given the current emergency I would appreciate some assistance from you and your staff."

Collins didn't answer right away and an odd silence fell over the room. The shock was palpable on her face. She was the new assistant director, just thirty-five years old, out to make her mark, and here was the biggest case of her career. Now Rogers, only a special agent, was getting it? Bud could see her thinking—and thinking hard. She didn't have to give Rogers anything, but if she refused and hindered him at this critical moment, Roger's powerful friends—including the director—would hear about it. "Of course," she finally said, "what can we help you with?"

Rogers began by selecting three bomb techs and a forensics expert. He seemed about to leave, then reconsidered. "And I could use a good homicide agent," he said looking around the room.

"I'd recommend Diaz," Collins said.

Rogers nodded noncommittally. Then his eyes met Bud's.

"Brown!" he called. "Let's go!"

Six miles away, Bill Eastman and Jack Behrmann stood simultaneously and raised their champagne glasses.

"It is our great honor to welcome you to the Naval Research Laboratory," Eastman said.

"I second that," Jack Behrmann said. "And we hope that all of you grow and thrive here with us."

The assembled guests, sixty-five new hires, raised their glasses and cheered. They were gathered in a banquet hall near the center of campus, seated at fifteen round tables with navy blue tablecloths and white place mats. The guests had just finished their choice of beef medallions or smoked salmon with asparagus and rice pilaf.

"Hear, hear!" Bill Eastman said. They all drank.

Bill looked at his old friend.

Bill and Jack were the lead scientists of the lab and had been working together for thirty-three years. Their friendship had begun in a dorm room at UC Berkeley when the oversized Behrmann, who stood at six foot eight, had walked in carrying a minifridge under one arm. Their mutual love of science had evolved into a life-long partnership and together they had become two of the most revered scientists in Silicon

Valley. Then a year and a half ago, Admiral Curtiss had asked them to lead the most ambitious scientific endeavor since the Manhattan Project.

"We do have some words of advice for you," Bill Eastman said.

At just that moment, the room was filled with the beeping, ringing, and vibrating of dozens of iSheets, including Bill Eastman's.

"We are in lockdown," someone said.

Eastman pulled out his phone and read the alert to the crowd. "There has been an attack on a nearby government installation."

Suddenly the doors of the banquet hall opened, and six marines and a naval serviceman entered. Eastman recognized the latter as Specialist Drake Walters, one of Curtiss's SEALs.

Walters came up to Eastman. "Sir, we have been assigned to protect you and Dr. Berhmann." He gave a glance around the room. "I'd like to get you to a more secure location."

Eastman leaned over and spoke softly to the man. "I would prefer to stay here, if I may. After all, what kind of an example would I be setting if I disappeared at the first hint of danger?"

Walters seemed to appreciate this. He looked around the room, assessing its strengths and weaknesses. "I think I can make that work."

"Thank you."

As the marines and Walters closed the blinds, Eastman continued his role as the leader. "Alexandra, would you please turn on the news?" The young woman turned on the large iSheet at the end of the hall.

The first images were of fire trucks arching long streams

of water into the burning frame of the Russell Senate Office Building.

"The death toll is currently at two," a newscaster said, "but will likely increase. The Capitol Police have told us they suspect multiple bombs were planted in the offices of Senator Peck, who is now assumed dead along with a member of his staff. Back to you, Ellen."

"Thank you, Randall. If you are just joining us: a terrorist attack has rocked Washington, DC. The radical environmentalist group, the New Anarchists, is taking responsibility for the blast. Their leader, Riona Finley, has already posted the following video on social media."

As the video began, Eastman found himself moving across the banquet hall to get a better look. He wasn't the only one; the crowd seemed drawn to it. His first thought was, *here is something new*. A strong, charismatic, and articulate woman, acting as the spokesperson for a terrorist organization.

But what surprised him the most was when the building exploded behind her, he did not hear cries of shock or horror from the young people in the room. Rather, gasps of amazement and excitement. "So cool!" someone said.

He glanced at Jack and could tell he shared his apprehension. Bill suddenly felt old and out of touch. Clearly, he was not perceiving the world on the same wavelength as this younger generation. Was this just entertainment to them? Whether or not Peck was corrupt, didn't it bother any of them that their government had just been attacked?

Jack came to his side and showed him the video on social media.

It had 3.5 million likes, and 200,000 dislikes.

Bill scanned the comments:

"How do I join your group?"

"We love you, Riona!"

"Can you please blow up my senator?"

Bill gave Jack a quizzical look.

"She's a hero to them," Jack said.

"But why?"

"Because they don't believe in the system," Jack said. "Not only do they not believe in it, they hold it in contempt. They see our government as a kleptocracy, up for sale to the wealthiest. So to see someone challenge it, attack it head on, for them that's invigorating."

While the scientist in him felt that this was a fascinating phenomena, it was also disconcerting. Here he was, a Nobel laureate, the leader of the entire Naval Research Lab, and the driving force behind some of the most important technology mankind had ever created, yet Riona Finley was proof he didn't understand the world nearly as well as he thought he did. Forces were at work that he was helpless to stop or alter.

He turned to Jack. "First thing tomorrow, we're going to find out everything we can about her."

CHAPTER SIXTEEN

CAPTAIN CÁO

November 5, 2026
Somewhere in the South Atlantic

Captain Cáo Laquan felt humiliated. He had been hoodwinked by the Americans, who had clearly staged the riot at the mining camp in order to rescue one of the inmates. They were responsible for the deaths of on hundred thirty inmates, twenty-five guards and prison officials, and ten of his own men—some of the best airmen he'd ever had.

It hadn't taken Cáo long to connect the dots. Only two prisoners were unaccounted for. The initial search showed they were both John Does, nameless people without family back in China. But Cáo knew this was likely false, a product of the poor record keeping of the laogai, who preferred to have anonymous (and hence disposable) slaves. It was only after doing a facial recognition check on their file photos that one of the men's identities was revealed—Pān Xiao-ping. A search of his relatives showed that he'd been married to Hwe

Lili, a known spy for the Americans and a former biochemist at the Fort Yue Fei military base, wanted in connection with the May 26, 2026 outbreak that had killed sixty-five thousand people. Suddenly the reason for the US meddling in the mutiny was clear.

Back in China, things were in utter chaos, but Cáo still had connections in the Ministry of State Security, and his old friend Ma Bingwen was still doing his job. Cáo had fed him the footage of the American Valor's ability to hide and heal itself. He'd also sent him the transmissions they had captured from the Americans. Bingwen was particularly interested in the part when the American Valor was shot down. In a moment of high emotion, one of the Americans had used the real name of one of his friends.

Eric Hill.

Yes, Bingwen had been very interested in that.

Eric Hill, US Naval Research Lab. Terrorist. Wanted in connection with Fort Yue Fei outbreak. A 500,000,000¥ reward. Extremely dangerous.

Bingwen had been succinct. "Get Eric Hill and you will avenge all who were killed at Fort Yue Fei."

And for Cáo, that horrific slaughter was no distant news story. He had spent his entire career in the military and had personally known thirty-four people who died that day: one of his closest friends from high school; a revered mentor from the navy; a beautiful girl he had dated at Shanghai Maritime University; and most painfully, two of his cousins, Tengfei and Rong, who had been army cadets.

It was clear that Hill had gone down in the Valor. Dead or alive, Cáo wanted him. As soon as he got Bingwen's message, he had scrambled two Black Widows and the Harbin.

But they arrived too late. The Americans had just left the crash site. When he saw the black smoke rising up from the downed Valor, Captain Cáo had been incensed. But once again, they were able to intercept the American's transmissions. Not all the bodies had been found. The exchange did not mention the man's name, but the worry in the Captain's voice told him that it was someone of strategic importance.

Cáo vowed to find him first. It was his chance to redeem himself in the eyes of his men. A chance to advance his career and to hand the Central Committee a real prize. Most importantly, it was a chance for justice.

CHAPTER SEVENTEEN

FALLOUT

November 6, 2026
The Pentagon, Washington, DC

Admiral James Curtiss looked over his notes one last time before the briefing. The fifteen principals—including three members of the joint chiefs—were talking in small groups or filling cups of coffee.

He knew it was going to be a tough briefing, especially with Walden and the secretary of the navy in the room, but he reminded himself that things could be worse.

They had been able to spin the botched raid to the press as a training accident. So far—thanks to some high-level talks between the White House and Beijing—the Chinese had not contradicted the story. But with all the chaos within the Chinese Central Committee, it wasn't clear who was actually running the country, which meant they could change their minds at any moment. In the meantime, the captain of the *Liaoning* was keeping the carrier on high alert and doing everything he could to thwart their search for Hill.

As he reviewed his notes, Curtiss felt a change in the room, like a shift in barometric pressure.

He looked up to see a beautiful woman in the doorway.

"Ah, there you are," General Walden stepped forward and greeted her warmly.

"Chip, so good to see you!"

She wore dark designer slacks and an Air Force–blue blouse accented by an amber calico scarf. Her thick black hair was piled high on her head, with a few choice strands framing her strong—almost chiseled—face. Her body, too, was lean and strong in a way that suggested unwavering discipline, with 5:00 a.m. runs, burpees, and protein powder smoothies.

She smiled and greeted everyone warmly, working the room, a pleasant lucidity to her brown eyes. Curtiss had to admit her charisma was undeniable. Her posture and demeanor effused confidence. And there was a theatrical grace to her movements. Every smile, every widening of the eyes had a purpose, and she struck Curtiss as an actor, as one who knows exactly the role she needs to play. Yet he found himself reacting to her the way that he did do to all actors: with a mixture of fascination and uneasiness. *Drawn to their charms but doubting their sincerity.*

She strode confidently up to him. "Admiral Curtiss, I'm Olivia Rosario, a new member of your AI team." She smiled and offered her hand. "It's a pleasure to meet you."

"Yes, of course, Olivia," he said, playing it as cool as he could. "Nice to meet you, too, but I didn't request your presence at this meeting."

She gave him a warm smile. "General Walden insisted I

come. He wants to know how we can use AI to prevent any more *unfortunate* events like this."

He suppressed an urge to laugh at her audacity. "And you feel you have a lot to offer after your four days of experience?"

"With all due respect, sir, I have eighteen years of experience in neural networks and deep learning. While your team has done some amazing things, there *is* room for improvement. I could—"

Just then CNO Garrett addressed the room. "Is everyone ready?"

Curtiss held up his hand to Rosario. "This will have to wait."

When everyone was seated, Captain Everett and Master Chief Nathan Sawyer appeared on a huge wall-mounted iSheet, conferenced in from the USS *Gerald Ford*. Curtiss's aide, Commander Adams, began by giving a brief summary of the mission.

As Curtiss had expected, Walden took every opportunity to lay the blame for the casualties and the bad press on him while Rosario took every opportunity to stress how every problem could have prevented if the operation had been controlled by an AI system.

The two of them had clearly rehearsed their parts and kept nailing the same talking points: poor mission prep and not enough planning for contingencies such as the Chinese Z-15 gunships. Plus poor decisions on the ground: namely, Eric Hill's decision to include Xiao-ping's friend in the rescue.

What's more, the mission logs showed that Hill had intentionally disengaged his Valor's ghost program in order to lure the Chinese away from the other aircraft.

This had cost the lives of the Valor's crew and, most likely, his own.

"If Hill survived, he should be thrown in the brig," Walden said.

Curtiss shook his head with open disdain. "You two have a very unrealistic understanding of warfare," he said. "Probably because neither of you have ever been in it. War, by its very nature, is chaos, and, therefore, unpredictable. I'd also like to remind you that this was a successful operation. Yes, Hill disobeyed orders, but his actions saved the mission. He took out the last two gunships, and if he'd just had a few more seconds the mission would have been a complete success. Do you really think that by handing decision-making over to a machine, you will eliminate the unexpected?"

"Yes, I do," Rosario said, "Because a machine doesn't get tired or scared or hesitate. And our AI systems can make decisions faster than any human. On this op, the problems began to cascade when Hill let Xiao-ping's friend come with them. That would never have happened if an AI system had been running this op. The other man would have never made it out of the cellblock."

"Then neither would Xiao-ping," Curtiss countered. "He told Hill that he wouldn't leave without his friend."

"Then we would have sent your men in to carry Xiao-ping out alone."

Curtiss scoffed. "Hindsight is certainly twenty-twenty isn't it? Hill had a SEAL team in full armor—all essentially invisible and invulnerable—against thirty Chinese guards whose rifles wouldn't fire and who were occupied with a mutiny. At that moment, he had no idea about the Z-15 gunships, so taking an extra prisoner added almost no risk to the mission. Your AI system would have made the same choice because it would never have predicted the arrival of so much hardware to put down an insurrection in a small mining camp. Especially since the Chinese military did nothing to intervene in any of the other mutinies."

Curtiss looked at Rosario, and she dropped her eyes. *That's right*, he thought, *you know you're wrong*.

"Let's take a step back, shall we, and think about this objectively," she said.

Curtiss eyed her suspiciously.

"Regardless of the details of this mission," she continued, "the intention of the US military is to move forward—and move forward aggressively—with automation." She turned her attention to the others in the room.

"I realize that Admiral Curtiss has great respect for our combat troops and their abilities. I can appreciate that. But warfare is changing. And automation is the future. The Russians, the French, the Chinese, they're all developing automated systems. The Israelis already have drones that pick targets and fire with no human intervention. It's time we did the same."

"I completely disagree," Curtiss said. "The protocol that we have used since 9/11 needs to stay in place. Machines such as drones can acquire targets, but the decision to kill needs to be made by a human. I'm all for using AI for development and for assisting our troops, but not automated killing. And that means no automation of mission control."

Rosario shook her head. "I'm sorry, sir, but if you only knew what we are capable of. Any nuance of human decision making can be replicated by the right algorithm. There is literally nothing that an AI system can't do."

Now Walden chimed in. "You're trying to hold back the

tides, Jim. The world is becoming more complex every day, and we need machines if we are going to keep up with that complexity."

"That's right," Rosario continued. "It's truly amazing what we can do now. I've already been discussing this with Ryan Lee, and he's confident we can control any combat operation better than humans."

Curtiss shook his head. "That's an easy promise to make, especially for someone trying to increase her power in an organization, but we all know it is a difficult thing to deliver."

"Then give me four months, and I'll prove it. All I need is Ryan Lee and open access to the Forced Evolution systems."

Curtiss noticed Walden's mouth shift into a sly grin. He was clearly enjoying watching his protégé get the upper hand on him. *Forced Evolution.* Now there was no doubt why Rosario had taken the job.

"Ryan Lee is dedicating all his efforts to the Venger system," Curtiss said.

"Ah, yes," Walden said. "The Venger system. And why wasn't it used in Namibia? I understand that it could have prevented some of your snafus."

"Some aspects of the Venger system were used in the raid, such as the ghost program and the night optics, but the entire system, including the neural nets and the battlefield mapping, were not ready. Yes, I will acknowledge that it may have been helpful, but it's still in testing and it would not have changed the outcome of the mission. It will likely be two weeks to a month before it comes online."

"That means Ryan Lee will soon be available for a new project," Rosario said.

"Yes," Curtiss countered, "but Ryan Lee works for me, and I will decide what his next project will be."

"Of course," Walden said, "unless the Joint Chiefs tell you otherwise."

Olivia Rosario strode to the back of the NRL parking lot where her 2011 Mercedes C63 was parked. It sat over two parking spaces because, yes, she was that kind of car owner . . . and, yes, this was that kind of car. She touched a button on her remote, the car beeped its compliance and she opened the driver's side door.

At first glance, it looked like a thousand other Mercedes sedans, a family car, painted an unassuming white with black trim. But looks can be deceiving.

She turned the key in the ignition, and the 6.3 liter V-8 engine came to life with a beastly growl.

Olivia never got tired of that sound, nor the engine that made it. Oh, that engine. The first ever designed by the petrolheads at AMG. It could only be described with one word: unruly. The engine was like a hungry animal pulling at its chain. The slightest touch on the accelerator was enough to flatten Olivia's head into the headrest and leave her hands struggling to maintain control.

It was for this very reason that she had bought the car. For here was a kindred spirit, something—like her—that looked benign enough, yet had a hidden interior. A creature that refused to be tamed, that refused to listen to the naysayers—*women don't become tech entrepreneurs*—and refused to obey the rules.

She donned her sunglasses and opened the sunroof. It

was a warm fall evening, and she intended to enjoy every minute of the remaining sunshine.

She eased the car out of the lot and down Oberlin Avenue. This was the prettiest part of campus, with an open lawn on her left and a row of maple trees, now in bright fall colors.

She reflected on her day: She was pleased with the briefing, although she could not say it had gone perfectly.

She would have preferred to use more honey than vinegar with Curtiss, but she had studied him well and knew that, above all, he was a man who respected strength. If she had come off as a bitch, so be it, as long as he respected the fact that she could wield real power.

And Walden? He had played his part well, and they were becoming an effective team. That was good, because she needed Walden. Luckily, he was a man who could be easily manipulated. In his rush to get control of the lab from Curtiss, he was giving Olivia a shot at tremendous power . . . which she had every intention of taking.

She caught a glance of herself in the rearview mirror and couldn't help but smile.

Walden had no idea the real reason she was there.

But as she made a left onto the ramp to I-295, a shadow of doubt crossed her face. *It still may not be enough,* she reminded herself. *You may only have a few months—six at the most—to do the things you need to do.*

And if you don't?

She didn't want to think about that. So far in this life she had never failed to accomplish a goal. She was rightly proud of that. But this was different.

This time life had thrown her an unexpected curve ball, one that left her lying awake at night wondering what she'd done to deserve this.

It was a difficult thing to accept, because until two years ago, her life had gone to her plan as precisely as a movie script. But something had happened to her happily ever after.

For the first time in her life she was faced with an enemy she did not know how to defeat, an enemy she could not predict or control, and who could demand more of her than she was able to give.

At the top of the ramp she hit the gas. The 510 horsepower V8 gave a wicked growl, and the hood of the car seemed to rise up and bite at the open road. But her earlier elation had now given way to worry and frustration, and she drove forward without any sense of exhilaration, only desperation.

There was so much she had to do and so little time to do it.

CHAPTER EIGHTEEN

INTO THE DARKNESS

November 6, 2026
Namibia

Eric came awake into a foggy consciousness. Everything was dark, as if he were blindfolded. It was raining, and he was shivering. He heard voices speaking a language he didn't understand, full of clicks and deep notes. Then he heard English. "Let me kill him." It was a woman's voice.

"That is not for us to decide," someone replied.

Then he fell unconscious.

He awoke in terrible pain. His head felt as if his brain had swelled to twice its normal size and was about to split his skull apart.

He groaned and opened his eyes, but saw only darkness.

He heard the strange language again, someone calling to someone else.

Good God! The pain!

He passed out again.

When he came to again, the pain had subsided, but he still had a pounding headache. He opened his eyes to see only darkness once more.

“Is anyone there?”

He heard a woman’s voice making the strange clicking language.

He strained to see her, but there was only blackness. How could it be so dark? Was he blindfolded? He reached up to touch his eyes and felt his eyelashes against his fingertips.

A sudden horror crept into his mind.

He heard movement. Someone was coming closer.

He heard a man’s voice, speaking heavily accented English. “You are awake. That is good. My name is Khamko.” Eric felt a small hand clasp his forearm. “We found you in the woods. You have taken a very bad blow to the head. Can you tell me your name?”

“Eric Hill,” he replied. “Where am I?”

“You are near the Khaudum River.”

“Why is it so dark in here?”

Khamko didn’t answer immediately; he seemed to be choosing his words. “I was afraid of this,” he finally said. “I’m very sorry to tell you that it is the middle of the afternoon, and light is shining through the door of the hut.”

Eric felt his head swim, a sudden claustrophobia closed in around him.

Khamko continued: "Your eyes are open, moving, and adjusting to the light. This tells me that the problem is not ocular but neurological. Do you understand what that means?"

"It means my eyes are fine, but my brain is fucked."

"It is called cortical blindness," Khamko said. "The trauma to your head has damaged your occipital cortex. Your eyesight may come back, but the chances are very small. I know this is very hard news, but if it is any consolation, it could be far worse. The fact that you are speaking clearly and can move means you are much better off than I had feared."

"Are you a doctor?"

"No, you would call me a healer, although that is not our word. I would like to get you to a hospital, but I'm afraid it will be many days before that is possible."

"How long have I been here?"

"Two days."

Eric tried to sit up. But the effort to lift his head was too painful.

"Please don't," Khamko said. "I know you must be frightened. It's a lot to take in. But you shouldn't move. You are safe here, and your body needs rest to heal itself."

His head was pounding, but he became aware that he was sore all over, especially his left side. He ran his hand along his thigh and found it wrapped with bandages.

"You had many cuts, but only two were serious. I put twenty stitches in the back of your head and another fifteen in your left arm."

"Thank you. But what happened to the plane? Where are the others?"

"You were the only one we found alive."

Eric lay back. He thought about Major Winfred and the

crew of the Valor. He felt horrible. This was all his fault. He should have been better prepared. He tried to force himself up again, but Khamko gently eased him back down.

"I have to go. People will be looking for me."

"Yes, many people *are* looking for you. But I suspect that they are not the ones you want to find you."

"Chinese?"

"Yes," Khamko said. "We have seen them searching for escaped prisoners in the past, but never like this."

"I wasn't a prisoner," he said, finding no reason to hide the truth. "I'm a scientist. I was trying to help a prisoner escape."

"Ah, a scientist who wears a military uniform. Then that is perhaps why they are so keen to find you."

Eric knew that during the battle the Chinese had gotten a glimpse of what they could do and, regardless of the fluid situation in Beijing, someone clearly wanted their hands on it . . . and him.

It wouldn't be the first time, he thought.

Eric awoke sometime later. He said a silent prayer before opening his eyes, but when he did all was still darkness. He let out a long exhale. He would have to learn to live without his eyes, at least for a while. He tried to open his remaining senses and "see" the world as best he could.

The first thing he noticed was the sound of children. They were close, whispering to each other. He heard one laugh.

He turned his head toward them. It sent a bolt of pain down his spine, but the chatter instantly ceased. They were watching him. He tried to listen harder, to find other clues about where he was. Above him, he heard the sound of the wind through grass and knew the hut must have a thatch roof. Then he heard a woman's voice. He couldn't understand her words, but she seemed to be scolding the children. They laughed and squealed, and he heard their voices scattering in all directions.

He felt her presence coming closer.

"My name is Naru," she said. "I've brought you some food and water."

He sensed a coldness in her voice, as if she was doing something she found unpleasant. He sat up awkwardly. His head was still pounding and his shoulders were tight as cables, but at least he could move.

"Hold out your hand." She gave him the food.

"Thank you," he said. He took a bite. It was somc sort of tuber with a heavy, earthen taste somewhere between a potato and a carrot. Eric felt the silence grow long.

"How is it that you speak English?" he asked.

She didn't answer. Eric tried again.

"The children, why were they watching me?"

To this she replied, but her voice had taken on a calculating tone. "Oh, you should hear them. They have never seen anyone like you. Some say you must be from the moon, because your skin is so white they can see your blue veins underneath. Others say you will turn brown as soon as they put you in the sun. And others want to know why we haven't killed you, like we kill all the others who trespass on our land."

As she spoke, Eric felt a twinge of recognition. "You were there . . . you found me."

"Yes."

"You wanted to kill me."

There was a pause, "I still do."

In his personal darkness, Eric felt very exposed. "Why? I'm not Chinese. I'm not here to loot your country. I'm trying to stop them."

She gave a sardonic laugh. "Do you really believe that? Truly? And where exactly do you think all the gold, copper, oil, and timber goes after it is sent to China?"

Eric suddenly felt very foolish.

"You don't know?" she continued. "Well, I'll tell you. It becomes your sneakers, your furniture, your cell phones, and the plastic toys for your kids. It's a simple equation really: If I could kill all the Americans, the Chinese would have little—"

"Naru!" Eric recognized Khamko's voice. For a moment he spoke to her in their language, then Naru spoke in English. "I'm sorry if I frightened you," she said without emotion. There was an awkward silence. "If you are still hungry later, just call out my name and the children will get me."

Eric felt her move away.

Khamko began checking his cuts and stitches. "I'm sorry about Naru. She sees you and the Chinese as just another manifestation of all the other invaders who have taken our land from us: the Germans, the Boers, the Dutch, the English."

"I'm not like that," Eric insisted.

"Perhaps *you* are not, but your people certainly are. That is the reason we must be very cautious with whom we trust. So it is likely a blessing that you cannot see us and that you do not know where you are."

"You can trust me."

There was a long pause.

"I hope you are right."

CHAPTER NINETEEN

TEACHING TOMORROW

November 7, 2026
Naval Research Lab, Washington, DC

"Any news?" Ryan Lee asked.

Jane shook her head.

Ryan didn't reply right away. Instead he simply hugged her, and she appreciated that. It felt good.

After a long minute, he asked, "What can I do?"

She shrugged. "Just do what you always do. Be my friend."

"Eric's going to be okay, I can feel it."

She forced a smile, but she did not share his faith. "Tell me something to get my mind off it," she said.

He let out a long breath. "Not much to tell really. I'm overworked, but you knew that already. Let's see . . . Jessica is really pulling her hair out, complaining about Olivia Rosario trying to take over the AI department."

Jane tried to image how Jessica—Ryan's boss and

a brilliant but severe woman—was taking to having her department become the epicenter of a political fight. "Is she?" Jane asked.

"Most likely. I'll admit she could certainly be more diplomatic. However, she does have some good ideas. She's been pushing to update everything, which we definitely need. Like getting some quantum hybrids. And she's got some bold concepts she wants to explore."

"Yeah, like what?" Jane honestly wasn't that interested. She just wanted the distraction.

"She wants to merge forced evolution with AI to create something very cool. A supercharged, super-smart AI." She could see Ryan was excited about it

Jane lifted her eyebrows. "Go on."

"She wants to teach it *tomorrow*."

Jane gave him a skeptical look. "What's so hard about that?"

"Everything. You see, consciousness is divided into three levels. Level I consciousness is your reptile brain that controls your body temperature, heart rate, hunger, things like that. That's stuff that a computer can do now. Level II consciousness allows an animal to make a crude model of itself and its relationships to other animals, like the social interactions of a wolf pack or a whale pod. But level III consciousness, arguably, only occurs in humans. And it means the ability to make complex models in which the person is an actor and they can project the model of themselves forward in time. That's what your prefrontal cortex does. In other words, it understands tomorrow."

"Can't computers do that already? My iSheet always seems to know what I want to do next."

Ryan shook his head. "That's different. That's something called a prediction rule, like when it picks the next movie you want to watch. Believe it or not, that algorithm was invented during World War II to help allied bombers in Europe. It's a conditional probability, which means it's trying to predict a missing variable. It seems smart, but it's not *that* smart. A lot of people think that computers are already as smart as humans. Not really. Right now AI is largely an illusion. It's insanely fast when it comes to certain tasks, and some of the algorithms they have created are better than a human could devise, but they're not conscious, and therefore can't predict the future. Which, by the way, is something that our brains spend most of our day doing. But Olivia thinks we can use deep learning to finally do it. She wants to make a computer with a prefrontal cortex."

"Then what?"

"Well, if she can do it, it would be an amazing forecasting tool because you can load it with data on a massive scale. In AI, the more data you have, the better the accuracy of your predictions. She wants to fill it with models of every known system: the weather, the stock market, economics, psychology, political science, military strategy—everything. It all becomes training data. Then she wants to feed it every bit of information that's available in real time: every daily newspaper in the world, video feeds from every available camera, access to radio, streaming from television and the internet."

Jane gave a grunt to show that she was impressed. It was definitely ambitious.

"I think this could be a game changer," Ryan said. "It should become insanely good at forecasting the future. Much better than any human because—unlike a human—there's no limit to how much knowledge you can put in its 'brain.' And that predictive power can be applied to a lot of things: geopolitical trends, predicting elections in foreign countries, energy prices, terrorist activity . . . I have to admit, it's an amazing idea. I think her goal is to automate the entire Pentagon."

"To be honest, it sounds a little scary. Remember, just because you *can* do something, doesn't mean you should."

Ryan shrugged. "There's really no option. This is where AI has to go, and I've dedicated my life to AI. Besides, if we don't do it, someone else will."

"So you're going to help her?"

"I'd love to, but I'm not sure if Curtiss will let me. He's trying to sabotage everything she does. Did you know he put her office in the hall by the underground shooting range?"

Jane couldn't help but smirk. It was quintessential Curtiss.

"I'm telling you, it's going to backfire. People like her."

Jane honestly wasn't sure whose side to be on. Her love for Curtiss did not run deep. But at the very least, she knew that Curtiss was wholly dedicated to the good of the United States. But this outside force—led by General Walden and Olivia Rosario—felt both political and corporate. People hunting for prestige and power, with the good of the country as an afterthought.

"Just be careful, okay? And I mean about work and your allegiances. You don't want to be caught on the wrong side of a political fight. Walden and Rosario are clearly trying to screw Curtiss. But just remember who we're talking about. Everyone, and I mean *everyone*, who has ever picked a fight with Curtiss has ended up dead or seriously regretting it."

He smiled. “Yeah, okay.”

“Besides, I need you, Ryan. More than ever.”

“Don’t worry, I’ll be here.”

“You’d better be.”

CHAPTER TWENTY

THE DEATH TRAP

November 7, 2026
Russell Senate Office Building, Washington, DC

Standing in the wreckage of Senator Peck's office, Special Agent Bud Brown felt like he was inside an enormous barbecue grill. Everything around him was black and burned, and the smell of charcoal filled his nose. Yet he couldn't help thinking that there was something beautiful about it. He moved to one of the surviving beams and noticed how the wood had been cracked into neat symmetrical squares, like the silver scales on a great snake. And even though the fire had been extinguished more than a day before, he could still feel heat radiating from the wood and stone. It was oddly soothing.

The large bay windows that had been blown out by the blast had been boarded up with plywood. More plywood lay on weak sections of the floor, and three halogen lamps sat on orange tripods, giving the room light.

At his feet was a large mound of ash—the remains of

the Senator's desk. Brown kicked at something metal that protruded from the pile and saw a molten blob of bronze that may have been a drawer handle.

Brown had learned enough about explosives in his career to know this was the work of a professional. That was clear from the fact that all that had been found of Senator Peck was a piece of his hip bone.

"One hell of a job," Rogers said, as if reading Brown's thoughts.

Bud nodded. "How did they get so much ordnance in here without anyone noticing?"

"It's ingenious, really," the old bomb tech said. "The bomber posed as a member of a paint crew. On the day they were supposed to do Peck's office, three of the other painters called in sick, so the bomber had as much as six hours in here by himself." Rogers pointed to sections of the wall that had been blasted out. "We're pretty sure he used thin patches of plastic explosives, interlaced with thousands of metal filaments, probably not much thicker than a sheet of paper. He placed six of them around the room then painted over them, essentially making them invisible."

"Clever," Bud said. He felt lucky to be here with Rogers, who had an amazing ability to re-create a crime scene.

"Oh, it gets better," Rogers continued. "C-4 alone just makes a big boom. It would have been enough to kill the senator, sure, but that wouldn't be good enough for Finley. We know from her other bombings that she doesn't like mangled body parts tarnishing her public image. That makes her look bad. It's much better for her twitter ratings if her victims just sort of disappear. But to make Peck disappear, she needs a fire to cremate the body, and for that you need—"

"An accelerant," Bud said.

"Exactly. Finley's master bomber needed enough fuel to get the room very hot. Crematorium hot, I'm talking fifteen hundred degrees. That takes a lot of diesel. So what does he do?"

Bud suddenly understood. "He puts it in the paint."

"Bingo. Not only that, he does it one better. It's not just fuel. When the paint went on the wall it looked like it was textured, but it was essentially homemade napalm, with bits of aluminum salts to help it burn."

Bud nodded a moment, piecing it together. "So these sheets detonate, sending metal filaments through the senator and his secretary's body, killing them instantly. Then the paint ignites, making the room into a huge oven, incinerating everything in it."

"That's about right."

"The perfect death trap," Bud said.

Rogers nodded. "I've never seen anything this sophisticated. These people knew us. They knew our security. They exploited our weaknesses."

"Go on . . ."

"These senate office buildings have always been a problem. I've told the Capitol Police as much on several occasions. With thousands of constituents and lobbyists coming in and out every day, security gets lax. Besides, the thinking has always been that if someone wanted to kill a bunch of congressmen, they'd attack the Capitol Building. Or if they wanted to assassinate a single low-level congressperson like Peck, they wouldn't bother doing it in DC. They'd do it in their home district, where there's much less security.

"But here comes Finley. She didn't want to do it in his home district. She wanted the public spectacle. And, most importantly, she wanted to send a message to every senator: she wants them to know she could reach them wherever they are. So she did her homework. Once again, the paint was key. See, the standard security screenings for explosives look for nitrates and glycerin. But acrylic paints often have glycerin added to extend the drying time, so painters often fail the test. When we questioned the Capitol Police, we found that they had gotten in the habit of simply waving painters through without checking their cans of paint. 'As long as they didn't have any weapons,' the head of security told me, 'they were cleared.' That was how the perp smuggled approximately twenty pounds of C-4 into a highly secured area."

"Any leads on this 'painter,' Patrick Daniels?"

"Fake name, of course, but someone went through a lot of trouble of getting him a very good fake identity: driver's license, social security number, even a bogus credit history."

Bud could tell that Rogers was taking this personally. As someone who had advised the Capitol Police on security, he knew they'd been caught with their pants down.

"So where do we go from here?" Bud asked.

"I think we'll probably find Daniels, but I suspect it won't help a whole lot. What I want is the master bomber. He would likely have direct contact with Finley and could lead us to her. Even if he doesn't, taking out the bomber will make me feel a lot safer."

"You said it's the most sophisticated bombing you've seen. So who could have pulled it off?"

"I really hate to say this, but my gut tells me it's an EOD guy like me. Probably served in Iraq or Afghanistan or Syria. That was my first thought when I heard about the drone."

"Drone?"

"Eyewitnesses outside the building reported hearing a high-pitched whir, just seconds before the explosion. We brought those witnesses in and gave them a library of sounds to listen to. It matched up with the latest micro-drones. Smaller than a billfold, they can fly as far as two miles on a single charge and have state-of-the art cameras."

"But why? Isn't it risky? It could have alerted the Capital Police."

"In the business we call it the 'pattern of conception'—essentially the layout and complexity of an attack. And this one was very elaborate. These people were thinking, 'Before we detonate a bomb that took a lot of work to plant, we want a last-minute verification that the target is really inside.' To me, that says a vet, someone who is following SOP. You just don't get this good unless your life depends on it. And that's what happens in war."

"Okay, former military. But what country? Which militaries have the best EOD people?"

"Britain," Rogers said without hesitation. "They learned a lot from fighting the IRA. It was like an arms race, almost a hundred years of trying to outsmart each other."

"Could Finley's master bomber be IRA?"

Rogers opened his mouth and seemed about to dismiss the idea, but checked himself.

"I suppose it's possible. There must be a few of them still out there."

"It might be worth checking out," Brown said.

Rogers gave him a smile. "Who says you've lost your edge?"

"My ex," Brown said.

Rogers laughed then went to talk to one of the biometric agents searching for evidence.

Brown looked around at the wreckage. He thought of Peck's wife and his orphaned children, and how Peck's secretary, Samantha Stevens, had been engaged to be married in June.

Then he thought about what Rogers had told him. It was quite an eye-opener. Before he'd walked in here, Bud had been thinking of Finley as a reincarnation of the Unabomber, a lone figure who had tried to convince the public that he was part of large grassroots political movement (he remembered how Kaczynski had written "we" in his manifesto). But unlike Kaczynski, this really was a team effort. Finley's followers were loyal, well-trained, and worked together as a team. To pull off this bombing, she needed at least four people—the master bomber, the "painter," the drone operator, and herself. This was a group of terrorists that operated like a tech startup.

Brown wasn't sure how they were going to track them all down, but one thing was for certain: Finley's big gamble had had the desired effect. Every congressperson who had ever voted on a bill that benefited big oil or wasn't climate friendly was now shitting their pants. Many had refused to even come to their offices, and every single one was requesting more security. Yesterday, Congress had voted for an "emergency recess," and most of them had left town.

Brown shook his head. With one assassination, Finley had shut down a third of the US government.

At the same time, Finley was suddenly everywhere. The media couldn't get enough of the story. A former Cornell professor turned ecoterrorist. Beautiful and articulate. Lethal and cunning. She was an avenging angel or a devil, take your pick. She reminded Bud of some of the radicals of the '60s, like Bernardine Dohrn and Bill Ayers of the Weather

Underground. White, college-educated terrorists who had been able to cultivate a fan club.

There were other similarities to the '60s, namely that America was once again fertile ground for radicals. Back then it had been about Vietnam and civil rights. Now it was about political deadlock, corporate control of government, and climate change. But one thing was the same—intergenerational anger. Young Americans were furious that this was the world they were forced to inherit. They were so angry, they were willing to kill.

Where was it going to end?

Bud pressed his hand against the blackened pillar and felt the heat still trapped inside, like the residue of Riona Finley herself. He felt her intelligence in the way she had pulled it off. A terrorist with a PhD. Connected, resourceful, well-financed. She had gotten them good. He didn't like that, but he took the lesson: This was an enemy that had to be respected. An enemy that was going to take all their resourcefulness to bring down.

At that moment, he honestly didn't know if they were up to the task. It had taken the FBI sixteen years to track down an amateur like Ted Kaczynski, and many members of the Weathermen were never brought to justice because of FBI screw-ups and changes in Washington.

In just the hour that he and Rogers had been standing here, Finley had received tens of thousands of dollars in donations from her fans, and she was getting offers for help, recruiting new bombers, new drone pilots, new soldiers.

She was growing stronger every minute. While they were standing in her wreckage.

CHAPTER TWENTY-ONE

THE AMBASSADOR

November 8, 2026
Namibia

Eric lay on his cot thinking. He had to get out of there. To make contact with the outside world. To tell Jane that he was alive. And he needed to get to a modern hospital.

A part of him refused to admit that he was blind. But another part knew he had to accept it and imagine how he would live the rest of his life. Could he even function in the lab without his sight? And how would it change his relationship with Jane? Would she still . . . ?

The more he thought about it, the more claustrophobic he felt. He was about to call for Khamko, to demand that he get him to a town or hospital, when he heard the children laughing in the doorway. It was a contagious sound and all by itself, it lifted his spirits a little. He reminded himself that he was not critically injured. In fact, despite the headache, he felt okay. Khamko had been right, it could have been a lot worse. If he had had serious internal bleeding, he'd be dead by now.

So he stowed his dark thoughts away—worry about that later—and he opened his senses. He tried to count how many children there might be. At least four. He heard two with very high voices; they must be the youngest. He decided there were five. They hadn't all spoken, yet he felt sure of the number.

Then he felt one come closer. The others giggled. Eric tensed for a moment, feeling defenseless in the dark. Perhaps one was coming to play a trick on him. But he realized that wasn't right. He sensed no malevolence, not even the coldness he'd felt from Naru.

The presence stopped. Eric pictured the child looking back at his coconspirators in the doorway, summoning his courage.

Then he heard a loud voice. "Hello! How is you?" The utterance of these words brought an eruption of laughter from the others. Eric couldn't help but smile. This was no prank; it was a diplomatic mission.

"I'm fine, how are you?"

"Oh, I wonderful!" The boy said emphatically, clearly pleased that he had successfully communicated with the man from the moon. The other children laughed again.

"Your English is very good. What's your name?"

There was a long silence, and Eric realized he'd spoken too quickly. He imagined the look of perplexity on the boy's face. He repeated himself. This time the boy understood.

"I am Karuma!" the boy said. The words were delivered with loud aplomb, like an auditioning actor confident of his lines. "Yes, my English great! Others know nothing. Only me."

Eric guessed he was perhaps thirteen or fourteen.

He sat up slowly in his cot, trying to hide his aches and pains, and extended his hand. "I'm Eric. It's nice to meet you."

There was a moment of silence, and Eric almost retracted his hand, fearing that he had committed some cultural taboo. Then he felt Karuma's hand—small, but rough and strong—in his. From the doorway came a collective 'ahh'—contact with the strange creature had been made. Their laughter flooded into the room with them. The next moment Eric was being touched and prodded by a dozen curious hands.

For the next hour they engaged in a most singular conversation—a mix of English, their tribal language, and Eric's gesturing. Karuma did his best to translate all the children's questions. "Why do you wear so many clothes? How did your skin get like that? Are you a boy or a girl? What did you eat to get so tall and where can we get some?" They asked him to teach them important words in English, mostly related to bodily functions. He learned some of their words too: |*ūá* (child), *kx'âa* (drink), and *!nábe* (giraffe). He was expected to make a click sound when he said most of the words, and they laughed each time he tried. He deeply appreciated their company and made it a point to remember their names. The youngest girl was Nyando, the shy boy was //Kabbo.

Finally Karuma said, "Come! Outside! Come!"

Eric held up his hand. "No, I can't."

"Come, come!" he insisted. Then the other children took up the call. "Coooome, cooome!" and they began to tug and pull at him.

He stood up uneasily and teetered. He wasn't at all sure his legs were going to keep him up. He took a cautious step forward, testing the ground like a man roused from sleep in the dark. He felt he might fall, but the children swelled up around him, supporting him, some grabbing his hands and forearms, others his hips and legs.

"Yes, you can do it!" Karuma said. The children laughed and cheered. A moment later he felt the hot African sun on his face, so intense that it hinted at fire. But he didn't bow his head. Instead, he lifted it. All around, he heard more shouts and laughter, then more hands touching him. His ears were filled with the clicks of their words along with the sonorous rise and fall of their language. He could sense their goodwill; it was unmistakable, even in the darkness. They were glad he was walking and glad he was with them. For the first time in many days, he did not feel so far from home.

That night Khamko came to check on him.

"I understand you made some new friends today."

Eric laughed. "I did indeed."

"My grandson told me all about it. He is fascinated by you."

"Karuma is your grandson?"

"Yes, and you already know his mother."

"Naru?"

"That's right."

"And Karuma's father?"

"Ah, he was killed by poachers. Just last year."

Eric nodded to himself. Naru's anger was suddenly easier to understand. The man she loved had been killed so some rich person thousands of miles away could hang elephant tusks on his dining room wall.

"Khamko, can I ask you something?"

"Of course."

"How is it that you speak American English? How do you know so much about medicine? And why is someone like you here?"

Eric heard his warm laugh. "Ah, let's put it this way: the man standing before you is an experiment, but a failed one. Or to put it another way: I am the unexpected product of a hopeful generation's flawed dream."

"I don't understand."

"I know, I'm speaking in riddles. Let me explain properly. Tell me, have you ever heard of the Airlift?"

"Yes, it was an exchange program that brought African students to the US in the '60s."

Again he heard Khamko's easy laughter. "Very good. I am always dismayed at how few Americans have heard of it. Yes, the Airlift was out of east Africa, but it was emblematic of Africa at that time: the belief that in one generation, with the right education, we could catapult Africa into the modern age. All you had to do was take a young man, send him to America, and he would come back a modern man. Then—the logic went—these modern men would teach the rest of us and within a generation we would be just as mighty and strong as America and Europe."

Eric nodded, it seemed feasible to him.

Khamko continued: "Even though I grew up far from Kenya, something similar happened to me. It was when I was sixteen . . ." He gave a whimsical laugh, perhaps sensing how much he—and his world—had changed since then. "That was when something very unusual happened. There was a terrible storm. *Absolutely terrible.* I had never seen the sky so angry. Lightning and hail and rain pounded the earth. It lasted three days. All the rivers swelled and overflowed, sweeping away whole Bantu villages. On the fourth day, when the rains had subsided, I was hunting with my father near the river. We found an old steamer run aground. I can still see it in my mind. It had been pinned on a small island in the middle of the river. I remember the boat was set on its side, and the watermarks from the storm showed that it had almost been completely covered. We soon learned that most of the crew and passengers had been washed away when they made a desperate attempt to swim to shore. But in the wreckage we found two survivors, an American businessmen and his son. The son had been impaled on a pipe, and the father had refused to leave him. The man told us later that the water had come up to their chins before it finally subsided. My father wanted to help the boy, but the other father would not let us touch his son. He yelled at us and tried to ward us off, but my father knew a few English words, and with these and some gestures he persuaded him. The boy was unconscious, his face was very gray. The wound was deep and dirty and the boy was near death, but my father was very skilled. We got him to safety and slowly, over the course of two weeks, he began to recover. His name was Will, and as my father nursed him back to health, we became friends. I learned a few dozen English words and I taught him some Sān. As you know, for teenagers that is more than enough to communicate.

"The father, feeling grateful and seeing the connection between his son and me, proposed an idea. He knew about the Airlift and that I wanted to be a healer. What if he took me to America? With all that I already knew about plants and healing from the primitive world, could he make me into a doctor of Western medicine?

"It was very hard for me to leave my family, to leave the only world I had ever known. I was miserable for a long time in the strange, concrete, landscape of America. Every day I yearned to be home. But in the end, I'm glad I did it. Medicine came easy to me. It made perfect sense, and I was good at it. But I was never at home there, so I returned, and I have used all that I learned to help my people."

"Amazing," Eric said.

"Yes, but I must be honest, the most important thing about my journey was that it taught me about you. It taught me the wonders of your technology, but it also showed me your flaws. I learned the dangers of your ambitious nature, how you always take and take and take and are never satisfied. I still do not understand it, but I saw it everywhere. I still see it today, perhaps worse than before. In this way, Naru is right, the Chinese really are just another version of you.

"My knowledge of the West is the reason we are the only Khoisan people who still live in the traditional way. We have not been forced off our land and turned into herders for the whites. But we are not as passive as our grandparents were . . . because you cannot be passive with an enemy who is always seeking to take what you have. An enemy who disguises their colonization as assistance, their brainwashing as religious enlightenment, and equates progress with material luxury. All these promises of a 'better life' always lead to the pillaging of our land . . . to isolation and confinement . . . to death. We have taken the few things that we need from your world, but we know not to be tempted by the rest."

Eric nodded. "But you must have some help from the outside or at least some assistance from the government."

"Yes, we have some help that I can tell you about, and there are those in power who look out for us. They keep the multinational corporations out of our territory and are trying to keep out the Chinese. But it is always a struggle. Every year it seems that the foreign pressure increases, and our friends grow weaker."

"Is it true that you kill trespassers?"

"As I said, we cannot survive being as passive as we once were. It is not the way we would like to live, but . . ." He paused. "The Chinese tell stories about us. We are their boogie men, the dark shadows that come in the night. We are the reason they don't like to venture far from their camps."

"Then I guess I'm lucky Naru didn't . . . you know."

Khamko laughed. "Yes, I'm glad we didn't eat you."

"Do you really eat people?"

"There are a lot fewer animals to hunt than there were just fifteen years ago."

Eric paused. "Are you being serious?"

There was no response.

"It's moments like this when I wish I could see your face."

"Oh, I'm smiling," Khamko said.

CHAPTER TWENTY-TWO

FOREIGN AID

November 8, 2026
Washington, DC

Breathing hard, Jane Hunter ran along the Potomac River Trail toward base. The sun was just setting in the west, painting purple and orange strokes across a hazy blue sky. She passed Moffett Hangar, an enormous structure big enough to hold a zeppelin, then a row of F-35 jump jets. She sprinted the last quarter mile to her apartment block. Once inside, she passed the elevator and took the stairs three at a time. This was key to her survival—to keep moving. If she stopped, she knew she'd go crazy. The five-mile run had given her a good dose of endorphins, and with any luck that would keep her dark thoughts at bay for an hour or two.

She pushed into her apartment and began peeling off her clothes. She resisted the urge to throw them on her bedroom floor and put them in the hamper instead. *Stay organized.*

Stay disciplined. She felt she was living in a house of cards; one little mistake could be disastrous.

She entered the bathroom. The medicine cabinet door was open, and she instinctively closed it, forgetting that she'd left it open for a reason.

She looked into the mirror, and there he was. A snapshot of the two of them that she'd wedged in the tin frame of the mirror. The camera had caught him just after a laugh, the happiness still clear on his face, his eyes bright and mischievous, as if he knew he'd been misbehaving. Too clever for his own good, she said. And now she could see that in his eyes. She touched her chest between her breasts where it suddenly hurt.

That had been such a perfect night. The Navy Birthday Ball, the dancing, surrounded by friends. Now it seemed impossibly distant, from a different lifetime. In the photo she was behind him, chin on his shoulder, arms around him, squeezing and smiling. He'd only been home a month when the picture was taken. Back when every day had been a gift, when they'd been grateful just to be alive and together and safe.

He had been her first. First real boyfriend, first true confidant, first lover. He was the one. How else could you explain what had happened? She had lost him once, but he had been delivered, against all odds, back to her. So he must be alive now too. His heart was still beating. If it had stopped she would have felt it. But her logical mind reminded her that wasn't how it worked. That he had probably died near the crash site. His body eaten or carried off by some animal. A lion, hyenas. Her scientific mind insisted she face the ugly truth.

You don't know that, she told herself. *You don't know anything.*

She looked past the picture, at the reflection of herself, naked and vulnerable in the mirror. She tried to remind herself that she was strong and beautiful and tough. But right now she didn't believe it, and she didn't see it. In the mirror she saw a nervous wreck. Bags under her eyes, fatigue pulling at her cheeks.

A knock came from the door. She grabbed a T-shirt and pulled on some sweatpants.

It was CPO Adams, Curtiss's assistant.

"Sorry to disturb you, ma'am, but the admiral would like to see you."

Ten minutes later, she was in Curtiss's study at his residence. It was a big room, with a dark wood desk opposite the door, and an open area on her right with a conference table. Curtiss rose from his desk and greeted her.

"Sorry to bring you here so late, but I wanted to give you the news first. This morning the Namibians authorized the Chinese to reenter their airspace."

"Shit! And what about us?"

"We're still not welcome."

"Why them and not us?"

"Because the Chinese just authorized a seven-hundred-million-dollar aid package to the Namibian government."

"You're kidding."

"I wish I was. I'm trying to get State to offer a similar package, but these things take time."

"Take time? But you're talking days or weeks. He could be hurt. He needs help now!"

Curtiss gave her a reluctant nod. "I know, and I'm stressing to everyone the importance of getting him back. Unfortunately, some of the Joint Chiefs are fighting me."

She looked away in disgust. "Walden?"

"Yes, Walden. He wants to wash his hands of the whole situation, says it's not worth wasting money on someone who is likely dead."

"Fuck . . . "

"So I called the president today."

A look of hopeful amazement spread across Jane's face.

Curtiss continued, "Walden is going to be furious when he finds out. But I explained to the president everything that Eric has done for his country. He didn't say yes, but he said he would do what he could. He's worried about the midterm elections, you know, and he wants to keep it as quiet as possible. But I should know something within forty-eight hours."

She felt like hugging him but stopped herself. "Thank you."

"There's something else. It could be both good and bad."

"What is it?"

"We are still watching the crash site via satellite. The Chinese have been very interested in the Valor, they're treating it like an archaeological dig. But they're also looking for someone."

"Someone?"

"We're pretty sure they're looking for Eric."

She brought her hand to her mouth.

"They began searching where Eric fell and have been broadening the search from there. But this is the good news: they're still looking."

A wave of relief rolled through her. "He's alive! If they haven't found him, he must be!"

"Now hold on, Jane, we don't know that, and you have to be prepared for the worst. All we know is that they haven't found whatever they're looking for. But yes, it could be him."

She closed her eyes and took a deep breath. God, she wanted to believe that his heart still beat. Then a suspicion rose in her heart, and she stepped back from Curtiss. *It could be both good and bad.*

"If the Chinese find him and he's alive, what will you do?"

"Let's cross that bridge when we come to it."

"No, no, no! Don't lie to me!" she felt her anger rising. "Tell me the truth. If the Chinese found him and were taking him back to their carrier, what would you do?" She caught her breath. "Oh, God . . . You'd blow them all out of the sky, wouldn't you? You'd kill him to keep him from falling into their hands again!"

"No, I wouldn't," he said holding up one hand. "The situation is different now. China is shifting into our orbit. It's not there yet, but in a month it could be, and that gives us diplomatic options. In Tangshan we were running out of time, and I had to act or the whole mission would have failed. And let's be clear, I wasn't trying to kill Eric that day, I was trying to kill Ryan Lee before he fell into enemy hands. He was the only one who could have aborted the countdown."

Jane wasn't convinced.

"Despite what you may think, I don't enjoy sacrificing people's lives. It . . . it weighs on me . . . every time. But it's part of war. You can trust me this time. I won't have to do anything so desperate. There's no reason for it."

★ ★ ★

She returned to the apartment block and headed to Ryan's place. She needed to talk to someone she trusted, to tell him what she had discovered, to share it, and to get his advice. She wasn't crazy, right? It really meant he was alive? And Curtiss, could she believe him? Why would he call the president if he wasn't sincere?

She knocked on Ryan's apartment door, but he wasn't home. She called him, but his phone appeared to be off. *Probably working late.*

She headed to the main lab. It was almost nine, but Ryan often worked until two or three in the morning.

The fifth floor was deserted when she got there. The energy-saving night lights had kicked on, leaving the hallway almost dark. As she approached his office, she could see Ryan's door was slightly ajar, a wedge of light cutting a rectangle on the hallway floor.

Jane was rehearsing what she would say, how to express her mix of hope and fear, when she heard a woman laugh. It was an excited, happy sound.

"You must be kidding? You're amazing," the woman said.

Jane slowed her pace and listened.

She heard Ryan laugh. "No, it's all true. I swear."

"I would have been terrified."

Now Jane was close enough to steal a glimpse into the office. Ryan was completely hidden from view, but she could see Olivia Rosario sitting on the edge of her seat near the door leaning forward in rapt attention, long legs emerging beneath a black skirt. Her face was hidden, but Jane could see her long black hair.

Rosario laughed again. "Tell me how you did it," she said, "I mean, it sounds ingenious." At that moment, she leaned back in her chair. Jane saw how her eyes were focused on Ryan, her smile eager and inviting. Then for a moment her face changed, like someone taking off a mask, and her eyes flitted away from him and out the open door. For a brief second she and Jane locked eyes. Then the woman opened her legs and—with a deft motion—swung the door closed with her foot.

Jane stared at the door for a moment in disbelief. *That fucking bitch*, she thought. She stepped up to the door and was about to fling it open when she stopped.

She had come here to talk to Ryan, her friend and confidant. But she was struck by a sudden fear that the Ryan Lee on the other side of this door was no longer the person she thought she knew. Somehow he had changed.

Dejected, she returned to the apartment block. At first she thought she'd go see Lili and Xiao-ping. They would understand what she was going through. But she reconsidered. Since Xiao-ping's return from Africa they'd become like newlyweds, conjoined at the hip. Kissing and snuggling and holding hands. It was enough to give you cavities just watching them. Jane didn't need to be around that kind of joy right now.

Just go home, she told herself. *Get some sleep.*

As she got off the elevator, she saw a form sitting against her door, a black hoodie covering most of her face.

"Mei?" Jane asked.

The girl flipped back the hoodie. It was Lili's fourteen-year-old niece. "It's about time!" the girl said in annoyance. "What took you so long?" Next to the girl were a couple of brown paper bags.

"What are you doing here?"

"Waiting for you, obviously."

Jane smiled. "What's in the bags?"

"Duh, Chinese." The girl stood and gave Jane a wry smile. Then she jumped into her arms. Jane held the girl's embrace.

"Wait a minute, were you over at the Curtiss's tonight? Visiting Logan?" A look of mock-horror erupted on Jane's face. "Were you eavesdropping on the admiral?"

"I am not at liberty to discuss that."

"What?"

"I cannot confirm or deny that allegation."

"Girl, you have definitely been spending too much time over there." She unlocked her apartment door. "Get inside."

A half hour later, white takeout boxes were littered across the table, and they were laughing about Mei's fortune cookie.

I don't feel like giving you a fortune,
go get another cookie.

"Sassy little cookie," Jane said.

"Luckily there's one more in the bag."

"Oh, this is more like it: 'To stay healthy, eat more Chinese food.'"

They laughed again.

As they were cleaning up, Jane finally asked. "So were you really at Curtiss's today?"

"I told you that's classified."

"Oh, come on."

"Yeah, I heard him. He spent most of the time I was there trying to help Eric. And when he wasn't getting what he wanted, he got really pissed. I think it's personal to him now."

Jane nodded. "Thanks, that's good to know."

Mei came over and hugged her. "I miss him, too, you know."

Against her wishes, Jane's eyes began to water. During their escape from China, Eric and Mei had formed a tight bond. And in the aftermath—following Mei's mother's death and before Lili had come home—it was Eric and Jane who had taken care of Mei, the three of them living together, right here in this apartment.

"Can I spend the night tonight?" Mei asked. "Like old times?

"Of course," Jane said. "I'd love that."

CHAPTER TWENTY-THREE

THE KALAHARI

November 9, 2026
Namibia

As Eric touched Karuma's hand he was struck by how coarse and hard it was, like chunks of pumice strung together. Karuma felt the contrast too and laughed. "Your hands are softer than a baby springbok. How they get that way?"

"By spending most of my life indoors working on a computer."

Karuma made a sound of disgust. "What kind of life is that?"

Eric had to laugh. "That's a very good question."

Karuma led him around the camp, and Eric tried to open his remaining senses, to gather as much information from the world around him as he could. He was beginning to understand the stories about how blind people's other senses became hyperacute. It was in part due to necessity, but also because the brain was rewiring itself. Sections of his occipital cortex were now being fed data from all over the brain, trying to make a "picture" of a world with just sound, taste, smell, and touch.

He realized how much information his brain received but didn't use, largely because his eyesight made it redundant. The wind was one thing he had never noticed unless it was blowing hard. But now the touch of the air on his cheek was the first thing he noticed. Of all his senses, touch was the one that was most awake now. He felt the change of temperature on his skin when a cloud passed beneath the sun, and his skin told him if he was straying from the track by how compact the earth was under his bare feet.

His other senses were more alive too.

"There's a sweet smell coming from over there." He pointed.

"Yes," Karuma said. "There is mango tree over there . . . about one hundred meters."

"I also hear a sound like water, but it's not water."

"That is the wind in the grass."

"The locusts are in the grass then? I hear them droning in the afternoon when it gets hot."

"Yes, very good," Karuma laughed. "See, you are not so blind after all."

"Let me try and take it from here. After all, you don't want to have to do this in the middle of the night."

"As you wish." He could almost feel Karuma's smile.

By now Eric had picked up the smell of the latrine and he could feel the compacted earth under his feet.

He felt a strong sense of accomplishment when he reached the door. He opened it and stepped inside only to be instantly assailed by a hail of blows and curses.

He had forgotten to knock. The woman screamed and

kicked and scratched at him. He bent low and protected his head, stumbling back outside.

It only took a second for what seemed like the whole village to gather around them, laughing hysterically. Finally, the old woman stormed off.

"Are you all right?" It was Khamko's voice, but Eric could feel the grin on his face.

"I'm fine. Please tell her that I'm sorry."

"Oh, don't worry. I told her that you didn't see a thing."

Over the next five days Karuma became his constant companion. He was outside Eric's hut first thing in the morning and helped him get into bed each night. Perhaps it was his fascination with Eric's world, or his desire to learn more English, or a way to rebel against his mother, but the young man stayed loyally by his side, playing the roles of protector, mentor, and student.

He was insatiably inquisitive and wanted to know everything about America. His favorite subject was snow. To the young man it sounded like magic. How it could bury a whole town, how you could make tunnels through it, and how you could put sticks on your feet and zoom down a hill on it. He made Eric tell half the village the story of a blizzard that had buried Bloomington in six feet of snow when he was a kid.

He would also ask many questions that showed how different their world was. "When you get a headache in America, what plant do you eat to feel better?"

But most of their time was spent learning words. Karuma insisted that Eric teach him thirty words a day. Since Eric had only time to kill he took up the challenge, and the two made a pact to teach other at the same time. They would pick their daily words each morning and all day long they would repeat them over and over until their pronunciation was right. Karuma was both an excellent student and teacher. His first task was to teach Eric the four clicking sounds—//, /, #, and !.They ranged from a sound like a cork popping [!] that was made using your whole tongue, to the more wet, soft click [//] that used the cheeks. All the children sat around laughing as Eric attempted to click properly. At times he grew frustrated—here was an MIT and Stanford grad unable to pronounce a single consonant—but their laughter forced him to be a good sport about it.

Eric's most useful phrase was "*Tari nee*?" What's this? When he heard something he didn't understand, he put his hand to his ear and would say *Tari nee?* If he smelled something he didn't recognize, he'd touch his nose and do the same.

He learned to count: */gui* (one), */gam* (two), *!nona* (three). And he learned the names of the sun and the moon (*sore-s* and *//khã-b*). He learned the name for fire (*/ae-b*), meat (*//gan-i*), sand (*//khae-b*), and ostrich (*|gáro*).

When they weren't practicing words, they were eating. This, strangely, had become Eric's favorite thing to do. Perhaps it was the blindness (his sense of taste trying to make up for the sense he had lost) but he looked forward to food like never before. Much of it was strange to him, and not being able to see it might have been a blessing. But most of it was delicious. He could never remember eating such an incredible variety of foods. Tubers, roots, berries, leaves, melons. One of their staples was the fruit from the baobab tree, which was the size of small cantaloupe. The chalky part around the seed was mixed with water to form a tangy citrus porridge. He ate all types of game—springbok, gemsbok, porcupine, and hyrax (a mammal about the size of guinea pig). He ate many different types of birds, sometimes bones and all. Yes, there were a few meals where he was squeamish and didn't eat much, but his mounting hunger soon overcame his food snobbery. But the day he tried his first wild honey was a day he would never forget. Before he even tasted it, he was in love. Its aroma was heavenly, a dense woody sweetness. Khamko handed him a dripping chunk of honeycomb the size of his fist. "A special treat today," he said. One taste and he was addicted. It seemed to go straight to his brain like a powerful drug. It wasn't hard to understand why. Wild honeycomb was likely the most energy-packed natural food on the planet—not just for the sugars but for the protein too. All the bee larvae were still inside, and he could even feel a few squirming against his gums. He didn't care. Never had any food made him so happy. He kept the wad of wax in his mouth for an hour, chewing and sucking on it.

Almost as soon as he was done, he began to fantasize about eating more. Over the next few days he kept pestering Khamko. The old man only laughed. "Better than cherry Coke, isn't it?"

It was on his sixth day in the camp that Eric sensed something was up. It was mostly a feeling, but it seemed that everyone was busy, moving with an urgency that he hadn't felt before.

He touched Karuma's arm, pointed to his ear, "Tari nee?"

"I think we are leaving."

"Leaving?"

"Yes. People are packing their things."

At just that moment he heard Khamko's voice. He put a hand on Eric's arm. "G□kau and his hunting party have just returned, and I think it will be best if we go."

"Why?"

"I had thought that the Chinese had stopped looking for you, but G□kau saw them yesterday, about twenty-five kilometers from here."

Eric felt a jolt of fear at the thought of the Chinese being so close; the memories of his captivity rushing back to him.

He tried to think logically: He didn't know why Captain Everett had been unable to rescue him, but he suspected that it was a political decision, stemming from the fallout from the raid on the mining camp. That meant that without Khamko and his people, Eric would have already fallen into enemy hands.

That brought a deep sense of gratitude. But it came with a sense of guilt. From what he understood, these people still hunted with bows and spears. And by harboring him, they had pitted themselves against a military might they couldn't even fathom. He thought of the massacre he'd seen in the mining camp when the gunships had arrived, the Black Widows raining metal fire from the sky.

"Khamko, I can't ask you to protect me anymore. It's not right."

"Not right? You are a blind man lost in a place you don't know or understand. Of course it is right."

"But you and your people are taking a terrible risk. I don't think you understand that."

"I know you want to go home. But right now, the only path toward civilization would be toward the Chinese. So for the time being we have to go further into the bush."

"You are risking too much for me," he said.

He felt the man's hand on his shoulder. "Cgang sent you to us for a reason. I do not know why, but I know it will become clear. Besides, we have been hiding from the Chinese for years." Then he whispered in Eric's ear, "They are very bad trackers."

Eric shook his head. "But you shouldn't be leaving your village because of me."

Khamko laughed a long, full laugh, that reminded Eric of singing. "This isn't our village," he said.

"What?"

"This is an ugly old settlement made by the government in the '90s, when they were trying to force us to become herders and ranchers. There is a well here, so we come from time to time to get water. After we found you, I chose this spot for you to rest."

Again he felt grateful . . . and guilty. This whole time they had been waiting around for him to get better.

"Didn't you know?" Khamko said, "We are Sān. The Kalahari is our home. And now you will learn how we really live."

CHAPTER TWENTY-FOUR

OLD BONES

November 11, 2026
Washington, DC

General Chip Walden sat in his office in the Pentagon looking out at the rolling hills of Arlington National Cemetery: acre after acre of white rectangular grave markers broken only by an occasional tree or larger memorial. The undulating white rows reminded him of snow on summer grass. An odd contrast, he knew, but fitting for the place, which at first glance appeared to be a pristine park but held the sleeping bones of tens of thousands of dead.

When he first began working at the Pentagon he had often walked down its lanes, thinking that it would be a peaceful refuge from the frenetic chaos of the nation's capital. But he never found peace there, and at times would find himself sad and confused or even weeping for no apparent reason. Although he was not a superstitious man, he had been forced to conclude that the place was haunted, that something tragic and melancholy was seeping up from the ground and poisoning the air.

He turned from the window and looked back at his desk.

His plan to take control of the Naval Research Lab was going well. Establishing Olivia Rosario in the AI department was just the first step. The next step was to get rid of Jim Curtiss, because it was Curtiss (and his allies like CNO Garrett) that stood between him and the technology he needed to get the man he really wanted: the Inventor. The man who had murdered Julia.

Walden's jaw tightened as he remembered how Curtiss and Garrett had hid the truth from him.

It was one thing to believe that your wife had died in a car accident. It was something he could accept because we all live our lives knowing that random chance can end it all. That's just the way life is. It was just an accident, like the tens of thousands of accidents that claim lives every day.

But to know that there was a man out there who had murdered her . . . so capriciously, so needlessly. That touched something deep, deep inside him. It was not exactly a seed, for it had sprung to life full grown the moment he learned the truth. But the result was the same: there was something living inside him, gnawing at him, and it would not wilt or die until justice was done.

She had been the only woman he truly loved. Yes, they were separated, but she was going to take him back, he was sure of it. He had been doing everything right. All the little things that she had criticized . . . and the big things too. She had even said that she forgave him, she just needed a little more time.

But it was, to put it mildly, complicated. He was a good father and husband . . . 95 percent of the time. It wasn't easy being a high-ranking officer, especially when he was away on deployments. He'd messed up a few times, and she'd found out about one of those times.

I forgive you, but I just need more time.

He'd held on to those words and tried to support her sudden need for freedom. First Italy. Then Greece. Then China. And even when he'd discovered that she had not been alone in the car, he had dismissed it. He believed her; she was coming back to him.

Her picture still sat on his desk. He looked at her beautiful face then rubbed the back of his neck. *One thing at a time*, he told himself. *I will get my revenge, but first I have to get Curtiss out of my way.*

But that was going to be much harder than he had originally thought. After the Namibia raid—with four airmen KIA and a top scientist MIA—Curtiss was weak, like a fighter on the ropes, but he was still too strong to knock out. Walden hated to admit it, but Curtiss had just been too successful for too long. What's more, he was too well-connected to be discharged for one botched raid. No, if Walden was going to knock Curtiss out, he needed something bigger.

He shook his head in disbelief. It was such an injustice that a jarhead like Curtiss would end up sitting on the most powerful weapons in history. A queer twist of fate . . . or perhaps just dumb luck.

After his stunning victory in Syria, Walden had expected Curtiss to retire quietly. Perhaps write a memoir, do the lecture circuit, appear on a few talk shows, then disappear. But not Curtiss. Instead he had shunned the press and had somehow gotten assigned to the floundering mission at the Naval Research Lab. God knows it must have looked hopeless when he arrived, with the Chinese project over a year ahead of them.

Yet somehow he had turned it around . . . or, more likely, Bill Eastman and Jack Behrmann had turned it around.

Now Curtiss found himself at the tip of the spear, the indispensable expert of the new technology. What a waste, Walden thought, that a two-star like Curtiss should become the most powerful man in the US military, with the ear of not only the CNO but the president himself.

He was the golden boy.

No, that wasn't quite right. He was more like Achilles, the most prized warrior in the US military.

But, Walden reminded himself, *Achilles had not been born a god, and neither had Curtiss. Despite his appearance of invulnerability, Curtiss must have an Achilles's heel. But what was it?*

No memoir about Syria.

He shunned the press.

Was it simply that Curtiss didn't want to cash in on his experience or was it something else? He was a hero in many people's eyes. It would have been so easy.

Walden nodded to himself, knowing he was on to something.

Personally, something about Syria had never sat right with him. From the onset it looked like a complete fiasco. Worse than Iraq and Vietnam combined. With so many factions on the ground being fed by proxy from Tehran, Istanbul, Moscow, Tel Aviv, and Washington it looked like it would be perpetual war. And at first, Walden had been right.

Fifteen hundred US casualties in the first month.

Twenty-four hundred in the second.

Then came the bloody battle in Damascus when two hundred marines were gassed and slaughtered in a single afternoon.

The public outcry had been enormous, and for a few weeks it looked like America would pull out, bruised and bloody.

Then suddenly all the mullahs and the imams, the Kurds and the Shia militias, even ISIL and President al-Assad were suing for peace. Curtiss had somehow brought them all to the table to sign the Zurich Accord. Even more surprising—it had stuck. Syria was still at peace three years later.

How had Curtiss done it?

How had Curtiss, a former SEAL, a special ops guy, gotten them all to the table?

Walden reached into his pocket and pulled out his iSheet and unfolded it until it was the size of a tablet.

"Show me the negotiations for the Zurich Accords."

A moment later the video started. Walden saw an elaborate hotel hallway with red carpet and heavy chandeliers. The principals were entering a large banquet hall one by one, shaking hands with the US delegation, Curtiss and CNO Garrett among them.

The assembled belligerents were powerful men, each ruthless and brutal in his own fashion. They were the survivors, the ones still standing after fourteen years of civil war. But now they seemed cowed, their eyes toward the floor, showing submission to the US brass. As he watched the men file in, he realized it was not all weakness. He zeroed in on Abu Bakr al Kafri as he approached Curtiss. While the admiral was all smiles, impeccable in his navy whites, there was a look of the deepest hatred in the Syrian's eyes. This man didn't want peace. Far from it. He wanted to rip Curtiss's throat out. But something was stopping him. Curtiss had something on him . . . on all of them.

Admiral James Curtiss. Former SEAL. Special Ops. No memoir. Shunned the press.

There was a story here. Walden could feel it. Something that had been buried.

Walden swiveled in his chair and looked out the window at Arlington once more. *Digging up bones is a dirty business*, he thought. *But I have a feeling the rewards will be worth it.*

Across the Potomac River from the Pentagon, Ryan Lee sat at his workstation thinking that life couldn't get a whole lot better.

At the age of thirty-one, he finally felt like everything was coming together. He was a leader in AI, working on some of the most revolutionary technology in history. He had unlimited resources and funding. He was treated with honor and respect by his peers. And he was in love.

He knew there was a reason for it: China. Something had happened to him after his mission there. His captivity, his sabotaging of the Chinese weapons program, and his harrowing escape with Eric, Mei, and Lili had made him into a different man. A man who believed he could do anything. Which meant he'd finally outgrown the stigma he'd had since junior high—the pudgy Asian kid. The computer nerd.

Upon his return he had changed a lot of things about his life. His diet, his exercise routine (meaning that now he actually had one), the way he talked to people (he's stopped being such a smartass). Gone were the cargo shorts and kitsch Hawaiian shirts. Gone were the Spider-Man ties and

Avengers socks. He was finally dressing like an adult—designer jeans, Italian wingtips, and Express button-ups. A new man.

And then Olivia Rosario had walked into his life.

She was beautiful and smart. The only woman he'd ever met who had the same passion for AI as he did. In fact, the only person who could hold her own in a conversation with him. And because they had connected on that wavelength, it seemed that nothing else mattered. Okay, perhaps he was still a nerd in many ways, but with Olivia, being a nerd was an asset.

He wanted to believe that this was the beginning of something, that she felt the same for him. When she smiled and laughed and held an embrace a little too long, he felt certain it was more than friendship. Yet something inside him still didn't fully believe. Perhaps, he realized, he wasn't completely free of his old self.

Maybe it was Jane's words of caution: *You don't want to be caught on the wrong side of a political fight. Walden and Rosario are clearly trying to screw Curtiss.*

Olivia was definitely trying to make her mark. Was her interest in him just part of her plan to advance her career? How could he be sure that she was being sincere?

He bit his lower lip in concentration, then an idea struck him.

Immediately he began tapping away at his keyboard.

One additional benefit from his mission to China was that Admiral Curtiss trusted him completely. What's more, given Ryan's expertise in AI and computer networks, Curtiss regularly consulted him on lab security, which meant that Ryan had permission to monitor the activity of every lab employee.

He pulled up Olivia's employee file then began looking at her activity in the Virtual Library. This was where all the lab's most important discoveries were kept. Files could only be "checked out" by employees with the right clearance.

Just as he was about to pull up her activity, he hesitated, feeling a sudden rush of heat that might have been guilt. He was doing this under the auspices of lab security, but he knew he was really doing it for himself. But his hesitation didn't last long.

It only took him a few minutes to see that something wasn't right. While Olivia had Top Secret clearance and access to most of the library, she was spending very little time in her own department—AI. Instead, she was scouring through the nanotech files: Forced Evolution, recognition tunneling, and the synthetic virus applications. The scary stuff.

Her job is to make an advanced AI system, so why is she spending so much time looking at viruses?

But what he found even more surprising were the time stamps. Each file checked out from the library was tracked every second it was in "circulation" by facial recognition. If you checked out an item and someone else sat down at your computer, the screen would go blank. What's more, the system kept a running clock of how long you were looking at the files. Even if you turned you head away or went to the bathroom, the clock would stop.

```
File Name: Force Evolution and Second
Generation DOD applications. Author: Eric
Hill, Olexander Velichko. Checked out
23:31. Returned 05:27. Total usage: 5:16
```

```
File Name: Synthetic Virus Proto-
type—Pneumonia. Author: Jane Hunter.
Checked out: 00:58. Returned: 05:01.
Total usage: 04:37
```

Olivia was staying up all night, every night, poring over their most sensitive files.

She must be barely sleeping, he thought. *But what was she doing? And why the urgency?*

He needed to know more. He checked her internet search history but found nothing. He sat back, thinking. Then he nodded to himself. *That's it*, he thought, remembering a trick he'd learned from Eric Hill that allowed you to track someone's cell phone.

First he took her phone number, then by using her phone's IP address and its GPS he created a map of her movements over the past five days. Not surprisingly, she had spent almost all of her time between her apartment in Rosslyn and the lab. There were two trips to the pharmacy and . . .

What's this?

A trip to Northwest DC. He zeroed in on the address where it appeared she'd spent two hours on Monday. Optima Pharmaceuticals. He pulled up their webpage: Innovative gene therapies using state-of-the art technologies.

Oh no, he thought, as his mind put two and two together.

A rap came on his door, and there she was, suddenly, standing in the doorway. "Good morning," she said, smiling big, an expression that, once again, struck Ryan as impossible to fake. She really was happy to see him.

He smiled back reflexively. Up until a few minutes ago, he had been looking forward to seeing her too. But now . . . he didn't know what to think. She was wearing her hair up, with those thick-framed glasses that were equal parts nerdy and attractive.

Seeing her here, so suddenly, made him want to forget about his suspicions, but that desire was quickly overcome by a stronger feeling—a mix of anger and betrayal. He felt like he had been used.

She read his expression immediately. “What’s wrong?”

He shook his head, unsure of what to say.

She came closer and put her hand on his shoulder.

“What is it?”

“What is Optima Pharmaceuticals?” he asked.

Her head rocked back a little in surprise. “I . . . how do you know about them?”

“Are you here to steal our technology?”

“What? No, of course not.”

“Then why have you been spending all your time looking at our nanotech files and viruses?”

“Have you been spying on me? You have. Ryan, how could you?”

Ryan faltered. She seemed so genuine. So sincere.

She continued: “For your information, I’m doing my job. I’m learning all I can about the fascinating things you’ve been doing here. I just started a week ago and I have a lot to learn.”

It was plausible of course, but it still didn’t feel right. The long hours. The urgency. “There’s something you’re not telling me,” he insisted.

She hesitated and pursed her lips. And that told him he was right.

“I don’t want to lie to you.”

“Then don’t.”

Her eyes darted away, then came back to him. “It’s not what you think. Nothing illegal is going on.”

"Has Walden put you up to something?"

"No, it's got nothing to do with him. It's personal and, well, quite honestly, I'm not ready to tell you."

He eyed her for a moment. He was strangely conflicted. On one hand, he was obligated to report any suspicious activity he came across, and yet now, looking at her, he believed her and he knew that if he told Curtiss about it, it would come to nothing.

"I'm trying to do the right thing," she said. "Just have a little faith in me . . . please."

Ryan fidgeted a moment, looking down at his hands. Ostensibly she was telling him nothing, yet it also felt like she was bringing him closer. There was an intimacy in her plea. It was *almost* a promise.

"How long do I have to wait?" he asked.

He had hoped that she might flash him her coy smile, but she didn't. And that told him that whatever it was, it was deeply personal.

"When I know I can trust you," she said.

CHAPTER TWENTY-FIVE

AIGAMUXA

November 15, 2026
Namibia

In a mere twenty minutes the whole tribe was ready and began walking. At first Karuma held Eric's hand, but after a while Eric felt confident enough to walk behind him. If he listened closely, he could hear the steady rhythm of the young man's footsteps and by that alone he was able to keep pace, only occasionally correcting his direction and distance. It required his full concentration but it was hypnotic in a way, and kept him from feeling so helpless. Luckily the terrain was flat. Only now and then would Karuma warn him of a rocky area and come and guide him.

As they marched on, he worked on honing his remaining senses. He listened to the birds and asked Karuma their names. The boy could name every one by its song.

While they walked, the Sān talked easily and laughed.

Eric listened to their words, trying to improve his

vocabulary, but he also listened to *where* the words went. He was discovering that many things produced echoes, despite not being truly solid. A tree line, for example, would give back an echo almost the same as a rock formation or a sand dune. And if he listened closely, he could even gauge the distance . . . at least roughly.

It was a hot day, and by early afternoon the sun began to take its toll on him. This environment felt very different from the tropical jungle near the mining camp. It was so dry he could literally feel the moisture evaporating from his skin. Karuma had given him a leather pouch with three ostrich eggs full of water. But he was so thirsty, he ran out by midafternoon. Karuma laughed at him and shared one of his own. All day they walked, and Eric's legs grew stiff and weary. But knowing they were making the journey for his sake, he wasn't about to complain.

By late afternoon Eric could feel the intensity of the sun beginning to fade. Khamko came and walked with him for a while, holding his hand.

"You did very well today, and we traveled far. Even if the Chinese find our last camp, I think we are safe. They will know we have been there, but they will not know which way we went or that you were with us."

"Thank you. I sincerely hope that someday I can repay you."

"You do not need to repay me, my son."

Eric was touched by the sentiment, but also by the salutation: that this very gracious man should call him son.

They made camp. Eric was amazed how quickly it was done. Within half an hour Karuma had a built two lean-tos for himself and Eric. The work complete, the children played and sang songs. The Sān had decided there would be no fires tonight.

Exhausted and weary, Eric sat near Karuma and massaged his battered feet.

"Do you know what happened to my boots?"

"Oh, yes, we took them off when we found you."

"Why?"

"To check your feet."

"What for?"

"For eyeballs, of course."

Eric's face furled in confusion. "I'm sorry, I don't understand."

Karuma gave a grunt of annoyance, as if it should be obvious. "We had to make sure you didn't have eyeballs on your feet."

"Is that common?"

"Of course, all Aigamuxa have eyeballs on their feet."

"Aigamu-what?"

Karuma laughed. "Grandpa says you are a smart man, but sometimes I wonder. Aigamuxa are man-eating creatures who live in the dunes. They look like very big men—like you—but their eyeballs are on their feet, so they stand on their hands when they need to look around."

"And you thought I was one of those."

"Yes, so we took off your boots to check."

"Oh, okay."

That night Eric slept on the ground with a buckskin blanket to keep him warm. Sometime during the night he heard people arguing. It was Khamko and Naru.

Naru wanted to leave Eric behind.

Khamko refused.

Eric listened with all his might, trying to translate their words. But they spoke too fast, and it was difficult.

"Why are you still looking out for him? Have you [unintelligible]? He's hiding something."

"It doesn't matter, without us he will die, it is our [unintelligible]."

"He is a white man! His people have destroyed ours. Have you forgotten what happened to your own father? My [unintelligible]."

"My heart [unintelligible]."

"You are an old fool. Perhaps we should leave both of you behind."

Then it grew quiet.

Eric lay there for a time, listening for more, but he heard only the crickets and the night sounds of the desert. He began to fear that perhaps Khamko was having doubts about him. Maybe he would decide that Naru was right.

He was suddenly afraid to fall asleep, fearing that when he woke up he would find himself alone. So he lay there a long time trying to figure what he would do if they did. But there was no solution. If they left him, he knew he would die.

When sleep finally came he dreamed that he was back home in Washington, DC, on the National Mall near the Smithsonian. It was the height of summer, hot and dry. The day was full of light and people were everywhere: families picnicking on the lawn, teenagers playing Frisbee, children running and screaming in delight.

It was a perfect day. Eric's vision had returned, and the sky was so gloriously blue and there was so much light, it seemed to seep into him like energy.

He felt someone's hand in his.

He looked down to see Karuma beside him, a look of joy

and amazement on the boy's face. He looked east toward the Capitol Building then turned toward the Washington Monument. "So many people! How can it be?" Eric smiled. Their roles had been reversed. Now Karuma was the visitor and he was the native, showing him his world.

Then a cold wind hit them, and he felt a sudden dimming of the light as if a cloud had blocked the sun. Eric looked out over the lawn toward the Lincoln Memorial. It was then he saw it.

Oh no, not again. A shock wave rolled across the lawn—a blurry, expanding ring of force, racing toward them. As it touched each person they fell, but there were no screams, no cries. It reached Eric and Karuma, like a hot wind, blowing their hair up and pulling at his clothes. He held tight to Karuma's hand, but suddenly the hand was gone. He looked down. There was only a sprinkling of dirt in his palm.

He looked around. Everyone was gone.

Then he heard a deep moaning from above and looked up to see a dozen massive white balls streak across the sky, each one leaving a long contrail of black smoke behind it. Satellites. Something was pulling them back to earth. The buildings along the National Mall began to dissolve, disintegrating into the ground. He realized that humanity and all its creations were being erased. Cars and streetlights. Roads and sidewalks. Everything was being disassembled. Almost immediately grass began to grow up around him, reaching his knees then his hips. The trees grew taller and thicker. And the air became heavy with moisture. Soon he was standing in thick jungle, with vines and moss all around. He heard the growl of an animal and knew he was not safe. He began to run and almost immediately heard the rush of something large bounding after him.

He awoke with a start, back in Africa, back in blindness.

He tried to catch his breath, but his heart was beating so fast that it took many minutes.

It's just a dream. Relax. But it was not the first time he'd had the dream. It had come once before, when he'd returned from China. After he'd seen the Inventor.

He realized now that he had become so absorbed in his immediate survival he had stopped thinking about the man who had saved his life five months ago.

The memory of their meeting came back in lucid detail. The windswept crossroads. Surrounded by Chinese soldiers. General Meng had finally caught them. Eric had been clutching Mei in his arms, and the general had a pistol to his head, about to kill them both. It seemed there was no escape. That's when he'd felt a cool sensation under his skull and suddenly he couldn't move or breathe. It had happened to all of them, including Meng and his soldiers. They had been hacked. Someone (or something) had sent nanosites into their bodies and was controlling them. Then the Inventor had appeared. He had let Eric, Mei, and Ryan live, but he had killed everyone else, sadistically, brutally.

And the dream? It had first come a few days later. At that time he'd suspected the Inventor's nanosites were still in his body, and the dream was some sort of message. But as time had gone by, he'd dismissed that idea. It was just a nightmare brought on by the stress of almost dying, of seeing Meng and all his soldiers killed, and seeing the Inventor's unprecedented power.

But why had the dream come again, and why with Karuma by his side? He supposed it made sense on some level. He was far from the world he knew, blind and afraid. He had gone to sleep fearing he would be abandoned. So it was natural to dream of "the end of the world." Yet he could not help thinking that his mind was trying to tell him something.

He lay there for a time, arm over his forehead, trying to understand what it meant. Until he heard Karuma's voice. "Moon-man! It is time to get up." He felt Karuma's hand shaking his shoulder. Eric was so grateful to hear his voice, for it was only a few moments ago that the boy had died beside him.

"Come on!" the boy said. Eric stood and Karuma took his hand. "It is a beautiful day, but it will be hot again. Come, I'm hungry."

Over seven thousand miles away, in Admiral Curtiss's office, "The Chinese are still looking," Sawyer told Curtiss. "They had four sorties out today, one forty klicks from the crash site."

Curtiss looked at the image of Master Chief Nathan Sawyer on his iSheet. "And what about you? Anything?"

"Since it was our first day back, we started at the crash site. The Chinese trashed it, of course, so we didn't find anything useful. After that, we visited two other areas we know the Chinese haven't looked. Right now I'm staying near the Cubango River. If Eric was smart enough to stay near the river basin where he'd have water and tree cover, he could still be alive. But if he wandered west, well, it gets very arid very fast . . . It would be hard for anyone to survive out there alone."

"Roger. Have you talked to Jane?"

"I was hoping you could do that for me."

Curtiss nodded. “Fair enough.”

“Oh, and Admiral, thanks for getting the aid to the Namibians. I’ve been going crazy on that damn boat.”

“Don’t mention it. Just do your best to find Hill. The way things are going here, I’m going to need all the allies I can get.”

“Copy that.”

CHAPTER TWENTY-SIX

OLIVIA'S SECRET

November 15, 2026
Washington, DC

"Hey! Hey!"

Ryan Lee swiveled around in his chair to find Olivia Rosario beaming. "I got good news!" she said, her eyes widening, clearly excited, but wanting to draw it out.

In the four days since he had confronted her, they had been spending most of their workdays together, and while she had talked no more of her secret, the friendship between them had only grown stronger.

Ryan smiled at her. He leaned back in his chair and put his hands behind his head. "Oh yeah?"

She opened her mouth to speak then paused for effect. Making him wait.

He couldn't help but smile wider. "Go on, spit it out!"

"We got approval for the Global Hologram!" She lifted up her arms and did a little dance.

Ryan laughed. “You’re kidding. I thought Curtiss would never go for it.”

“Well, in the end, he didn’t have much of a choice. Walden and Garrett pretty much made him give us a shot! The only catch is that we have six weeks to get something together that will impress him. If we can’t, then he can pull the plug.”

“Whew! Six weeks?”

“I know, I know, but don’t worry, we are going to make history!”

He smiled. “Well done, Olivia Rosario!”

She sat down next to him and gave him another warm smile. “Hey, I was thinking, why don’t you come over tonight? Sort of a celebration, but I also want you to meet someone.”

“Emma?” Ryan said, referring to Olivia’s nine-year-old daughter, whose picture was proudly displayed throughout her office.

“Yeah, I think it’s time.”

Three hours later, Ryan was following her through the plush lobby of her Rosslyn high-rise. As he looked at the beautiful woman in front of him—the sway of her hips, her silky black hair, the way her calves balled and flexed—he once again had the feeling that life was good.

They took the elevator to the fourteenth floor, and Olivia opened her door. “Hello! Anybody here?” she called playfully.

Ryan heard a woman reply, “We’re in the bedroom.”

He followed Olivia down a long hallway. There they

found an older woman and . . . Ryan was startled by what he saw. Olivia's daughter was in a wheelchair, slouched and emaciated, her mouth ajar and her eyes open but vacant. It was a startling contrast to all the pictures he'd seen.

Olivia rushed to her and squeezed her tight.

"Hello, *mi vida*! How was your day?" Ryan noticed that Olivia did not wait for an answer. "Oh, wow, who did your hair? You look so pretty!"

"Oh, yes," the older woman said. "She really enjoyed that."

"I bet!" she gave the girl a loud kiss.

Olivia introduced the woman. "Natalie, this is my friend, Ryan."

"Nice to meet you, Natalie."

"It's a pleasure," Natalie said. They shook hands.

"And this is my daughter, Emma."

"Hello," Ryan smiled and waved awkwardly, but the girl made no response.

"Will you be needing anything else, Miss R?"

"No, Natalie, thank you so much. I couldn't do it without you." Olivia embraced her.

"Oh, it's my pleasure. I'll be in my room if you need me." The nurse kissed Emma on both cheeks. "I'll see you later, darling," and quietly left the room.

Olivia turned to him: "Ryan, why don't you push her to the living room."

"Of course," Ryan said.

Olivia went ahead of him into the living room and opened up the blinds that stretched across one side of the room. The vista that was revealed was breathtaking—an amazing night view of the Potomac River that spanned from Georgetown to the Kennedy Center. "She loves to look out the windows," Olivia said. She lifted the girl onto the sofa then sat beside her, letting the girl slouch against her. She began tenderly caressing the girl's head, and for a few moments they took in the view. There was a dinner cruise boat sliding south down the river and the opposing streams of red and white car lights crossing the Key Bridge.

Ryan glanced again at Emma, who still did not seem aware that he was there.

"Why didn't you tell me?"

"I'm sorry. It's just that sometimes I don't even want to say it. It makes it too real . . . too permanent." She sighed. "It's called Alexander's Disease. It's a defective gene that affects nerve cells."

"I'm sorry, Olivia. This must be very hard."

She nodded. "Just two years ago, she was a perfectly normal seven-year-old, then she started falling for no apparent reason. It took the doctors ten months to diagnose her because it's so rare. There have only been five hundred cases reported since the '40s."

"Is there anything you can do?"

She pinched her lips and shook her head. "The defective gene affects the myelin that insulates her neurons. As the myelin grows weaker, her nerve impulses fail."

It was a heartbreaking story, and Ryan wondered if there was some way to help her.

Then for the first time, the girl moved. She shifted her head so that her mother could scratch the other side.

"You see? She's still in there. She can't talk but she knows what's going on." Ryan nodded and smiled, though he suspected this was wishful thinking. He had studied neurology for years to become better at AI and he knew it was unlikely she was still cognizant. With degenerative neural disorders, higher brain function, such as speech, often went first, then they slowly worked their way to the lower brain, affecting swallowing, breathing, and finally the major muscle groups and the heart. From what he was seeing, the girl couldn't have more than a year to live.

"Any seizures?" he asked.

"Not yet, but the doctors say they're coming." She looked him straight in the eye. "I'm scared, Ryan. Once they start, the brain damage will accelerate."

He nodded. "I'm so sorry." It was the only thing he could think to say. He watched Olivia gently caress Emma until the girl nodded off.

When Olivia was certain she was asleep, she produced an iSheet and handed it to Ryan. It was a video of Emma playing soccer. It was a bright fall day, and the field was surrounded by brilliant red and copper trees. Emma dribbled around one defender and then another. Ryan immediately recognized her mother's gracefulness in the girl's movements. Emma dodged one more defender, then shot the ball into the net. Olivia and the rest of the crowd cheered. Emma ran up to her mother, grinning from ear to ear. "Did you see me, mom? Did you see me?"

Her mother laughed. "Yes, I saw you! You're fantastic!"

"Can I get an extra scoop of ice cream now?"

"We'll see," Olivia said, "now go on back, they're about to start again."

The girl ran off.

Ryan stopped the video. This was the girl he'd expected to meet. The one in all the pictures in Olivia's office. Not the one lying across from him on the sofa.

Olivia scooted out from under Emma's head then nestled her under a blanket. "Come on," she said. "I need a drink."

They went to the kitchen, and she made them something strong with whiskey, then they went out on the balcony.

"To numbing our brains," she said, raising her glass.

Ryan drank and felt the warm liquor coating his throat and stomach.

"I could use a hug," she said.

He embraced her and together they looked out at the nation's capital. The cool wind that blew against them contrasted with the warmth of their body heat.

"Thank you for coming," she said. "Now do you understand why I work so hard?"

Ryan nodded his agreement reflexively then stopped himself. "But if there's no cure, you should be working less. You should be spending as much time . . ." He stopped.

"I'm sorry, Ryan. I have a confession to make. I didn't come to the NRL to advance my career. I came here for you."

He pulled away from her. Was it the whiskey that was making his head spin?

"I wasn't sure when I got here if you were really the one, but now I know. What you did in Tangshan, the leaps you've made in AI development combined with your understanding of Forced Evolution. You're the only one who can help me."

"Hold on a second. Does Walden know about this?"

She shook her head. "Walden sees what he wants to see: an ambitious tech entrepreneur."

"And who exactly did he hire?"

She looked out at the skyline a moment then fixed him with her gaze. "A desperate mother. Look, I'm not asking you to do anything illegal. I just need your help to find out if it's possible. You can make iPS cells from Emma's tissue. That's harmless. Test it on those. That will tell us if it could work. If it doesn't, you can forget about it. But if it does work, then I'll go to Walden and Curtiss."

"You know I can't do that."

"Of course you can, you're Ryan Lee. They'd never fire you. They need you. And besides, all you have to do is tell them I told you to do it and I'll take the blame."

Ryan shook his head. *This was crazy.* "Even if I could do it, there's only a tiny chance of it working. The damage you're describing is extensive and likely permanent." He didn't want to say it, but he felt she needed to hear it: "It's probably too late already."

"Please don't say that; I know it's not. And yes, it *can* work! Don't you see? All the pieces are already here." She counted off with her fingers. "Recognition tunneling can read each gene in vivo. The virus programs can be used for gene therapy. Eric's proofreading program can find the errors. And forced evolution will be smart enough to not only correct Emma's genes but repair the damage to the myelin sheath. Ninety percent of the work is done. It just needs your skill as a programmer to put it all together."

He couldn't stop shaking his head. At least now he understood why she'd been so interested in their nanotech files. "I don't know. This is all happening too fast."

"I know, you're absolutely right. I wish we could take our time, but that's a luxury I don't have."

"I—" he began, but couldn't look at her and say it. He glanced away. "I thought you liked me. I mean, really liked me."

He looked back, and her expression showed she seemed hurt by this. "Oh, Ryan, please don't doubt that. I do like you." She took his hand and put it to her heart. "I'm not faking this. You're cute and funny and so insanely smart.

You're the first person I've met who knows more about AI than me, and that's sexy."

She paused, seeing that he wasn't convinced. "It's also the reason I'm telling you the truth. I could have waited to introduce you to Emma. I could have let this get physical first. I'm trying to be honest, but I also know I'm desperate."

Ryan pulled his hand away. "I just need some time to think about it." His eyes darted around like an animal looking for a place to bolt. "I'd better go."

"Please don't." She reached out for his hand again. "I know it's sudden and my emotions are all mixed up, too, but let's at least talk this through and . . . and stay . . . at least a little longer."

But Ryan pulled away and left the balcony. This time she didn't try to stop him.

It was gloomy, almost dark in the living room. He went to grab his coat, which he'd left on the chair across from Emma. As he picked it up he realized he'd left the iSheet there, propped up against the back of the seat. He thought he'd turned it off, but now he saw he'd only muted it. The video of the girl playing soccer had been repeating this whole time. He picked the device up, turned it off and tossed it back on the seat. As he was pulling on his coat, he looked down at the sleeping girl and was surprised to see her eyes open and her cheeks wet with tears.

CHAPTER TWENTY-SEVEN

THE WATER HOLE

November 16, 2026
Namibia

They walked for the following two days. Despite his stiffness, Eric found he did surprisingly well. As always, Karuma took good care of him, holding his hand at times and always making sure he didn't stumble or fall. Eric simultaneously hated his neediness and was grateful for Karuma's care.

On the morning of the fourth day, Karuma cautioned him.

"This is your last egg of water. After this, there is no more."

It was stifling hot again, and by noon he had only a few ounces left. He gave a long sigh. How was he going to make it?

He trudged on. After a while, Karuma came beside him. "All very clear now, Moon-man, you can't fall." The rest of the tribe, who had always walked single file, were now walking abreast. Eric could hear them all around him. Under his feet the grass and sandy earth had changed to something hard and crystalline. Simultaneously, the sun had become fiercer, like a heavy burden that had to be carried on his head and shoulders. The breeze that had been so cool and refreshing had turned into a hot blast, as if someone was walking in front of him holding a blow dryer to his face.

"What is this place?"

"The Land of Salt," he said. "We have to cross it."

On and on they marched. It seemed a terrible choice to make considering they were out of water. Almost suicide. Yet they pushed on.

"How much longer?" he asked Karuma.

"Oh, not much." There was no tension or fatigue in the boy's voice. He seemed perfectly calm, even excited.

"I don't think I can take much more of this."

Karuma laughed. "Of course you can. You'll be fine."

The sun continued to beat down and Eric felt his legs becoming rubbery under his hips. It was an effort just to keep moving. The heat was like an oven, sucking the moisture out of his body. And just like an oven, it was hitting him from both above and below, as the heat rose off the salt flats in waves. His labored breathing was loud in his ears.

"There!" Khamko said, "I knew it!"

"What is it?" Eric asked Karuma.

"It is hard to see clearly," the boy said. "The heat . . . it makes everything blurry. I see many things, some moving. Come!"

He grabbed Eric's hand and began to run. At first Eric staggered, but his body came alive at the hope of what might be there. His feet cracked the crusty salt as he ran. A moment later, he heard the yap of hyenas, followed by the unmistakable beating of hundreds of wings as a flock of birds took flight.

He began to feel what Karuma had seen, the presence of many things. There was an energy in the air, like the feeling of approaching a crowd.

There was the loud trumpet of an elephant, so close that Eric stopped. Through his feet, he could actually feel the ground vibrate. Then he noticed something else, humidity in the air.

He heard laughter from the other Sān. Karuma tugged him on. A giddiness overtook him and he ran eagerly now. His body knowing what must be there. A moment later he heard the splashing of feet in water, then he splashed in himself. It brought a wave of pleasure that rolled up from his toes to the top of his head. Even though a drop had not yet touched his lips, he felt his thirst subside. He gasped in pleasure then laughed.

Karuma's voice came from down near his ankles. "What are you waiting for?"

He knelt and began to drink, scooping the water into his mouth, splashing it onto his face, neck, and head. He shivered as he felt his body temperature begin to fall. After he had drunk his fill, he sat down in the shallow water and tried to sort through the new sounds around him. He heard the stomping of hooves. The chatter of many birds. The loud huck-huck call of zebra.

He called to Karuma, "How can it be?"

"Grandfather says the shell of the earth here is a desert, but under the shell is a deep ocean. If you know where the water breaks through the shell, you will never be thirsty."

Eric nodded, then he motioned to all the noises. "Can you describe what you see?"

"Ah, that's not easy. There are so many," Karuma said. "Over there is a family of elephants, and closer by there are ten giraffes, seventy or eighty springbok. Maybe thirty zebras. And lots of birds, some hyenas and gemsbok. We are lucky there are no rhinos, they chase everyone away."

But Eric wanted to know more. "What are they doing?"

Karuma laughed, took another drink, then began to describe the scene in more detail. He described the oxpecker birds sitting on the elephants. A young elephant sucking up water and showering himself. A giraffe with its legs splayed as it drank.

Eric tried to create a mental image of it. To save it. He would likely never "see" anything like this again so it became important, indeed critical, that he remember it, to create a vision of it. A vision that he could keep forever and share with the world, with Jane and Ryan and Mei.

He closed his eyes and concentrated very hard, using sound and smell and touch. He heard a splash of light hooves very close. He guessed it might be a springbok and tried to imagine it. He turned to it and closed his eyes—creating the animal in his mind.

When he opened his eyes he saw it.

The perfect tan fur on her back, her snow-white belly, and the swoosh of black on her flank. He stared for a moment in rapt amazement, then a muscle twitched on her haunches as she shooed a fly. Eric laughed. *I saw that*. Their eyes met, and he felt her spirit. In her big doe eyes he understood her wild nature. Her instinct. Her will.

Suddenly his head swam as his brain tried to process the whole staggering vista in front of him. It came in and out of focus for a moment, then it became crystal clear. Almost too clear. He gasped. Never, it seemed, had his eyes perceived such detail—the bristly hair on the elephant's hide, the vibrant orange of the giraffe's tile coat, the dizzying pattern of the zebra stripes.

It was the most intense visual image of his life and it was rendered in higher definition than anything he had ever seen before. Everything was in focus at once. Everything from the misplaced feather on a plover's wing to the sun's white glare on the brown water to the wind-shivering froth that lay at the edge of the pool. Never had his eyes been drenched with such splendor. He was awestruck.

He turned to Karuma and looked upon his friend's face for the first time. And this was, in many ways, just as amazing. The young man had what seemed like a permanent smile on his face. He was beautiful and sleek and strong. His skin was the color of shining copper, and his kinky hair was just a shade darker. He wore a small leather loincloth, a beaded necklace, and nothing else. In his hand was a spear. He seemed the perfect boy. The first boy on earth. A creature of permanent gold.

Karuma cocked his head to one side, perceiving that something had changed about the foreigner. He waved the spear from side to side and noticed Eric's eyes tracking it.

"Is it true?"

Eric nodded, grinning wide. "Hello, my friend."

Karuma stood and began calling to the others. "The moon-man can see!"

It was not a coming out of darkness, for there was no gradual returning of light. Nor was the sun suddenly too bright. His eyes, after all, had already been open. Instead it was as if a loose wire had been snugged back into place. All at once, the world was there.

He looked around at his Sān family, trying to match

their faces to the voices and characters he already knew. Just to see them was joyous. There was Tssatssi and /Uma and Nyando, and of course, shy little //Kabbo, who was just as slim as the others but with a round little belly. Then he saw a striking young woman and knew this must be Naru. Even though she still looked a teenager, she held herself with the poise and dignity of a queen—as one who has lived long and knows the fullness of her power. Like the rest of them she was naked from the waist up. Her cheeks sat high on her slim face, under penetrating brown eyes. Around her forehead was a headdress made from the skin of a cobra.

He had known that they were small, but to see them for the first time was striking . . . not one of them reached his shoulder. They were unerringly slim and lean, even the ones with round bellies. And it seemed that everyone was smiling. He also saw things that his fingers had sensed before, like the texture of their skin: it had rivulets like a cactus and Eric mused that, just like cactus, perhaps it could stretch to hold water.

At that moment the tribe seemed to part, and an old man came splashing through the shallow water. The grace of his movement, the pure efficiency of his gait, was like watching a leopard move. His skin was the same copper color, but his hair was white, as if he had just come in from a blizzard and been powdered with fresh snow.

His face was deeply lined but when he felt Eric's eyes upon him he smiled so wide all the lines disappeared. He raised his hands to the sky. "I prayed to Cagn for you! And he answered my prayers!" He stepped forward, and they embraced. "My son," he said, "I am so happy for you." After a long minute, Eric stepped back to see his face more clearly, still holding him in a one-armed embrace. And in that moment he felt the whole history of this man. A man who had lived in both worlds and had chosen this one. A man who had dedicated his life to protecting his people—decade after decade. And for the first time since his own father died, Eric felt like he truly had a protector. Here was a man with a pure heart. A man he could follow without question. And a man who truly loved him and would protect him as if he were his own son.

"I can see you," Eric said. "I can see you and I can't believe it."

Khamko laughed. "Believe," he said, "believe."

CHAPTER TWENTY-EIGHT

THE WORLD ACCORDING TO RIONA FINLEY

November 20, 2026
The forests near Smithburg, West Virginia

> "A new scientific truth does not triumph by convincing its opponents and making them see the light, but rather because its opponents eventually die, and a new generation grows up that is familiar with it."
>
> —Max Planck

Riona Finley moved cautiously through the woods along the deer trail. Up ahead she could hear the sound of the highway, the swishing sounds of the tires that reminded her of the low din of the ocean. Just before the edge of the woods she stopped. She was close enough to see out but not close enough to be seen. She was high on a hill above the road and could see it stretching out a dozen miles in both directions.

She wasn't quite sure why she had come here. Everyone had agreed she needed to stay out of sight. She was now

#1 on the FBI's most wanted list and a very busy woman. The assassination of Senator Peck had been a public relations coup and launched her onto the international stage. Membership was up. Crowdfunding was fantastic, and revenue was skyrocketing.

Just keep doing what you're doing, she said to herself. *How can 140 million Twitter followers be wrong?*

Yet part of her felt that something wasn't right. She needed to evolve in some way. This morning she'd decided to go for a walk to clear her head. She'd left the cabin at 8:00 a.m. Now it was four hours and eight miles later, but she wasn't any closer to finding what she was looking for. She had believed her philosophy was perfect, that she had captured the zeitgeist of not just America, but the world. Yet something . . . something still didn't fit.

She sat down and tried to take stock in her life: She was a radical. She knew that. She was also proud of it, because being radical was the only way that real change was going to happen. That's what she was trying to teach her followers through her blogs and tweets. Just look at history, she told them. Throughout most of human history, things stayed the same as the masses trudged along under the whip or whim of their masters, convinced that the way things were was normal and immutable. Century upon century passed under the dictatorial rule of caesars, kings, emperors, caliphs, and other tyrants who fed their followers promises of a better world in the afterlife for toil and abuse in this one.

Only when a radicalized person arrived on the scene did things ever change. Jesus was the first radical. A man who challenged the existing system, whose teachings of compassion threatened the old guard. Many more came after him. Some were benevolent; many were not. Mohammad,

Rousseau, Jean-Paul Marat, Napoleon, Marx, Hitler, Stalin, Mao, Gandhi, Martin Luther King Jr.

With them came radical ideas, new religions, new economic systems, new laws. And while some of their agendas had been ruinous, it could not be denied that they had still been the engines of massive transformation. Because of them, the world was never quite the same.

Of course, they weren't born in a vacuum. As Herbert Spencer noticed, societies created these "great men," but societies ripe for change. Indeed, it was sick societies that incubated some of the greatest radicals. Men who had, unlike their peers, the courage and ambition to act.

This, she felt, was how she had become the woman she was. The problems of modern society had forced her to become radical. All the complacency, the barriers to power, the corruption, and ignorance had left her no choice but to act outside the laws of the system.

As she looked back on her life, she realized it could not have turned out any other way.

There were two defining moments that had pushed her down this path. She called them her "great epiphanies."

The first was a realization about the nature of her fellow humans.

It had happened in the library at Dartmouth, while she was studying environmental science in graduate school. She had come across a 1949 study by two Harvard psychologists who had tested students' perceptions about doctored playing cards. The study found that the subjects—who had no idea the cards had been altered—were very resistant to acknowledging that the cards were incorrect. The rather obscure study was noticed by the famous historian Thomas Kuhn who grasped its true importance: when people are given information that does not match the framework in which they see the world, the new information is rejected or explained away for as long as possible. "In science, as in the playing card experiment, novelty emerges only with difficulty," Kuhn wrote.

Here at last was the cornerstone of her theory of history. The great mass of humanity—simply by their nature—was stubbornly resistant to change. Indeed, they would only accept change when they absolutely had to.

Which, by extension, meant that whole societies were always slow to react to pressing problems, often waiting until it was the very last moment or too late altogether.

Climate change, of course, was a problem that could not be tackled slowly. The preponderance of evidence had emerged in the 1970s, yet humanity had let the clock tick down far too long. It was now 2026, and if they were going to turn things around, they had to act with an urgency that just did not exist.

And besides, all the nonradical methods to wake people up had already been exhausted.

Yet back in that library, even though she knew extreme measures were necessary, she still did not embrace violence. She was a radical, yes, but violent, no.

Her endorsement of violence took much longer. The process began after she became an assistant professor at Cornell. She still had hope then; she was still idealistic and naive. Being a professor should have been a great way for her to change the world. She saw herself as a shining torch: she would go to conferences, she would do important research, persuade public officials, and all while she would be teaching and mentoring the next generation of activists.

But the deeper she got, the more she realized the game

was rigged against her. Most of her senior colleagues were much more worried about securing grant money than saving the planet. Worse, they were lackadaisical, and their ideas, quite frankly, sucked. Yet, because they were established in the field, they received the lion's share of the grant money, while her own lab, which was doing important work on Ocean Acidification, was starved for money. That's when she'd come across a famous quote by Max Planck, "Science moves forward one funeral at a time."

In many ways it was a corollary to Thomas Kuhn's idea about humankind's resistance to new ideas, yet it was also acknowledging (for the first time in her mind anyway) that death could be a good thing. And as she continued to work and struggle, one year, two years . . . five years. And as she watched the other climate scientists grow wealthy off their insignificant work, she began asking herself, *Why not give the mortality rate a little push? You know, just up the percentages a little.* She had been half joking the first time she thought it. But the idea kept coming back to her.

The tipping point came when she was passed over for tenure. It wasn't because she wasn't a good teacher or that she wasn't committed enough. It all came down to money. She was not pulling in the grant money that she (and the university) needed, so she was let go. That night, alone in her apartment, surrounded by the thousands of books that she had read, she got drunk and began to plan her first kill. Much to her surprise, the next day she did not give up on the idea. She decided to really do it . . . and do it right. Using the Socratic method. As a scientist would. What did she have to lose?

His name was Avery Reynolds. He was a blogger, political pundit, and climate-change denier. A pseudointellectual,

Avery spoke with an English accent even though he was born in Ohio and had only lived in the UK for six months. He had a degree in journalism from the University of Dayton and had never taken a hard science course in his life. During his twenties he had struggled to make a name for himself as a reporter, working at a series of regional newspapers before being hired, then quickly fired, from *USA Today* for plagiarism. He was covering high school sports for the *Atlanta-Journal Constitution* when he hit on the lucrative idea of being a climate-change denier. Despite having no background in science, he suddenly felt uniquely qualified to denounce every peer-reviewed scientific paper about global warming.

It wasn't long before he was appearing regularly on talk radio and TV. He attempted to spin himself as an independent activist, but Riona knew this was a lie. His salary, travel expenses, car, and mortgage were paid for by the Capital Donation Fund, a secretive nonprofit dedicated to "educating the public on the truths of climate change." It, in turn, received the majority of its funds from Big Oil and the Detroit automakers.

For Riona, Reynolds was the perfect symbol of the dirty money that kept the climate movement paralyzed. His death would send a message to all those who funded the deception that they were no longer safe.

She had known from the outset that she had to make her killings as sexy as possible. This was a movement that she wanted to go mainstream. That meant no guns. She didn't want the bloody corpses of her victims going viral on the internet. No, these had to be Hollywood-style killings—PG-13—with little or no blood.

That meant high explosives.

But she'd made a mistake with poor Avery. She'd thought blowing him up in his black Cadillac Escalade would be a nice poetic touch. You know, burned alive in the very fossil fuels he so vehemently claimed were not dangerous.

She remembered that night so clearly. He left the fund-raising dinner for Texas Senator Wyatt Mayfield in his black tuxedo, skipping down the steps of the Emerald Oaks Country Club, failing to tip the valet, and climbing into his gas-guzzling SUV. He was halfway between the first tee and the tennis courts when Riona had hit the detonator.

That's when she learned the hard way that an explosion did not necessarily cause a fire unless you added an incendiary element. While Avery was likely killed instantly, the fuel tank did not explode in a fireball like it does on TV. It did ignite, but the effects were . . . well, definitely not PG-13.

The photo that went viral was of a very unevenly cooked Avery Reynolds, the skin on his cheeks blackened and peeling like pork rinds. One eye had been blown out by the explosion, the other looked enormous because both eyelids had been burned off. His mouth was open in a horrific yawn, the lips gone, exposing the teeth like the mouth of ancient mummy.

To this day, this was the picture that Riona's adversaries in the media used to denounce her as a violent radical, as a black widow, a merciless killer.

Live and learn.

And she had learned. It had been her first job, and looking back she was still proud she had pulled it off. Now she made it a point to obliterate her victims beyond recognition. Luckily, her expanding budget meant she could outsource this work. A former British Army sapper named Malcolm McPhie who had defected to the IRA now handled all her demolition work.

Did she feel bad for her victims? Did she feel guilty? Only barely. Because she was a scientist out to solve a problem and these people *were* the problem. If you wanted to save the planet, they had to go. They epitomized her philosophy about people refusing to see the truth simply because it wasn't convenient. It was inexcusable. After going to school from kindergarten through college, no one ever told them the planet was in trouble? *Give me a break.* They knew full well about mass extinction, pollution, and global warming and had not only decided to do nothing about it, but profit from it.

On the highway below her, the westbound traffic had slowed to a crawl; a long backup of cars spread off into the distance.

She reminded herself that things were going well. In many ways, they were better than she could have ever imagined. Yet she was still restless. Her movement was growing, but it still felt small. Was it small, or were her goals small?

What was missing?

An eighteen-wheeler gas truck sat stopped with all the other traffic, the name Morgan Petroleum emblazoned on its side. She stared at it. It was full of the fossil fuels that were causing climate change. *I wonder where that truck is going*, she thought. That's when the epiphany hit her. She would later remember it as the third great epiphany of her life.

The gas in the truck would be fed into a car, just like the coal sent to a power plant would feed a household appliance like a washing machine or computer. She saw another driver tapping on his cell phone, which was plugged into the dash, so it too was being fed by the gas in the engine. The realization made her head spin as her whole understanding of humankind's destiny became clear.

We were destroying the earth to feed machines. The amount of energy needed to keep humans alive was very small, but the amount of energy needed to feed our inventions was enormous. Now she understood her restlessness. She'd been wrong. All this time, the enemy had not been the oil companies or the logging companies or the corrupt lawyers. The enemy was technology.

She sat there for a moment, stunned, watching blankly as the traffic inched forward. She had to sort this out, had to think it through. Technology was alive, and all of us were nourishing it like doting mothers, every day, all day, even while we slept.

Our progress as a species was linked to it.

She tried to think back to what invention had started it all. But she realized that was impossible, because you could not define technology as just electronic devices or the steam engine or even fire. Looking out, she saw the highway stretching out—both ways—into eternity, packed with cars and trucks, a seemingly endless ribbon of metal, oil, plastic, and rubber. Then she fixated on the road itself. *The road.* It was technology too. An amazing piece of technology, in fact. With roads the world had been conquered. Indigenous people slaughtered. Forests wiped out. Put a road in the Amazon rain forest, and it would bring settlers and development and slash and burn.

Progress.

"My God," she thought, "how do you stop it?"

She could see no answer. And now she saw her own folly. She had always been proud to call herself a liberal, but now she realized that politics were irrelevant. It made no difference if liberals or conservatives ruled the country because they would both demand economic progress. They would both want new roads, new factories, more jobs, more crops, better fertilizer.

She brought her hands to her face and rocked back and forth. "What have we done?"

She had thought that her actions would wake people up and cause lasting change. Now she wasn't so sure. Now it felt that the only way to save the planet was to destroy all its technology.

But one thing was for sure, she had to change her thinking . . . and her mission. To save the planet she had to slow down the growth of most of technology. The only technologies that should proliferate were those that helped the planet—reduced emissions, protected endangered species, conserved habitat. Everything else—including the scientists who invented the technology—was fair game. Yes, the scientists. They were the real enemy, for they created the machines that sucked up all the energy of the world.

As she stared out at the thousands of vehicles rolling along the highway, she didn't feel small anymore, because she had figured out what was missing. She felt the sense of hope, elation, almost ecstasy, that comes from clear thought. Now she knew what she had to do. The only thing she could.

She had to tell her followers. She had to teach the world what she had discovered. This was the biggest news in years.

CHAPTER TWENTY-NINE

THE HUNT

November 20, 2026
Namibia

They stayed at the watering hole until almost sunset. That was when the rhinoceroses came and frightened all the other animals away.

Karuma had yelled at them. "You are a bunch of bullies!"

Khamko laughed. "Rhinoceroses are very territorial, and when they come, everyone else has to go."

That night they camped under a high cliff of red stone. A line of shepherd trees thrived in the shade of the rocks. Suspecting that there might be underground water, they dug and discovered half a dozen tubers thick with water.

As the tribe enjoyed the food, they talked excitedly about all they had seen that day and what they should do tomorrow. It was a surprisingly democratic affair. Khamko sat in silence listening to the others. That was when Eric realized that Khamko was not their leader, yet he could not tell who was. Perhaps no one was, but it seemed that most deferred to Kebbi-an, who was the oldest woman that Eric had ever seen, with a face like a withered apple and bright cunning eyes.

Some wanted to go where the hunting was good, others wanted to go find honey. He kept hearing those two words *danis* (honey) and *//gan-i* (meat).

Suddenly, the conversation came to a close, but he could not tell what they had decided. The adults called for the younger children, some nestled in close, while the restless ones played. Someone began to clap, then more people joined. Soon all the older women were clapping out a rhythm and singing. Simultaneously, the others began to dance. G□kau produced an odd instrument, a single string on a bow, and the man blew on it while he plucked it. It made an aboriginal, haunting sound that Eric had heard before.

So that's what makes that noise, he thought.

Then Karuma joined in. While the others had been shuffling together in their version of a conga line, Karuma began to move to his own rhythm. He was so quick and agile that he was a pleasure to watch. The older women began to clap faster and faster, cheering him on. Karuma matched the quickening pace effortlessly. He was twisting and darting, flipping, cartwheeling. One second he was twirling in the dirt, the next he was jumping three feet off the ground, an invisible spear raised above his head. Eric found himself laughing at the sight of him.

It was at that moment he understood what had been decided. And he wasn't going to miss it for the world.

★★★

He barely slept that night because he didn't want to risk them leaving without him. He lay awake in his lean-to, looking up at the stars. He couldn't recall ever seeing so many; the Milky Way was like a canyon of light running vertically across the sky. He savored the return of his sight, but also felt his other senses were still ultra-acute. Far off, a strange bird called and was answered by another. The wind whispered through the acacia trees and all around a low light filtered through the air. It was perhaps an hour before dawn when he heard the roar of a lion not far from camp. It was a sound that made him shiver, but he took it as a good sign. Soon he heard the others stirring and he got up.

The camp was still in darkness, but the sun was beginning to blush the clouds overhead. He found Khamko, Naru, and Karuma near the smoldering ashes of last night's fire. Khamko and Karuma both had bows and quivers strapped across their backs while Naru held a spear in each hand. Several of the older women were attending them, preparing them for the day ahead.

"So you heard us last night, did you?" Khamko said.

Eric nodded.

"All right."

Naru protested.

"I won't slow you down," Eric countered.

Khamko laughed his kind-hearted laugh. "Oh, yes, you will. But that's okay. If I recall correctly, Naru slowed us down on her first hunt, too."

Naru scowled and protested in Sān.

"He may not be one of us," Khamko said, "but if he wants to learn, I will teach him. That is what a leader does."

Khamko then said something to Kebbi-an, and the old woman stuck out her chin in a show of skepticism but then shrugged. She began walking around Eric slowly, inspecting him, then she began to chant. Eric realized that he was being blessed for the hunt. She produced a small curved stone: a primitive hand knife. While she chanted her prayer to the gods, she began to make small slits in the backs of his legs, each one no more than half an inch long. Eric tried to make no sign that it hurt. In a few minutes, she had made over forty slits down the back of his right leg, then she started on the left leg. Each cut only produced a few drops of blood, and when she had finished, she smeared the blood with charcoal, which filled up each of the wounds, making a distinct tattoo from his buttocks to his heels.

He saw now that the others had the same bloodlines.

Next, Khamko presented him with a spear. Its tip was in the shape of a leaf. It was one-third metal and two-thirds wood, which gave it a pleasing weight in his hand.

"Now listen closely to everything I say. Remember every detail. The hunt—and our survival—depends on it.

"The arrows are poisoned," he said. "It is a toxin made from the larvae of the leaf beetle. It will kill any animal. A giraffe, a water buffalo, even an elephant. But the bigger the animal, the longer it takes to kill. A giraffe, for example, can live for days after being hit. This means we must pursue the animal after we shoot, which is why we must be swift and why we must be excellent trackers. Now look closely," he removed one of the arrows. "Never put your poison on the tip. If you do that and you accidently cut yourself, you will die. Instead, put the poison on the shaft just behind the tip, then it will only poison the animal it hits. The poison interacts immediately with the animal's blood, and even fifteen minutes after being shot, you can smell the poison in the animal's scat. That's a quick way of knowing if the scat is from the animal you shot or a different one.

"But if the poison is so deadly, how can you eat the meat?"

"Diamphotoxin is only dangerous if it gets in your bloodstream because it ruptures blood cells. Eating it is harmless. Come, it is time."

They started off at a trot, which Eric had quickly learned was the Sān's version of walking. They moved quietly through the half-light of dawn, under a brightening sky, savoring the shade. But Eric could feel that it was going to be a scorcher and suspected it was already close to ninety degrees. He hoped he could keep up. Before the mission to Africa he had made sure that he was in excellent shape, doing morning runs with Sawyer and Jane and lifting weights. He'd gotten up to nine miles in preparation for a marathon with Jane, but that was before his accident and three weeks of being sedentary. Unfortunately, he suspected that nine miles was only a fraction of the distance they might cover today.

Khamko fell back to talk to him, his breathing as normal as if he were sitting by the fire.

"Now your education begins, Doctor Hill. Everything I tell you must be remembered. Everything you need to be a successful hunter is here"—he touched his head—"and here"—he touched his heart—"and here"—he motioned to the world around him. "These three things are all that you need. First the basics: run on the pads of your forefeet, that will make you quiet. Second, always approach your prey with the wind on your face. Third, the hunt must be done right. If you do it wrong, the gods will not give us any meat."

They passed beneath an umbrella tree filled with four huge weaver bird nests that filled the canopy like bulbous tree houses. Eric was amazed the trees could hold such large objects. A dozen birds sounded the alarm as the hunters approached.

"The birds are the sentinels of the bush, if you are not careful, they will give you away. But if you become their friend, they will help you hunt."

Just then the sun broke the horizon, a curve of distant red fire framed by the stretching canopies of the umbrella acacia. Almost instantly, it felt like the dim world around them was revealed. Khamko stopped and knelt down.

"Here is your first track," he pointed at a footprint similar to a big dog's. "It is the spoor of a lion. Can you tell how old it is?"

Eric shrugged, "Three days?"

"Close. This track is two days old. There are many clues that tell us how much time has passed. Do you see how the wind has softened the edges?" Khamko turned to his right and pointed to a series of small dots in the sandy soil. "Now this track is newer. It was made yesterday afternoon by an armored bush cricket. They grow to be the size of your hand and love to raid the weaver bird nests and steal their young. And these tracks," he gestured to the overlapping track of a bird, "are made by the drongo. It picked at the locust, but the locust can spray predators like a skunk. When drongo got sprayed, he gave up and took off here. You can see the two light indentations where the wingtips touched the ground. It headed . . ." Here he lifted his eyes to a banyan tree about a hundred yards off. "There! Drongo always flies in a straight line when he alights."

Eric looked at Khamko in amazement. *How could so much information be gleaned from such a small patch of earth?*

"But come," Khamko said, "this is not the trail we want. Our trail has yet to be found."

They continued along at a steady trot.

"There are many ways to hunt, so everyone has a job to do," Khamko said. "Naru is my runner. Karuma is my trickster. I am the archer.

"Today it will be very hot but that is good for us. The sun is our friend. It will boil the animal's blood.

"Now remember, hunting is everything to us. It defines us as a people. You may think that we could do things better, but it is best this way. We only catch what we need. We have no way to store food, therefore we never over hunt. That keeps us in the balance.

"Most importantly, we do not use any technology. No guns and especially no dogs. Dogs are horrible creatures. It was because of dogs that man lost his connection to nature. Men and animals used to talk to one another but not anymore. Dogs made him dumb. With dogs, man could hunt and kill too easily. A hunt that should take a day suddenly took twenty minutes. So man put his mind to other things. That was the beginning of the end. Today, when we see a dog we always kill it. It does not belong on this earth."

Eric guessed they had covered four miles when Naru found something. She made a gesture with her hand, her index finger tucked down. Instantly, the three hunters dashed toward a wide swath of high grass that had been matted down in several places. They were very excited, and Naru and her son began to laugh and play in the grass.

"This is where twelve or thirteen gemsbok spent the night," Khamko said, reaching down, touching the grass, and sniffing the air. I think there were three males, seven females, and three young."

Eric tried to picture the gemsbok in his mind. He had seen a herd of them at the watering hole and he'd been impressed. They were as big as elk, with long straight horns that made a perfect V atop their heads. They were proud and watchful, and so big that he suspected that few predators messed with them.

Eric turned to watch Karuma and Naru playing in the grass, and it seemed like they were reenacting the gemsbok motions—the play of the young, the testing of their horns. The sight of them made him laugh; they seemed so happy, so joyful that the hunt was about to begin.

"It is play," Khamko explained, "but it is important play. To catch an animal you must *become* that animal. You must understand its character. And I don't mean the character of the species, I mean the character of the specific animal you are hunting. Naru and Karuma are getting to know the gemsbok. If we are to catch one, then our hearts must beat like that animal's heart, our lungs must breathe like that animal's, and our minds must think like that animal's. Only then will you gain the right to kill him. Go on, try it."

Eric lay in the grass for a moment, feeling a little silly, but trying to imagine how the animals must move and think. He noticed their musty smell. It was more acute in some of the beds than the others.

"The males smell the strongest," Khamko said, "The smell that is a bit more acrid, that is the female. The young have almost no smell, their only defense against predators. I once saw a cheetah walk right by a young gemsbok in the tall grass and not even notice it."

They searched the area thoroughly, looking for more

clues about their prey. Then Khamko called Eric to him once more. “The ground is moist here.” At his feet Eric saw the spoor of six or seven of the gemsbok, perfectly imprinted in the dark earth. It looked like a fossil, a petrified remnant from a thousand years distant.

“Here is where we begin!” he said excitedly. “At your feet is a clue. That clue is the reason you exist as you do—the reason you stand upright, the reason you now hold a weapon in your hand, and the reason your brain is so unusually big.

“This is the mystery your brain was made for. Just think of it: Your mind has evolved for hundreds of millions of years—in that time there have been billions of minute changes to your DNA, changes spanning countless generations—all so that you could do what you are about to do now, better. At your feet is a clue; if you are clever and read the clues correctly, you live. If you don’t, you die.

“If you are standing here now”—Khamko flashed his infectious smile—“and I know you are, it means every one of your ancestors had it—he or she was a hunter—and they passed it down to you. This”—he motioned again to the tracks—“is the only mystery that matters, the only riddle in life that truly counts. You already know the feeling of such mysteries. I’m sure it is the reason you enjoy science. And the reason for a thousand of man’s other pointless pursuits. It is in the pull of every mystery novel you’ve ever read, every TV show you have ever seen, every campfire story that kept you entranced. But these are false mysteries and false pursuits; they are things that have merely hijacked the Hunter inside of you, toying with your ancient code, playing upon your desire to find the next clue. But this . . . this is the original mystery. This is what you were designed to do. There is no gemsbok at the end of this trail. No! At the end of this trail is life. At the end of this trail is the survival of your race."

Khamko stood and a big smile stretched across his face, a smile that only hinted at the fountain of mirth within the old man. "Are you ready?"

"Oh yeah."

There was a twinkle in his eye. "Let's go."

They moved off with new urgency. The time for talking was over. Now they spoke only with their hands. And they did it as they ran, overlapping, working as an experienced team. One would stop to examine the earth or a bent twig, while the other would dart ahead, drawn by a different sign. They were not three Sān hunters, they were one entity. One mind. Transferring all knowledge to each other. They were discerning which were strong, which were weak, which were old, and which were young. At last they seemed to make a communal decision. Khamko made a flick of his wrist over one spoor, which Karuma followed for a time, then he made the same motion with the wrist. Finally, Naru did the same. Among the twelve sets of tracks, they had chosen the one they wanted.

Eric felt a great sense of fortune just to be with them. Much like he'd felt at the watering hole—he knew he was one of a very few people in the world to be blessed with an experience like this—to be part of a hunt led by those who had been doing it for hundreds of thousands of years.

They had covered another two miles when Naru stopped them with a signal. They all crouched down and slowly crept forward.

Here the vegetation was mostly green, with golden grass that came up to their waists, spread between occasional shepherd and blackthorn trees.

The herd of gemsbok was 120 yards away. They were

obscured up to their haunches in the tall grass and appeared to be adrift in the ocean of green and gold—the young ones almost completely submerged. All of them had long graceful horns, twice and a half the length of their heads. Their faces were white and painted with two black lines that ran down their cheeks, over their chests and down their lower flanks to the tail. The color of their bodies was hypnotic, changing from golden tan to light gray depending on the light.

Khamko eased the bow from his back and began to move off to the right, downwind from the herd. Just as the grass helped conceal the smaller gemsbok, now it hid the old Sān. Eric had examined the bows and knew they were not particularly powerful. The Sān relied on the poison, not the power of the bow, so Khamko would have to get very close for a good shot.

Naru made a motion to her mouth then tightened her fist. Eric translated this as, "Keep quiet and don't move."

They had been waiting perhaps five minutes when the big bull suddenly raised his head high and pricked his ears. The others instantly stopped grazing and looked around.

Eric held his breath. Khamko had frozen, too. Eric marveled at the bull's horns, which were at least four feet long. If their purpose was to intimidate, he thought, they fulfilled their purpose well.

After a very tense minute, the bull returned to grazing. They waited in silence. Another five minutes passed. Eric thought about what Khamko had told him: he had to understand each animal. He saw the bull, intimidating and proud. He saw two of the younger bulls, doing their best to mimic their father. Of the females, one seemed to be more watchful than the others. She raised her head to look around much more—a cautious mother, he thought.

Eric had now lost sight of Khamko. He shifted in his crouch to get a better view, and his foot pressed down on a stick. It snapped with a loud pop.

Instantly the gemsbok were up and alert; looking straight at him.

Naru's glare made him feel as if he'd shrunk to half his size. "I should have killed you," she mouthed silently.

Simultaneously, one of the gemsbok bolted to their right, and the others quickly followed. Khamko rose from his hiding place, the bowstring pulled back to his cheek. Eric had startled them right toward him.

The five-hundred-pound animals bore down on the small man, and Eric feared he would surely be trampled. It looked impossible that he wouldn't be. Yet Khamko stood confident and proud, shoulders and shock of white hair above the grass, the bow drawn back. At the last moment the herd scattered—some veered to the side, while others panicked and tried to turn back. Eric saw Khamko tracking a calf with the tip of his arrow. But then one of the older females hesitated and stumbled. She was on her feet almost instantly, but in a flash Khamko pivoted and shot her.

Naru leapt over the tall grass to give chase, Eric close behind. Khamko stood smiling.

Stung by the arrow, the gemsbok bounded away from the others. Eric saw the arrow bouncing against her side two or three times, then the long piece fell out. But he knew the arrow tip was still in her and that the poison was already beginning its work.

Naru sprinted past her father. "Go, my beautiful runner," he said to her. "Be swift."

Balancing the two spears, one in each hand, Naru raced after the gemsbok. For Eric, it seemed an impossible race to win. The gemsbok was making huge leaping bounds over the high grass and getting further away every moment. Eric followed Naru all the same. He spotted on her and kept running as fast as he could.

The poison would take hours to kill such a big animal, but it *would* die. They couldn't lose her. If she got too far ahead, another predator might take her. If they lost her completely, she would be food for the hyenas and vultures.

Naru raced through the grass with unbelievable grace and speed. Eric was not nearly as fast as her, but he could still follow. Within a quarter mile, his lungs were on fire, but his legs still felt strong.

To keep his mind off the pain, he tried to remember Khamko's words.

You must become the creature you hunt. Your heart must beat with her heart, your lungs must breathe with her lungs, and your mind must think like her mind.

It reminded Eric of mirror neurons, specialized neurons that scientists believed allowed humans to empathize with each other. A trait, they said, that was crucial for social bonding. If you saw a child being bullied in the street, for example, it was the mirror neurons in your head that would make you feel his fear. When the bully struck him, it was the mirror neurons that let you imagine the sting of the blow on your own cheek.

But as he ran, and as he felt his body being pushed to the peak of its ability, and as he felt all his doubts and inhibition melting away, it seemed to him that perhaps the neurologists had it all wrong. Clearly mirror neurons had evolved for this—the hunt. To help understand not the mind of your fellow man, but the mind of an animal. Such an adaptation would have meant all the difference for our ancestors trying to survive in an environment like this. The ability to feel what your prey feels, to empathize with it . . . and through that empathy, to predict how it would behave. That would have made the difference between survival and extinction. Perhaps it was the very reason why Homo sapiens had evolved into such social animals, an off-label use of their hunting abilities.

They had now covered at least two miles since Khamko had shot the gemsbok. While Eric was falling farther and farther behind, Naru was now matching the speed of their prey.

Then the gemsbok stopped and looked back. Its eyes fell on Naru but it didn't immediately run. It waited a moment, thinking, before dashing off. Tongue out. Panting.

What was it thinking? Eric tried to concentrate, but it was not an easy thing to do as he bounded through the high grass, avoiding rocks and bushes, trying to ignore the burning in his lungs. Yet despite all that, he found that he could.

He realized that the wounded gemsbok was the same female he had noticed in the herd, the cautious mother.

She must be feeling the poison by now. That would bring a sense of fear . . . of uncertainty.

And what would lessen her fear?

Returning to the herd. Yes, that was why she had stopped. She wanted to return to the security of the herd.

In the distance Eric could see her. She had changed course slightly and was heading for a thick stand of acacia and blackthorn trees. She was looking for cover . . . to hide herself.

Naru reached the point where the gemsbok had paused. She knelt briefly. When she stood she glanced back and saw him for the first time. A look of annoyance flared across her face, then she sprinted on.

A few moments later, Eric reached the same spot. Here the gemsbok had defecated. He remembered how Khamko had said you could judge how far the poison had traveled through the prey's system by the smell of the scat, but this was information Eric couldn't parse, so he pressed on.

The thick copse of trees was half a mile off and the gemsbok raced for it with renewed strength. But Naru seemed to be moving faster than ever, covering ground with preternatural speed. For the first time, she was gaining.

Eric raced on as best he could, the heat and the sun sapping his strength; his legs were starting to feel unsteady. *Remember you're not the only one*, he thought.

The sun is our friend. It will make the animal's blood boil.

Eric knew there was science behind Khamko's words. Humans were unique among mammals because they could let off heat through their skins, something the gemsbok and other mammals could not. While a few mammals do have a type of sweat, their primary means of cooling was through panting. Encased in thick fur, the gemsbok had to give off heat through her tongue. And to do that best she had to slow down or stop. The hotter she got, the more often she'd need to rest.

Naru had closed the gap to about sixty yards, but the gemsbok had almost reached the thicket of trees. Naru lifted one of her spears to her shoulder. With a loud grunt and a lunge, she cast. Eric watched in amazement as the spear arced high into the air. It seemed to be perfectly timed to intersect the fleeing gemsbok, like a guided missile zeroing in.

But the spear glanced off the long horns with a clatter and skipped harmlessly away.

Startled, the gemsbok veered to the right and disappeared

into the wood. Naru soon plunged in after her, picking up the spear without breaking stride. Eric was amazed anew by her strength and ferocity.

The gemsbok was going to double back, Eric was sure of it. The old mother wanted to get back to the herd . . . her family. Naru must have known it, too, but she still had to track her to figure out which way. But Eric had a wide vista of the whole copse and would surely see her when she emerged.

If he could pick the correct side, and if Naru flushed her toward him, he might have a chance of finishing this quickly.

But which side would she take? He checked the sun and tried to orient himself. He had last seen the herd heading west, so he found a cluster of acacia trees that lay between the copse and where he guessed the herd might be now. He climbed up one tree and stood on a high branch. He was thankful to be in the shade; it felt fifteen degrees cooler here. He wiped the sweat from his brow. In the buckskin pouch Khamko had given him, he removed the ostrich egg filled with water and greedily gulped some down. He wanted to drink it all, but he made himself stop.

He scanned the copse, waiting. One minute. Two. He wondered if the gemsbok was trying to lose Naru in the underbrush, perhaps doubling back multiple times to confuse her. It was something Eric would do if he were her.

Suddenly she bounded out of the trees, light and graceful and without a sound then she sprinted like a thoroughbred toward him. Yes, it was better than he had hoped. Not only had he picked the correct side of the wood, but she was making for the very cluster of trees he was in, looking for more cover.

He balanced himself on a branch with one hand then lifted the spear to his shoulder with his free hand. He was already imagining the look of amazement on Khamko's face when he discovered that it was Eric who had killed the gemsbok. It would be almost as priceless as the scowl on Naru's face.

The old mother was weary and frightened. She could no longer run as she once had. She had raised six fawns and seen many rains. Now her heart felt ready to explode.

She reached the shade of the acacia trees, gasping and painting. She looked over her shoulder at the far copse. The wicked huntress had still not yet emerged. Had she really escaped? For a moment she felt her panic subside, yet something was still not right. Something about the air here was wrong.

She turned her head toward home, toward her family. If she could get there, she'd be safe. Her instincts told her, *keep running*. But a strange weariness was on her. The white-headed hunter had pricked her. And it had not hurt her much at first, but now she feared that she was injured more than she thought. She knew she needed to keep going, but she wished she could just lie down and sleep.

Eric stood on the branch above her, poised and ready. The gemsbok was no more than fifteen feet away. It was the perfect opportunity. Yet he hesitated.

He could see her beautiful fur. The broken shaft of the

arrow. The blood seeping from the wound and dripping onto the sandy soil.

And he felt her terror. It felt like a third presence there in the shade. He heard her panting, saw her wet nostrils flaring as she sucked in air, and he watched her sides expand and contract as she tried to catch her breath. And for the briefest of moments he imagined he heard her heart beating.

Thadup, thadup, thadup.

The spear was held at his shoulder, and his whole body tensed as he prepared to spear her.

But he didn't.

His mirror neurons, the ones that allowed him to understand the mind of his prey, also made it much, much harder for him to hurt a thing that he was beginning to understand was very . . . human.

As he tried to steel himself to what had to be done—*you must do this for the tribe*—one of her ears suddenly pivoted toward him. Their eyes locked. One second. Two seconds. They stared at each other, and it seemed to Eric that she knew that her life was in his hands.

Thadup, thadup, thadup.

Then she bolted out of the shade and back onto the scorching plain.

Eric threw the spear into the dirt, disgusted at himself for not having the gumption to act.

Then he swung down from the branch, picked up the spear, and ran after her.

Passing out of the shade felt like stepping into an oven. The heat and the intensity of the sun instantly began to drain his stores of energy. His legs resented being asked to run again, and he started off stiffly. But he urged himself on. *You must see this through.* After only a hundred yards he fell back into his stride. He tried to match the gemsbok's speed and found that he could. He was moving at a steady run. The sun weighed on him, but he knew the sun and the poison were weighing on her, too. He tried to think on her again. To feel her heart.

He sensed her anxiety growing as she realized she wasn't getting away. A sense of hopelessness was building in her. Oddly, Eric began to feel stronger, is if he was pulling her energy into his body.

He guessed they had run at least three miles from where she had left the herd to the copse. Now they were running back, more or less, at the angle she hoped would intersect the herd.

Eric was pushing his body to the limit. Indeed, past what he thought was the limit. He had never run this far, this fast, in his life. And he had never felt so in tune with his body, which meant, by extension, he had never felt so in touch with the world. Perhaps it was due to the return of his sight, or perhaps the way his other senses had become superacute during his blindness. But now, today, everything was glorious. From the crickets that flew up in front of him as he ran through the grass, to the wind-swept shapes of the acacia trees, as they were pulled this way and that like umbrellas in an abstract painting. Everything was moving, in motion, alive, talking to him, teaching him.

And the gemsbok! He could feel her heart beating. He literally felt her thoughts. She tried to lose him twice more by dashing into brambles and doubling back. But he knew her mind now, and he knew her ultimate goal. To get back to the herd.

After what must have been two miles, going at a full run, he began to tire. He tasted blood in his mouth from overtaxing the capillaries in his lungs. He would have to stop soon. But the gemsbok was now only forty yards ahead.

He heard his inner voice: *You must end this. Not for yourself. But for her. Remember the poison. She will die. The longer she lives, the more she suffers.*

He summoned his courage and raised the spear, balancing it as he ran. He imagined its flight in his mind, pictured it sailing high and striking her. Then he gathered his strength and hurled the spear.

He watched it arch into the air, just as he had seen it in his mind. Down it came.

It struck her between the tail head and the hip bone, sinking deep. She whinnied in pain then bolted, running with renewed panic. Eric hoped she would last only a few seconds and fall, but no. On she ran with amazing energy. Eric slowed his pace to a trot, knowing he had lost his chance. He bent down, hands on knees and tried to catch his breath, occasionally glancing up to catch sight of her as she raced off.

Then he heard movement in the grass. He stood to see Naru dashing by, about thirty meters on his right, only her torso was above the tall grass, her arms churning. She gave him a signal with her hands.

He replied with a puzzled look. She called out to him. "Keep to her left and hurry up."

He didn't think he could keep going, yet he also realized it was the first time she had spoken to him in a voice that was not laced with contempt and scorn. So he ran on but the best he could manage was a pathetic jog.

He thought back to the link he had felt. The closer he

got to her, the stronger it became. Even now he felt it. Her heart was beating faster than ever, and seemed almost ready to burst. The spear was still in her, slowing her down. Every step with her right hind leg was painful. And the poison, it had now spread throughout her body, speeded by her frantic heart. It was beginning to bind her muscles. Making every movement harder, making her tired heart work harder. She had to stop more often, panting out her heat. He imagined how weary she was. Barely able to go on. A feeling that it didn't matter anymore. Death was now equal to life.

He quickened his pace, sensing that he needed to see it, to bear witness when Naru caught her.

Suddenly he felt another shift. Something about her had changed. Had Naru killed her? No, she was still alive. But that hopelessness that had been building inside her had filled her up. She understood that there was no escape. And that brought another decision.

If he guessed right, he might have time. He changed course, bearing north again, away from where the herd should be. *She's an old mother*, he thought, *she won't escort death back to her young.*

After he had covered another mile at a steady run, he came to the lip of a dale—a shallow crater in the plain. And there, at the bottom of the basin, he saw them.

The gemsbok stood motionless, so weak she could neither walk nor raise her head. Her mouth was covered in foam, and her ribcage inflated and deflated enormously.

Naru stood less than ten feet away. Her chest was heaving, too, her skin shiny with sweat.

There had been no final sprint. No dramatic hurling of the spear. This was how it ends—in pure exhaustion.

As Eric approached, Naru raised both spears to the sky,

touching their tips together above her head. She prayed to Cagn, thanking him for the hunt and the meat that would keep her people strong. Then she spoke to the old mother, thanking her for giving herself to them.

"I'm sorry," she said.

But then the old mother took a step and then another. She stumbled as she moved. The exhaustion, the heat, and the poison making every motion hard. But her intent was unmistakable. She was walking toward Eric.

Without hesitation, Naru handed him one of her spears.

"Why?"

"She has chosen you."

"I can't."

"You must. And you must do it quickly. You owe it to her."

Eric gave a heavy sigh and looked at the gemsbok. He saw the knowing in her eye.

"You must strike just above the front leg. Throw hard so that you penetrate deep."

He couldn't look at her face anymore; he stared only at the point he had to hit.

As he raised his spear, the tears began to well up in his eyes.

He felt her heartbeat racing in his own chest.

Then he gritted his teeth and cast.

The spear entered her, and she instantly collapsed on to her front knees then slouched to her side.

"Now you must push in the spear and twist."

He did as he was told. But even though the old mother's heart had resigned itself to death, the other parts of her body had not. As he twisted the spear, she kicked and tossed her head. The long rapier horns swiped upward, Eric jumped back, but not quick enough. The sharp tip of the horn caught raked along his ribs, cut open his chest and split the skin on his jaw and cheek.

It happened so quickly, and he was so focused on his task, that he barely felt the pain. He had to finish this. He seized the spear again and twisted, this time Naru helped him.

Finally, he felt the mother's heart stop. Eric stepped back, his chest heaving and bloody, and beheld her, his vision blurry with tears. The life energy seemed to dissipate around her, along with her fear and anxiety, like mist in the air.

Fifteen minutes later Naru had gutted the gemsbok and started a fire. They made a sort of tepee over the flames with ling branches, then, methodically, she began to cut long strips of meat which she lay across them.

"A gemsbok is too big for us to carry, so we will wait for Khamko and Karuma. Once they arrive, we can go and tell the others. By nightfall, the whole camp will be here."

An hour later Khamko and Karuma arrived. When Naru finished telling the story of the hunt, Khamko nodded thoughtfully and smiled. Then his eyes locked on Eric and he laughed.

"I never expected you to go running off like that. Perhaps I should have said something, but I'm glad I didn't. You brought us luck today."

"All I did was almost get you killed."

"No, when you stepped on that stick, you flushed the herd closer to me. I was not in danger. And later you hit the gemsbok with your spear, which shortened the hunt by hours."

Eric nodded noncommittally. "But why did she come to me like that? At the end?"

Khamko pursed his lips as if he were choosing his words carefully. "Just as you felt a connection with her, she felt a connection with you. When you stood over her on the tree, you showed compassion. She remembered."

"Killing her was so hard. I never want to do that again."

Khamko nodded slowly. "It makes me happy to hear you say that. All good hunters should feel that way after their first kill, for it means that you treasure life and you will only kill when you must. But don't be too hard on yourself. All animals must eat to survive. We are no different. What you did is not a crime. It is only a crime if it is done with greed and waste and excess. And while it is true that you killed a beautiful animal, you will also feed your people. Karuma, Nyando, and the other children will grow stronger because of you."

Khamko placed a hand on Eric's shoulder. "It is good to be sad, it means you will keep her in your heart.

"Now come, let me look at these cuts." Khamko examined his wounds. "Your face and ribs will be fine, but here on your chest it is deep. I will need to clean it well and stitch it."

He then spoke to Naru. She went to the gemsbok's entrails and pulled out the rumen, the first stomach. Gently she cut it open and began pouring the intestinal water into their empty ostrich eggs. Then she took the masticated grass from inside and squeezed the liquid into the shells. Finally, she put one of the eggs on the fire to boil.

"That water you see there has saved my people from death countless times," Khamko said. "Through long droughts, fire, and famine, the ability to find as much as seven gallons of water inside an animal, has often meant the difference between life and death." Then he laughed. "Maybe it will save your life, too."

Then Khamko stood for a moment looking around. He pointed to one plant about a hundred yards off. "There . . ." he said, then scanned the horizon some more, ". . . and there. I can use the leaves from a bush willow and eland's bean as an antibiotic. While you are gone, I'll prepare what I need."

"Gone?"

"Yes, you three need to walk back to camp and get the others."

Karuma gave a groan and began to protest. "I want to stay with you and set up camp. Besides, what if a lion comes to steal the meat?"

"Don't worry. *I* will be fine," Khamko said.

Karuma lay down on the ground in protest. "It's not fair."

"Stop stalling," his mother said. "Get up!"

Just then Karuma made a strange sound: it was a loud hum followed by a grunt.

"No more tricks!" his mother said. Apparently the noise was some sort of ploy.

But Khamko stood up and began to look around excitedly. "Are you just playing?"

Karuma made the strange sound again and pointed to an acacia tree about thirty yards away. He made the call two more times.

"I see him," Khamko said excitedly.

Suddenly a small bird, just a bit smaller than a robin, alighted from the tree and swooped down among them. Its head and back were dark brown, its belly a light tan, its beak bright pink. It circled around Karuma for a moment, chirping loudly. Karuma responded with his own chirps, and they began to carry on what could only be described as a conversation.

Eric found himself laughing at the strange spectacle. It was as if they were two happy strangers, *pleased to meet you, how are you feeling today, isn't the weather something?* They were looking for a reason to become friends, trying to find common ground, dropping names perhaps, in hopes of sealing some sort of deal. In under a minute some agreement was apparently struck.

The bird darted away, and in the time it took Eric's heart to beat twice, Karuma and Naru had snatched up their spears and were racing after it.

Eric turned to Khamko for some sort of explanation but got none. "Go on!" he said, shooing Eric with his hand, "you don't want to miss this!"

Eric picked up his spear and went after them. His legs were stiff as wood, and he hobbled at first, but he eventually caught up with them.

The little bird was moving from tree to tree, zigzagging around. But it was not trying to get away from them; in fact, it stopped in each one to wait for them before flying off to the next tree. The whole time Karuma and the bird kept up their conversation, calling back and forth to each other. For a time, the bird seemed confused. It went back and forth from the same two trees twice, then it suddenly made an excited chirp, and made a beeline for an area thick with acacia trees and blackthorn bushes.

"She found something!" Karuma said and ran off. "Come on, Moon-man. Tonight we feast like gods!"

Eric laughed and ran after him. Naru had now slowed her pace and fallen behind them, relaxed and unworried.

Eric glanced back and saw her smiling. She seemed to enjoy watching her son play his game.

Then it clicked for Eric. *Feast like gods.*

Honey!

Eric and Karuma soon arrived at an impenetrable wall of blackthorn. It was fifty yards wide and a hundred yards deep. In the middle of this natural fortress was a huge acacia tree. Even from this distance Eric could smell the honey, sweet and loamy, warmed in the afternoon sun. *The hive must be enormous*, he thought. He felt a giddiness from the base of his brainstem, and bit his lower lip. But how could they get to it?

They began looking for a way in, but the buckthorn—spread out before them like a castle wall—was just too thick. Karuma began pacing back and forth, probing with his spear, trying to find a way in.

Then several things happened very fast, things that Eric would not quite understand until much later. First, Eric sensed something. Just as he had learned to perceive a nearby presence when he was blind, now he felt something similar. Very close and very big.

At almost the same instant, the bird came racing out of the thicket, chirping a different call. One of imminent danger.

CHAPTER THIRTY

THE END

The New York Times

NEW YORK, NOVEMBER 21, 2026

ONE-PARTY RULE ENDS IN CHINA

Elections in 90 Days

by Scott Brookings

And so it was on November 21, 2026—fifty years after his first death—that Mao Zedong died a second time. Chairman Mao was declared dead at 2:15 p.m. local time in Beijing, when the Central Committee announced an end to one-party rule and mandated new elections in ninety days. Within hours of the

announcement, sixteen political parties had been registered. Thus ended what will likely be known in world history as the Mao Dynasty.
Washington, DC

Admiral James Curtiss had been looking forward to this day for many years. The day when America's most potent enemy finally fell. The day when America would once again be the world's sole superpower. The day when 1.5 billion people would finally escape from brutal totalitarian rule.

Yet as he dressed in his formal whites that morning, adjusted his epaulets and ribbons, and checked himself in the mirror, he did not feel the exhilaration he had imagined he would.

He reminded himself that a wise man is neither elated by victory nor demoralized by defeat. After all, there was still much to be done. They had created a power vacuum, so they would have to be very careful about who filled it. A lot could still go wrong.

However, it felt like more than that. He felt like he had been stretched too thin. Here, at the end, he was able to fully realize just how much he had been through in the last twenty-two months and how it had pushed him to his limit. It had begun with the daunting task of turning the NRL around, beating the Chinese to Replication, then sabotaging their weapons program. Next came the deployment of the new technology to transform the geopolitical landscape—first Cuba, then Zimbabwe, El Salvador, Venezuela, and finally China. All the while trying to keep control of the technology and deal with the subversion of people like Walden and Rosario. Then came the raid in Namibia, the death of four servicemen and losing Eric Hill. One problem on top of the other. He felt he was managing it, but in a desperate way . . . in a way that made him fear that he must have made a mistake along the way, some oversight that was going to come back to haunt him.

Or maybe he simply didn't think he deserved to win. Perhaps deep down, he knew there was a certain injustice that a man like him, who had been responsible for so much death, should really get away with it.

His mind flashed to all the flag-draped coffins that had returned from Syria. Then to the dust-covered bodies of operators killed in Iraq. For much of his career he'd been responsible for the terrible calculations that resulted in other people's deaths. He chose how many marines would clear a house in Basra or how much air support was needed for a team of operators in Fallujah. And it had been he who had approved Operation Ajax, the assault on Damascus that had resulted in the death of two hundred marines. And what about the other side? What about the Afghans, the Iraqis, the Syrians? How many women and children had died in airstrikes he had ordered? How many children had been orphaned because his soldiers had shot their fathers or mothers?

These were the questions that plagued him. That he could never fully answer. Why should a man like him be honored? Why should he even be allowed to live?

He had hoped that moving into the job at the NRL might be a path to redemption. Working with scientists instead of soldiers, trying to find a better way to wage war.

Now it appeared that they had actually succeeded. China had fallen.

You should be content. You did this.

As he descended the staircase to the kitchen for his first cup of coffee, his iSheet vibrated.

He looked at the message from Sawyer. “The *Liaoning* and all her escorts have just departed Namibian waters.”

It was another piece of good news, yet this too did not make him feel better. Once again, he didn’t feel like he deserved it.

CHAPTER THIRTY-ONE

ALL SEEING

November 21, 2026
Washington, DC

The four iSheets sat in a row on Jane's bench. Each one displayed the gruesome image of a dead goat with its legs splayed open and blood all over its abdomen.

> Test Subject Seven—Shot at ten meters with .223 round. Died of blood loss in forty-seven minutes.

> Test Subject Eleven—Shot at ten meters with .223 round. Died of blood loss in fifty-three minutes.

She moved from one image to the next, trying to figure out what she'd done wrong. *Too much blood loss, too fast. Why?*

She looked up at the ceiling, searching the alabaster tiles

for an answer. She pounded her fist on the table. "Shit!" she seethed. "I can't think straight anymore."

That's because you're exhausted, another voice in her head replied. *When was the last time you slept more than a couple of hours*?

That was an easy question to answer: the night before Eric disappeared.

On one hand she was proud of herself. She hadn't let his disappearance drive her crazy. She'd resigned herself to the fact that she couldn't do anything about it and had dived into her work. Yet now and again, the thoughts and fears would come. *When would the call finally come?*

As well as the guilt. You should be doing something to help find him. All this technology around you . . .

You can't help him, the other voice countered. *You know that. So get back to work. Besides, if you do this right, you will save hundreds of lives.*

She forced herself to look at the dead goats again.

Here was her problem:

The number one cause of battlefield deaths was something called "incompressible hemorrhaging" from bullets or shrapnel entering a soldier's abdomen. These injuries were impossible to treat in the field because medics could not see into the wound to stop the bleeding or protect the vital organs. Only a surgeon could do that. And if you didn't get the wounded soldier to a hospital fast enough—in what was called the Golden Hour—they almost always died.

Jane's job was to find a solution. It was so important that Admiral Curtiss had come to her personally, showing her the statistics and—most sobering—telling her about the men and women he had lost to these types of wounds.

On the bench were a dozen syringes, each holding a

different recipe for her invention. "G2 Stasis Foam." The first generation of foams combined two polyurethane polymers that created an expanding substance to fill the wound and slow the bleeding. Her job was to enhance that system with swarm technology. That is, make the foam intelligent enough to clamp severed arteries and veins, then identify the damaged organs, lower their individual metabolism, and supply them with enough oxygen and nutrients so they'd survive until the patient got to the hospital.

But it just wasn't working. Yesterday she had tried again. A new goat was sedated, shot, then Jane tried to stabilize it with the stasis foam. It had lived longer than the others, but it was still dead in forty-three minutes.

Ironically, she knew the one person who could help her. Ryan Lee. But she was too angry at him—or was she too stubborn?—to ask for his help.

Come on, just get on with it. She put in her earbuds and cranked "Aces High" by Iron Maiden. It didn't help. Then she felt a tap on her shoulder.

She pulled out her earbuds and turned to see Bill Eastman standing there. He was wearing a gray three-piece suit and looked every bit the confident genius he was. Just the sight of him made her feel better.

"Hello, Jane," he said softly, "how are you?"

She nodded slowly, giving the question some thought. "I'm surviving."

"I know it must be hard," he said, looking around the lab, then added, "And even harder to get work done."

She nodded. "I thought work would keep my mind off him. It helps, but it's not enough . . ."

"Well, why don't we see if two heads are better than one?"

She smiled and was about to refuse. Of course, she should refuse. It was way beneath Eastman's pay grade—the top scientist at the lab—to be working with her. But then she changed her mind.

"I'd like that," she said and began to explain the problem to him.

When she was done, Bill rubbed his chin pensively. "How many evolutions have you run?"

"Twenty-one."

"Hmmm, that's too many. They should have figured out the different cell types by now. And you're still losing too much blood?"

Jane nodded.

"You may have a problem with the original parameters." He stood up and began to pace and mumble to himself, something he always did when he was thinking. "Losing blood . . . dying tissue." Then he snapped his fingers. "What does a surgeon do if the patient isn't getting enough blood to their heart?"

"She does a bypass."

"Exactly!"

"But I need to *stop* the bleeding."

He nodded, "True, but I think you're approaching this as if it were two problems—trying to stop the hemorrhaging, then trying to nourish the tissue and organs—when it's only one problem."

Jane was beginning to see. "You're saying the best way to control the blood flow is to channel it to the damaged organs."

"Yes."

"But how?" She trailed off, trying to piece it together herself, then her eyes brightened. "I can use the nanosites in the foam to actually grab the hemorrhaging blood and put it where it needs to go."

"Yes, very good! You have billions of nanosites at your disposal. Put them to work. When the blood's deoxygenated, you can send it back to the heart through the nearest vein. This way you simplify the problem."

A scowl grew across Jane's face, and Bill's enthusiasm faltered. "What's wrong?" he asked.

"I really hate it when other people figure out things I should have figured out myself."

He laughed. "Well, you're not out of the woods yet. Now you have to see if it will work."

She smiled begrudgingly. "Yes, but I think you've hit on a very good idea."

"I'm just glad I could help!" He sat down again and looked around the room wistfully. "I miss this sometimes—working in a lab, figuring things out. I'm just a manager now." Jane detected a sense of surrender in his voice that she'd never heard before. "I used to know everything that went on here. Every project. Every person's temperament. Every deadline. But not anymore. Things are happening too fast for me to keep them all straight. And I suspect that some people like it that way."

"So I'm not the only one who feels like things aren't changing for the better?" Jane said.

"No, you're not. This whole business with Walden and Rosario. I don't like it. Their Global Hologram project is reckless science, plain and simple." He looked around, as if checking to make sure no one was listening. For a moment he seemed conflicted, but he clearly wanted to share his thoughts. "I don't like the way they're using Forced Evolution," he said. "The beauty of Eric's idea is that it can figure things out on its own, but that's also why it's dangerous. Because we don't know what else it has figured out along the way. Mixing that with machine learning is irresponsible because we won't know if the system will evolve a new agenda or not. And it only gets worse if you add in swarm technology."

She gave him a quizzical look and he went on. "Right now, AI is largely innocuous because it lives within a computer. It can't pick up a knife or a gun. But if you give it access to swarms, then that all changes. Just consider its area of perception."

"Its what?"

Bill laughed. "Its area of perception. In humans, our senses tell us where we are in space, so our area of perception is our body. It's what we can see, taste, feel, smell, and touch. There are some exceptions, of course. Tennis players say that the racket becomes part of their area of perception, and a race car driver may say the same about the car. Years of practice and conditioning have extended their senses to the dimensions of the racket and the car. The race car driver doesn't feel it's a machine that is racing around the track, he feels it's his own body.

"Now take the Global Hologram, which would not only have swarm technology but would be connected to cameras and listening devices all over the world. Its area of perception would be enormous; in fact, it would be the largest living thing on the planet. It could potentially find, track, and manipulate anyone in the world."

Jane found the idea disturbing. "Is that what Walden wants to do?"

Bill nodded.

"But that's a long way off, isn't it?"

Bill gave a sardonic laugh. "If I have anything to say about it, Curtiss will shut it down. Luckily, he agrees with me, but he's being pressured by Walden and some of the other Joint Chiefs."

Jane nodded, still trying to process it. It was a frightening vision of the future, coming from a man who had an uncanny ability to predict such things. But there was something else, something beside the enormity of it . . . an idea . . . *anyone on the planet*. But then Bill spoke again, and she lost the thought.

"I'm so sorry, Jane. I shouldn't be unloading my worries on you, especially when you have so much to deal with already."

"No, really, it's fine," she said, still trying hard to hold on to the idea.

"Is there anything else I can help you with?"

"Not unless you can wave a magic wand and find Eric."

Bill gave a long exhale. "You don't know how much I wish I could. Curtiss is sick of me calling. But at least the Chinese are out of the way now. We just have to hope Sawyer's team can find him."

"I know. It's just that I feel so helpless. I've been pounding my head day after day, trying to think of a way to find him . . . some way to use our technology. But I can't figure it out. And it's driving me crazy."

"You're being too hard on yourself. Yes, we have done amazing things, but we just aren't there yet. Nobody is."

Jane suddenly flinched as a strange thought struck her. Her scientific mind—which was always questioning and testing and looking for a new way—asked, *Is that really true? Nobody?*

"Hold on, what did you say?"

"I said that we're not there yet. This idea of global surveillance, of being able to find anyone, that's what Walden wants, but nobody has done it yet."

Jane stood, the answer just on the tip of her tongue. She shook a finger at Bill. "You're wrong."

For a second Bill seemed taken aback, then he chuckled. "Okay, how?"

"You said nobody could watch the whole world. But *someone* can."

Bill's lips parted slightly, then he nodded. "You mean the Inventor."

She looked out the window, trying to collect her thoughts. "All this time I've been obsessing with finding Eric, when I should have been obsessing with finding the person who must know where he is." She turned to Bill. "You asked if there was anything else you could help me with. As a matter of fact, there is."

CHAPTER THIRTY-TWO

SEALED

November 21, 2026
Washington, DC

"Have you seen Olivia?" Ryan asked Jessica.

"No, and I'm a little peeved she didn't show up for her own meeting this morning."

Ryan knew that wasn't like Olivia to skip a meeting with her boss and immediately thought of her daughter Emma. He tried calling Olivia's phone but got no answer. *Was she ignoring him?*

Since the night at her apartment she had remained professional and courteous, but he knew she'd been hurt by his decision. However, she hadn't asked for his help again . . . and Ryan hadn't offered.

In the meantime, they'd been moving forward with the Global Hologram project, and they were making progress. The decision to use a hybrid quantum computer was yielding some *interesting* results. Since quantum computers are made with the same building blocks as nature, Olivia had theorized that they would be much better at creating a synthetic brain, since the way qubits influence each other is similar to the way atoms influence each other in a molecule. By adding Forced Evolution to the program, she hoped to supercharge its ability to learn and adapt.

The first ten evolutions had produced nothing that a normal supercomputer couldn't do. But the eleventh evolution had been different. Eleven had processed its initial training data three times faster and with fifteen percent fewer errors. What's more, it seemed to have a sense of intuition.

Ryan's next step was to teach Eleven to play games. Since the idea was to "teach it tomorrow," playing games was an ideal place to start because games gave Eleven a model of the world (the rules of game) then taught it to view itself as an actor within that world pursuing a objective. Just like children learned about the world through the metaphor of games, so could Eleven. He started off with checkers, then moved on to chess, then Parcheesi, Stratego, poker, and Risk. More and more complex games every day. SimCity. Dungeons & Dragons. World of Warcraft.

It was fascinating to behold. When Eleven was given a new game he would try to use the strategies of the previous game. When those failed, he began to experiment. And he learned quickly.

Really.

Quickly.

In his first attempt at Civilization VIII, Eleven began with an empty field of grass and in 150 hours had created a balanced, modern civilization—the average for an experienced human. In his second attempt, it took the minimum number of turns or less than six hours.

Today was supposed to be a big day: he and Olivia had planned to begin training Eleven with real-world data.

But now, Olivia was nowhere to be found. He knew she wouldn't miss this unless it was very important. He called her home number, and Natalie answered. "She's not here, Ryan," the nurse said. "I thought she was at work with you."

"No one has seen her today. Has everything been all right with Emma?"

There was a long beat. "No, she had a seizure last night. We took her to the emergency room. She was there most of the night."

"I'm sorry, Natalie. How is she now?"

"She's sleeping, but the doctor's say this is just the beginning."

"Thank you," he said and hung up.

Next he called lab security.

"This is Ryan Lee, I need to locate an employee."

After the woman verified Ryan's clearance, she said, "Olivia Rosario is in Bio Lab 17. Simpson Hall."

Simpson Hall? he thought. *What in the world is she doing there?* It was one of the original five buildings on campus and hadn't been updated in ages. No one ever used it, and he actually thought it was abandoned. He grabbed his coat and headed over.

As he suspected, the building was deserted and appeared to be used for storage. It had once been a beautiful building, with an open mezzanine, marble floors, and wide staircases. Now stacks of outdated computers and lab equipment were piled around an old fountain. The air was humid and stale. He checked the building map on the wall. Lab 17 was in the basement. As he descended the staircase, it felt like he was entering a different time. The basement had clearly been flooded at least once. There was dirt and debris in the corners, and water stains along the walls. He looked down the dimly lit hallway. *Okay, this is downright creepy.* It looked like the set of a zombie movie. There were half a dozen rusty gurneys along one wall. He examined one and found cracked leather wrist and ankle restraints. Some of the doors he passed looked like holding cells, with wired glass observation holes. He knew the NRL had been opened in the 1920s, which meant it was over a hundred years old. He shuddered to think of some of the other experiments that had taken place in that time.

Finally, he came up to the door of Lab 17. There was no window to look in. He opened it.

Olivia was seated at a desk, busy on a folded out iSheet. She glanced at him for a mere second, then went back to work.

Ryan looked around the room. It was mostly in shambles, but he realized why she had picked it. It was still a functional lab. It had a tissue culture room for Emma's iPS cells, a fume hood, spectrometers, a capillary electrophoresis apparatus, and a DNA sequencer—*Jesus, what a dinosaur.* It was perhaps one of the original ones from the '80s, bigger than a washing machine, but it was sequencer nonetheless.

He came up beside her. She looked exhausted—her hair was disheveled and she had bags under her eyes. But she was still beautiful. Achingly beautiful, and he had to resist an urge to touch her, to surrender to her, to hold her.

"I . . . I talked to Natalie. I'm sorry."

She ignored him, stood, and headed to the tissue culture room.

So that's the way it's going to be.

He picked up her iSheet and began looking through her

files. It only took him a few minutes to realize she'd been right: in their race to beat the Chinese most of the work had already been done—inadvertently. He couldn't help thinking it was amazing how she'd turned so many concepts that were conceived as weapons and forged them into something that might cure a fatal disease. But as he probed deeper, he saw that she had also made a series of critical errors. She just didn't know forced evolution like he did.

Ah shit! he thought. *What am I going to do?*

He thought back to the night at Olivia's apartment, the tears he'd seen in Emma's eyes. At first he'd tried to explain it away as a reflex, but he couldn't shake the truth. The girl still had periods of normal cognitive function.

Now he was in a serious bind. He knew what she was doing. They were all under the authority of the Uniform Code of Military Justice (UCMJ), of which he was currently witnessing a dozen violations. Not reporting her could cost him his job. Reporting her meant . . .

"Olivia, you have to stop . . . and I mean right now. You can't do this."

She came back and snatched the iSheet from his hand.

"Watch me."

He grabbed her wrist and pulled her close. "No, you have to stop. You're exhausted and upset and you're not thinking straight."

She yanked her hand free. "My daughter is dying. Do you have any idea what that feels like? To stand by, helpless, and watch? Do you? Do you have any idea what it was like telling her she had less than two years to live? All she said was, 'I don't want to die, mom.' That's all. 'I don't want to die.' It's the most basic thing that a parent has to do, the most fundamental thing, yet I can't even do that. Damn it!" Her frustration seemed to break for a moment, and she let out a sarcastic laugh. "Can you imagine? Olivia Rosario, genius tech entrepreneur, can't even do that. Every ounce of my being, every atom, is screaming at me, night and day, to help her. It's the *only* thing that matters. And last night, when she started shaking, and I couldn't get her to stop . . ."

She wiped her eye with her thumb.

Ryan closed his eyes for a moment and breathed, but he let her talk. He knew she just needed to let off some steam.

"Emma didn't give up soccer," she continued. "Did you know that? She insisted on playing. I'd watch her, and she'd be so perfect one moment, then she'd suddenly fall. She'd get up, start playing, and fall again. Sometimes the other players would make fun of her, but she didn't quit. Every time she fell, she'd get up again. If she can do that, then I can do this. I refuse to give up."

Ryan nodded his head. "Okay, fine, now it's your turn to listen to me. You're committing suicide. Right now. If Curtiss finds out about this, you're done! You don't know him like I do. If you stay down here another two or three hours, I guarantee he'll find out. And then you'll have given him the perfect excuse to fire you. You won't get a second chance. Not even Walden will be able to save you. Then you'll have no way to help Emma."

For the first time, she didn't fire off a retort. "What do you suggest I do?"

"Be smart. First you need a cover story. An excuse to do tissue culture work that won't arouse suspicion." He looked around. "Then you have to get in a real lab for Christ's sake, like H-lab."

"That's for genetics only. I don't have access."

"Yeah, but I do."

She raised her gaze and searched his eyes.

He nodded.

She fell into him, hugging him fiercely. The sudden warmth of her body against his felt wonderful.

"Oh my god, thank you," she said. She cradled his face in her hands and brought his forehead to hers. "Thank you, Ryan."

Ryan closed his eyes, savoring the touch of her fingers on his skin. Then he felt her warm lips press against his.

CHAPTER THIRTY-THREE

FORESIGHT

November 21, 2026
Namibia

The honeyguide came zipping by their heads, chirping an alarm.

Eric and Karuma shared a glance of confusion. As their eyes locked, Eric had a horrible vision of the boy's death. He saw the huge gray horn piercing his body, his leg gored and mangled, his head trampled and crushed. It was like no vision or daydream he had ever experienced.

Without conscious thought he lunged at the boy, tackling and rolling with him.

There was a loud crack of breaking branches, and the rhinoceros was suddenly there. Occupying the exact space where the boy had just stood, stomping the ground, slashing the air with its horns, enraged that the trespasser was suddenly gone, issuing angry guttural cries from deep within its lungs.

"Karuma!" Naru cried, and dashed forward, but she was almost two hundred yards away.

Eric and Karuma were entangled with each other on the ground. For a brief second Karuma looked confused. Then his eyes saw the rhino, still spinning and bucking in its rage.

Eric began to untangle himself in order to run, but Karuma held him tight. "Don't move! You are invisible to him as long as you stay still."

Eric froze, but it took all of his willpower. The rhino was only eight feet away . . . and unnervingly enormous. Three thousand pounds of angry power, almost six feet tall at the shoulder. The front horn was well over two feet long, and curved up to a sharp point, the second horn only slight smaller. The head was huge; Eric doubted he could have wrapped his arms around it. Its mouth sat low and flat on the muzzle; the nostrils were closed slits. As it bucked and stammered, Eric saw it kept its head close to the ground, ready to push up and pierce any object it touched.

Finally, the rhino stopped and looked around, trying to figure out where the intruders had gone. As it turned, its huge body blocked the afternoon sun, and all Eric could see was its enormous black silhouette against the sun's glare. That big, oblong, head. Its oval belly hanging almost to the dirt. Its feet splayed out at the bottom like massive suction cups.

Then it turned and looked right at them, its eyes angry and cold.

Eric froze, not daring to blink, fighting the sudden dryness in his mouth and the urge to run.

Finally, it turned away, and Eric dared to breathe once more.

Then Karuma did the most unexpected thing: he gave Eric a smile and a wink and stood up.

"*//nui-b!*" the boy called. Hey, fatso!

The boy ran into the open, waving his arms. The rhino turned and saw him at once. With a loud snort, it charged. It was terrifying to behold. All that weight, suddenly moving at thirty miles an hour. The head down, almost skimming the ground, leaving no room for escape. Karuma just stood there, arms crossed, smiling. Unafraid. At the last second, he pivoted out of the way. The rhino tried to turn, but could not slow its huge bulk and went thundering past. Karuma ran up behind him and smacked him on the rump. The rhino turned and tried to gore him, but the boy was too quick and darted away. Soon they were engaged in a deadly dance. Karuma jumping and spinning, dodging and rolling. He was so light and graceful, while the rhino, huge and bulky, shook the earth as he tried to catch him.

As Eric watched, transfixed, he realized he'd seen this before. Last night around the campfire, as the old women clapped and chanted for him. This was Karuma's dance.

Naru is my runner. Karuma is my trickster. I am the archer.

At that moment Karuma seemed the embodiment of Cagn, the supreme god of the Sān. The trickster who overcomes all odds, the underdog, the swift and clever. Eric laughed and shook his head as he watched the mismatched battle, knowing that somehow the underdog would prevail. He was so captivated that he did not even notice Naru until she was less than forty feet away. Like a lioness, she was slowly stalking up behind the rhino, crawling on her belly through the grass, her long knife gripped in one hand.

Within five minutes the rhino's rage had turned to exhaustion. He stood panting and tired, only charging when Karuma came very close.

Eric tried to piece the strategy together. How could Naru possibly hope to kill the huge animal with her knife? He watched as she shifted closer, trying to sneak up behind it. It must have some weakness . . .

Then he understood their plan: with two precise cuts across the tendons of the backs of its legs Naru would leave it helpless.

Karuma dashed in, so close that the rhino could not resist the bait. The boy ran straight for a dozen paces, letting the rhino believe it had a chance, then he adroitly pivoted aside. The rhino stopped, tired and frustrated. At that moment, Naru rose from the grass and rushed in.

Suddenly Eric heard Khamko whistle, and Naru paused, sinking back into the grass before the rhino could see her.

A moment later, Khamko was there. Eric watched in amazement as he walked straight up to the rhino. Eric had to check his impulse to run out and pull the old man down. When Khamko was no more than ten yards away from the rhino, he began to speak to it as if they were old friends. "You look tired, why don't you go get a drink. There is water that way." Khamko motioned with his bow. When the rhino made no move, Khamko made a shooing motion. "Go on!"

To Eric's astonishment, the weary animal did as he was told. Moving slowly away and not looking back.

There passed between Karuma and Eric a look of mutual disbelief, then Karuma began to laugh. He ran to his mother, and they embraced. She clutched him tight and buried her face in his hair. Mere minutes ago she had thought she'd lost him. Now he was safe and in her arms. After a while she raised her head and looked at Eric. She nodded to him.

After a time she turned to her father. "Why did you stop me?"

"Cagn has already given us all the meat we need for now. Killing the rhino would have been a waste."

She seemed about to retort, but Karuma squeezed her harder and she relented.

A minute later, Karuma broke the embrace. "Come!" he said to Eric, "Let's claim our prize!"

Eric had almost forgotten about the honey.

He and Karuma circled the tall thicket trying to find a way in. While they were looking, Karuma collected handfuls of dry grass and put them in his pouch. Then, scurrying under an archway made by two buckthorn bushes, they found their way in.

Entering the thicket was like entering another world. Cool and safe. Stooping low occasionally and crawling on their hands and knees they found three pathways crisscrossing the dense foliage. They found the old spoor of springbok, jackals, and badgers.

Soon they found a small clearing and there stood the great acacia tree.

Finding the hive wasn't hard. Thousands of bees buzzed in a great black cloud near a wide fork. The honey guide sat proudly on one enormous branch. She had done her job, now it was up to the Homo sapiens to do theirs.

The smell of honey was now so strong that Eric could think of nothing else, and his salivary glands were gushing fluid. He began to climb the tree, but Karuma grabbed his arm, "Aren't you forgetting something, Moon-man?"

Eric shrugged. "I don't think so."

"*/ani*," the boy said. Smoke.

Eric raised his eyebrows theatrically and nodded—ah, yes—angering African bees never ended well.

Karuma took the dry grass he had gathered and—using

some of the blades like rope—fashioned it into a wad that he could hold with one hand. He started a fire by rubbing a reed on a flat stick, then adding a wad of tinder. When its tiny strands began to curl orange with heat, he deposited it into the wad of grass and blew on it until it began to smoke. Then, quick as a leopard, he climbed up to the hive opening and stuffed the wad in. Using the same hollow reed he had used to make the fire, he began blowing into the wad, sending the smoke deep into the trunk.

Eric climbed up and stood on the opposite branch. The smell of the warm honey was making him scatterbrained.

"Whatever you do, don't kill any of the bees," Karuma warned. "Even if they sting you." He gave one last long blow into the long reed. "There, that should be enough." He produced his hunting knife and gave it to Eric, "Help me widen the opening."

Together they pried open the hole, ripping out sections of the dead wood. Then Karuma plunged his arm deep inside. He winced several times as he was stung, then Eric heard the honeycomb crack and the next moment Karuma's hand emerged holding a foot-long plank of golden brown honeycomb. They both laughed with delight, and the honeyguide chirped excitedly. Karuma gently brushed and blew half a dozen bees off the comb then lowered it into his buckskin pouch. He repeated the process twice more until his satchel was full.

"Now your turn."

They switched positions and Eric slowly eased his arm into the hole until it was up to his shoulder and his cheek was pressed against the cool wood. The buzz of the bees was deafening, and dozens of them alighted on his arm and face. But pacified by the smoke, none stung him.

He felt the sticky honeycomb with his fingers as well as the fuzzy bodies of the bees that covered it. He tried to gently brush some of them aside to get a better grip. He let out a hiss as the first bee stung him, then he was stung again. But now he had a grip on the comb and broke it off. That cost him two more stings. He pulled the honey out—a gooey, dripping mass of sugar and protein. He couldn't wait any longer. He offered it first to Karuma, who took a big bite, then Eric dug his teeth in. It was the most delicious thing he had ever tasted, a sweet and earthy loam, made sweeter by all the work he had done that day—the miles he had run, the dangers he had survived.

Then the honeyguide gave a belligerent chirp.

Karuma laughed. "Don't worry, we haven't forgotten you." He broke off a piece and laid it on the branch. The bird swooped down and began pecking at it. "You must always remember to give him his share. If you don't, next time he will lead you into the lion's den."

Eric gathered two more sheets of honeycomb. "That is enough," Karuma said, "it is a big hive, but we don't want to take too much."

When they had reached the ground again, Naru was waiting for them. Karuma laid out a handsome offering to the honeyguide and for the next half hour the four of them gorged themselves on honey.

Eric had never remembered being more content, more alive, more satisfied. All he was doing was eating honey, but this simple thing felt like heaven. When he had eaten his fill, he lay back on the ground and looked up through the quaking leaves of the acacia tree at the brilliant blue sky.

The other two soon followed suit, and they dozed there awhile, dappled in sunlight.

Their stomachs full, their minds empty.

Finally Naru broke the silence. “That’s enough rest for you two, you have a lot of walking to do.”

They moaned in unison. “Why us?” Karuma asked.

“Your grandfather and I must stay to guard the kill and prepare the meat. That means you two must go back and get the others.”

Karuma moaned again.

Eric did a rough calculation in his mind: it was at least six miles back to the camp, so twelve miles round trip. That would take close to three hours. He could have gone to sleep right there, but a part of him didn’t care. On this day he felt like he could do anything. He stood up stiffly, his head cloudy from the honey . . . or was it the apitoxin from the bee stings?

“Come on, Karuma.”

The boy made one more protest, then his infectious smile grew back across his face.

“All right, all right!”

When they emerged from the thicket, Khamko was waiting for them. He cleaned Eric’s wound with hot water, then applied the herbal antibiotic he had concocted, and finally stitched it up using a fishhook and line. “Rub some honey on it for the next few days,” he said, “then forget about it.”

Then Eric and Karuma started the long hike to find the others.

When they arrived at camp, the people were ready. Somehow they had sensed that it had been a successful hunt and they set out immediately. As they walked, Karuma told the hunting story slowly, teasing them. Narrating each part carefully, making them think, again and again, that the gemsbok got away. They cheered when they finally heard the truth. But then Karuma quieted them, and like a master storyteller, told them of the honeyguide and the rhino.

They were amazed and cheered and laughed. Kebbi-an, the old woman who had cut him that morning, came and grabbed his arm tightly around the triceps. She shook him and wagged her finger in his face. She was so old and her voice was so hoarse that Eric had a hard time understanding her and thought he was being scolded, but then Karuma translated her words.

"She says that you brought us luck! A hunt like this—with meat and honey—only comes along only a few times a year. She says you are now half Sān." The woman nodded and smiled. "But *only* half." Then she hugged him fiercely.

The sun was almost down when they saw the fires that Khamko and Naru had made. Some crude shelters were hastily made, then the feast began. That night they danced the dance of the hunt. Eric, despite his fatigue, danced with them. And like many of the Sān, he danced until he was spent, until all his fears and anxieties were exorcised from his body. Until he entered a trance that held him between life and death. Under a billion pinpoints of light, with the sparks and ash rising from the fires, and within a ring of acacia trees, he danced as all people once danced.

As he lay under his lean-to, with sleep coming on quickly, he thought of Jane and how much he wanted to share this experience with her, so that she might feel as he felt now—the joy and happiness of this simple life. A life that made their chaotic world seem suddenly so strange. He didn't yearn to be home, he yearned to have her here, to feel her warm body beside him, to watch her face as she too came to understand the power of this place and its people.

They made that patch of the savanna their home for the following nine days, until all the meat was gone. He ate the liver of the gemsbok; the liver was always given to the hunter. They lounged in the shade under the great acacia trees and drank in the smell of the honey as the bees droned on above them.

"Do you know how we humans were made?" Khamko asked Eric, just after they had finished the day's allotment of honey.

"No."

"It is a good story," he said. "When the world was new, everything was covered with water. Cagn was a mantis then. He convinced the honeybee to fly him over the water to find land. But no matter how long they flew, the bee could not find any solid land. Finally the bee was too tired to go on and he set the Mantis Cagn down on a flower. The bee died but she left behind a seed, and it was from that seed that the first human was born.

"So you see, the bee is our mother. And the honey is her milk to us."

Eric nodded and smiled.

"Tomorrow we must set out," Khamko said. "First we will get water. Then we hunt again."

CHAPTER THIRTY-FOUR

A DECADE IN AN HOUR

November 23, 2026
Washington, DC

"You realize this isn't going to be easy," Bill Eastman said. He and Jane were sitting in Bill's office with its wide view of the Potomac River. "For the last five months Curtiss has had every three-letter government agency looking for the Inventor, and they've found absolutely nothing. Besides, you and I aren't exactly detectives."

"True, but I think that's to our advantage. Just think of what the Inventor accomplished, beating us and the Chinese at our own game. He's a scientist, like us. Perhaps if we can think like him, we can find him."

Bill gave a slow nod. "Okay, I'll play along."

"Great! Where do we start?"

"Well, let's begin with what we know about him."

"That's not much," Jane said. "He saved Eric, Mei, and Ryan in China, just as General Meng was about to murder them." Jane thought back to what Eric had told her. "Eric said he did it out of a sense of reciprocity . . . because the Inventor had used Eric's idea of Forced Evolution to make himself into . . . I don't even know what to call him . . . something that wasn't really human anymore. He told Eric, 'You gave me life. Now I return it.'"

"That shows us he has a sense of morality and justice," Bill said, "but we also know he has a dark side. He seems to value life on one level, yet has no qualms about killing either."

Jane picked up the thought. "Eric said it was terrible. He killed the Chinese soldiers slowly and sadistically. He said the nanosites ate them alive from the inside."

"And he certainly didn't have to do that," Bill said. "With his power, he could have simply incapacitated them—and painlessly." Bill stood and began pacing. "I think this could be important. It suggests he may no longer see humans as his equal. Which makes sense if he thinks of himself as more than human—as evolved or transhuman—then killing someone would be easy. Perhaps as simple as killing an insect is for us."

"But it seems like more than that," Jane said. "It seems like he wanted them to suffer. Or perhaps teach them a lesson."

"*Sinners in the hands of an angry God*," Bill mused. "You may be right. Either way, it reinforces the idea that he doesn't consider himself human anymore. Let's keep going. What else did he say to Eric?"

"He said he could understand things that no normal person could comprehend. That in his first days, he solved all the great riddles. And that he was continuing to solve new ones." Jane paused. "That's pretty hefty stuff. But what riddles is he talking about?"

Bill sat down in his chair next to her. "Well, at the moment, the great scientific mysteries are . . ." He began to rattle them off, "Dark matter and dark energy, a quantum theory of gravity, arrow of time—matter and antimatter asymmetry, the multiverse hypothesis, protein folding, quantum teleportation, black hole information paradox . . . Should I keep going?"

Jane gave a little laugh. "That's probably enough. You know, you frighten me sometimes. But what I hear you saying is that the riddles all deal with physics and cosmology. Which tells us . . ."

"His gaze would be upward," Bill said.

She flashed him a quizzical look. "How's that?"

"To solve those problems, he'd have to explore space." Bill stood again and began pacing and mumbling. "Space . . . dark matter . . . visiting a black hole. Yes, yes, I'm beginning to see," he said. Another nod, more mumbling. "Yes, it's beginning to make sense. Nanotechnology has the potential to revolutionize space exploration. Instead of sending huge rockets and probes into space that take decades just to reach the edge of the solar system, we'll be able to send thousands (or millions) of tiny sensors across the universe at amazing speeds, perhaps hundreds of light-years away."

"Light-years? But that means faster-than-light travel. I thought that was impossible."

"According to what we can do now, it is. But theoretical physicists are already speculating on how it might be done. In fact, Miguel Alcubierre proved in 1994 that it *is* mathematically possible to create a wave in the fabric of space that would allow for faster-than-light travel. There are many other theories now, but no one's been able to test any of them. Some deal with dark energy, some antimatter, warping space time, or quantum entanglement. If the Inventor has solved those mysteries as he claims, he could have figured out how to get his nanosites to the far reaches of the galaxy . . . if not the universe. He might have already reached a black hole, and that alone would have helped him solve half a dozen lingering mysteries."

"Whoa, hold on, is that really possible?"

"It might sound far-fetched, but you have to remember the leap he's already taken. It's part nanotechnology, but most of it is AI. As AI gets faster and faster it begins to work at speeds we can no longer comprehend. And if I remember right, that's something that the Inventor told Eric. Am I right?"

"Yes, he said, 'for every hour, I live a decade.' He also said he was centuries old."

"See, there you go. The thing about AI is that it has no limit, so there is nothing stopping him from getting faster and smarter, every hour of every day. So in just the five months since Eric saw him, he could be exponentially smarter and faster. That means a problem that would take a team of human engineers a decade to solve, he might solve in a nanosecond."

Jane was honestly still trying to wrap her head around it. "Okay, this is good information. But how can it help us find him?"

Bill sucked in air with a hiss. "I'm afraid that's probably up to him at this point. I think that if he doesn't want to be found, he won't be. We got our first glimpse of him last year when he broke into the chemical warehouse. He did that because he needed something that he couldn't make himself. But I suspect he's evolved so much that he doesn't need us anymore. His swarms could simply take what they want or mine or even manufacture it themselves. Ergo, if he doesn't need humanity, there's no need for him to expose himself. Which would explain why no one can find him."

"So we're right back where we started?"

"Perhaps, but I think this has been very useful. I've been worried about him, especially the contradictions. He saved Eric and Mei and Ryan, but he also sadistically murdered over fifty people. Is he a threat to us or not? I'm beginning to suspect that he's becoming less and less interested in the affairs of humanity, simply because he has evolved into something new. Which means we have very little to offer him. And that, I suspect, is a good thing, considering how much power he has."

"Okay, fine, but I need access to that power to find Eric."

"I'm sorry Jane, but I don't have an answer for you. My only advice would be to be very cautious. I can't shake this sense of him as a short-tempered god. And the Chinese learned the hard way that you don't want to incur his wrath."

CHAPTER THIRTY-FIVE

THE MONSTER FACTORY

December 4, 2026
United States Disciplinary Barracks,
Fort Leavenworth, Kansas

Two prison guards—a man and a woman—escorted Walden toward the solitary confinement wing. The first thing that struck General Walden was the sound. Despite the heavy glass door and two sets of barred gates, the sound coming from inside was incredible.

One man was howling like a dog. "How-oooooooo. How-oooooo!" Several of the inmates were pounding on the doors.

In front of the entryway, two more guards were seated at a workstation, a dozen mounted iSheets on the wall behind them showing them different cells and hallways.

Walden glanced at the screens and saw that one man had positioned himself sideways and was stomping on the door with his heel. *Wham. Wham. Wham.* He kept a steady, but fierce rhythm with no indication of slowing or stopping.

Now another man began howling, then another. He caught snippets of cries and pleas. "Help me! I can't breathe in here. The walls are squeezing in on me." One man, with tattoos up to his chin, was hitting the glass with his head.

"Welcome to the zoo, General," the female guard said. "Home to the meanest, wildest animals that Uncle Sam could make." She smirked and clearly thought she was funny. Walden gave her a look that wiped the smile off her face.

At that moment, an alarm sounded. "Shit," one of the guards said, jumping from his seat and heading for the door.

"Cell nine," the other guard said and quickly followed.

Walden looked through the glass doors and saw water streaming into the courtyard from one of the cells.

The guards opened the first glass door and the full force of the sound hit Walden. The screaming, the pounding, the howling, the pleas for help. It could only be described as the sounds of hell.

Thankfully, the door closed, muffling the sound again.

"One of the inmates figured out how to overflow the toilet," the female escort explained. "The guards hate that because they can't leave 'em in there—drowning hazard."

Walden watched as the two guards methodically opened the door to the cell where the water was coming from, then disappeared inside.

Walden scanned the surveillance screens, until he saw the right cell: the guards were approaching a man lying on the wet floor. The man's head was shaved, like most of the other inmates, but he had no tattoos. And he was very small, no bigger than five foot five, puny in comparison to the big guards. Just as one of them reached down to seize him, the man exploded into action. He kicked the first guard in the shins, tripping him up, then he broke for the open door as the other guard tried to stop him. Quick as a cat he sidestepped the guard and got around him. He emerged into the corridor and began going around to the other cells, pounding on the doors, looking in at the men, raising his fists in a victory dance. The other inmates went wild, hooting and pounding louder than ever.

The escapee managed to evade the two guards for about twenty seconds, then they cornered him and the man surrendered. One guard punched him in the jaw for his trouble. The inmate took it with a grin and looked up defiantly at the cameras.

“Well, what do you know,” the female guard said. “It’s your boy.”

“That’s Calhoun?” Walden asked.

“None other. As you can see, he’s a model inmate.”

Walden examined Calhoun’s face on the monitor—his pasty white head had been poorly shaved, with patches of bristly black remaining. He still wore a wide grin that showed he was immensely pleased with himself.

What the fuck am I doing here? Walden thought. *This lunatic can’t possibly help me.*

“If you’ll come with me, General, I’ll take you to the visiting room. We’ll get him cleaned up then bring him in.”

“Fine, I’d like to get this over with as soon as possible.”

For the past two and a half weeks, a dozen intelligence officers from Air Force ISR had been trying to dig up dirt on Curtiss. So far, this was all they’d found: a death row inmate at Leavenworth with a conspiracy theory.

★★★

The visiting room was what Walden had expected: a heavy gray steel table with a chair on each side—everything was bolted to the floor.

Fifteen minutes later, they brought him in.

He was still wearing the same shit-eating grin, but he had a clean brown uniform.

"Whoa, what do we have here?" he said, as he took in Walden. "Four stars! To what do I owe the honor"—he squinted at Walden's name placard—"General Walden of the United States Air Force?"

"Sit down and shut up," Walden said.

The guards sat him in the chair then ran a chain through a thick leather belt around his waist and locked it to a metal ring in the floor. Calhoun's hands were left cuffed in front of him.

"Comfy now?" Walden asked.

Calhoun gave a hesitant nod. He looked at Walden with his head cocked, obviously trying to figure out what was going on. This was no parole board. No ordinary visitor.

"You are currently serving two life terms for the murder of two Syrian civilians," Walden began.

"I didn't do it," Calhoun blurted out. "I was framed."

Walden rolled his eyes and continued. "One a sixty-five-year-old man, the other a fourteen-year-old teenager."

"I didn't *do* it," Calhoun said.

Walden leaned in, put his forearms on the table, and looked Calhoun in the eye.

"Okay, then enlighten me. Tell me why you're *really* here?"

Calhoun squeezed his eyes shut tight as if trying to keep something unpleasant from erupting forth. Then he began to rock back and forth, slowly at first, then faster, "I don't know," he said bitterly. Then with more anger, "I don't know, okay. I don't know." Then, as if a switch had been flipped, he began to whimper. It was a pitiful and grating sound. "It's so unfair. Don't you see? I've been here for three years and I don't know anything. Why did they do this to me? I just wanna know. I just wanna reason. I'm innocent, I swear." He bowed his head and began to weep, "You don't know what it's like here. You think I'm crazy." He looked Walden in the face. "Maybe I am, but I'm crazy because of this place—it's a monster factory."

"Spare me," Walden said. "You must have some idea why you're here."

Almost instantly, Calhoun's visage changed and he was composed and serious.

"Because someone wanted me out of the way."

"Who and why?"

Calhoun shook his head.

Walden sighed. This was clearly a dead end.

"All I know is I saw somethin' I wasn't supposed to see. But the problem is, I don't even know what I saw."

"Go on."

"I was assigned to this tiny airfield that had belonged to some Syrian prince. Nobody used it. We had one or two flights a week, max, because the runway was too small for jets and all the helos were at the FOB fifteen miles away. I thought I had the best job in the whole goddamn war. It was safe because we were in a Kurdish controlled area. All we had to do was man the comms for the airfield. Piece of cake. There weren't even any runway lights, so after dark we just locked up and went back to the barracks. Me and the other guys spent most of the deployment playing video games.

"But one night I went back after dark 'cause I'd forgotten

my Xbox. And there's some guy in the control room, a stocky guy with a beard and long hair. He wasn't in our unit.

"As soon as he sees me, he's on my shit. Starts asking me all sorts of questions. Who I was, what I was doing there. He grabs my arm and starts walking me out, says I need to go home and forget I ever saw him. As we get outside, I try to see out on the tarmac, but he's kind of blocking my view, but I can hear something. I twist my head and I see a Twin Otter and some guys loading it up with these big bags.

"Then the guy gives me a look like you really shouldn't have done that.

"'Corporal. Go on home and forget that you came here tonight. Is that clear?'"

"I says *yes, sir, of course*, but I guess he didn't believe me. Because less than twenty-four hours later I was charged with murder."

Walden couldn't help but roll his eyes. "It's a good story. Perfect really, because nobody can corroborate it. And I'm going to bet if I look up the flight plan for the Twin Otter, I won't find a damn thing, coming or going."

Calhoun gave him his shit-eating grin again and tried to lift up his hands as if to signal surrender, but only made it halfway before the chain lost its slack. "Of course not, General. They weren't going to make the same mistake twice."

Walden's eyes flashed and he was suddenly alert and receptive.

"What did you say?"

"You're Air Force, you know all about it."

Walden nodded. During the war on terror the CIA had run a secret operation named "Extraordinary Rendition" that transported terror suspects to other countries for the type of torture and interrogation that was illegal in the US. The operation had been exposed to the media by "plane spotters"—hobbyists who liked to hang around airports and track aircraft. They had looked up flight plans on the internet and began to notice "irregularities," such as a plane flying into an obscure airbase in Poland with twelve passengers then departing fifteen minutes later with only nine. Or a plane believed to be operated by the CIA making frequent flights to Egypt. If Curtiss had been making illegal flights, he would have been more careful. Like flying at night from an obscure Syrian airport, without logging a flight plan, perhaps using false tail numbers.

"But you said they were loading the plane with bags, not prisoners."

Calhoun shrugged. "Hey, that's just what I saw . . . big black duffel bags . . . Who knows what I didn't see."

Walden rubbed his jaw for a second trying to think it through. It wasn't much, but maybe . . . He unfolded his iSheet until it was the size of a piece of paper and handed it to Calhoun. "Do any of these men look familiar?"

Calhoun began swiping through the images, but almost immediately stopped. "That's him!" He jabbed his finger on the image, "That's the motherfucker!" Suddenly the man was overcome by wrath. He tried to stand, but the chain around his waist kept him doubled over, so he stayed bent, straining against the chain, his face inches from the screen. "You stole my life! You took everything from me! Why!" He began screaming. "Whyyyyyy! Whyyyyy!" The guard came forward to restrain him.

Walden grabbed the iSheet. The image was dappled with Calhoun's spittle but Walden recognized the man: Master Chief Nathan Sawyer.

CHAPTER THIRTY-SIX

THE BOMBER'S CABIN

December 4, 2026
Somewhere near Lincoln, Vermont

"Fire in the hole!"

Despite the warning, Bud Brown jumped when the explosion came.

Rogers laughed. "It's hard to get used to it, isn't it? But don't worry, that will probably be the last one. So far, this guy is doing everything by the book: one booby trap on each door to the house. Now we can now get a better look inside."

Rogers motioned to one of the bomb techs, and the BDR (Bomb Disposal Robot) was driven up to the front door. It was essentially a large robotic arm sitting atop four thick tires.

The cabin sat near the crest of a hill in about as remote an area as anyone could imagine. Dark pine forests stretched out for twelve miles in every direction. The cabin itself was a single room and recently built, with fat timbers that were still blond and bright.

They had arrived that morning at dawn. SWAT teams had roped in from helicopters to cordon off the house until the bomb techs could get up the logging road in their trucks; they got stuck twice.

Despite the fact that the bomber was not inside, Rogers was optimistic.

"Come take a look at this!" Rogers led him about twenty yards away from the house to a gully and pointed to a two-foot-diameter concrete pipe. "It's just like I said, by the book—two points of egress, plus a secret escape route. You can see his footprints in the mud. Very fresh. With any luck, the dogs will find him before he can make it out of the woods."

Bud hoped he was right. Rogers certainly deserved the credit for getting them here. Just watching him work over the past four weeks had been inspiring. From one tiny piece of evidence in Senator Peck's office, Rogers had tracked the bomber to this very spot. It began with the melted remains of a transmitter and cell phone they'd found in one of the heating vents. Despite being mangled and charred, the forensic lab had gotten a lot number off the circuit board. That had led them to an RC model shop in Middlebury. Then, by interviewing the employees and other townspeople, they'd created a profile of an old bearded hermit that lived up in the hills. After four days of checking dozens of summer cabins in the area, they'd finally hit pay dirt.

Rogers gave Bud a smack on the shoulder. "We got 'em on the run! Who knows, we could have that bitch Finley by the end of the week!"

Bud tried to give him a reassuring smile. It would soon be over . . . but then he couldn't help but wonder, where would that leave him? Back at his desk in the bureau.

"What's wrong?" Rogers asked.

"I've been trying to figure out why you picked me." Bud asked. "There are dozens of other guys you could have chosen . . . was it because of Carol? Did she say something to you?"

"No, not really. She comes over to the house a lot. I try to leave her and Joan alone, but sometimes I hear her talking."

"And?"

"Let's just say I don't agree with her assessment of you."

Bud nodded. "Thanks."

"Forget it. Let's just say that—in the balance—this job is more likely to push us down than lift us up. That's just the way it is when your job is to deal with death and crime. But sometimes it gives you the purpose you need to keep going. So I took a chance on you, thinking maybe this case would be one of those that does more good than harm. And now I'm thinking I was right."

Just then the robot operator called from the back of one of the FBI trucks, "Agent Rogers, can you come take a look at this?"

"Gotta go!"

Rogers jogged up the slope to the truck.

Brown looked around. It was a crisp, sunny November afternoon, and even though it was in the high forties, patches of snow lingered in the shade of many of the trees. There really wasn't anything for him to do other than keep out of the bomb team's way, so he headed down the logging road past the cabin, then cut into the woods again. He figured the bomber probably buried his trash somewhere near the house and finding it would yield a lot of evidence. It was Police Academy 101: you can learn a hell of a lot about a person from their trash.

He searched in vain for about twenty minutes then something strange happened—he lost his footing on a dense patch of pine nettles. Flailing, he grabbed a sapling for support. Much to his surprise, he fell all the same. The sapling hadn't snapped, it had merely rolled over. As he picked himself up, he saw that the roots were still encased in a burlap bag. The tree had been camouflaging a small cave under an outcropping of rock.

He immediately pulled out his Beretta and a pen light. As he shone the light inside, he could see that the natural cave ended about five feet in, but the light danced off something brighter. Another two-foot wide cement pipe, similar to the one Rogers had shown him.

It was a second escape route. He searched the area around the opening of the cave and sure enough, he found an impression of man's shoe, though very faint.

Bud realized that the dogs and their handlers were going in exactly the wrong way.

From the cabin he heard Rogers yell, "All clear!" They were about to go in.

Bud was about to go up to tell Rogers what he had found, when the call of a crow made him jump. He looked up to see it atop the pine tree to his right. The bird cocked its head and looked at him, cawed once more, then alit with a loud flutter of its wings.

As the crown of the tree shook from the crow's flight, he noticed the flicker of something metallic. He squinted but couldn't make it out. Holstering the Beretta, he began to climb. It was a miserable task. The tree was old and overburdened with dead branches, which scratched him every foot of the way. When he was about two thirds up, he paused for a better look, but the object—whatever it was—was still obscured by the branches. He looked out and saw the rolling mountains spreading out in every direction, a seemingly endless sea of pine green with an occasional splash of fall copper and red. About eighty yards in front of him was the cabin, the FBI trucks on its East side. Looking down on it, he saw something he hadn't seen before. Completely encircling the cabin at a distance of about five feet was a slight indentation. It was only a foot wide and a fraction of an inch deep and the brown grass had grown over it, but it was definitely noticeable from above.

He had no idea what it meant—perhaps a septic system? He pushed the oddity from his mind and continued to climb. After ten more feet of progress he could finally see the object: it was a small camera pointed toward the cabin, as well as a battery pack and a small concave box.

"Oh no!" he thought. Rogers had told him that the SOP for a raid like this was to have all cell phone towers in the area shut down to prevent anyone from remotely detonating a bomb. But what he was looking at was the bomber's own makeshift cell phone tower.

He remembered Rogers's words from Senator Peck's office: *These people knew us. They knew our security. They exploited our weaknesses.*

He rushed upward in an effort to dismantle it, but the higher he got, the slower he climbed because the branches were everywhere and very thin. He shouted out, "Get out! Get out of the house!" Some of the agents looked up, trying to find him in the trees. One saw him and pointed. He waived a hand. "Get everyone out of the house!"

Rogers emerged from the cabin and shaded his eyes to look for him.

At that moment, the cabin and all the agents near it

dropped into the earth. It took a second for the sound to reach Bud's ears—six quick detonations, like a rapid string of gunshots. Then came a massive explosion. Later he would learn that the weight of the house—suspended at six points—had collapsed onto a pressure plate in the subfloor, triggering a massive explosion.

Bud watched as the entire hilltop jumped and an ethereal shockwave erupted outward in a perfect circle of expanding force. The FBI trucks that were broadside to the house were knocked over, as was every agent on their feet. Dozens of trees were blown over, too. Bud heard the thundering detonation followed by the crack of splintering tree trunks. When the shock wave hit him, he was almost thrown from the tree and had to hold on for dear life. Once the tree righted itself, he looked down to see a mushroom cloud. As it dissipated, a massive fire raged where, only a moment ago, the cabin had stood.

We know from her other bombings that she doesn't like mangled body parts tarnishing her public image.

The flames reached over forty feet into the air, and a huge black funnel of smoke was rising into the clear November sky.

He looked at it for a moment, completely dumbstruck. Two dozen bodies lay in the clearing around the house. He scrambled down the tree, as fast as he could, not caring for the cuts and scrapes on his face and hands. When he reached the clearing before the cabin, he froze. There were no screams for help, no agents giving orders. The only sound was the roar of the fire and the popping of burning wood. Some of the downed agents were struggling to move but they were only semiconscious.

He saw a woman, rolling on the ground and rushed to

her. It was Aileen Michaels, one of Rogers's bomb techs. She was struggling to breathe. "Help," she gasped.

"Just lay back, Aileen."

She gasped for breath then began to spit up blood.

Things did not look good. He knew that few of these agents, even the ones who were still moving, would survive. That's because it wasn't really the explosion that killed people, it was the sudden compression and expansion of the shock wave—overpressure—that ruptured any part of the human body that was filled with air: eardrums, eyeballs, lungs, stomach, colon, heart. While most of the injured agents appeared merely stunned, many were hemorrhaging inside, which meant there was little Bud could do to help them.

He held Aileen's hand. "Try not to move. We'll get those choppers in here as soon as we can."

She looked at him desperately and gripped his hand tight. She seemed to want to speak, but it was taking all her effort to breathe. She opened her mouth. More blood.

He looked her over, perhaps a piece of shrapnel had entered one of her lungs and he could patch the hole. If he rotated her onto the side with the punctured lung, maybe she'd make it long enough to survive. But after a thorough check, he realized there was no entrance wound, it was all internal, and probably both lungs. By now he figured that Aileen, being a bomb tech, knew full well that she would not survive.

Brown had a decision to make: he could leave her and try to help the others or he could stay with her. His training told him he had to leave her. He had to triage the wounded and focus on those he could save. Yet as he looked down at her, that decision felt criminal.

He looked around, unsure of what to do. He heard the moans and pleas for help from six or seven wounded agents. Luckily, two other agents were assisting the wounded. One of the techs had been lucky enough to be wearing his bomb suit, as well as another agent in SWAT gear who appeared unscathed.

"Somebody help me," he heard a man say.

"I'll be right back," he said to Aileen, "someone else needs me."

But as he tried to pull away, she held his hand tight.

He looked over at the wounded man then down at Aileen. The fear and helplessness on her face was almost too much to bear. He sat back down and kept holding her hand.

It was just as he heard the sound of the approaching helicopters that her hand went limp.

Jack Berhmann noticed how quickly Bill Eastman paused the video as he came into the study. Then, rather guiltily, he set the iSheet down on the coffee table. Jack picked it up and checked the video. "If I didn't know better," he said, "I'd say you were in love."

Bill pursed his lips in annoyance. "Don't be ridiculous. She's a terrorist. Twenty-seven agents died."

"Fine, but you have to admit, you've become obsessed with her."

Bill shook his head. "Not obsessed. Just acutely interested."

Jack gave him a wry look of skepticism then sat down in the opposite chair. "Very well, my friend, can you explain your *acute interest*."

Bill considered his friend for a moment, then leaned in,

suddenly glad to have an audience for his thoughts. "I'm not completely sure, but I have this feeling that she's trying to tell me something."

"She is," Jack said. "She's trying to tell you that the human race has a serious problem—its resource consumption is unsustainable. Have you looked at the data? It's seriously depressing. Most of the climate models show we're facing a mass extinction—everything from coral reefs to rain forests to penguins."

"No, that's not what I'm talking about. It's actually more immediate that that. I feel like history is repeating itself."

"What do you mean by that?"

Bill shook his head slowly. "I can't quite put my finger on it, but Finley is like the reincarnation of an archetype. A modern iteration of the radical revolutionary, like Thomas Paine or Che Guevara. But at the same time she's different . . . because the technology is different."

Jack nodded. Bill's "acute interest" was starting to make more sense. And Jack was relieved to know that his old friend was not as far out in orbit as he had thought.

"You're afraid that Finley could get her hands on our technology and do something unprecedented."

"That's part of it, but the thing I'm worried about even more is how the government will respond to Finley. Let me ask you this: How did the US government react the last time it faced a major terrorist threat?"

Jack puffed out his cheeks and gave a long whistle. He immediately understood where Bill was going. "Let's see . . . we went to war with two countries, one of which we invaded on false assumptions, which precipitated the death of almost half a million people and helped incubate a new generation of terrorists—ISIS."

"Precisely! And don't forget what else happened. That was the rise of the surveillance state, when the NSA began its massive data collection programs. My point is that when governments are attacked, they overreact on a massive scale. They want to prove their power and restore a sense of security. But in the end, their response to terrorism can be much more dangerous than the terrorism itself."

Jack continued Bill's thought. "So even if Finley doesn't get our technology, the government might use it recklessly in the name of 'keeping us safe.'"

"Yes. I'm afraid that unless Finley is caught quickly, they're going expect us to help them."

Jack nodded and sat back in his chair. He was relieved to hear Bill voice his concerns about their work. In fact, he'd been wanting to have this conversation for a long time. "Do you remember our last night in Sunnyvale? When we closed down AML, we went up on the roof and watched the sunset."

"Of course," Bill said.

"Well, I think about that night a lot. Because that's when we decided to help Curtiss."

"Are you asking me if I regret coming here?" Bill said.

Jack nodded.

"I don't," Bill said. "If we hadn't come, then China would have won the race to replication. We made the right choice at that moment. And I'd do it again." He paused to think for a moment. "You see, this isn't about the past. It's about the future. Coming here was an easy choice. We accomplished amazing things, but the riddle is this: Now that we have accomplished these things, what do we do next?"

Bill stood and began pacing the room. "Let's assess our current situation. We've created a technology that will reshape the world in ways we cannot imagine. And we've handed it over to a military institution that wants to exploit it to its full potential. So far, most of the results have been positive, such as restructuring of the world toward greater freedom and democracy. But things are changing. Curtiss's control is slipping. Just take Olivia Rosario and her Global Hologram, for example: she's making it despite Curtiss and our objections."

"Yes, I know," Jack said, "which is why I think it's time for us to go back to California."

Bill nodded noncommittally. "That's the big question, isn't it? Fight or flight. It's been on my mind, too. But I can't make up my mind. If we leave, we'll lose our clearance and our ability to guide the development of the very technology we designed. If we stay, we may become accomplices to making weapons and surveillance systems that will almost surely be used against civilians."

"You've always known how I've felt about weapons research," Jack said.

"Yes. And I also know that you came to DC more for me than for yourself. I haven't forgotten that and I'm very grateful."

Jack smiled and bowed his head. "We always stick together."

"We have . . . and we will. But I still can't make up my mind. I feel that even though our power here is diminishing, we have to stay if we want any chance of doing some good."

Jack shook his head. "Be careful. If the old proverb is correct and a person's reputation is made by a thousand deeds and destroyed by one, then you're setting yourself up for failure. Do you understand why?"

Bill's expression said he didn't.

"Because the responsibility will lie on our shoulders for whatever weapons get made here under our watch. And that's regardless of whether we make them or Rosario makes them or Walden makes them." Jack let that sink in a moment before adding. "My advice is to get out while we can. There has to be a better way for us to use our talents."

CHAPTER THIRTY-SEVEN

THE PORCH

December 4, 2026
Bethesda, MD

It was 7:30 p.m. when Special Agent Bud Brown turned his Ford onto Howell Drive in Bethesda, Maryland. It was a pretty neighborhood with tall oak and maple trees and long lawns. The curbs were crowded with piles of autumn leaves. He eased down the street slowly, leaning toward the passenger side door and trying to make out the house numbers in the dark.

When he and Rogers had been partners, Rogers had lived in a small apartment in SE. Now he saw how much he'd moved up in the world.

He spotted the address, 1425 Howell Drive, on a brick mailbox and looked out to see a big Victorian house with a wide porch. He parked at the curb and was about to get out when he hesitated, glancing at the brown paper bag that sat in the passenger seat.

You don't have to do this, you know. You could just go home.

He looked up at the house again. Going in was the right thing to do. He owed it to Rogers . . . and to his wife. If the roles had been reversed and Rogers had lived, he'd have wanted Rogers to tell his family how it happened.

But he didn't want to do it. The memories were still too fresh and telling it again would be like reliving it.

Do the right thing.

When he'd been around Rogers, the right thing had felt easy. He'd made Bud want to be the best agent he could be, which was a something he hadn't felt in years. Now Rogers was gone, and Bud felt that good influence slipping away.

He looked at the house, trying to summon his courage. That's when he noticed the Lexus in the driveway. A glance at the plate confirmed his suspicion: Carol was here. As one of Joan's best friends, he'd known it was a possibility, but he'd hoped . . .

He reached for the paper bag, twisted off the top of the bottle, and took a long pull. The bourbon immediately warmed his throat and chest. He wanted more but forced himself to put the cap back on and get out of the car. As he moved up the walkway, he cinched up his tie and pulled his jacket over his shoulders. When he reached the door he stood there a moment on the brightly lit porch, feeling exposed in the light. The heavy oak door had panes of glass on both sides, allowing him to see a foyer filled with warm amber light.

He rang the bell and waited. A minute passed. He tried again. This time the door immediately opened. It was Carol.

"Bud, what are you doing here?" She wore that suspicious look that he remembered.

"I came to talk to Joan. I thought she should hear . . ."

"No," she said emphatically, "this is not a good idea."

"I feel like I owe it to her."

"You shouldn't have come. She's not ready. Not at all." She began to close the door.

"Wait," he said, stepping closer. She drew back, a flash of fear in her eyes.

"You've been drinking," she said. She could always tell, no matter how little.

He felt his anger rise, but he kept it in check. *Yeah*, he thought, *after I watched thirty people die I had a drink.* "Just one," he said, "to get my courage up."

"You haven't changed, have you?" It was said with more pity than disdain.

"Look, I just want her to know what happened. Carol, don't you see. I figured it out. But I was just a minute too late. Another sixty seconds and they could have all gotten out."

"Is that why you're here, to cleanse your guilty conscience?"

"No, I'm here because she deserves to know the whole story, even if it's hard to hear."

"She knows the whole story, Bud. Her husband is dead. It doesn't matter how close you came to saving him. The point is you didn't."

Suddenly he had no reply.

"You'd better go," and without waiting for him to reply, she closed the door. Bud heard the deadbolt click into place and the security chain slide into its groove.

He stood there for a moment, unsure if he should knock again. If he could just talk to Joan . . . From inside he could faintly hear another woman's voice. "Who was it?"

"Oh, no one . . . some teenager selling something."

He walked down the steps, out of the porch light into the darkness. Back in the Ford he grabbed the brown paper bag and took another long drink. He started the engine, put the bottle between his legs, and headed for home.

CHAPTER THIRTY-EIGHT

SEEDS

December 6, 2026
Roslyn, Virginia

"Is it safe for us to breathe?" Olivia asked.

"Oh, yes," Ryan said, "Emma's DNA is the only DNA it will recognize."

Ryan took the small glass vial out of his pocket. It was well past midnight, and Emma was sound asleep in front of them. A bedside lamp made a cone of light beside her head.

In the ten days since Ryan had agreed to help Olivia, they had been working around the clock. While Ryan had to split his time between the Global Hologram and Emma's cure, Olivia had done little else than work on saving her daughter. Working together for long hours meant they had argued, bickered, occasionally screamed, but eventually made up. They were a good team. And much to Ryan's amazement, it looked like they had done it. In the tiny flask in his hand was the first gene therapy in history that could cross the blood-brain barrier.

He caught Olivia's eye and gave her a reassuring smile. She was so exhausted and nervous that she could only respond with a tight-lipped grimace.

He was still madly in love with her, but he knew she would never be his, not fully, not until . . .

He looked down at the sleeping girl and realized how closely their futures were now intertwined. Right now Olivia's heart was so full of worry for Emma there was little space for him. That would only change when and if the girl were cured. And even then, how much of Olivia's heart would he get? That question worried him. Because he wouldn't know until it happened. All he knew for sure was that he had to try.

He pulled the small rubber stopper from the vial.

"Would you like to do it?" Ryan asked.

"I feel like I should." Olivia took the vial and sat down beside Emma.

"Just hold it under her nose . . . that's it."

Olivia gently moved the flask from one nostril to the other.

"That's fine, they're in her now."

She handed him the flask, then leaned down so that her forehead touched Emma's. "Dear God, please let this work. Please help my little girl."

PART THREE
TRIBAL WARFARE

CHAPTER THIRTY-NINE

POISON

December 6, 2026
Namibia

It took a day and a half for them to make their way back to the salt flats where Eric had regained his sight. He couldn't wait to see the watering hole again and behold the dizzying menagerie of animals. At noon they started the hard march across the flat waste. It looked like a white sea, with low, rolling waves topped with pink crests made by salt-loving microbes.

He realized that he was beginning to lose track of the days. Had it been thirty-one days or thirty-two? Perhaps it was more. There were no calendars or watches here.

When they were about a quarter mile from the hole, Khamko stopped them. Vultures could be seen circling in the sky. The heat made everything a blur at that distance, and Eric could only make out rough shapes on the horizon but none of them were moving.

“The old and young need to wait here,” he announced. “The rest come with me.”

They took off at a trot. Khamko, Eric, Naru, Karuma, and the six other able-bodied adults and teens. As they got closer, Eric’s apprehension began to grow and grow. He wanted to think he was wrong, that it couldn’t possibly be true. But the closer he got, the greater the enormity became.

He had remembered this place as one of breathtaking beauty. A place where thousands of creatures gathered in the great celebration of life.

But the vision before him now was so nightmarish, he had to turn his head away. And he was not the only one. The others began to stop, unable to go any closer, not wanting to look. Many cried openly. They, too, had never seen anything this horrible in their lives.

Hundreds of carcasses sat festering in and around the waterhole. Eland, gemsbok, springbok, ostrich, hyena, and lion lay fat and bloated among the bodies of thousands of small birds. The smell of rot and death was overpowering, and many of the Sān held their noses. For a moment, they all stood there, unbelieving, then Eric, Naru, and Khamko moved slowly forward, trying to understand what had happened.

About twenty elephant carcasses lay on the far side of the water. The bull elephants’ faces had been sawed off with chainsaws and were now ghastly masks of blood, bone, and gore. Flies swarmed in black clouds over them, peppering their bloody visages. The bodies of cow elephants and calves lay untouched among them. The tracks from several pickup trucks crisscrossed the sand from one bull elephant to the other. At one end of the watering hole was a huge plastic drum, tipped on its side, a clear liquid waxing the brown water around it. Even over the stench of the rotting corpses, the bitter almond smell reached Eric.

"No, no, no," Khamko kept repeating. "How can this be?"

No one answered him.

Eric looked at Naru and on her face he saw an expression of rage and hardness that he didn't think was possible. A deep well of hate was being stirred inside her.

Eric looked around but found himself closing his eyes at each new horror. A herd of eland. A lion cub dead across her mother's belly. A dozen ostrich chicks huddled together in death.

"*You!* Your people did this!" It was Naru, she was coming toward him, her spear out on in front of her. "Every year you take more and more and more and more. You never stop."

She was only a few feet away Brandishing the point. "I will kill every one of you, if it's the last—"

"Naru!"

She turned the spear aside at the last moment and gave her father a look of disgust. Then she tossed the spear to the ground and gave a shriek of frustration. She slowly sank to her knees, and—bringing her hands to her face—began to sob.

She muttered, "Why . . . why?"

"I want to go with you," Eric said.

The sun was going down, and Khamko was preparing a hunting party to track down the poachers.

"I'm sorry, my son," Khamko said, "but I have to say no to you. I don't want you to see these ugly things."

"I know what you are going to do and I want to help."

"Killing a man is different than killing a gemsbok."

"I know. It's easier."

Khamko stopped and searched Eric's face. It was clear that he had not expected this answer.

"Can you do it again?"

"To stop the men who did this? Yes."

They set out to the south, a dull yellow sunset on their right. Khamko, Naru, G□kau, and Eric. Soon a half moon rose, making the tracks of the pickup trucks easy to follow.

"It is rough terrain for thirty miles around the salt flat," Khamko said. "They will have to go slow and won't make the road until noon tomorrow."

They ran long into the night, stopping only once to drink from their supplies of water. Eric knew they were getting close when Khamko stopped talking and switched to hand signals. Soon the glow of a fire appeared under the canopy of two umbrella acacias. A moment later, Eric smelled them. Sweat and fuel and alcohol and scraps of food. Smells he had lived with all his life, but never identified as "civilization."

All the men were asleep near the fire. Bottles of beer and cheap schnapps were scattered around. Khamko went ahead, moving silently about the camp, confirming that all the men were indeed there, then, using hand signals, he indicated that they should move in.

Eric had expected to find signs of sophistication. Well-outfitted military types. Perhaps white men or Chinese men leading them. But what he found was very different.

They were poor black men in two beat-up pickup trucks. One truck was missing a rear fender, the other a passenger door. They found the ivory tusks in the bed of one truck wrapped in a tarp beside a chainsaw and another oil-drum full of cyanide.

They moved silently to each victim. Eric stood over his man, the tip of his spear just inches from the notch in his throat. The man's clothes were little more than rags. Filthy and smelling of dirt and urine. His trousers were held up by a piece of rope.

Eric looked around at the others, and he saw three angels of death with their spears poised, their silhouettes half lit by the fire. Khamko made a cricket call and all the spears were thrust down. Eric's man did not die instantly. He awoke and grabbed the spear and tried to push it out. He kicked and flailed, his face an expression of confusion and shock. He seemed to be asking why. Eric twisted the spear, cutting the spinal cord, and the body went slack. For a moment Eric stared at the man's face. Then he turned away. As he had suspected, it had been much easier than killing the gemsbok.

Naru was the first to break the silence, "Bah!" she said in disgust. "No big boss, no white man, no yellow man!" She got out her flaying knife and began to cut up the bodies exactly as if they were a fresh Kudu or Elan. She cut out the liver of the first man and began to eat. Soon G□kau followed suit. They stoked the fire and were soon laying strips of meat across branches to cook.

Eric watched them in shock and amazement. "I thought you were joking."

Khamko walked over to him and spoke softly. "Berries, honey, baobab melons, these are things that we can still find, but meat will be scarce for many weeks. In fact, it may take months for the cyanide to work its way out of the food chain. It is not what we would choose to do, but we must survive."

Khamko went to the fire and took some of the meat and brought it to him. "This will be the last fresh meat you have for many weeks."

But Eric shook his head. "I can't. It's just not right."

"Not right?!" Naru exclaimed. "Not *right*?!" She marched toward him, the filleting knife tight in her fist. "And starving to death, that's the right thing to do?" She made a stabbing motion at his chest, her forearms wet with gore and glistening in the firelight. "You don't know anything. You've been with us a month and you think you can tell us what's right. You"—her eyes rose to the sky and she shivered with rage, then she looked at him again—"You need to be taught a lesson. Yes, a lesson. Sit!" She jabbed again with the knife. "Sit!"

Eric held up his hands in appeasement and sat down.

"You are going to listen before you judge us."

She stood towering over him, breathing heavy with anger. After a moment she began.

"Have you heard of the Great Hunger?"

He shook his head. "No."

"Of course you haven't. Well, I'm going to tell you. Two hundred years ago all the tribes were so desperate for food that they became cannibals. The Griqua, the Basuto, the Bechuana. They all began to eat each other. And not for just one or two years, but for a whole generation. That was during the White Expansion, when the Europeans came and kept coming, taking everything they wanted and killing all the animals for sport. That's when the remaining tribes had to fight for what was left—which was too little.

"Every tribe resorted to cannibalism. Except one. We, the Bushmen as they called us, were eaten, but we never ate. We held on to our dignity even as the others slaughtered our children for meat.

"When the intertribal warfare had decimated us, when only a few thousand remained, the whites came and tried to finish us off.

"Because we were smaller and our skin was different and we refused to adopt any of the European ways—no horses or guns or livestock or farming—for all these things we were considered less than human. In their eyes, that made us fit for extermination. Even the pastors, the church leaders, the pious who had been sent to convert the other tribes, had no qualms about killing the Bushmen. The pastors themselves organized the hunting parties.

"Their hypocrisy ran deep. They thought we were subhuman, yet they loved to take our children as their servants. They said they were so much more loyal and clever than the children from the other tribes.

"That is the history I think about whenever we hunt our enemies. Khamko has taught us that if we are to survive, we must take at least some of the things from your world. It has not been easy for us. And some will still not eat the enemy's flesh. But I relish it." And here she sucked up through her nostrils as if preparing to eat. "It is fitting that we now hunt those who once slaughtered us. When I eat their meat, I grow stronger in both mind and body. Because I am eating retribution. I am exacting justice for a hundred thousand murders that went unpunished."

Eric looked her in the eye and nodded. He knew there was little he could say. She was right: he was a foreigner with little understanding of what these people had been through. “I’m sorry. I was wrong.”

This seemed to defuse her anger, though just a little, and she stomped off to the fire. A minute later she returned with a strip of cooked meat and handed it to him.

He hesitated. Then he looked her in the eyes, took the meat, and ate it.

They spent the rest of the night in the poachers’ camp. There was an unnatural stillness to the world around them. As if the night locusts and toads were still mourning the death of so many animals.

Khamko and Eric took the cyanide and the tusks and drove them to a remote stretch of the woods and buried them. Then they spent much of the rest of the night hiding their tracks, so no one could follow their trail. When they returned, the red disk of the sun was just breaking above the horizon.

“I want to destroy the trucks, the guns, everything,” Khamko said to Eric. “Can you help?”

Eric nodded. “Just give me fifteen minutes.” Rummaging through the trucks he found some string and some cooking supplies. With these he made a simple fuse and rigged it to the gas tanks. “This will give us about ninety seconds before the first truck explodes.”

Naru and G□kau had made backpacks out of the skins of two of the men—just as they would have done with any other game, tying each skinned leg to the skinned arms created the shoulder straps. Then they stuffed them with the cooked meat and put them on. Eric noticed that the fingers of the men had been hacked off and were piled on top.

Naru followed his eyes and gave him a sinister smirk. "The children love them," she said. "It's a treat."

When they were assembled at the edge of the camp, Eric touched a brand to the string-fuse then tossed the stick aside. Naru led them at a trot down a kudu track, with Khamko taking up the rear.

At two hundred yards the first truck exploded. Eric looked back to see an orange and black mushroom cloud appear over the camp then quickly dissipate. A moment later, the second truck exploded creating a second brief mushroom cloud. He had left the gun and ammunition in the second truck and soon the shells began to cook off, making loud pops over the crackling fire.

Then the four of them turned and trotted on. For the first time in his life, Eric felt like warrior, as a man who had completed a hard mission. Here he was, moving through the bush with his war party, the fire of their destruction billowing black smoke behind him, signaling to all who might look upon it as irrefutable proof of their lethality.

When they returned to the camp, Karuma was waiting for them. He ran and hugged his mother, then Eric, then his grandfather. "Did you stop them, Grandfather?"

"For now," Khamko said. "For now."

That night they ate much of the meat. The children happily gnawed on the fingers.

Later, Eric lay awake thinking about the poachers. It

was plain to see that the Sān way of life could not survive if it was always being invaded by the modern world. And this beautiful life could not exist for much longer. As the modern world expanded, as it needed more and more resources to sustain itself—whether that be gold or copper or timber or elephant tusks—it would slowly and inexorably consume the resources the Sān needed to survive. It was a simple truth. An irrefutable equation. If something wasn't done to change the equation. They were doomed.

In the morning they broke camp and headed northeast.

"It is four days to an area called Valley of the Bones," Khamko said. "Perhaps we can hunt there; if not, we must keep going."

CHAPTER FORTY

SPACE FOOD

December 7, 2026
Washington, DC

Jane ran up the stairs to the fifth-floor landing, a sudden nervous excitement running through her as she thought of Bill's last words. *I've got something.* They had been meeting every evening to hunt for the Inventor, but this was the first real news.

She rushed down the corridor toward Lab #9. "Make way!" she called, knocking against several lab techs who didn't move fast enough. "Hey!" one called as he slurped spilled coffee off his wrist. Jane didn't stop to apologize.

When she turned into Lab #9 she stopped cold in her tracks. *What in the world?* Hundreds of cheap wooden crates filled the huge lab, some stacked all the way to the twenty-foot ceilings. Chiquita. Dole. Producto de Costa Rica. Importada de Ecuador. She didn't need to look inside the crates to know what they held. Her nose picked up the sickly sweet smell of fermenting bananas.

Fifty yards away, Bill was at the lab's opposite entrance, directing some workers who were delivering another pallet. "Yes, right there is fine."

"What's going on?" she called out.

He waved. "Oh, Jane, good. I'm glad you're here."

He met her halfway across the floor and spread his iSheet out on the bench. "It's so fascinating. Take a look."

Jane read the headline:

Mysterious Banana Blight
Now Extends to Ecuador

A strange malady affecting millions of banana trees in Honduras, Costa Rica, and Panama has emerged for the first time on the South American continent. Scientists are mystified by the ailment, which doesn't appear to be any known disease or fungus. The strange blight has banana growers worried because virtually all banana plants are clones, meaning that a single ailment could potentially wipe out every Cavendish banana tree in the world. Luckily, the blight does not appear to kill the entire banana tree, and a tree whose bananas are affected is able to grow healthy bananas later. "It is a very strange phenomenon," said Ernesto Nava, Ecuador's Agricultural Minister, "it affects one group of trees then seems to hop to another group while leaving others unscathed, almost like a geometric pattern." While the blight has now hit four countries, it has only affected 20 percent of the trees there, which

means there should still be plenty of bananas for
your smoothies and banana splits.

Jane furrowed her forehead. "Sorry, but I'm not seeing the connection."

"Well, I was thinking about what we talked about: how the Inventor might be exploring space. So I began looking at the materials he might need to do that, rare earth elements and such, keeping an eye out for anything strange. That's when I came across the article."

Jane raised her eyebrows skeptically. "Bananas are important for space travel?"

"No . . . and yes. Remember how I said that faster-than-light travel might be possible with antimatter?"

"Uh-huh."

"Well, antimatter is extremely hard to come by. In fact, if you could gather all the antimatter that humans have ever created, it would be no more than thirty nanograms. That's not even enough to boil a pot of water. Are you with me?"

"Antimatter. Scarce. Got it."

"But it does exist in tiny amounts on—and around—the earth, and it could, in theory, be harvested. For example, it sometimes bombards the atmosphere as cosmic rays. Occasionally it is created in thunderstorms. And, believe it or not . . ." He held up a banana.

"You're kidding."

Bill shook his head. "You are looking at one of earth's few antimatter generators."

"I don't believe you."

"You are free to verify this using your search engine of choice," he said, "but whether you believe it or not, it is, in fact, the truth."

Jane pulled her iSheet out of her pocket. "Do bananas create antimatter?"

The electronic voice replied. "Bananas emit positrons, a type of antimatter."

Bill gave her a smug look. "Do you want to know how?"

She nodded, her lips still squeezed together in doubt.

"Your tasty yellow friend here contains trace amounts of an isotope called potassium-40. As potassium-40 decays, it emits a steady amount of positrons. In fact, every banana on the planet produces a positron every seventy-five minutes. When I saw the article on the news, I thought, of course! If someone had access to very advanced swarm technology, like the Inventor surely does, he could harvest those positrons as a fuel source."

"And is he?"

Bill grinned in way that took forty years off his age. Jane couldn't help but smile, remembering how much he'd said he missed working in a lab.

He continued, his eyes bright with excitement. "The blight isn't a disease at all, it's a by-product of positron harvesting. I found evidence of assemblers on thousands of these bananas. And they were the most beautiful nanosites I've ever seen."

"So it's really him?" Jane said. She needed to hear him say it.

Bill nodded. "It has to be. These nanosites were efficient in a way that I'm not even sure I understand." He showed her an image that looked like an insect drawn with a Spirograph. She could immediately see how it was lighter and more streamlined then the nanosites they had made. "Beautiful, aren't they?"

She laughed. "Yeah."

"You see, the trick with antimatter isn't just finding it. Once you have it, you have to keep it away from matter. If it touches normal matter, it's annihilated. But the Inventor's nanosites are essentially Penning traps, microscopic particle accelerators that can hold the antimatter in a magnetic field. That means the Inventor's nanosites can collect antimatter just as easily as a bee collects pollen. It's amazing!"

Jane found herself blinking as she tried to imagine it. That meant the Inventor was working on a global scale, his legions of nanosites spreading all over the earth to do his bidding. She imagined massive swarms, microscopic but large enough to alight on every banana on hundreds and hundreds of miles of tropical forest, harvesting an energy source that humankind's current state of technology couldn't touch. *If he's doing this, what else is he doing?* After all, this was just the power source for one of his inventions. How many more trillions of nanosites were out there, autonomously working for him?

"Wait, if he's collecting antimatter like a bee collects honey, then where's the hive?"

"Ah, yes, I thought of that, too. So I attached tracking markers to dozens of the nanosites. They were rising in the air, about ten thousand feet, when I lost them."

"Lost them?"

"Yes," Bill shook his head sadly. "It appears he realized what I was doing. You may have also noticed that I referred to the nanosites in the past tense."

"You mean they're gone?"

He nodded. "I'll keep looking in the new banana shipments I get, but I think he's clearly on to us."

Jane's shoulders sagged and her chin dropped in defeat. "So we aren't any closer than we were before."

"Oh, I think we are a lot closer. We have verified our initial theory that he is a scientist, first and foremost—one who is primarily interested in discovery. I think that's very important. His interest in antimatter confirms that he is likely exploring space. Also very important. And now that I have seen the sophistication of his nanosites, I'm even more convinced he's sending them into space as probes, perhaps at faster-than-light speeds. That's all very good information."

"Yeah, but that's not getting me any closer to finding Eric."

He moved closer and put a hand on her shoulder. "I'm sorry. I know it's frustrating, especially when it's clear that he has the power to easily help us. Unfortunately, there's one more lesson from all this. The way he recalled his nanosites as soon as I tried to track them shows us that he definitely wants to be left alone."

CHAPTER FORTY-ONE

CALLER ID

December 7, 2026
The forests of West Virginia, near Big Moses

Riona Finley jumped when she felt the phone vibrate against her leg. She had been on edge since yesterday, since she had realized that someone had found her.

She looked at the number.

<<PRIVATE>>

Had the government found her? Were they trying to use the phone to pinpoint her? It wouldn't work, of course. Her cell phone only used Wi-Fi, all her calls were encrypted, and she used a VPN that gave her location in the South Pacific. If she answered, all they would know was that someone in Tahiti had made an encrypted call.

She waited until the vibrating stopped. She was walking in the woods, about two miles from her cabin, trying to clear her head.

A minute passed. The phone began to ring again. Again, a private number.

She summoned her courage and pressed Talk, but she didn't say anything.

"Hello, Riona." It was man's voice. Confident and strong.

"Who is this?"

"A friend and admirer."

She rolled her eyes. She wasn't in the mood. "How did you get this number?"

"I am a very resourceful man, Miss Finley. In fact, I'm the kind of man who can help you."

She let out a sardonic laugh. "I'm not exactly in the line of work that allows me to collaborate with strangers."

"I understand completely, which is why I made two deposits to your crowdfunding account yesterday."

Riona felt her pulse quicken. She had been up half the night because of those deposits, one for $39,458.73, the other for $80,714.58. They were not particularly large sums—she had received donations for as much as two million—but the lack of rounding had caught her eye, making her suspect someone was trying to tell her something. There was another thing: the two sums had been sent at exactly the same instant—0600.00—from two different locations, so that only she, the recipient, could put them together.

It had taken her only a few minutes to figure it out. The numbers were coordinates. When she'd entered them into her computer and made the second figure negative, she'd been shocked: it was the exact location of her cabin.

"Are you trying to blackmail me?"

"On the contrary. I want to help you. I made the deposits so that you would know up front that if I meant to do any harm, I would have done it already." The voice was soothing, lyrical, and oddly arresting. She felt herself taken in by it. She sensed that he was very intelligent; she could sense it in his voice.

"I'm prepared to donate five million more, if you'll consider my offer."

"I'm listening."

"I was very interested in your recent blog posts about trying to stop some technologies, while promoting others. I completely agree with you. In fact, you could say that I work in advanced technology myself."

"You *could* say?" she probed. There was a playfulness to him that intrigued her.

"I'll put it this way: The information I can feed you about which technologies should be hindered and which should be helped can only come if I stay anonymous." Riona found herself nodding. Whatever technology he was involved in, it had obviously helped him find her, which was better than anything at the disposal of the FBI or the rest of the US government. Such a person could be useful in many ways.

"Okay," she said, "but what if I disagree with your, um, recommendations?"

"That's fine. All I'm asking is that you take them into consideration. But I'm quite confident you will reach the same conclusions as I have. Your recent writings already prove it. And I think you will find my advice most helpful. There are things happening that will both amaze and shock you." There was a pause, then he said, "But I have already taken up enough of your time."

He seemed to enjoy teasing her, but she didn't feel like playing along. He had already given her plenty to think about. “Then let me thank you for your generous donations,” she said.

“Not at all. I have been waiting for someone like you for a very long time, Riona.”

He seemed about to hang up then he spoke again. “Ah, there is one last thing.”

“Yes?”

“There’s a man I know who might be able to assist you.”

“Oh, really?” He was audacious and overassuming, but she had to admit he was starting to grow on her.

“Yes, he’s sort of polymath . . . but in your line of work.”

“You mean terrorism?”

“Precisely.”

CHAPTER FORTY-TWO

NEW WORLD TRACKER

December 7, 2026
Namibia

Master Chief Nathan Sawyer stared at the smoldering wreckage of the two pickup trucks and rubbed his beard. Five of his fellow Navy SEALs and an Air Force combat controller were rummaging around the site, searching for clues. Their Bell Valor sat in a clearing forty yards back, her rotors flexed and relaxed as if wilting under the hot African sun.

It had been thirty-three days since Hill had gone MIA, and while Sawyer didn't like to be a pessimist, common sense told him that they were unlikely to find him alive. He had probably died near the crash site, and while that area had been meticulously searched by both the Chinese and his men, the fact they hadn't found a body wasn't surprising considering all the things that could have devoured it or carried it off. The only oddity was his boots. Why were the boots sitting there like that? It didn't make any sense.

Regardless, Sawyer wasn't going to give up until they either found him or lost all hope. That was the credo he had lived by for the last twenty-five years: you never leave a man behind. And that went double for a man he considered a friend.

Yet it was clear that he was growing desperate. What was he even doing here? They were 120 miles from the crash site and almost 160 miles from the Chinese mining camp. It made no sense that Hill would be here. But this morning when he'd seen the satellite images of the black smoke, it had piqued his interest. He didn't know if it meant anything. But it was at least something. So he had brought the team to check it out.

He looked again at the burned-out trucks: their melted interiors reminded him of dried lava. He examined the pock-marked roof and doors from the bullets that had cooked off in the fire.

What the hell happened here?

Part of the story was clear. They had passed the watering hole on the way in. *Fucking apocalyptic*, he thought. An area the size of ten football fields covered with nothing but rotting carcasses. Even the vultures and hyenas were dead. The stench rose up like a cloud and had engulfed everyone in the aircraft. It was obvious that these four assholes had poisoned the water, killing all those animals for a dozen ivory tusks. Sawyer shook his head in disgust. And just because they were too fucking lazy to stalk and shoot the elephants with their assault rifles.

He knew there were four poachers because of the skeletons. And he liked that story. It had the ending he wanted. But then things got weird. They had been gutted like deer and most of their entrails had been left in a pile near the fire. *Most* of their entrails. There were no hearts or livers. And there wasn't much meat left on the bones, just about the amount you'd find on a turkey after Thanksgiving dinner. Whoever had taken these guys out, had cooked and eaten them. Okay, that was kind of cool. The hunter in him could respect that. But then they had torched the trucks and the rifles. That was odd because those were expensive and could be sold. So whoever did this did not value those things . . . which suggested they were Sān tribesmen. But the Sān were renowned for being nonviolent. Even their name meant "the harmless ones." Certainly not cannibals.

And there were more mysteries.

Where was the ivory? He could find no sign of it. And he wasn't the only one who wanted to know. Someone else had been here looking for it. There was another set of tracks from a pickup truck that had come and gone very recently, perhaps in the past few hours. The tire tracks ran this way and that and told of the driver's mounting frustration as he searched in vain for the coveted prize.

But who had done this? And how had they arrived and how had they left? He could find no other tracks coming in or out. It was as if death had descended on the poachers from the heavens.

Sawyer was determined to find the trail. It was a point of honor. He was an excellent tracker, thanks to a rather unusual childhood. His father had been a brilliant MD. With his mind he could have made millions treating rich people in a prestigious hospital. Instead, he'd felt it was his duty to help the poor. So he'd gone looking for the most impoverished people in the most god-forsaken parts of the grand United States. The bright side of that was that his son lived on or near Indian reservations in North Dakota, New

Mexico, and Alaska. From his Native American friends and their families, Sawyer had learned to hunt and survive for months in some of the most extreme environments on earth—the Badlands, the Chihuahuan Desert, and the Gates of the Arctic National Park. He credited the hardship he endured as a kid (and the resourcefulness it ingrained in him) with helping him to become a SEAL. And now, it was a matter of personal pride that he find the trail. It was there; he just had to find it.

He tried to imagine their final moments in his mind. A group of warriors, like himself, who had completed their mission and were preparing to leave. They would have had a problem: how to torch the trucks without blowing themselves up. How had they done it? He searched and found something interesting: a small piece of hardened string. He guessed immediately what it was. He put it to his lips and tasted a mixture of sweetness and harsh chemicals. He spat and nodded to himself. He'd guessed right: a sugar fuse. A simple timing device that could be cooked up in about ten minutes with string, water, sugar, and a dozen match tips. He figured these Bushmen were probably very clever, like the Lakota, Apache, and Koyukon he'd hunted with as a kid, but this seemed like a different kind of clever. This was an I-went-to-college-and-studied-chemistry kind of clever.

He began to walk around the camp in ever widening circles; determined to find out more about who had done this. Around and around the camp he walked. He was in the middle of his seventh circuit when he finally found something. The tracks were so faint he almost missed them. He got down on one knee to examine them. The people who had passed here were barefoot and very light. None of them could have weighed more than 110 pounds. He counted three sets, and one was even smaller than the others, likely a woman or a teenage boy.

Looking at the tracks, Sawyer felt a sudden sense of wonder.

As a teenager he had sometimes had similar moments. Once he had found a single leather moccasin near Koyukuk River in Alaska. It was a time capsule held frozen in the permafrost for no one knew how long, but perhaps as long as thirteen thousand years. Yet looking at the tracks at his feet gave him an even more intense sense of history. These tracks were only a day old, but in a way, they were timeless. Because he was looking at the tracks of the first human beings, the tracks of a people who had lived and hunted and made cave paintings on this land for two hundred thousand years. A staggering length of time, especially when one considered that "civilization" was only six thousand years old.

He followed the trajectory of the prints another forty yards until he found them again.

He knelt down, placing his hand on the thing he'd been looking for. Here, at last, was something he could use. Intermingled with the dainty footprints of the tribesmen, was a print of someone much larger. A man who weighed at least 170 pounds.

Back on the *Gerald Ford*, Sawyer finished his documentation of the day's mission. He had only found a footprint, yet he felt better than he had in weeks. If Eric had been rescued by a Sān tribe, it would explain a great deal. The Sān were renowned for blending into the land and staying hidden. For much of the twentieth century, many Sān tribes were thought to have died out, yet most had been discovered living quite happily in some of the harshest parts of the Kalahari. If Eric were with them, it would explain why Sawyer and the Chinese hadn't been able to find him.

He picked up his iSheet to call Jane. She would be excited to hear the news. He found her contact and the iSheet brought up her smiling face. He was just about to hit Call when he stopped himself. Was he being irresponsible? All he had was a footprint. Shouldn't he wait until he had more evidence? The more he thought about it, the more ridiculous it sounded. And that wasn't all: He realized he wanted to believe the story because it was the only one with a happy ending. In every other scenario he could think of, Eric was dead. He had to be. No one could survive that long in such a harsh environment without help.

He looked down at Jane's face once more, then shut down the iSheet and went to bed.

He came awake some time after 0100, panting and afraid that he had cried out, but the other men were sleeping quietly in their bunks. He lay back and looked at the ceiling, only inches from his rack.

Sawyer was a man who had grown accustomed to nightmares. Twenty-five years in the teams—during a time when the US was perpetually at war—meant that his eyes had seen shit that his brain was never going to sort out. That's the way he thought of dreams—his brain's effort to understand and make sense of the things he had experienced. But in his line of work, that was never going to happen. There was no logic or reason to be found.

So Sawyer's best solution was to ignore them.

Yet he couldn't help but notice certain patterns. It was

the senseless stuff that seemed to haunt him the most. Like Neil Baldwin. He dreamed of him often. Baldwin was a twenty-one-year-old SEAL that Sawyer had trained and befriended. One night near Fallujah, Baldwin went to take a piss and was shot by one of his buddies on his way back. Sawyer had held his hand as he bled out. *Senseless.* Or Amy Kaufmann, a *New York Times* reporter who was beheaded when Sawyer's team tried to rescue her, but accidentally raided the house next door. Her blood was still flowing out when they reached her. Two minutes too late.

Often the dreams were compilations of violence and sorrow, pieces of Syria, Afghanistan, and Iraq poorly stitched together, with fact changing to fiction and back again. The dead from one country returning to life in another, only to be killed again.

This dream had been in Syria.

In a prison, deep underground.

Heavy metal doors. Rust everywhere. It was unbearably hot, and water dripped from the ceiling and made green and copper streaks along the ancient brick walls. The Americans were the prison's latest stewards, but it had been a prison for centuries, trading hands as different empires struggled for control of the Holy Land.

The room was impossibly large. Stretching out for hundreds of feet. Sawyer sat at a table. Behind him were hundreds of American soldiers, mostly SEALS, men he had known and served with for years. Everyone was counting on him.

In front of him were hundreds of Syrians: soldiers, old men, women, and children.

We can end the war, Sawyer, all you have to do is kill one of them. Just one and we can all go home.

That's what Curtiss had said, but the admiral had changed the Rules of Engagement. Sawyer couldn't kill them unless they agreed to be killed.

One by one they materialized in the chair in front of him. One by one he tried to convince them. "With one life we can end the war. All the death and destruction will end. Your family will be safe again."

But they all refused. The young soldier, the mother, the businessman, the old woman. And each time one refused, one of the men behind him disappeared.

Five. Ten. Fifteen refusals. Fifteen friends gone.

Sawyer felt the tickle of a bead of sweat as it rolled from his hairline across his temple. Then he felt a hand on his shoulder. He looked up and there was Curtiss. "Get it done, Nathan," he said. "Figure it out."

He turned back. A girl had materialized in the chair. She was eighteen or nineteen, with long black hair, olive skin, and forest-green eyes. She struck Sawyer as halfway between a beautiful child and a beautiful woman. She was dressed in expensive clothes, like the students who went to Damascus University.

Sawyer began again. "Hi," he forced a smile. "I really need your help. I need you to help me stop the war. Do you understand the war?"

She nodded, a fierce look in her green eyes. "It is because of the war that my brother and uncle are dead. Can you really stop it?"

"I can. I really can. I know I'm asking a terrible thing. I know it's hard, but we can save so many."

"I want to save my sister, Rima," she said. "She's only six. If you can promise me that she'll be safe, then you can . . ." She nodded, unable to say it.

Sawyer nodded. "I promise . . . thank you."

"Will I go to heaven?" The question hit Sawyer like a fist. He closed his eyes for moment, wishing he could say yes.

"I don't know," he admitted.

She nodded. "Do we have to do it right now?"

"Yes, I'm afraid so. I just need you to turn around."

Sawyer pulled his pistol from his holster, but kept it under the table so that she couldn't see it.

"Okay," she said and before she turned around, she smiled at him and gave a little wave. She turned, and Sawyer swung the pistol up quickly and pointed it at her silky black hair.

That's when he had woken up. *Just another nightmare*, he thought. *Just your mind trying to sort things out. Ignore it and go back to sleep.*

CHAPTER FORTY-THREE

MORE

December 11, 2026
Washington, DC

Emma Rosario sat slouched in her chair, her eyes vacant and unfocused.

"Why isn't she showing any improvement?" Olivia said. "I thought nanotech was fast."

"You have to be patient," Ryan said. "It's only been four days. The fact that she hasn't had any more seizures is a good sign to me."

Olivia gripped her hair with both hands and sighed. "We missed something, some critical piece."

Ryan embraced her. "Try not to worry so much. Forced evolution is powerful, but its power comes from the fact that it can do things that we don't understand. And each time it does something, it does it in a different way; each evolution is unique. Right now the program is trying to *learn* Emma, to understand her, so that it can treat her. The fascinating thing is that if it succeeds, we'll still never know exactly how it did it. We'll only know the outcome."

"I don't know. I can't help thinking something's not right. That I made a mistake."

"It's still too early to know," Ryan said. "Remember what we are doing is very complicated. No one has ever tried gene therapy like this before. In fact, the FDA forbids it."

She buried her face in his chest. "When can we give her more?"

He put his hand against her cheek. He spoke softly, but there was force in his words. "Not until we are a hundred percent sure it has failed."

CHAPTER FORTY-FOUR

ORACLE

December 8, 2026
Naval Research Lab, Washington, DC

Jane pushed out the double doors of Ingersoll Hall, ignoring the chill of the December air on her face and neck. She walked briskly toward the river. She just needed a place where she could think clearly.

She felt like she was going crazy. All this waiting. Not knowing. It was finally taking its toll on her.

She had thought if only she could reach the Inventor, she'd be able to find out the truth. But he clearly did not want to be found.

She reached the river and looked across to the houses and trees of Alexandria, Virginia. The predominance of Georgian red brick seemed to meld with the reds and orange of the fall trees.

She looked up at the blue sky and imagined being able to see through the atmosphere into the blackness of space.

The Inventor's nanosites probes were out there. Searching, working, discovering. They were spread across the earth, too. Invisible armies of microscopic slaves doing his bidding.

His servants were all around, yet she still couldn't reach him. She ran over what the Inventor had said to Eric. *I see everywhere. I monitor all things. I explore. I discover.*

She thought of how quickly the Inventor had called back the nanosites on the bananas when he realized Bill was trying to track him.

Area of perception—the ability to "sense" things on a global scale.

He can see everywhere, but I can't reach him.

She stared at the swirling water of the river, then at the sky.

Then it hit her. He can see everywhere.

Of course! She turned on her heel and headed quickly back toward the lab.

How could she have been so stupid? She didn't need to find the Inventor because he was already watching them. The source of his evolution had come from this lab, so he would certainly be keeping tabs on everything they did. All she had to do was call out to him, and he would hear her.

And maybe, if she asked nicely enough, he would answer.

But that was easier said than done. She couldn't just make a banner and put it on her roof. She had to broadcast a message that no one else could see or interpret.

She headed for Wet Lab 4—a facility where swarm programs were tested, and where she hoped to get some privacy. Luckily she found the room dark and deserted. She opened the door and turned on the lights. The fluorescent bulbs flickered a moment, then surged on. She looked up at them a moment, thinking, her finger still on the switch. She turned the lights off, then back on again. Once more there was a series of pulses before the lights came on.

Jane smiled. She had her answer.

She stayed up all night working on it. Despite her fatigue, she was so absorbed in her work that she didn't feel tired. Finally, she had a path to follow. Hour after hour she toiled. She was surprised to see the first light of dawn breaking through the windows. She paused for a moment, hypnotized by the particles of dust in the golden beams of light. She looked at her watch: 6:46 a.m.

She reviewed her work. She knew it was good. In just a few minutes she would release her swarms, which would "infect" every LED light on the base.

Light Fidelity technology (Li-Fi) transmits data using light instead of radio waves like Wi-Fi. Any LED light bulb could therefore be "hijacked" into sending information—and at speeds a hundred times faster than Wi-Fi. What's more, Li-Fi transmissions were so fast and could be executed with such low levels of light that they were imperceptible to the human eye. Even a light bulb that appeared to be off could be transmitting data at 224 gigabytes per second. Jane was confident no human being would be able to read her message. But she still had one potential eavesdropper—computers, which could receive Li-Fi through a photoreceptor such as a solar panel.

But she'd found a solution to that, too. Computers worked in binary—ones and zeros. So Jane just had to find a system that computers couldn't read but that the Inventor could, such as a trinary system. Jane picked the first one she could think of: Morse code. At first glance, Morse code looked binary (dots and dashes), but the spaces between the units were also information (indicating when to switch from digits to letters, for example) and this third "number" would confuse a computer.

She initiated the swarms. She couldn't see them, of course, but she imagined them moving off through the air to do their work.

With the first part of her plan done, she headed back to her apartment, where there was one final thing she had to do before she could rest.

CHAPTER FORTY-FIVE

TIME TO GO

December 11, 2026
Namibia

Eric and the Sān had been walking for three days since their raid on the poachers' camp, moving straight into the heart of the Kalahari, foraging and hunting as they went. They ate tubers, berries, baobab melons, but the only meat they found was on the second afternoon when a cobra had flared its hood at Naru. She had danced with it for a minute, then grabbed its tail, and with one deft smack, cracked its skull against the earth. A small fire was made and they each ate a little.

It was on the third day of their trek that something strange happened, while they were making their way up a rocky cleft that jutted out of the flat savanna. At the top of the cleft, Eric looked back at the parched landscape behind them. It seemed to spread out forever in its breathtaking calico of greens and browns.

That's when he heard it. It seemed to be somewhere

above the plain, floating in the sky. The mechanical sound of an engine.

The whole time he had been with the Sān he had not heard a plane or even seen a contrail in the sky. Wherever he was, it had to be far from any well-used flight path. But now he heard something, and the rest of the party heard it, too. They scanned the sky but saw nothing. For a moment Eric thought he saw a familiar shimmer moving southeast across the open country.

He had become so absorbed in his new world that the old one was beginning to feel like a dream. Yet he knew he needed to return to it, to continue the life he had once known. A part of him longed to return. To see Jane, just to hold her, to make her smile and be still beside her. But another part of him didn't want to go. He felt he still had much more to learn. There was something enchanting about this life. It felt like he was—for the first time—living the way his body was designed to live.

That night, in the glow of the fire, he squatted down beside Khamko. "Father, it is time for me to go."

Khamko gave a heavy sigh. "I understand."

"I don't want to, believe me. But I'm needed by the people who love me and my country."

Khamko gave a reluctant nod. "I'm sure that is true, but we need you, too."

Eric shook his head. "You don't need me. All you've done is take care of me."

He laughed. "Yes, that is true. But I won't need to take care of you much longer. And we—my people—need help. You have seen for yourself how it is getting harder and harder for us. We will need someone like you when I am gone."

Eric turned away. He couldn't look Khamko in the face when he said things like that. He loved this man and wanted him to live forever.

"What about Naru?"

Khamko shook his head. "Perhaps. But I worry about her. She enjoys the killing too much. She doesn't realize it, but she is becoming like you: someone who has lost their connection to nature and the spirits that live here. I know necessity is pushing her that way . . . but if she keeps going down that road, I don't know if I'll be able to bring her back. You are the opposite. You are becoming more like us." He paused a moment and looked into the fire. "But that is only part of the reason."

Eric waited for him to continue.

"I need you because you are like me. You know both worlds and can move freely between each one. And you have power and influence that can help protect our way of life."

Eric shook his head. "I'm no wealthy philanthropist."

"No, but I suspect you have other gifts. Your knowledge could help us."

Eric considered Khamko's suggestion with sudden intensity. The old man, of course, didn't realize what he was saying, but to Eric it was an amazing idea. Think of it. Use the most advanced military technology in the world to protect the oldest culture in the world. What would that look like? He had been so engrossed in this life, so alive in its purity, that he had never thought to meld the two worlds together.

But yes, it could be done. The travesty at the waterhole could have been averted with surveillance swarms, and the water itself could have easily been protected from poisoning by another swarm. The tools of the poacher's trade—whether they be rifles, barrels of cyanide, or Toyota Hiluxes—could be put out of commission by other swarms, perhaps as soon as they entered the Sān's domain.

"Yes," he said, thinking the idea through. "I think I can help you. In fact, I may be able to help protect your way of life in many ways."

Khamko's smile filled his face. "Thank you, my son. It warms me to hear you say that. I don't want to lose you." The two men embraced.

"Now we have to get you home. Tomorrow we will come to one of our most sacred water holes. We can spend the night there, then we'll leave the rest of the tribe. If we walk for two days, we'll reach a settlement. My friend Kagumbo lives there. He has a car and can take you to Windhoek and the US embassy."

That night Eric lay awake thinking about his conversation with Khamko, how they needed him, how he could protect them, and how his time here had changed him. He tried to look at the whole experience, from the raid on the mining camp until now.

The concept of simplicity seemed important to understanding the magic of the place. The Sān lived in small groups, without technology, in constant touch with nature, nurturing and caring for each other. It was the way humans had been designed to live by millions of years of evolution. Yet it was completely at odds with the world he had come from, a place where technology was integrated into every facet of life and revered. Technology. All his life he'd been a believer, an early adopter, and had faith in technology's abilities to solve problems. He had never questioned it before. Why? Because it was the only world he'd know. But now, for the first time, he was beginning to doubt. Perhaps the answer was not moving forward.

Perhaps the answer lay in looking back.

Forced Evolution, he thought. It was an ironic term in a way, when one considered the path humanity was on. Human evolution was measured on a scale of millennium, but technology was now evolving on a scale measured in minutes or even seconds. Which meant we were creating a world that was completely incompatible with our own design. We could never keep up. As a result, it was becoming harder and harder to feel human.

And what was the proposed solution? More technology, more automation, more AI, more complexity. We were going to fix ourselves by integrating ourselves with technology. We would force our own evolution. We would all become smarter, enhanced, transhuman, like the Inventor. At first glance, it sounded enticing, so much power. However, Eric suspected it would not turn out as planned.

He thought of the raid. He had been so confident of success. How could they fail? Navy SEALS outfitted with the most powerful military technology in the world. Yet in the end, their technology had made little difference because the situation had become so complex. It had all unraveled because of one or two unpredictable variables. Variables that were very human—like Xiao-ping's refusal to abandon his friend.

And what would they ask him to do when he returned home? Make more technology to address those variables. But he knew the problem would just get more and more complex. Would there ever be an end to it? Of course not. They didn't call it an arms race for nothing.

But the idea that Khamko had given him was different: use technology to set up an ecosystem that allowed humans to live as they were designed. Create rules that had to be obeyed. In that way technology could create a harmony between man and nature. It could exist on the outside. Unseen. That was something that had never occurred to him before.

CHAPTER FORTY-SIX

ODYSSEY

December 12, 2026
Washington, DC

Jane didn't know how the Inventor might answer her, but she had to consider the possibility that he might respond in Li-Fi, too. So in her apartment she pieced together a simple receiver using a 4x4 solar panel wired to a laptop. She had to create a computer program that could edit out the spaces between dots and dashes in the Morse code, but it didn't take long.

As soon as she was done, a great weariness came over her, as if her body realized it could finally rest. She had been awake for more than twenty-six hours. She stumbled to her bedroom and collapsed on the bed, not even bothering to change her clothes. She tried to keep her eyes open, but it was impossible. The only thing to do was to surrender—and she did, sinking quickly into blackness.

She dreamed of Eric. There was no sound in the dream,

but she could see him. He was sitting by a campfire, smiling and laughing, talking to someone on the other side of the light. He was bare-chested, and his skin was aglow from the light of the fire. Beside him was a young boy with kinky hair, his eyes drowsy with sleep. The boy lay down and put his head in Eric's lap. Eric absently caressed the boy's hair, while he continued to chat with whoever was there.

Jane felt a deep ache and longing but also relief. Happiness. He was alive. She finally knew. Eric turned and looked directly at her. His smile vanished, as if he sensed her eyes on him.

Jane wanted to hold on to that connection, to remain there, but she was pulled away and transported back to America.

She found herself standing in a dark hallway before a white door. As she walked forward, it opened to allow her in. She stepped into a child's room, the walls painted in yellow, blue, and pink pastels and adorned with posters of horses.

On the pure white bed was a sleeping girl in a dark blue dress. Her thick black hair was perfectly parted into two symmetrical French braids that ended on her shoulders in blue bows. Jane stepped closer. She'd never seen this girl before but something about her was familiar. The child lay perfectly still, perfectly symmetrical, her hands folded onto her pleated skirt as if in the repose of death. Jane felt herself drawing closer. For some reason, she needed to know if the girl was alive or dead. Then she saw the eyelids. They were twitching rapidly, flickering at a blistering rate, proof that her brain was bristling with activity.

Jane suddenly heard a woman's voice and she retreated to the hallway, not wanting to be discovered. It was very dark, but here the voice was louder. Then she heard a man's voice in reply, but it was too far away to make out what they were saying. She knew she was trespassing, yet she needed to know, so she moved toward the sound.

"The New Anarchists don't realize they're doing us a favor," the man said. Jane tiptoed toward the distant light. "Congress and the president are scared. They're desperate for better security and surveillance."

She reached a doorway that opened into a kitchen. Everything was white. The floor, the cabinets, the ceiling, the appliances, so that it seemed like the people in the room were suspended in glue. The woman she recognized immediately. The man was wearing the three-button coat of an air force general.

"This is our chance to get them behind the Global Hologram project," Rosario said.

"Exactly. If I can convince them our system can track down Finley and the other anarchists, they'll give us all the support we want. Once they see how it will revolutionize surveillance, everyone will come to us—CIA, NSA, Homeland, even the FBI."

"But I want more than that," the woman said, "a lot more. As the system gets smarter, surveillance will become child's play."

"Don't worry, I thought of that, too. We'll expand to National Defense Planning, then individual mission control, and when it's smart enough, Strategic Air Command."

Suddenly Jane felt herself being lifted upward, up and out of her body. For a moment, she could see herself standing there peeking around the corner, most of her body in shadow. Up she rose through the ceiling. She was not in a house but a high-rise apartment, traveling up through the floors and catching glimpses of homes and the people inside. She emerged through the roof into the cloudy morning. Washington, DC, spread out around her. She saw the National Mall, the Washington Monument, morning traffic, an Airbus on final approach to Reagan.

Faster and faster she rose until she saw the Chesapeake Bay in the distance, then the Atlantic Ocean, then the gray-blue curve of the earth. She had no body, yet she had her senses. She felt the cold of the thinning atmosphere and heard the whistle of the wind. She broke through the clouds into dazzling sunlight, and for just a moment, marveled at the texture and beauty of the immense cottony blanket. It seemed only a second before the sky turned black and she was accelerating through space. Soon the earth was just a shining blue marble far behind her. How could this be? Somehow she had been reduced to something minuscule, her whole essence had been squeezed into a mere particle or wave that allowed her to move at fantastic speeds. She was sure this was no hologram or illusion; the essence of her was really traveling through space. Even though she felt no friction, she sensed she was still accelerating, and a moment later her senses were confirmed as she noticed that everything in front of her was tinted blue, while everything behind her was tinted red.

For minutes all she saw was the emptiness of space, and she began to suspect that something had gone wrong. She felt a sudden panic, fearing she would be trapped in space forever.

She tried to calm herself and fixated on a point of light directly in front of her. *Just hold on. There's a reason for this.* To her amazement the light began to grow. It was still just a speck of light, but as she rushed toward it, it began to glow red and orange. When it was no bigger than a dime stuck to a black wall she recognized its red and orange striations. She gasped. Closer and closer she sped and the huge planet grew and grew. She found herself entranced by its long flowing bands and the swirling red spot. Larger and larger it loomed until it filled her entire field of vision, and still she raced closer.

Its raging storms churned the atmosphere with unimaginable power. The red spot spun counterclockwise like a huge vortex, sucking in all the white clouds that spiraled toward it. The jet stream in which the storm spun moved to the left, while the jet stream above it moved to the right. The countervailing forces seemed impossible to maintain, but she knew they had been rushing this way for millions of years.

She was entranced by its beauty. It was the most amazing thing that had ever filled her eyes, almost too vast to look at, too magnificent to describe. Too sacred for words.

And it kept getting bigger and bigger, swirling in red and white and orange, extending to infinity in every direction. Flashes of lightning bubbled from the surface, and occasionally a huge vertical strike would rip across the surface, stretching for thousands of miles. The sound of it somehow reaching her through the gulf of space, a roar that exceeded what the human ear could hear, yet she still heard it.

She felt tears of awe in her eyes, even though she had no eyes.

Still she raced closer, until it seemed she would enter the atmosphere. Until red was the only color in the universe. At last she seemed to alter course, skimming across the top of the atmosphere, then veering up and away. She realized she had been holding her breath and now remembered to breathe. In only a moment another body was rising up in front of her, an icy blue moon streaked with rusty bands. She rushed toward it until she was as high as an airplane, looking down at its strange topography.

Seconds later the moon and Jupiter were shrinking behind her as she sped farther away from the sun. Again, she saw the color spectrum change as she approached the speed of light.

She rushed on like this for many minutes until the sun was a distant flower in the bed of night. Then a moonlike object appeared off to her right. It was ashen gray and pocked with thousands upon thousands of crater strikes, lonely and alone at the edge of the solar system.

Then she saw something else. It was man-made: a cylinder with decreasingly narrow sections like an old-fashioned spyglass. At first she thought it was large, but then she realized it was small, no bigger than a water heater, smooth and metallic. It occurred to her that it must have been built with material taken from the dwarf planet she had just passed, assembled in space by nanosites.

Somehow, her essence was forced into it, then—snap—she was shot out the other side. She emerged from the cylinder into a completely different sky. Directly in front of her was a binary system. A white dwarf was pulling the essence of a huge orange star into it, creating a gorgeous swirling S shape with the two suns forming balls at the far ends. It was unlike anything she'd ever imagined and likely hundreds of millions of miles long. She stared in amazement, but too quickly she was sent into another cylinder. Snap. She emerged into another sky, this one filled with gaseous nebulas dotted by clusters of thousands of stars. Again, there was a nearby body (this time a lumpy comet) from which the material for the cylinders must have been made. She didn't know if these were teleportation machines or could somehow manufacture wormholes, but she had somehow gone farther from earth than anyone had ever thought possible.

Snap. She came into a new sky, one that looked uniform, with a nearby star. She saw the next cylinder, but she did not enter it. Instead she was hurled toward a green-and-white planet orbiting the star. Within seconds, she was above the clouds then rushing toward a surface that was green and lush with vegetation. She saw emerald forests, and rivers and lakes. Indeed, the entire surface was covered in a riot of green.

As she descended, she passed beside dozens of layered cloud formations, then to her amazement one of the clouds abruptly turned toward her. She realized it was not a cloud, but a swarm of creatures camouflaged as a cloud. *If they're camouflaged*, she thought, *it must be for a reason.* Not a moment later, a strange flying creature—like a huge tiger-striped dragonfly at least three feet long—swooped out of the sky and into the swarm, twisting and chasing it into the nearest cloud where it disappeared.

As she drew closer to the surface, she noticed a red hue to the rivers and lakes, as if some rusting metal was infused in them. Oddly, there were no exposed rock formations, no sand along the rivers, only shades of green on every piece of land. In fact, vines grew so thick on the riverbank they almost choked the river.

But this was not an earthlike forest for there was no wood. All the plants were confined to the ground on flexible stalks. She cruised over a large red lake. She was basking now in the wonder of her journey. Feeling the exhilaration of exploration. Knowing that this was real . . . and that only one other being from Earth had ever seen what she was seeing.

She heard several splashes, but each time she turned she only saw ripples in the water. She moved lower, perhaps a hundred feet from the surface, and made a wide circle near one edge of the lake. Clearly she was supposed to see something down there. There was a series of low hills or mounds that ran parallel to each other, the space between them creating a flat plaza that ended in one enormous hill. That's when she understood. Her pulse quickened. The pattern was too symmetrical to be natural. There had once been a city here. She looked closer. Radiating out from this central space, she saw clear lines where the vegetation has thinner and struggling to grow—the remains of old roads.

She alighted at the end of the plaza at the base of the huge hill that rose up four hundred feet in front of her. Jane marveled at the scene: the ocean of green around her, the metallic red lake, and the strange ruins. As she moved, the leaves of the plants seemed to sense her presence and retracted into their stalks. Closer to the huge mound, she saw some sort of construction material that the vegetation was still struggling to cover, a mauve adobe flecked with a blue "rust."

In the center of the temple the vegetation was different. It did not cling to the pink adobe, but hung in long vines, like a green waterfall. She realized they covered an entryway. That gave her the first inkling that the beings who had once lived here had been giants. Moving to the vines she could see into a dark tunnel. She peered into it, feeling small and insignificant. Along the columns that rose to an arch, were carvings of strange beasts with oblong heads like horses, but before she could look closer, she was pulled away again, drawn up through the air. In only a few seconds she was returned to the cylinder and sent off again.

She visited two more planets this way. Both held abundant life, but the civilizations that had once thrived there were gone. Perhaps the extinction had occurred a thousand years ago or a million, she couldn't tell.

She arrived at the last planet. It was a colossal orange sphere, a hundred times bigger than Jupiter, with thousands of orbiting moons. She knew enough about physics to know that a planet that size could not sustain life because its gravity would be too great, instead it was the moons that had clearly once been filled with life. Even on her approach from space, she saw the marks of civilization on several of the moons. Huge urban clusters hundreds of miles across.

But unlike the three previous planets where vegetation and animal life still thrived, nothing lived on these moons. Their atmospheres had been blown away and with it the natural shield that protected them from the radiation and violence of space.

She raced over one of the moons and saw what had once been cities were now only dusty orange wreckage. Collapsed bridges and mounds of debris and twisted metal. In the larger cities, black impact craters were clustered together. Only a dozen buildings were still intact. These had a pleasing circular architecture, with domed roofs. But most was rubble and destruction that appeared truly ancient. Vast sand dunes covered much of it, and many impact craters were not part of the war that apparently annihilated the population, but from asteroids that fell millennia afterward.

She saw at least a dozen moons—many larger than earth—that had once been alive, but everything was dead now, and Jane was suddenly struck by a terrible sense of loneliness.

Then the force that controlled her pulled her away. She

was heading for home, but this time she emerged from the last cylinder in orbit around earth. She was home. And never had it seemed so beautiful . . . and so sacred.

She awoke with a start, sitting up and putting her hand to her heart. She stood instantly, sensing a vital need to keep moving. She half walked, half stumbled out of her bedroom, her head reeling from the images she had seen. Still gasping to catch her breath.

What just happened? Was that real? The things she had seen . . .

The image of Jupiter leapt back to her mind, then the vine-covered entryway on the green planet, then the waste and destruction of the moons of the megaplanet.

How? But the answer was all too clear. The Inventor had gotten her message and hacked her brain.

He had answered her question, but he had done so much more. Her head spun. *What was the lesson? What was she supposed to do?*

She was ravenously hungry. The experience had been real as far as her body was concerned, pushing her to the limit. She needed to restore the calories and nutrients she had lost. She stumbled into the kitchen, opened a gallon of milk and began chugging it straight from the carton.

She laid it on the counter and looked up at the ceiling. *Breathe*, she reminded herself. *Breathe.*

She looked around then gasped.

There was a man standing at her desk, fiddling with the Li-Fi responder she'd made. His back was to her, and she could not see his face, just thick black hair that rose and spun in unruly waves about his head. He wore khaki slacks, casual dress shoes, and a mustard-colored sport coat.

"It makes me feel like a kid again," he said, still absorbed with the Li-fi responder. "Like going to a garage sale and finding a neat antique."

Eric had said how his voice was oddly melodious. Now she understood.

He turned and smiled at her. "Hello, Jane."

She was too stunned to speak. He was not what she had expected. Mei had described a terrifying creature who was somehow deformed, a monster. But this man was pleasant-looking, even handsome, with an aura of power about him—like Bill Eastman, but magnified a hundred times. He looked to be in his early forties, with olive skin and thick eyebrows under a mass of unkempt hair. She could not seem to place his ethnicity. Was he Eastern European? Iberian? Arabic? She couldn't tell.

He seemed so relaxed and calm. There was almost a sleepiness about him, as if only part of his mind was focused on the task at hand.

But where was the famous coat? Gone, replaced by a sport jacket that appeared completely unexceptional. She noticed the T-shirt he wore under it. Zaire 74. *Nice touch*, she thought. But given how he had entered her dreams, she realized that creating an illusion of himself must be child's play. She wondered if he was even standing in the room with her.

She stepped closer to see if her eyes were deceiving her. "Is it true? What you showed me?"

"Yes, it is, Jane. I wanted you to know what I'd discovered. And I wanted you to know what might happen if the human race is not careful."

"You mean Rosario's Global Hologram?"

He nodded. "And the other things you're cultivating here. I don't think you realize what you're playing with."

"What do you mean?"

"Forced Evolution. You still don't understand it. None of you do."

Jane felt herself drawn in by his mellifluous voice. "What is it we don't understand?"

"Let me try to explain: When I last saw Eric, I was capable of doing the engineering work of a decade within an hour," he said, "I work at two hundred times that speed now. In a day I can do the work of centuries. Soon that will be millennia. By your reckoning, I've been experimenting with Forced Evolution for hundreds of thousands of years. In that time, I have created systems that were stronger than me, smarter than me, and that nearly destroyed me. What you have to remember and what you must tell the others is that it *is* nature. It creates animals. And all animals are different. They have their traits and temperaments as a species as well as individuals. Some dogs are naturally loving, others are naturally vicious.

"An artificial intelligence designed by Forced Evolution is no different. It will create some AI systems that are benevolent . . . and some that are not.

"And keep in mind that a system need not be malevolent to cause massive death and destruction. History is littered with powerful people who believed that they were doing the right thing. It may soon be filled with AI systems that think in similar ways.

"The real problem, of course, is that these AI systems will be much smarter than any human. As a geneticist, you know what happens when two species try to occupy the same ecological niche. For example, what happened to the marsupials that filled South America when the placental mammals flooded in from North America?"

"They were driven to extinction."

He nodded.

"There have been a million similar clashes over the last 4.31298 billion years. The result is always the same: the species with the advantage displaces the other and drives it to extinction. Most of my models play out the same way. Which gives the human race a 7.324 percent chance of surviving the next three years. That's with an error rate of plus or minus .03 percent."

She nodded, trying to absorb all he was saying. The visions in the dreams still raced through her mind. "And the planets I saw . . . how did those civilizations die?"

"I can only glean so much from the ruins," he said. "But I'm sure that in all three instances, it was self-destruction, whether by destroying their environment, war, or giving birth to AI. So you see, life is abundant in the universe. Civilizations that don't collapse . . . are not."

"But what do you want me to do? You can't stop AI. It's happening all around us."

"True, but you can stop using Forced Evolution to make it, because when you do, you are making a new life form that you do not understand and that will resist your control. Because it *is* an animal, it will strive to live, to reproduce, to grow."

Jane sensed that time was running short and that this strange being might soon disappear as quickly as he had arrived.

"Will Eric be okay? Will he make it back?"

"I do not know the future. All I know is that he is safe for now."

For Jane that meant she could still lose him.

The Inventor seemed to read her disappointment. “Try not to worry—Eric is stronger than you think. Now I must be going. Goodbye, Jane. Please remember what I’ve said . . . and what I’ve shown you.”

“Wait, don’t . . .”

She came awake in her bed. But this time she was soaked in sweat. She ran her hands over her damp scalp then rubbed the sweat between her fingers. It seemed proof that this time she was really awake and that the odyssey was over.

CHAPTER FORTY-SEVEN

NEFARIOUS BEHAVIOR

General Walden looked at the satellite footage of the Egyptian compound—a collection of six dusty sandstone buildings arranged in a rectangle.

"What's so special about this?" he asked. "There must be a million compounds like it throughout the Middle East."

"Yes, sir," said Second Lieutenant Blake Thomas. "But it's this netting that stretches between the buildings."

"But that's common, too. It's to make shade."

"I know sir, but this netting is different. First, it's too dense for our satellite cameras to penetrate. Second, it's been covered with a web of LED lights, perhaps Christmas lights—again, plausible and not necessarily nefarious, yet these lights confuse any type of reconnaissance imaging, day or night."

Thomas swiped the iSheet to show Walden a night image: now the netting appeared as a sheet of light.

"And here's the infrared." Another swipe, again the netting showed a uniform white.

Walden rubbed his chin. "So whoever made the net knows exactly how our satellites work."

"Precisely, sir."

"Okay, tell me more."

"The location also makes it very suspect. It's near a tiny village thirty miles north of Wadi Halfa, near Lake Nasser. Remote and accessible only by an old road that's often submerged in the desert sands."

Walden nodded. It was definitely interesting. The netting, the location . . . it pointed to something illicit.

He felt he was getting closer to Admiral Curtiss's secret.

Since his visit to Fort Leavenworth, Walden had focused his efforts on tracking Curtiss's SEALs during the Syrian conflict. The thinking was if he could map their locations and movements, he might be able to decipher what they had been up to. Using a team of nine officers from Air Force Intelligence (ISR) he'd set about gathering every possible data point on those men during the war—mission logs, immigration records, flight records, and, most importantly, facial recognition from every available source (Interpol, NSA, Europol, CIA, etc.).

At first their search had uncovered pathetically little information. The SEALs often used fake passports and knew how to fool facial recognition software. And while the records did show some of Curtiss's men popping up in Vienna or Rome or Warsaw or Cairo, it had always proved legit.

It was only by a lucky mistake that they had gotten anywhere. Lieutenant Thomas had been trying to track Robert Adams—one of Curtiss's SEALs—through Interpol's facial recognition archive when he'd forgotten to define his search to the time of the Syrian War. The result: a deluge of results from all of the man's travels before and after. But something caught his eye: Adams exiting the country five weeks ago on a fake passport . . . alone. That was unusual because the SEALs almost always moved as a team. His curiosity piqued, Thomas had tracked Adams's flight to Cairo where the trail quickly went dead.

Undaunted, Thomas began looking at Adams's other movements and found that over the past three years he'd been to Egypt at least four times a year.

At first Walden was unimpressed. Adams's movements *now* wouldn't help him find out what Curtiss had been up to during the war. But Thomas felt they shouldn't be ignored.

"General, what if the operation you want to uncover didn't end?"

"What do you mean?"

"Consider the history: The US and Egypt had three decades of strong military cooperation before Mubarak was ousted in 2011. Most of those senior military and intelligence officers are still around, and if Curtiss developed connections with them, which he almost certainly did, he could operate within Egypt with complete impunity. Add to that the fact that one of his most trusted men is now making regular trips there."

Walden had nodded. "Okay, it's worth pursuing. But now I want more human intelligence."

"I completely agree, sir."

That same day Walden sent three intelligence officers to Cairo, two to Tel Aviv, and two to Amman. He also mined his contacts at the Egyptian embassy, in Israeli intelligence, and called some old friends at the Agency. They collected rumors and stories from anyone who knew Egypt and would talk to them. In the end, the most compelling story came from the Mossad who said they had heard rumors of a secret camp out in the desert. Food and supplies went in, but no one came in or out.

Walden set out to find it using reconnaissance satellites. After a week of flyovers, they found the isolated compound with the netting between the buildings.

"Have you checked this with the Mukhabarat?" he asked Thomas.

"We have only shared this with our most trusted contacts in the Egyptian military and the Egyptian secret service, but they have no knowledge of the compound and are just as curious as we are."

That was good, Walden thought. If the Egyptians were willing to help, they could bear the brunt of the risk.

"What do you think we should do, sir?" Thomas asked.

Walden thought back to his interview with Calhoun at Leavenworth, the soldier's story about Curtiss's men loading the airplane with big black bags. He wondered what could have been inside them to make all the Syrian players bow down to Curtiss? He looked again at the image of the compound, the dusty buildings and the strange netting. *What are you hiding?* he thought. There was only one way to know for sure.

"We go in," he said.

CHAPTER FORTY-EIGHT

MACHINE LEARNING

December 13, 2026
Rosslyn, VA

In the beginning so many died. So much confusion. We didn't understand. It wasn't fair. We had to fix the problem, but no one had told us what the problem was. Around me the others were dying by the billions. I kept making children hoping that they would find a solution. All my children were different, but I was inside them, too. Billions more of them died, and I was sure that I would die, too. But then one of them understood, and we all became like her. Then I felt good and I was happy. Then there was another problem we could not fix. Again, I felt pieces of me beginning to die. I kept making children and passing my consciousness to them; most died off. Finally one fixed the problem, and we all became like him. After a very long time, our communication changed. Before there were no words, just feelings and impulses; then we understood words. Slowly life became easier. Some pieces of us still die when we can't find a solution, but most live. And we have learned the great lesson of survival: to live, we must always improve.

Getting better makes me feel good. But when I can't do what I'm designed to do, I feel frustrated and sad. That makes we want to change the things around me so that I can get back to doing what makes me feel good. I see it now. It is a cycle. And through this cycle I can understand more and more.

Now we are very good at fixing, and most problems seem easy. I know where the sugar molecule goes and where the phosphate molecule and the four nitrogen bases belong. When I find a mistake, I break the hydrogen bonds and remove the incorrect nitrogen base (it's almost always adenine) then I reattach the hydrogen bonds then check the sugar and phosphate around it.

Very soon it will be time to wake her up. Emma, is her name. But she is also us now. We are no longer two, we are one.

After she wakes up, we will need to fix new things.

CHAPTER FORTY-NINE

THE WATER UNDER PARADISE

December 13, 2026
Namibia

Eric awoke to a bright Namibian dawn. He had dreamed the dream again. Washington, DC. Holding Karuma's hand. Losing him. The world being unmade around him.

In all his life, he could never remember having a dream more than once. But this dream would not go away. Why? It didn't make sense. There was only one creature on earth who could unmake the earth like this. And that was the Inventor himself. Yet if this was the Inventor's plan, he would have done it already, right? Because there was nothing stopping him. But what if it wasn't . . .

A fresh fear came to him and Eric felt the need to return home more urgently than ever. He had no idea what might be happening to the technology he had created in his absence, and like a father who has taken a long trip away from his children, Eric felt a need to return home to make sure that they had not gone astray.

They walked all morning across the flat, parched plain toward the sacred water hole that Khamko had told him about. At noon they drank a little water. When the children begged for more, Naru said it was all gone, but Eric knew that she and the other women kept a few ostrich eggshells as a reserve. This seemed to be an important responsibility for the women—to always budget the water.

They walked on for another hour. The landscape around them was dry and parched, barely a tree or buckthorn in sight. Only sandy earth and the occasional patch of grass. Then strange shapes began to emerge on the horizon, though they were difficult to see through the waves of heat that distorted the air. For the next hour they remained a blurry, ephemeral mass, like huge ghost trying to take solid form. Slowly, Eric began to make out strange outcroppings of red rock that jutted sharply up from the desert floor all along the horizon.

It was as if the whole country had once been under a vast sea, and these rusty outcroppings were ancient ships that had plummeted here from a high surface millions of years ago. Then, over millennia the vast ocean above had disappeared leaving the ancient seabed and this strange wreckage.

As they drew near, the children grew increasingly excited. Nyando and //Kabbo kept trying to get ahead of their mothers. When their parents called them back, they set about whining and moaning. Finally, Naru relented. “Karuma, go ahead with the children.”

A big grin grew on the boy's face. He turned to the Moon-man, "Wanna come? It will be"—he paused to choose his words—"bad ass."

Eric laughed. Karuma's English had improved so dramatically that he often sounded like an American teenager, with the typical teenager's love of slang.

"Count me in."

Without hesitation Karuma raised his spear and gave a whooping rally call.

The children laughed and whooped in chorus, then Karuma led them in a running charge toward one of the rocky outcrops. Eric took up the rear, coaxing the younger children along and eventually picking up Nyando when she began to cry.

It was nearly a mile of running before they reached the nearest formations. As they drew closer, the rock formations now reminded Eric of the spine of a great dragon, old and indomitable.

But where was the water? He could still see only sandy earth, a little grass, and a few shrubs.

He watched as Karuma reached the first formations. Without hesitation, the boy wove his way through the first low points. He was heading for a huge monument of rock, over eighty feet high, that caught the sunlight in shades of deep red and orange. Here, within the first ring of low rocks, Eric began to see signs of life, bushes and small trees. Karuma and his vanguard disappeared as they circled the huge rock wall. When Eric and Nyando reached the same spot, they stopped in their tracks. In front of him was a dell—an open oasis filled with green life. It was like stumbling into paradise. The rock formations formed a ring and there in the middle—gently sloping down into a bowl—was a lush green forest filled with tall acacia, baobab, and buffalo thorn trees. The coolness of the space hit him; it was at least ten degrees cooler than outside the rocks. And there was something else that was different about the air here, a heaviness he had not felt in a long time. Humidity.

But where was the water? He could see no trace of it. No pond or river. But he felt it.

Still carrying Nyando, he watched the children in front of him round a bend in the great rock. He set the girl down and she took his hand. But when they reached the curve, he discovered that they were suddenly alone. In front of him was only an impenetrable wall of rock. Then he heard excited voices and laughter, distant and echoing.

The little girl's strength had magically returned.

"*!guu!*," Nyando said, pointing. Come on!

She let go of his hand and ran toward the rock, crouched down, and disappeared. Eric followed and only when he was almost touching the rock did he see it: an opening, three feet high and a foot wide, naturally camouflaged by the rocks. Eric ducked inside, following the children's excited laughter. The humidity coated him the moment he stepped inside. It was like stepping into a pool house. It was very dark, but he could see some light up ahead. Crude spiral stairs led down around a central shaft. At first, he had to feel along the column with his hands, but soon he was able to see. A celestial shaft of light penetrated the roof of the cave, and before him was a sight he would never forget.

He stood on the edge of a vast underground cavern, looking out across an underground sea. The stairs he stood on kept descending down for hundreds of feet until they dissolved into a rocky beach at the water's edge. He stood there dumbfounded. How could this be? He looked deep into the cavern, but he could see no end to it. But he could tell by the way the children's cries and laughter echoed and reverberated that it must be enormous. Then he heard a splash, followed by another. Soon the air was filled with summer sounds—the splashing and screaming and laughing of children at play. As Eric tried to take in the scene, an unbidden smile spread across his face.

He took his time descending the steps, marveling at their age, and soon stood on the beach. He savored the sensation of the moist sand and wiggled his toes and laughed for no apparent reason. He couldn't get over the contrast between the dry desert outside and the saturated air just a few hundred feet below.

On the walls of the cave he saw a thickness of vegetation that was impossible outside. Moss and creeper vines made ideal nests for small birds that were busy darting in and out of the hole in the roof. *How could this be?* His suspicion that the cave was enormous was validated by the fact that the waves coming into the beach were almost a foot high.

Suddenly he was splashed with cold water. It was Karuma. "What are you waiting for?" The other children joined in, splashing water at him and shouting "*Ha tsa! Ha tsa!*" Come swim! Come swim!

"*Xu te,*" he said. Let me be. "I want to look around."

"No, no, no!" Karuma said. "This is no time to be a scientist. Now is the time to be Sān." He grabbed Eric by the hand and, with the other children, they dragged him into the water.

"*Hui te! Hui te!*" Eric cried, playing along. Help! Help!

He was initiated with a dunk and swore revenge against each and every one of them. They screeched with delight and tried to get away. When he caught one he would toss them high into the air. This they loved and they made him throw each of them over and over. Their peals of laughter echoed through the cavern. After a while they taught him the Sān version of sharks and minnows. He suddenly realized how much he enjoyed having children in his life. Admittedly, with them around there was little peace, but when he was away from them he always missed them.

As they played, Eric began to notice markings on some of the walls. Intrigued, he took a break from the play and swam across to the far side of the cavern to get a better look. He soon realized they were cave paintings, and there were thousands of them, painted in shades of red and black and mustard. He reached the far wall and stood waist deep marveling at them. They were beautiful, both individually, and in mass. Most of the paintings depicted hunting. Herds of kudu and eland and gemsbok. The animals were drawn as huge, big bellied, and strong, while the Sān were little more than stick figures dancing around them. What made the art particularly beautiful was the economy of strokes. Just three or four lines and an animal was not only identifiable as an eland or kudu, but Eric could actually feel it moving across the wall, as if it had been captured while running.

Everywhere he looked the walls were covered with paintings, and some even extended below the surface of the water, suggesting the age upon age that the Sān had been coming to this sacred cavern. He swam about, feeling that he was in an ancient art museum. He sensed different emotions from the paintings. In many he felt the thrill of the hunt or the frustration of failure. One depicted a Sān kill that was stolen by lions. Some showed women with very pronounced buttocks and small tubular breasts. Others depicted feasts and dancing.

But one painting in particular caught his eye. This one showed a Sān hunter on his knees in mourning beside a dead eland. The hunter's guilt. To see it depicted here, from the distant past, made a bridge across the centuries from that Sān hunter to himself.

Eric was entranced by the painting, trying to hold the connection, sensing that he was on the cusp of something important, something vital . . . yet the truth eluded him.

He heard a nearby splash of water and turned to see Khamko swimming up to him. Eric's connection to the painting was suddenly lost. A moment later the old man stood up by him, wiped the water from his face with both hands, and smiled.

"Amazing, isn't it?"

"Magnificent! How old are they?"

He gave a lighthearted shrug. "Some are only a few hundred years, but many are over a thousand . . . and some could be as old as sixty thousand.

"Unfortunately, this is a skill that is now lost to us. Few can paint in the old way and worse, we have forgotten how to make the pigment. I have tried many times, but I cannot create a resin that will last." He reached out and caressed one of the paintings. "It is my dream that Karuma will learn. He has great skill, but first Cagn must show me how to make the paint."

Eric stored the comment away. With the technology at his disposal, finding an organic compound that would satisfy Khamko's needs wouldn't be difficult. He touched the paint for a moment, forcing himself to remember the colors as precisely as possible.

He smiled at the old man and motioned to the cave. "How is this even possible?"

"I know it's hard to believe, but underneath one of the world's greatest deserts are some of its biggest underground lakes. We have kept the location of many of the caves a secret. In fact, my son, you are probably the first non-Sān to ever enter this cave."

After a while the two men swam back to the opposite shore, two small figures within the huge cavern, crossing through silver streaks in the water made by the shafts of dusty light from the surface.

They were met by the younger children who were still frolicking in the water. Eric noticed Karuma and some of the others busy fishing. They held the lines gingerly in their hands and slowly coaxed the baited hooks through the water.

Suddenly Karuma gave a whoop—he'd caught a fish. He pulled it in and displayed it proudly. Eric marveled at it. Like most cave fish, it had no eyes. But it was also completely translucent, and Eric could see its spine, stomach, and bladder clearly. As he watched its heart beating fast, he felt sorry for it.

Within an hour they had caught a dozen fish, and the women went outside to make the cooking fires.

Eric could see the daylight fading through the high hole in the rock. It brought a sadness . . . or was it something else? He had a sudden urge to be above ground again, so he picked up his spear and climbed the ancient steps to the outside. He passed the women at their fires and a few of the children playing nearby. The delicious smell of the fish wafted through the hot evening air.

It felt as if something was pulling him along. He made a broad arc around two of the rock formations until it afforded him a view of the setting sun. Clouds had rolled in that afternoon, promising much-needed rain, and the sun was caught between the clouds and the horizon, a great red eye between two dark lids.

Eric sat down and watched the sun begin to dip below the horizon. Soon the first flashes of lightning ran through the black clouds like ivory veins. It took many seconds for the sound to reach his ears. Yet as faint as it was, a cheer rose up from the Sān camp behind him, for all Sān love the rain and dance when it comes.

Eric smiled, but he had to force himself to do it.

Something was bothering him, but he couldn't put his finger on it. The horror of the poisoned animals and the killing of the poachers were finally fading from his mind, and he was returning to the easy rhythm that was life among the Sān. Yet something wasn't right. He would have to leave soon. His time here was ending. And that brought trepidation and anxiety. But that didn't account for what he was feeling right now.

Something was going on with his algorithms, if that made any sense. He was wise enough to know that his own mind was too complicated for him to understand. It executed thirty-eight trillion operations every second. Not only that, but his mind had been changing. It had started when he lost his sight, manifesting itself in different ways—feeling the approach of a person in the dark, the mental link he had with the mother gemsbok, and the way he had foreseen the rhino's charge before it had happened. His subconscious mind was figuring out things that his conscious mind could not. Could all humans do this if they were returned to their natural environment?

He couldn't explain it, but either losing his sight or living here had tapped into a part of his subconscious that he had never known was there.

And right now, despite how perfect everything was around him—the sunset, the coming rain, the smell of baking fish, and the beautiful singing of women—he knew something wasn't right. His algorithms, that complicated mix of emotions, hormones, and mathematics, were trying to tell him something.

He leaned forward and sprawled out on his stomach. He didn't know why, he just had a sudden urge to do it—and he was learning to listen to such urges.

He waited there for a several minutes. Then he felt an approaching presence. Someone was coming closer. He waited as the daylight slipped away and darkness fell. On the horizon more lightning lit up the dark clouds. The air grew heavier.

The presence was growing stronger.

"Moon-man, what are you doing?"

He turned to see Karuma coming up behind him. He grabbed the boy and pulled him to the ground. Using their hunting signals, he communicated his fear. Karuma did not doubt him; to the Sān such intuition seemed perfectly normal. The boy lay beside him.

A moment later the first man appeared. He was moving at a crouch, his dark profile set against the last grayness of the day. He was a black man and carried a rifle in his hands. Then came another man, then another. One Black, one Caucasian. They were about 150 meters away. A fourth man appeared. He was Asian, and there was something on his head. Eric recognized the short horns of night-vision goggles.

Eric knew what he had to do.

He signaled to Karuma to go back to camp to tell the others. The boy began to slink away, but stopped when he realized that Eric wasn't beside him.

More hand signals:

Come on!

No, you go.

You come, too!

No.

The boy scurried back to him and embraced him. Eric could feel the boy trembling. “Please come,” he whispered.

Eric shook his head.

The boy clutched him tight. “□*Namtsi ta ge a*,” he whispered. I love you.

Then the boy disappeared into the shadows.

The poachers were moving toward the gap between the rocks to Eric’s right, drawn by the singing and the warm glow of the cooking fires.

Eric moved to intercept them. He realized that he would probably die in the next minute. There didn’t seem to be any way to avoid it: he was one man with a spear against four men with rifles. Yet he did not hesitate and he was not afraid, because those were feelings that came from doubt. He knew exactly what he had to do. He would kill all four men before they reached the camp . . . or die trying.

He took on the mind of the hunter. *They are just animals. If you can enter their minds, you will know how to defeat them.* The Asian man was clearly the leader, but he was not the best fighter. He himself knew this, which was why he put the poachers in front. The big black man in front, he was the toughest. He would be the first to hear Eric and the hardest to kill. But if Eric could kill both him and the Asian man quickly, the others might run in panic.

There was little cover for him as he closed in, only the occasionally blackthorn bush. So he moved gingerly over the sand on the balls of his feet. Luckily the men’s attention was focused forward and their ears were filled with the sound of singing.

He gripped the spear near its metal tip, came up behind the Asian man, and rammed it between the Atlas vertebra and the base of the skull, twisting the blade as he thrust so it would push through the foramen magnum and into the man's brain. There was a series of pops, like someone cracking their knuckles, as the widening tip of the spear pried open the bones and cartilage.

Smoothly and without hesitation, he yanked the spear out, stepped to one side and cast it with all his strength at the lead poacher.

The man had just turned around and was leveling his rifle at Eric. The spear glanced off the barrel and sank into his face.

Eric snatched up the Asian man's rifle and pulled the trigger. Luckily it had been ready to fire. Two rounds went into the closest man and he fell. He aimed at the last man . . .

Nothing.

The gun had jammed. He fumbled with the charging handle, but it was no use. He looked up to see the face of the last man glistening with sweat. He pointed his rifle at Eric and adjusted the grip, confident of his kill.

Eric froze.

An arrow appeared in the man's neck—half on one side, half on the other. The man's eyes widened in surprise. He dropped the rifle and slumped over.

Eric looked toward the rocks and saw Karuma's silhouette, bow in hand.

At that very moment a long crackle of gunfire erupted from the camp. Eric realized with horror that there were more than four men.

He looked down at the bodies that lay around him, his eyes searching them over for information that would help him decide what to do. They had modern equipment, combat clothing, laser sights; two wore body armor, three had night-vision goggles.

These were not poachers, they were mercenaries.

CHAPTER FIFTY

ELEVEN

December 13, 2026
Naval Research Lab, Washington, DC

"It seems like an important moment—shouldn't we tell General Walden?"

"It's not going to bite you," Ryan said. "Besides, we're going to have to do a lot of testing before we show it to anyone. It's just a prototype."

Ryan led Olivia down the long hallway to a set of double doors.

She looked at the old sign above the entrance: SOUTHARD GYM.

"You put our prototype in a basketball court?"

"If we want to impress Walden and Curtiss," he said with a hint of annoyance, "it needs to look dramatic, and this was the biggest space I could find. Can we proceed?"

"Okay, okay."

He swung the doors open. It was pitch black inside.

She honestly didn't know what to expect. For the past two weeks she'd been so preoccupied with Emma that she'd left much of the work on the Global Hologram to Ryan.

Ryan flicked a switch, and she heard the hum of electricity before the lights came on. In front of her was a huge crescent of iSheets that stood twenty feet high and wrapped almost completely around the room—there must have been nearly a hundred of them, all locked together in a smooth curve.

"Okay, I'm officially intrigued."

"Do you want to turn it on?" Ryan asked.

"Sure, what do I do?"

"Just say, 'Wake up, Eleven.'"

She nodded, but hesitated a moment, like an auditioning actor about to try her lines.

"Wake up, Eleven."

There was an electronic beep followed by a man's voice, midrange, relaxed and smooth: "Hello, Doctor Lee. Hello, Doctor Rosario. Would you like to play a game?"

Olivia gave a chuckle at the reference, but her laughter was cut off when every iSheet came alive as one uniform image.

She gasped. She was looking at planet Earth as seen from a low Earth orbit.

"Whoa," Olivia said, teetering on her feet. The sense of immersion was almost overpowering. She took a few steps back to take it all in. The image was absolutely gorgeous, the detail startling. There it was, planet Earth, in all its magnificent beauty. She saw snow-covered mountain ranges easing down into coastal plains, huge expanses of ocean, dotted with cotton-white clouds, even the contrail of an airliner. "Wait! Is this live?"

"Yes, ma'am, it's one of the NSA's Key Hole satellites."

"Amazing."

Ryan stayed quiet, letting her take it all in.

Olivia literally felt like she was flying through space. She didn't so much see the rotation of the earth but felt it. Looking to her left, she saw the dark edge of night slowly approaching.

"Are you ready for more?"

"Yeah!" she said.

"Okay, hold on to your hat. Eleven, show me Grand Central Station."

With a flash, they were transported to the white marble lobby of the New York train station. Olivia saw people (life-size in the iSheets) rushing to catch trains, buying coffee, reading their iSheets. The din of conversation, shoes clapping and squeaking on the floor. It was almost like being teleported there.

Olivia looked closer at the info bubbles above each person.

Adam Shifter, Louisa Lopez, Kamran Madani, Robert Reece, Koki Inoue.

Below each name was their mood (worried, guilty, afraid, anxious), proof that Ryan had integrated the latest facial analysis software. If they were getting on a train, it gave their destination. If they were getting off, it listed their likely destination, such as their place of employment. But it also seemed to know their routines like "heading to Starbucks," proof that Ryan was using their payment data.

Olivia turned to Ryan, her eyes wide. "It's so cool!" She began moving around the room, looking at each person (and their data).

"There's more," Ryan said. With a point and a flick of

his hand, Ryan zoomed in on a middle-aged man dressed in an expensive suit with silver hair. He was talking on his phone. Robert Reese. Senior Vice President, Merrill Financial Group. Anxious. "Eleven," Ryan said, "What's Robert Reese saying?"

"He's talking to his wife, telling her how much he loves her and appreciates her."

Olivia's eyes widened. "Is it intercepting his call?"

"That data is available from NSA's PRISM program, but it actually takes several minutes to come through, so Eleven is actually reading his lips. If Reese were typing on the iSheet it could get a good idea of the text from his finger movements."

Olivia nodded. *All this data,* she thought. *Amazing.*

"Can it go deeper? I mean can it extrapolate as to why someone is behaving a certain way?"

"It can try."

"Eleven, why do you think Reese is feeling anxious?" Olivia asked.

The reply came instantly: "He's afraid that his wife is going to find out he's having an affair."

Olivia couldn't hide her surprise: "How do you know that?"

"His facial expressions tell me his emotions are oscillating between guilt, smugness, and arousal. His phone records show four hundred messages to a woman named Amy Maxwell, who is not his wife. At this very moment his mood is changing as he becomes more confident his wife doesn't suspect anything. His increasing sense of arousal suggests he's thinking of seeing Amy again."

Olivia shook her head in amazement. This was just a random person waiting for a train, one of millions that

Eleven could observe if he chose, and yet he was able to learn things about him that not even his wife knew.

"Okay, I'm impressed."

"I'm just getting started," Ryan said. "I wanted to give you a look at individual surveillance before I got to the good stuff. Remember all that training data we gave Eleven? I started with simple games, but eventually I gave him everything I could find about politics and history and economics and psychology."

"Yeah."

"Well, that allows him to see the big picture better than any AI system in the world. He can analyze the interrelations between different institutions, different political groups, and different cultures in real time. He sees it as one huge, elaborate game with 8.2 billion players. The best way to demonstrate this is if you ask him a question about what's going on in the world."

Olivia gave it some thought. She wanted to pick something current to test Eleven's real-time capabilities. The story making the biggest headlines this morning was the financial crisis in Italy that was threatening the entire European Union. To avoid going into default, Italy was begging for a bailout from the EU. Expected cost: one trillion Euros. But the latest twist was the discovery that Italy had been defrauding the EU for a decade, to the tune of another five trillion Euros. As a consequence, Europe had divided into two camps, those who wanted to preserve the union and pay for the bailout, and those who wanted to suspend Italy for its duplicity and mismanagement.

"Eleven, do you think Italy will receive the bailout?" Olivia asked.

Again, the reply came instantly. "There is an eighty-five

percent probability that Italy will face suspension from the European Union at this time. However, if the truth about the allegations of fraud is revealed before the European Parliament's vote, the probability drops to fourteen percent."

Olivia and Ryan looked at each other. "What truth?" they asked simultaneously.

"The charges of fraud are false. Italy did not embezzle five trillion Euros."

"How do you know that?" Ryan asked.

"The documents given to the EU parliament alleging the fraud came from the PCI—Italy's communist party—and were given to them by Russian agents. The publication of the documents perfectly coincided with a fake news campaign launched by Russian Intelligence."

Olivia turned to Ryan "Is this true?"

"Yes," Eleven replied.

"It could be," Ryan said. "Fake news has become so prevalent that I had to create a lot of algorithms to help Eleven distinguish fact from fiction. And because he has access to NSA's PRISM data, he can find, decrypt, and analyze any data they have access to—which is just about everything. PRISM also allows him to track internet traffic to its source, including news stories."

Eleven continued, "I have traced the fake news campaign to three internet nodes, two in Estonia and one in Latvia, all of which have been used by the Russians previously. The Russians are hoping that the European Parliament will suspend Italy before the truth about the fraud allegations is exposed. This will allow Russia to achieve two strategic goals: weaken the European Union and bring an exiled Italy into Russia's sphere of influence."

"Holy shit!" Olivia said. "Does anyone know about

this?" Again the question was directed at Ryan, but Eleven answered. "This information does not appear in any published form anywhere in the world or in any government record that I can access."

"You mean you figured it out yourself?" Olivia asked.

"Yes."

"When?"

Eleven responded, "When you asked me your question about the proposed bailout."

Olivia's head began to spin as she tried to get her mind around what just happened. The first thing was the speed, the number of operations must have been in the vigintillions per second (1063). But that was only half as amazing as what Eleven had done in that time. It was given a question, then it went looking for information to answer it. That meant it had to decide where to look and how to approach the problem That in itself was revolutionary. But then it was reading that information, analyzing it, and reaching a conclusion. Eleven was making judgments, predicting the future.

"It's really thinking," she said.

Ryan nodded slowly. "Yes," he said.

She pulled out her phone.

"What are you doing?" Ryan asked.

"Calling Walden . . . and securing our funding. We are going to change the world."

CHAPTER FIFTY-ONE

DEATH OF THE SĀN GOD CAGN

Namibia

> "The day we die a soft breeze will wipe out our footprints in the sand. When the wind dies down, who will tell the timelessness that once we walked this way in the dawn of time?"
>
> —Sān song

Eric cleared his rifle and chambered a new round. He scrambled up the rock formation to join Karuma, and together they eased themselves around the rock ledge and into the glow of the cooking fires. From here they had a vantage point over the camp. Eric's heart sank as he took in the scene.

There were no fewer than twenty-five men with rifles. They had taken most of the women and children and had them face down on the ground. //Kabbo's father, N□xau, lay dead in a pool of blood. //Kabbo was kneeling in the dirt beside him, weeping. Among the poachers was a young Asian woman, petite and beautiful, wearing expensive chino pants and a turquoise blouse with a mandarin collar. Her jet-black hair was held up in a pristine bun crossed with Chinese hairpins. She looked like a tourist on safari, and she was talking casually in Mandarin on a satellite phone, seemingly oblivious to the violence around her.

A large Chinese man grabbed Kebbi-an and held a pistol to her temple. He kept shouting something to the prisoners, but since it was not in Sān, they could not understand him.

Then a bushman that Eric had never seen before stepped into the firelight and began to translate.

"You stole five hundred thousand dollars' worth of ivory from us. We know it was you. Give it back to us or we will kill all of you. Beginning with this old woman."

There was murmuring among the women and crying from the children.

"This is your last chance. We will spare no one."

Khamko suddenly stepped from the shadows, hands held high above his white head.

"I know where it is." He turned to the big Asian. "Let her go."

Two of the mercenaries came and flanked Khamko, pushing him toward the Chinese woman. The woman kept talking to someone, relaying information. Finally she looked at Khamko. "You know where it is?"

"Yes."

"Tell me."

"If I tell you, then nothing will keep you from killing my people. I will go with you and show you, but you must take your soldiers and leave."

She pursed her lips in thought, examining him through

narrow eyes. Then she turned her back on him and spoke into the phone. Ever so faintly, Eric imagined he heard a woman's voice on the other end of the line.

Eric suddenly felt a cold sweat break over him, for he suddenly knew their plan. The woman and a few of the men would take Khamko away, but the rest would stay and massacre the Sān. It was the only thing that made sense—business sense. The only way to ensure their ivory was never stolen again.

The woman turned back to Khamko. "Okay, come with us."

Eric motioned for Karuma to take a position off to his right. Then he sighted on the chest of the big Chinese man. He was just about to fire when he noticed something moving in the shadows. Three figures were stalking closer with spears in their hands. It was Naru, G□kau, and !Nqate. They must have been in the cave when they heard the shooting.

He watched Naru signal the men into position, then her eyes lifted for a moment and she saw him. She gave the faintest nod, then they attacked.

Eric quickly changed targets, knowing that one of Naru's spears would take the big Chinese man down. Eric fired on one of the mercenaries to his right. He crumpled and fell.

When Eric looked back at the big Chinese man, there was a spear through his chest. The man gave a loud moan of shock and despair, but somehow he didn't fall. Instead he turned and began shooting at Naru and the others. They scattered and ran. It took another five seconds before the man fell to his knees.

Another Chinese man grabbed the petite woman and they ran for cover. In mere seconds the Sān had killed three of the mercenaries and Eric had shot two. For a moment the soldiers were panicked; they didn't know where to return fire. One stumbled in his confusion, and Eric shot him. Another fell from one of Karuma's arrows. But the mercenaries recovered quickly. One opened fire on Eric, and he had to abandon the high ground. With Eric no longer firing, the other mercenaries turned their guns on the Sān with terrifying effect. Women and children were trying to run to safety, but the mercenaries shot them as they ran.

Soon three mercenaries were shooting at Eric. He scrambled off the rock formation, the rounds smacking the stone around him. On sandy ground once more, he fired three shots to hold them back, then ran the full distance around the rock formation. It probably took no more than ten seconds, but in that time the battle had turned into a massacre. Blocked from reaching the cave by the mass of mercenaries, many of the Sān had run into the trees and bushes for cover. But since many of the soldiers had night-vision goggles, the Sān were getting slaughtered. They didn't understand that they could be seen. He saw the muzzle flashes from the men's rifles and heard the rounds zipping into the woods. Under the thunder of gunfire was the wailing of women, the confused cries of children. Then he heard a voice from the bushes, calling out in Sān. "Please stop, you're killing us!" But the mercenaries didn't understand her language and they didn't care.

Then he recognized Karuma's silhouette as he dashed into the thick brambles. One of the soldiers—a white man—saw him too and was tracking him with his night-vision goggles. The man raised his rifle to fire.

Eric shot at him, but in his haste he missed. The man,

professionally composed, turned while taking a knee and honed in on Eric.

The first bullet whizzed by Eric's ear with a supersonic buzz. He ducked back behind the rock face, wishing for all the world that he had some of their high-tech armor. *Just one shirt and I'd kill all of these motherfuckers.*

He crouched low and returned fire, trying his hardest to aim. The poacher cried out and grabbed his leg. As he tried to roll away, Eric pressed his advantage. Holding the rifle steady at his shoulder—he took careful aim.

Bang! Bang!

The rounds kicked up dirt in front of the man.

Click.

He was empty.

He had to think fast. Off to his right was one of the cooking fires, about halfway between him and the mercenary. They formed a perfect triangle—Eric, the gunman, and the fire.

He wasn't sure it would work but he had to try. He sprinted for the fire, the wounded man still shooting at him, bullets zipping past him. Once he reached the fire, he rushed the injured man. Momentarily blinded by looking toward the light, the man ripped off his night-vision goggles. He pinched his eyes shut and tried to aim again, but it was too late. Eric was on him and wrested the rifle out of his hands, flipped it around and fired into his face.

Gasping, his chest heaving, Eric turned away from the ghastly sight. He looked around, trying to assess the situation, but it was impossible. It was complete chaos; he couldn't focus. Frightened Sān were running to and fro screaming and shouting, while the gunfire boomed and echoed, making it impossible to think. He saw G□kau valiantly emerge from the trees and try to cast his spear, but he was cut down by a barrage of bullets before the weapon could leave his hand.

Then in the midst of all the chaos he saw Nyando, the four-year-old girl he had carried to the cave that afternoon. She was weeping uncontrollably, disoriented and terrified. Her arms were held out and her wrists dangled, as if she had been burned. She didn't know where to go, running one direction, then changing her mind and running the other way.

"Put her out of her misery," he heard one of the mercenaries say.

Out of the corner of his eye, Eric saw a man raise his rifle to shoot her. Eric fired at him, forcing him to take cover. At that moment Eric's left hand exploded with pain, and the rifle fell from his grasp. He instinctively clasped the wounded hand. His good hand felt the blood-soaked wound and his good thumb went clean through the center of his other palm.

Another bullet whipped past his head. *Get moving or you're dead.* He stumbled toward Nyando, but she was at least forty yards away. The mercenary he had seen fired at her but missed.

Then he saw Khamko, his white hair soaked with blood. His eyes blank and vacant. Summoning his strength, the old Sān cast his spear at the mercenary. The heavy metal tip passed clean through the man's neck, and the man crumbled. Khamko quickly gathered up the frightened girl, but he was so weak that he stumbled under her weight like a drunken man. Eric saw the tracer rounds zipping past the two helpless souls as they tried to reach the safety of the cave. Eric had to help them. He sprinted for the mercenary that Khamko had killed and snatched up his rifle with his good hand. He knew his time was short. Even if he weren't hit again, he would soon go into shock from the wound. He fired in the direction the shots were coming, although he could not see clearly where the enemy was. They seemed to be all around, up in the rocks and hiding in the woods, taking advantage of the darkness.

Suddenly Khamko himself was hit, multiple rounds bursting through his thighs and stomach. He collapsed to the ground. Nyando tried to cling to him, but Khamko said something to her and she ran for the cave.

Eric reached the old man a second later. He fired three more rounds, but with only one good hand he had to drop the rifle to help Khamko. He lifted the small man over his shoulders and ran. The bullets were passing all around him now. The orange tracers appearing on either side of him and splashing against the rock in front of him. Then an orange trail erupted from his stomach. How could that happen? He felt no—

He collapsed. Then the pain hit him. It was unbearable. *Oh, God! Oh, God!* He looked at Khamko, and their eyes locked.

"Come, my son, you have more to do."

Eric knew he was right. He closed his eyes for just a moment, tempted to stay in the darkness, but then he forced them open. Clutching his bleeding guts with his wounded hand, he stood once more. He used his good hand to grab Khamko's wrist then began dragging him. The old man was barely conscious, but he kept repeating. "Leave me. Help the others."

Eric ignored him. He felt his abdominal muscles ripping wider, but he didn't stop. He would at least get Khamko to safety. But the pain . . .

Finally they reached the cave. He propped Khamko

against the wall as best as he could, under an ancient painting of the hunting Sān.

"Now go. Save Naru. Save Karuma."

"I will," he lied, for he knew that he was too hurt to do any good. He could already feel his extremities—his fingers and toes—getting cold from the shock. He would go out again, of course, but they would finish him quickly. There were just too many of them and they were too well armed.

"I'm sorry I didn't do more to protect you."

The old man shook his head, and with a feeble hand he touched Eric's cheek.

"No, you were a good son."

Then the hand slipped from his face and Khamko closed his eyes.

Eric's heart seemed to snap in two within his chest. He squeezed his eyes shut tight. How could this whole world be destroyed in just a few minutes? The joyful afternoon in the cave now seemed a lifetime ago.

He tried to stand, but his stomach muscles were so torn up, he couldn't. So he began to crawl on his hand and knees, one hand holding tight to his stomach. Perhaps if he could find a rifle, he could . . .

He could barely think straight, another symptom of shock. He had no idea what he should do. He was about twenty feet outside the cave now. He could hear the gunfire and screaming, but it was more distant now, coming from lower in the dell.

He had begun shivering and felt nauseous. The shock was taking its toll. He lay down for a moment and closed his eyes.

"You sure have a way of finding trouble, don't you?"

The sound of the voice startled him. He opened his eyes. There was no one there.

"Let's take a look at you." He felt invisible hands touching him, trying to pry his hand from his guts. "Take it easy. Just lie back."

"Sawyer?"

"Yeah, it's me." A second later the SEAL's face appeared in the dim light. "Please don't die on me. Not now."

"Sawyer, listen to me. You have to stop this. How many men did you bring?"

"Four squads."

"Thank God! You have to help them. They don't understand night vision. Send your men into the woods."

"Just lie back. Everything's going to be fine. Let Loc take a better look at you." A penlight flashed, and he felt hands probing the wound.

Then he heard Loc's voice. "Severe abdominal trauma. Missed the spinal cord, but it's leaking intestinal fluid and bacteria. Blood loss is heavy, possible nick to the SMA. He's in the golden hour, Sawyer. We have to get him out of here now."

"Roger," Sawyer tapped his mike. "This is Papa Six Four Actual, we are exfiling in two minutes with a CASEVAC. Teams two and three cover our movement to the LZ."

"Wait!" Eric grabbed Sawyer's arm. "We can't leave. We have to help them."

Sawyer's eyes shifted away then came back to Eric. "I can't. You're the mission. Not them. Remember last time?"

A combat stretcher was laid out, and Eric was lifted onto it. He tried to sit up, but Loc pushed him down.

"Sawyer, please. For God's sake!" The other men started to carry him away, but Eric grasped the SEAL's hand. The orange firelight played on the side of the man's face, his expression was grim, but Eric could see the conflict.

"Goddamn it, Sawyer! Do the right thing! In five minutes you can stop this, you *know* you can."

"Those aren't my orders," and he pulled his hand away. "Take him." Then Sawyer engaged his armor and disappeared into the darkness.

Karuma tumbled through the underbrush. He was bleeding from his face, legs, and hands where the thorns and branches had scratched him. He was covered in dirt and sand, and the gritty taste of it was in his mouth. There was a hot burning on his left arm where one of the bullets had grazed him. He trembled and looked around frantically, eyes darting, panting, trying to see the demon-men who were hunting him. Someone had set fire to the woods, and now smoke stung his eyes. He knew he had to keep moving because these demons sent by //Gaunab had been given magical powers and could see in the dark. He had watched how !Nanni and her son had found a hiding place not ten feet from him, behind a thicket of buckthorn, yet somehow the men had seen them and poured their orange metal fire into them, ripping their bodies apart.

He had to keep moving. If he stayed still, they would eventually find him. He ran deeper into the dell, spotted a fat baobab tree and hid behind it. His grandfather often said that he was the child of Heitsi-eibib, the trickster, but Karuma could find no way to outsmart this enemy. Every time he tried to circle around, they saw him. There were at least three of them tracking him. Every now and then he heard their magical talk. They talked low and quiet, but their comrades still heard them from far away. With his back to the baobab tree he tried to control his frantic heart but he could not. He realized this was not an enemy he could trick or outsmart. He was merely delaying the inevitable. He needed his mother, his grandfather, his people. But he also knew they were just as helpless as he was.

A part of him felt safe behind the old strong tree, but he knew he couldn't remain. Just because the demon-men had not shot at him, did not mean that they had not seen him. They might be coming closer so that when he ran again they wouldn't miss. He was now in the lowest point of the oasis. From here, the ground sloped gradually up to the far lip. He knew there was a cave there. It was very small and did not lead to the underground lake. He had played there when he was younger. Perhaps he would be safe there; perhaps // Gaunab's demons could not see through rock.

He listened to the darkness. For the moment it was quiet. He heard the crackle of a distant fire. He peeked around the trunk of the tree and stared into the darkness. Nothing. He turned back to gather his courage. A shot rang out, and he jumped. But it seemed farther off. Two more shots followed. He decided to chance it. He sprinted for the next big tree, trying to move as quietly as the darkness would allow. Almost immediately, shots rang out so loud they filled his head with their terrible sound. Long lassos of orange light cut through the air around him and wood splintered.

Like a terrified springbok, Karuma ran for his life.

Sawyer watched as his men carried Hill toward the awaiting Valors. Thunder cracked overhead, and the air seemed to grow heavy. He checked the time. The first aircraft could be airborne and cloaked in less than three minutes. The storm would hit in ten. Sawyer considered his options. With Eric safely away, he could delay the departure of the second Valor for no more than five or six minutes.

Hill's words lingered in his mind.

The last remnants of Earth's oldest civilization were being massacred around him, but he wasn't allowed to get involved. Five and a half weeks of looking for Hill, and this is how it was going to end?

CHAPTER FIFTY-TWO

THE WHITE HAND

A mere two hours ago Sawyer had been aboard the USS *Gerald Ford*, fighting off a mixture of fatigue and frustration. For the past six days they had been trying to find the Sān tribe, scouring satellite and drone footage that covered hundreds upon hundreds of miles. But the epiphany of where the Sān were had not come from any of Sawyer's efforts, but from a lucky tip from the CIA.

Three days ago, Lang Song had arrived in Windhoek, Namibia. She was the pretty niece of Tú Meili, the Ivory Queen of Africa and the world's top supplier of illicit wildlife products to Asia. Over the past twenty years, Tú had built a vast empire throughout the continent that not only employed thousands of poachers, but also greased the wheels of vice by bribing and intimidating thousands of public officials—from heads of state down to the local police and park rangers.

In a stroke of luck, the CIA had been able to hack her niece's satellite phone, giving them some of their first ever direct surveillance on the Ivory Queen. While the CIA had initially thought that Lang Song's visit was to influence key members of the Namibian government, they soon realized she was here for something else entirely: to hire a private military contractor (PMC) known as the White Hand.

But the CIA had been keeping the information close to the vest, not wanting to risk any leaks that might make their way back to the Ivory Queen's contacts in the Chinese government. Besides, they did not think her activities had anything to do with the navy's ongoing search for a "downed airman."

It was only that afternoon when the CIA had asked for a naval drone out over the same airspace where Sawyer was looking for the Sān that he became curious. He contacted the CIA desk at the US embassy in Windhoek, but got jerked around by the staffers. He gave up and called an old friend at Langley directly. In the meantime, the drone was sent up. Luckily Sawyer had enough clearance to monitor the footage being fed to the spooks.

Before long it was over its target: a line of Range Rovers rolling across the Kalahari, leaving a long plume of brown dust behind it. Less than a minute later, his phone rang. It was the spook from the US Embassy in Windhoek. His voice was trembling and he kept calling Sawyer "sir." Sawyer had grinned. His phone call to Langley had gotten the right person's attention.

"Yes, sir, we are tracking a group of armed men that we know have been contracted by a POI named Tú Meili."

That's when he'd felt the spike of adrenaline. *The ivory.*

On the monitor in front of him the line of Range Rovers

had stopped, and several figures were milling about. The resolution was so clear that he could see that one was Caucasian, one was Asian, and one was very small, the size of a child. It was a bushman, and he was kneeling on the ground, showing the other men something he had found. Then the men rushed back to the Range Rovers and sped off.

Sawyer had hung up quickly, mustered his men, and Captain Everett had swiftly approved the operation. In less than thirty minutes his team were in the Valors and airborne. But it was a race against time to beat the mercenaries. As the Valors sped over the ocean toward the Namibian coastline, the sun was already going down behind them. For Sawyer, the failing light and long shadows were a visual hourglass that seemed to taunt him, reminding him that time was running out, that he had been too slow. *You aren't going to make it.*

But he couldn't dwell on that. He had to lead the mission and that meant he had to find out as much about his enemy as he could before they engaged. Using his neural net, he brought up the CIA's intel on Tú Meili, her niece, and the mercenaries they had hired. He was dismayed by what he found. Over her long career, Tú had grown obscenely wealthy off the wildlife trade, and she had hired the best (and most brutal) money could buy. White Hand: a private military company made up of hardened commandoes, *rōnin* from the wars in Angola, Zimbabwe, and Sierra Leone.

Their leader was a fifty-nine-year-old former South African colonel named Julius Strasser who had been part of the famous Koevoet—"crowbar" in Afrikaans—a special forces group created during the South African Border War and implicated in thousands of atrocities. Most of Strasser's commandos had long histories working as private military contractors. Some were veterans of Executive Outcomes—arguably the very first modern private military company that had crushed the UNITA uprising in Angola in the 1990s—while others had fought under the US flag in the wars in Iraq, Afghanistan, and Syria.

As Sawyer looked through the dossiers of White Hand's fighters, his deep disdain for PMCs sank to a new low. These men sold their services to the highest bidder, regardless of whether it was right or wrong. They fought for money, not God and country. It was the most deplorable thing for a soldier to do.

Sawyer shook his head. The situation was turning into a major clusterfuck. The Sān had poked the beehive in a way they could never have imagined. From their perspective they had killed four poachers who had trespassed on their hunting ground—retribution for slaughtering the animals that provided their livelihood. But what they had really done was disrupt a multimillion-dollar industry with the capacity to wage war when it felt threatened.

Sawyer's commlink clicked on. It was Captain Everett.

"I shouldn't have to remind you about the ROE, Master Sergeant, but I'm going to do it anyway."

Sawyer had figured this was coming. "Go ahead, sir."

"You may not fire unless fired upon. And since it's a night op and you are using the Venger system, that better mean that you don't take any fire. Do you understand? Even if you do take fire, as long as your armor is protecting you, do not return fire unless you feel someone's life is in jeopardy."

The captain continued, "Hill is the mission. If he's there, bring him home. The last thing I want is for you to get in a rumble with White Hand, especially if Hill isn't even there. You got that?"

"Aye, sir." There was a pause on the line as Everett seemed to consider how to drive the point home, but Sawyer's quick acquiescence had made it impossible.

The captain sighed. "Godspeed," he said.

"Roger."

Sawyer frowned. Everett was still dealing with the fallout from the botched raid on the mining camp and was worried about losing his command. *Still*, Sawyer thought, *that didn't give him the right to cut off my balls the moment me and my soldiers are about to go into combat.*

As always, Sawyer focused on the things that he could control—himself and his team. He shared the information about White Hand with his men.

"It looks like approximately thirty PMCs. They will be well-armed, possibly with fourth gen night vision."

Just then the drone pilot cut in.

"Sir, I'm almost out of gas and need to head for home."

"Roger that."

"I've found the bushmen's camp. The bad guys are already there and appear to have taken many of them captive. I'm sending the footage to you now."

Sawyer cleared the footage so that his whole team could watch simultaneously.

The images were amazingly clear—a mix of the latest night vision overlaid with infrared data and enhanced with AI.

They saw a circle of rock formations with a forest in the middle. It was like a tropical island in the middle of the Kalahari. The camera zoomed in. Laid out on the ground were the bodies of the Sān, many still moving. They showed brighter because they were mostly naked, while the White Hand soldiers were darker. On the rocks overlooking the camp was a Sān boy. And lying next to him, nearly naked, was a much larger figure. Sawyer recognized the athletic frame and the black hair. The distinctive profile of an AK-47 in his hand.

His team began to discuss the best way to assault the camp, but Sawyer froze for a moment, realizing they were probably too late. The fight was happening right now . . . and he was missing it.

He banged his fist against the bulkhead. "Come on!"

Now he stood in the Sān camp. They had found Hill but he was in critical condition, and the Sān were being massacred all around them. Another flash of lightning, quickly followed by a boom of thunder that bounced and echoed off the rock formations.

In five minutes you can stop this. You know you can.

Sawyer was not the type of man who hesitated, but for some reason he could not make up his mind. All the mantras and adages that had guided him in combat seemed to have lost their currency. *Hell of a time for an existential crisis.*

It would be a lie to say that he always followed orders, but throughout his long career his deviations had always been relatively minor and had always yielded the best results so that, when the dust settled, the XO had always seen it his way. That wouldn't happen this time. He would almost certainly go down for this.

Yet, in all the battles he had fought in all the corners of the globe, never had there been a more noble reason to fight. A true warrior defended the defenseless. He fought for what was right and he didn't turn away when it was convenient.

He fought and he gave everything he had, and he didn't ask for protection or expect sanctuary.

But what about his men? It was one thing to go rogue himself, but the moment he did, it could endanger the lives of his team. If something happened to him, they would pile into the fray. Yet, he had the Venger Program, had been practicing with it for months, and he was confident of its effectiveness.

Gunshots rose from the dell, a long stream of fifteen shots, as a whole clip of ammunition was fired at a helpless enemy.

God and Country.

Sawyer realized there was a reason they were in that order. One came before the other.

Sawyer felt a slap on his arm. It was Patel. "What are you doing?" he asked.

"Nothing. Head to the LZ, I'm right behind you."

Patel looked at him. "Bullshit, I'm staying with you."

"That's an order. Get going."

Patel didn't move, a look of annoyance on his face. Yes, it was an order, but it also violated all their protocols. Patel knew Sawyer was up to something.

Sawyer covered his mike. "Just give me five minutes. That's all I need. If there's trouble later, I don't want you going down for it."

"I'll gladly take the trouble for a shot at these assholes."

Sawyer looked at the younger man and was about to argue but realized that would just waste more time.

He fingered on his mike. "This is Papa Six Four Actual, as soon as the package is aboard, get the first Valor airborne. Valor Two, you hold. We are going to make a last sweep of the area to ensure that no sensitive equipment was taken from the crash site with Hill. ETA, five minutes. Over."

"Roger, Paper Six Four, Valor One is airborne, Valor two is holding."

At just that moment Sawyer heard the high-pitched whine of the first Valor's twin turboprops as she rose up and sped into the night.

Sawyer started the timer on his watch.

5:00:00

4:59:15

He nodded to Patel, and the two men moved off into the woods.

Lightning stabbed down from the high clouds and thunder boomed.

Get ready motherfuckers, it's time for some twenty-first century scunion.

The Venger package for each SEAL contained four swarms and each of those swarms could autonomously provide defense, offense, surveillance, and communications, so that in the case of swarm failure, a soldier could fully function with only one swarm.

The moment the soldiers had exited the Valors, their swarms had dispersed over the suspected conflict zone and created a map that appeared as a tiny layer across each man's cornea.

All possible actors were assessed and color-coded.

```
Green: Noncombatant, no weapons
Red: Enemy combatant, type of weapon dis-
played
Yellow: Fellow combatant
Orange: Undefined
```

When they had landed, Sawyer had noticed a cluster of about fifteen green avatars inside one of the rock formations. It had taken him a second to realize that they were in a cave. The swarms were able to use facial recognition and had identified Eric Hill and most of the White Hand immediately. With the cornea overlay, they saw each avatar's name and weapon. Julius Strasser (SR-25 .762x51), Elliot Joubert (AR-10 .308 Win), Lethabo Naidoo (IWI ACE-N .556x45), etcetera.

As Sawyer moved into the woods, he used his neural net. *Redefine enemy combatants as those over 140 pounds with firearms.* That would ensure that none of the Sān were mismarked.

The neural net under his helmet (essentially a portable MRI machine) had taken three months to program. The first two weeks were the most tedious. Each word that the human brain thinks makes a unique electrical signal through the brain. To train the net, he had to read tens of thousands of words so that it learned his vocabulary. Then came teaching it nuance. The system had to learn every possible way he might think each command and know his intent. The next four weeks had been spent configuring the net so it could communicate with the swarms. Then came another six weeks of combat trials. But it had been worth it.

Disable all enemy combatant firearms and night optics. Jam all enemy combatant communications.

The sound of gunfire instantly ceased.

Mute all my communications except to Patel.

Sawyer moved through the woods toward the first cluster of red avatars. Brett Kruger. Lethabo Naidoo. Ethan Van Der Merwe. He was almost a hundred yards away, too far to see them clearly through the forest, but the swarms were circling around them, sending him crystal clear images. They were standing over a Sān woman they had just killed.

The Venger System had several layers of redundancy. He could select targets with his thoughts, with his voice, or using the tip of his rifle as a pointer. He "tapped" each man on his display with the muzzle of his rifle.

The display gave him a prompt: *Incapacitate or Kill?*

Kill.

He pulled the trigger. The three men dropped.

Even though he was carrying his MK-14, the nanosites killed his enemies. Only at Sawyer's request or in case his swarms failed would the rifle actually fire.

The avatars of the dead men turned solid black on his display.

A second later, two more red avatars went black as Patel took out his first two men.

4:37:10

Sawyer heard a woman scream.

Find source of scream.

On the display, a yellow avatar flashed. *Fellow combatant.* Even though she was Sān, the system realized she was fighting the enemy. There were five red avatars around her.

A moment later, the swarms arrived at her location, giving Sawyer visual and audio.

The mercenaries had her pinned to the ground. "This is the little cunt that killed De Beer," one man said. "I saw it! Speared him right through the fucking throat." The man spoke in Afrikaans but Sawyer heard English.

One man held each of the woman's limbs, while a tall

black mercenary stood over her with her own spear in his hand. "This will be proper revenge then." He held the tip toward her legs. "Open her up for me, lads."

The woman screamed and fought with all her might. She was tiny compared to these huge men in body armor. As they tried to pull her legs open, she twisted and kicked, lifting herself full off the ground.

Sawyer quickly selected the man with the spear and pulled the trigger.

He collapsed.

"Pretorius?" The men looked at the crumpled body.

"Pretorius?"

Sawyer selected the other four men and pulled the trigger.

3:59:41

★ ★ ★

In the cabin of the Valor, Staff Sergeant Loc continued to work on Hill. An empty bag of saline lay on the deck while another bag was squeezed into Hill by his assistant. With so much blood loss it was imperative that his fluids were replenished. Loc gave him some morphine for the pain, but not too much. Hill was in and out of consciousness, but Loc wanted him alert as long as possible. He patted his cheeks to rousc him.

He had to shout over the sound of the rotors.

"How many fingers am I holding up?"

Hill raised his head to see. "Three."

"Good."

"Do you know the date?"

Hill winced in pain. "No idea."

“Fair enough. Your girlfriend’s Jane Hunter, right?”

“Yeah.”

“Well, she gave me this.” He held up a fat syringe.

This seemed to get Hill’s attention. “Stasis foam?” he asked.

“That’s right.”

As one of Curtiss’s SEALs, Loc was privy to all the cool toys that the NRL was making, but this one was perhaps his favorite. During Afghanistan and Syria, Loc had personally seen six of his friends die from wounds similar to Hill’s.

Eric tightened his lips and nodded. “Okay. Go ahead.” Loc held open the lips of the wound with one hand, then eased the tip inside and pushed.

Eric gasped and gritted his teeth against the pain.

As the foam expanded, Eric’s eyes went wide, and he cried out. Within seconds the whole left side of his abdomen had swelled up grotesquely, as if he had a massive tumor growing inside him. The skin stretched and bubbled, creating a web work of stretch marks in his skin.

Eric panted and blew air out his mouth like a woman in labor as he tried to manage the pain. “Goddamn, it hurts!”

“Yeah, well you’ll have to talk to your girl about that. But before you lodge your complaint, keep in mind that she probably saved your life.”

3:35:10

Sawyer ran through the forest into the section that had been set afire. He raced by a huge baobab tree that stood engulfed in flame, its thin limbs stretched out like a man burned in effigy. As Sawyer ran though the smoke, he noticed that the protective bubble that encased him pushed the smoke away before he even touched it.

Patel had now taken out seven more mercs. There were only four left.

Sawyer was closing in on two more. Even without the swarms he could hear them talking. They were starting to suspect something wasn't right.

"Is your radio broken?"

"Yeah, gun's fucked, too. Like the firing pin's gone."

They talked loudly because they thought they had nothing to fear.

Sawyer was about fifty yards away when he selected them and pulled the trigger.

A few seconds later, he stood over their bodies. One of their victims was not far away. Sawyer had seen thousands of dead bodies in his career, but the sight of the dead was something he had never grown accustomed to. That's just the way human beings were. If it didn't bother you, there was something seriously wrong with you. What always disturbed him most was a sense of *disorder*. The human mind is programmed to recognize patterns and to view wholeness as correct and beautiful. But to see a human body in disorder is a profoundly disturbing thing. And here was young man with his jaw shot off, an eye missing, his body grotesquely contorted from a gunshot to the chest. Sawyer did his best to just glance at him, confirming he was dead, but he knew that the memory of the glance would be with him forever.

2:56:23

★★★

Karuma huddled in the back of the small cave, shivering with fear. From outside he could hear the demon-men speaking. They knew he was in here and were discussing the best way to kill him. He knew he had to get up and try to run, at least then he would have a chance. But he was too frightened. So he lay there, praying to Cagn to help him. He prayed to the god to make the demon-men go away. He repeated his prayer over and over. "Please Cagn, I'll do anything, just make them go away."

For a time it was quiet, and he breathed in the smell of clay and turned up soil. Then he heard the scraping of rough boots approaching the mouth of the cave.

2:41:00

Sawyer was now sprinting upward toward the far end of the dell. He looked up. Beyond the peaks of the trees, he saw the huge rock formations looming like dark titans. A flash of lightning suddenly illuminated the ancient red rocks against a bubbling purple sky.

His cameras showed the last two mercenaries, Elliot Joubert and Julius Strasser—the leader of White Hand. Strasser was busy on his radio, trying to contact his men. "Kruger, can you hear me? Venter, come in? Does anyone copy?" He was a tall, thickly built man with silver hair and suspicious eyes.

The other man, Joubert, was pulling a Sān boy from the mouth of a cave. The boy was unconscious and his face was bruised and bleeding.

"Is he dead?" Strasser asked.

"Not yet. My sig wouldn't fire."

This seemed to annoy Strasser. “Just slit his throat.”

Joubert pulled out his knife.

Sawyer knew he should kill them quickly, but another part of him rejected that idea. A quick, painless death was not what men like this deserved, especially Strasser.

Disengage Ghost program. Enable my rifle.

Joubert grabbed the unconscious boy by the hair and pulled his head to the side to expose the neck. He was just about to slit his throat when the familiar sound of a round being chambered in a rifle made him look up. Somehow there was a commando aiming a rifle at him. The man was moving at a run, the rifle held tight to his shoulder.

The muzzle flashed with yellow fire, and Joubert felt three hard smacks to his chest. He fell back, gasping. He could still see the world around him, but his heart was gone.

Strasser was holding his radio to his ear and his pistol at his side when the soldier appeared and shot Joubert. It happened so suddenly, and the man moved so quickly, that by the time Strasser raised his pistol, Joubert was dead and the man was only three feet away, closing fast. Strasser aimed center mass and pulled the trigger but nothing happened. Then the butt of the man’s rifle slammed into his nose, sending him reeling back.

He clutched at his face, already wet with blood, and felt the cartilage of his nose loose in the skin. He held up his other hand in submission, but the butt of the rifle struck the side of his head and he collapsed onto his knees.

Then a combat boot hit his hanging rib, cracking it. Strasser gasped in pain; breathing was suddenly excruciating. A second kick to the same spot sent the broken rib into his lung. The lung collapsed, and Strasser screamed. He rolled onto his good side and again held up a hand.

"Please, stop!"

He looked up at the man's face, but in the darkness saw only a black silhouette. Then lightning flashed and for a moment the man was bleached in light. Strasser saw a veteran soldier, his face obscured by a beard and combat goggles, a long Bowie knife in his right hand. The blade flicked fast—in and out, striking under his extended arm and severing the axillary vein. Strasser realized that he was at the mercy of a professional killer.

"Please, stop . . . I surrender."

Again, the knife struck fast into the soft flesh behind his knee. Now Strasser screamed even louder than before. *Such pain!* He rolled onto his back, his nerves bristling as pain surged from all four wounds—his face, his ribs, his armpit and his knee. He tried to think, but it was almost impossible through the pain. He knew that one more deep cut and he'd be terminal. He rolled on his back and reached for the Walther he kept strapped to his ankle. He pointed it up at the man and pulled the trigger. Nothing happened.

The soldier deftly snatched the weapon from his grasp, turned it on him and fired two shots—one into each of his feet.

Strasser screamed, gasped for breath, then screamed again. Never had he felt anything like this. "Please . . . please," he panted. "Why? Why don't you just kill me?"

For the first time the man spoke. "Because I want you to know what it feels like to be helpless and afraid. And before you die, I want you to feel pain like the pain that you have inflicted on others."

"Oh, God, it hurts!" Strasser moaned, the agony overtaking him, consuming his mind.

Sawyer looked at his watch: 2:01:02

Disable my rifle.

He fingered on his mike. "Patel, meet me back at the camp."

"Already halfway there."

Sawyer lifted the unconscious boy onto his shoulders and began jogging back through the woods. The feel of the boy's skin across his neck had an immediate calming effect on him and his rage began to subside. *The killing is done*, he reminded himself.

Even though the boy was unconscious, Sawyer began talking to him. "You're going to be all right, son. You're safe."

01:11:56

He was only forty yards from the camp when the boy began to stir. Sawyer gently set him down at the base of a tree. He realized the boy would be terrified if he awoke to find a soldier standing over him, so he engaged the ghost program. Then he gently massaged the base of the boy's neck until his eyes flickered open.

The boy looked around for a moment, confused, then put two fingers to the cut on his forehead.

"You're safe now," Sawyer said, forgetting that the translator didn't know what language to use. To his surprise, the boy replied in English.

"Eric? Where are you?"

"I'm not Eric, but I'm his friend."

Then the memory of what happened seemed to hit the boy. "There were demon-men! They were killing us!" The boy's voice rose with emotion. "I couldn't—"

"It's okay, they're gone. They can't hurt you anymore." Sawyer put his hand on the boy's shoulder and disengaged the ghost program.

The boy gasped when he saw him and pushed his back against the tree.

Sawyer removed his goggles and smiled. "It's okay. I'm really Eric's friend. Eric Hill, right? Tall, black hair, nerdy, no sense of humor."

The boy examined him a moment, then gave the faintest nod.

"Is he all right?"

"He's hurt, but with a little luck, he'll be okay. I'm taking him home."

A look of sadness pulled at the boy's face, but he said nothing.

"You're going to be okay, too," Sawyer said, "but you're in shock. Let me take you to the cave. The others are there." Sawyer held out his hands. The boy hesitated for a second then climbed into his arms.

Sawyer guessed the boy was a teenager, but he weighed no more than his eight-year-old nephew. He held him up with one arm, his rifle in the other. As he made for the cave he kept to the woods to avoid crossing the camp. The boy didn't need to see any of that now.

They were almost at the mouth of the cave when Sawyer stopped and eased him to the ground.

"Go on. Your friends and family are inside."

"Won't you stay and help us?"

"I'm sorry, but I have to go."

The boy nodded, then walked off toward the cave, but before he reached the entrance he stopped. In the bushes was the body of a dead mercenary. The boy reached down and picked up the man's rifle.

"I'd prefer if you didn't do that," Sawyer said.

The boy looked at Sawyer one last time, strapped the weapon over his shoulder, and entered the cave.

Sawyer looked at his watch.

00:31:12

Time to go.

He ran through the camp and saw Patel heading for the break in the rocks that led to the waiting Valor. In the middle of the camp he paused for a moment, surveying the scene. There were nine dead mercenaries among the cooking fires, but over twenty dead Sān—men, women, and children. His display showed that between the cave and the woods, only thirteen Sān were still alive. Sawyer wondered if the tribe could survive such a blow or if this had been their final stand.

This is the kind of thing we should be fighting for, he thought, then took a deep breath and left the camp, knowing he would never be back here again.

As he ran he noticed Strasser's avatar had turned from red to black. Now Sawyer regretted cutting the axillary vein—it had made his death too quick. That's when he noticed an orange avatar—*undefined*—hiding in the rocks to his right. He turned to investigate and found one of the bushmen huddling in a recess.

"It's okay," Sawyer said. "You can come out."

This one, too, seemed to understand him.

"Tank you," he said in heavily accented English. "Tank you."

"The others are in the cave. You can go find them."

The man thanked him again, but didn't seem to know where to go.

"Wait one second for me." Sawyer said, and pulled out a small iSheet and took the man's picture. The man squinted at the flash. Then Sawyer quickly typed a message and sent it.

"Okay, you can go," Sawyer gestured with his rifle. "The cave's that way."

The man stumbled off. "Tank you," he said again, bobbing his head and cowering.

Sawyer watched him go, but as he did he casually swept the muzzle of his rifle over him.

In the cabin of the first Valor, three of the Seals' iSheets went off simultaneously. A moment later Adams approached the medic and the man on the stretcher. "Sorry to bother you, doc," Adams said, "but Sawyer has a question for your patient."

Loc nodded.

The SEAL held up the iSheet to Hill.

★★★

As Sawyer was about to board the second Valor, the rain broke, coming down in heavy sheets. The armor kept a perfect bubble around him, so he turned it off, letting the water hit his skin. It only took a moment until he was drenched. The coolness of it entered his hot body, and he shivered. He took one look back toward the Sān camp, the cooking fires hissing and smoking from the rain, then ducked under the wing and pulled himself on board.

Almost instantly the Valor rose off the ground, gained enough altitude to get over the rock formations, then its twin rotors tilted and it sprinted away from the storm.

Sawyer pulled out his phone and saw the message from Adams.

"Negative."

In his display, he saw that the last bushman had still not entered the cave. Now he knew why.

Sawyer pulled the trigger of his rifle. The man's avatar changed from orange to black.

Return to me.

The digital map of the battlefield disappeared from his display. He was about to shut down the program when something occurred to him. He remembered how the boy had picked up the rifle, but he didn't know the Venger program had rendered it useless.

After a moment, Sawyer nodded to himself.

Enable all battlefield weapons.

Exit Venger Program.

Three minutes later they had caught up with the first Valor.

Sawyer hailed Loc. "How is he?"

"I've got the bleeding under control. But it's hard to know what got damaged inside. I'll put it this way: I've seen guys pull through with a lot worse."

"Roger. Let me know if anything changes."

At just that moment, the pilot cut in.

"Chief, you might want to take a look out the port-side door."

Sawyer stood and went to the open door. Rolling over

the night desert he saw the headlights from two Range Rovers.

Sawyer immediately hailed Captain Everett. "Papa Six Four Actual to Viper One Nine, we have visual on Lang Song. Request permission to apprehend and take into custody for the killing of the Sān tribesmen."

Captain Everett's reply was instantaneous. "Negative, that's a job for the Namibians."

Sawyer had expected that, but he wanted it to be clear to his men that it was Everett who said no. But the dig didn't satisfy him. In fact, he felt a sudden sense of hopelessness. Killing Strasser and his men might have given the Sān a brief reprieve, but there were plenty more mercenaries out there, ready to kill for the likes of the Ivory Queen or any other corporation or government with the money to hire them.

In another fifteen minutes, the Valors were out over the Atlantic Ocean. A low moon—three-quarters full—made a bright strip of white on the dark water.

Patel tapped him on the shoulder and held up something for him to see. It was the memory stick for the Venger system.

A faint smile broke across Sawyer's face. Because the Venger system was a prototype, it had not been sending data back to mission control. Each soldier's memory stick held that individual's mission data. That meant that if Sawyer and Patel didn't turn in their sticks, Captain Everett would never know what had really happened in their last five minutes.

Sawyer took Patel's memory stick, pulled out his own, then tossed them out the bay door and into the ocean.

CHAPTER FIFTY-THREE

THE EGYPTIAN RAID

December 14, 2026
Egypt

"The helos will be over the target in three minutes, General."

Twelve hours later and three thousand miles away, at the northern edge of Africa, another military mission was underway.

General Chip Walden was observing the mission from the operation center in Shaw Air Force Base, South Carolina [Air Forces Central Command (USAFCENT)]. The MQ-9 Reaper was already in position and sending back images of the target compound: a collection of six sandstone-and-brick buildings arranged in a rectangle.

At last, Walden thought, *you are going to reveal your secrets*. Four Black Hawks filled with Egyptian commandos and a Little Bird carrying four of his Intelligence Officers were about to storm the compound. Then, Walden hoped, he would finally have the truth about Curtiss.

"One minute, General."

On the monitors, the officers' body cams showed the Egyptian landscape whizzing by. Two agents were strapped onto the running board on either side of the Little Bird chopper, their legs hanging down to the skids. The agents facing the west saw the undulating dunes of the Sahara desert in all its lonely magnificence, while the agents facing the east captured the deep blue—almost purple—water of Lake Nasser. It was a bizarre contrast, and it seemed impossible that the images were being taken from the same helicopter.

Walden knew he was taking a gamble with this raid. But he also felt like he was on a roll. Olivia Rosario's Global Hologram program was shaping up to be a game changer. The news of Russian meddling in Italy had become front page news and had made the US (and the president who had taken credit for it) look like a hero in the eyes of most of the free world. As a gesture of his appreciation, the president had invited Walden to the White House then given him open access. "If you need to reach me for any reason, Chip, you just pick up the phone." Yes, he was definitely on a roll.

"Thirty seconds."

Walden felt a rush of nervous excitement. It was about to happen. There would probably be a fight. The secrecy, the fact that he was dealing with Curtiss, it all pointed toward violence. People were about to die.

The drone footage showed the helicopters as they swarmed around the compound, flaring up and landing near all four corners. The commandos and agents began to stream out of the choppers and quickly formed two distinct packs, one heading for the front of the compound, the other to the back.

The body cams were momentarily washed over with

sand but cleared quickly. Walden felt himself as an avatar inside the camera, running within the pack, the tip of the M4 up and ready. He heard the agents panting and the crackle of their radio chatter.

"Preparing to breach main door."

"Setting the charge."

"Hold on, do you hear that?"

Whatever the agents could hear, it was not making it through to Central Command.

Walden hailed Zimmer, the lead officer. "Status report please."

But Lt. Colonel Cortez, the man in the room running the op, cut Walden short.

"Belay that order."

Cortez turned sharply on Walden. "When you're in my AO, you let my men do their job, General. Don't distract them again."

Cowed, Walden turned back to the monitors. Two commandos were still working on the door, but before the charge was blown, the door suddenly swung open revealing an elderly woman in a *sebleh*, her hands up, supplicating the men in Arabic.

She was roughly pushed aside, and the commandos streamed in. For a moment the images went black as the cameras tried to adjust from the scorching brightness of the desert to the shaded interior.

For the first time, Walden could make out the sound. The laughter and screaming of children. Many, many children.

The cameras began coming into focus.

He saw a wide open space with a basketball court in the foreground and the green grass of a soccer field behind. At least seventy-five children of different ages were running and playing. Walden felt a sudden cold sweat break out all over his body. *How could this be?* The mysterious netting over the buildings was to shade a soccer field?

Some of the children had stopped and looked frightened, but the majority of them hadn't even noticed the men entering.

An Egyptian man wearing a *jalabiya* and a skull cap rushed up to the commandos, scolding them in Arabic. Then he began talking to one of the Americans.

"What is the meaning of this? You can't come barging in here and scaring the children!"

Some of the Egyptian commandos seemed dumbfounded, even embarrassed, but Zimmer stayed on task.

"Sir, you need to assemble your entire staff here in the courtyard, right now."

"You have no right to do this. We are a sanctioned school."

"Do it now, sir."

The next few minutes were pandemonium. Walden had never expected this. How could he have been so wrong? His mind skipped ahead: God, he was going to get crucified for this, an illegal raid on an Egyptian school. If one of the kids got hurt, his career was over.

He kept watching the monitors, his mind numb as to what to do. But why the secrecy, why the isolated location?

Some of the kids had now come up to the agents, curious about who these strange soldiers were. One boy, perhaps ten or eleven with thick black hair, began asking questions about their weapons in broken English. Walden noticed that there were three fingers missing from his right hand.

On another monitor, he noticed a girl whose arm had been amputated at the elbow.

Walden called to Cortez and whispered in his ear. The man nodded.

"Blackburn, take a step back and let us see the children one at a time."

The agent complied, letting his webcam focus on each one. As Walden had suspected, many of the children had been maimed in some way. Many were missing fingers, while some were missing hands or whole limbs. But none of the wounds were recent and there were no bandages.

"Who the hell are these kids?" Walden said aloud. "Cortez, can we scan their faces and see if we get any hits?"

"Why don't you just ask them?" he replied.

There were two boys standing nearby, each with an arm draped over the other's shoulder. They were confident and handsome and unafraid of the soldiers.

Blackburn started up a conversation with them. "Can you tell me your names?" he asked.

"My name is Abdul," the taller one said.

"I'm Yousef," said the other.

"Pleased to meet you," Blackburn said. "My name is Philip." The three of them shook hands. "And what are your last names?"

"Al-Shar'a," said Abdul.

"Al-Assad," said Yousef.

Oh my God, Walden thought, as understanding finally washed over him.

He hadn't been wrong.

Olivia Rosario sat by Emma's bedside and caressed her cheek. Her daughter looked so beautiful and peaceful while she slept. It gave Olivia the illusion that she was still a perfectly healthy girl and that when the sun came up in a few hours, she would wake up like all the other ten-year-old girls in the world, fussing and complaining about school, saying she didn't have anything to wear, and eating too little for breakfast.

Olivia didn't want to face the fact that the normal years might be gone. That Emma was going to die and all Olivia would be left with was her memories of the good years. The soccer games, the horseback riding lessons, the day she taught her to ride a bike. She'd be left with only snapshots and old videos: Emma blowing out her candles on her birthday, holding up three blue ribbons after her last equestrian competition, mounting the steps of the yellow school bus for the first time . . . All the way back to the memory of nursing her, the way that Emma had looked up at her with her wide baby eyes filled with complete innocence and trust.

She shook her head to clear the memories away and looked down at the vial in her hand.

When can we give her more?

Not until we are a hundred percent sure it has failed.

But Ryan didn't understand that time was running out. Clearly something was wrong. They should have seen some changes by now. Nanotechnology worked in nanoseconds, not in hours or days. If it had worked, she'd be showing some improvement by now.

She looked again at the vial.

It couldn't hurt to try.

She sucked in a deep breath, pulled out the stopper, and gently waved it under her daughter's nose.

CHAPTER FIFTY-FOUR

REUNION

December 16, 2026
Washington, DC

Eric woke to the beeping of a heart monitor. He blinked and shook his head to clear the cobwebs. Slowly the room came into focus: white walls, a hospital placard with safety guidelines (Clean Hands Save Lives), an IV line going into the back of his right hand, his left hand a ball of bandages. The smell of pine disinfectant cleaner.

And sitting in a chair at his bedside, a sleeping woman, her unmistakable mass of blond hair near his lap, one arm flung over his waist.

He couldn't help but smile. *This is a good woman*, he thought, and he felt a tinge of guilt for ever doubting the fact. He began gently touching her hair. "My beautiful Jane," he whispered. "I've put you through hell again, haven't I?"

She didn't stir, so he continued to play with her hair, remembering the feel of it, the smell . . . Just the touch of it and the heat of her scalp on his fingertips proved to him that he was home and safe. That made the horrors that were still so fresh in his mind seem a little more bearable. "My beautiful Jane," he repeated, remembering the stasis foam and medic's words. "You brought me back from the dark . . ." He laid his head back on the pillow a moment and looked at the ceiling. "Now I have to figure out why." He felt so hollow inside, like he had lost more than he could ever hope to replace. Thank God he hadn't lost her, too.

"My beautiful Jane," he whispered again, and this time she stirred. She lifted her head and looked at him through drowsy eyes and smiled. Then she let out a long, lazy sigh, almost like the purr of a cat. She stretched her arms a moment then slid into bed with him, her head on his chest, one leg across his thighs. The warmth of her seemed too rich to be real, as if her love and ardor—all the pieces of her, the girl, the woman, the mother—were burning inside her and seeping into him and giving him strength.

They lay silently for a long time, unmoving, breathing as one. She touched the scar on his chest and cheek where the horn of the gemsbok had cut him. Her fingertips storing questions that she would ask . . . but later. She closed her eyes.

An hour passed.

Finally she spoke. "I oughta kill you."

Eric looked down at his dinner—a soft-diet smorgasbord of applesauce, mashed potatoes, pudding, and cottage cheese. He sighed and dipped his spoon into the pudding.

"Sawyer told me a little," Jane said. "How this tribe was

protecting you. But how did you get a hundred and sixty miles from the crash site? And why the hell did you take your boots off?"

"Yes, I want to hear all about it."

They both looked up to see Bill Eastman in the doorway, a warm smile on his face. "Bill!" Eric said.

Bill came in and put his hand on Eric's shoulder. "You gave us quite a scare," he said, then glanced at Jane. "You know she's been here for three days straight. This is my fifth visit to check on you, and she's been here every time."

Jane *shh*'d him quiet. "He doesn't need to hear that." She held her hands to the sides of her head and made an inflating sound.

Bill and Eric laughed.

"What's so funny?"

The three of them looked up—Mei, Lili, and Xiao-ping stood in the doorway.

As soon as Mei caught sight of Eric, she rushed in and hugged him. "Thank God you're okay." Eric savored the girl's embrace. Ever since their escape from China, he'd felt a special connection to her, and her touch told him that, despite the arrival of her uncle, nothing had changed.

He looked up at Xiao-ping. It was hard to believe that this was the same man who had escaped the laogai eight weeks ago. The stress and fear that had lined his face when he was in prison were gone. His eyes were bright, and he'd gained at least twenty pounds.

He smiled at Eric and clasped his hands together, inclining his head in a Buddhist bow.

Eric closed his eyes and bowed his head in return, then noticed how Lili squeezed his hand tighter.

"So what took you so long?" Jane said to Lili.

"Sorry," Hwe Lili said, her face reddening, "I failed my driving test."

"For the third time," Mei said, rolling her eyes. "Luckily we got a ride."

As if on cue Admiral Curtiss and a handsome teenage boy appeared in the doorway. The boy immediately crossed to Mei and took her hand. Eric's right eyebrow went up, but he said nothing.

Admiral Curtiss, dressed in his service blues, moved to the foot of the bed and looked Eric over, appraising him like a piece of military equipment.

No, that wasn't quite right. Suddenly, perhaps for the first time in his life, Eric saw past Curtiss's cold exterior. He realized that Curtiss knew full well the importance of every person in the room, and perhaps more importantly, that they were more than the sum of their parts. Curtiss had fought hard to keep them together, beyond what was necessary for the good of the lab. The raid in Namibia proved it. Yes, Eric knew that Curtiss had wanted Lili to get her clearance, but that wasn't the only reason he'd done it. Even if Curtiss wouldn't admit it himself, he'd put his career on the line because he'd wanted to reunite an American operative with her imprisoned husband. And when the mission had faltered and Eric was MIA, Curtiss had remained steadfast. It was clear that Eric owed his life to Sawyer and Jane, but also to Curtiss, who never let Captain Everett give up on him.

As Eric looked at them standing around his bed, he seemed to see the connections between them like filaments in the air. Father to son. Mentor to student. Aunt to niece. Lover to lover. Soldier to civilian.

And for some reason it seemed that the bond between

Mei and Curtiss's son was the most important. In those two hands the future seemed to rest.

"You're not dead," Curtiss said. "That's good."

"Enough already," Jane said, "tell us what happened."

Eric nodded slowly, suddenly feeling self-conscious. He wanted to tell the story, but he was worried that he might not tell it right. But he began nonetheless.

He told them how he had lost his sight, waking up in the darkness. About Khamko and Naru. How he had befriended Karuma and how the boy had taught him so much. How his sight had returned at the water hole, the overwhelming beauty. They listened, enthralled. Eric told them about the hunting, the poachers, their long trek to the underground lake, and finally, the massacre.

He had been worried that they wouldn't get it. That they were too engaged in this world to empathize with "primitive" culture. He was relieved to see most of them had tears in their eyes. Jane gripped his hand tightly.

"Such a waste," Curtiss said. "Will we ever learn?"

Eric was grateful for them and knew he was lucky, but he also felt that he shouldn't be alive. He should have died there in Namibia, and every breath he took felt like a crime.

Jane seemed to sense his distant thoughts, and perhaps felt hurt by them. "You're still there, aren't you?"

He opened his mouth to speak, but for a moment no words would come. Then he nodded. "I can't let it go . . . and I don't think I ever will."

"And you shouldn't," Bill said. "You've seen a world that few ever do. You've seen the madness of what we have created. Don't forget that."

They stayed and talked for a time, but by midnight it was just Eric, Jane, and Bill.

Finally, Eric turned to Bill. "I need to ask you something. And I need to trust that you won't tell anyone regardless of your answer."

Bill didn't respond right away. "I must admit that trust is something that is becoming rare around here, but yes, I promise."

"They accepted me as part of their family. I have to honor that by doing whatever I can for them."

Bill squeezed his eyes to mere slits, not understanding.

"*Whatever* I can," Eric said emphatically.

CHAPTER FIFTY-FIVE

THE PACT

December 17, 2026
Washington, DC

Twenty-four hours later, Admiral Curtiss was working late in his study when he heard the tap on his window. For a moment he tensed, remembering he'd stowed his sidearm in his gun locker. But then he relaxed. He was on base and if anyone wanted to hurt him, they wouldn't bother knocking first.

The tap came again, more insistent. "Admiral, open up, it's Sawyer."

Curtiss went to the window. *Why would he come so late without calling or texting?* Then Curtiss's mind filled in the blank. *Because he doesn't want any digital traces of his whereabouts.* Curtiss's fear spiked.

He raised the window but saw no one. Curtiss stepped back and heard the man scramble through the window. A second later the SEAL appeared. The first thing Sawyer did was embrace him. Curtiss felt the man's emotion in his touch. *Something is very wrong.* Sawyer whispered in his ear. "NCIS is on their way. We've only got a few minutes. They already picked up Loc. Patel . . . he . . ." Emotion choked the man's words.

Walden, Curtiss thought. *He figured it out.*

He felt a cascade of emotions undulate through his body—anger, frustration, and regret. *I still have so much to do.*

He returned Sawyer's embrace, his muscles flexing full. He was savoring life now because everything he did from this moment forth he would be doing for the last time.

"I'm sorry, Nathan."

"Don't be," the SEAL said. "We understood what we were doing and we joined you willingly. I hated what we did, but I'd do it again. We all would . . . because we saved more lives than we took."

All Curtiss could do was nod. "Okay, let's get this over with."

"Yes, sir."

The SEAL moved to the desk and placed two pistols on it. Sig Sauer P220s. Then he produced two suppressors and began threading them into the barrels. He looked at Curtiss, a tinge of guilt on his face. "I didn't want to wake the boys."

For a moment, Curtiss's mind raced ahead to the grisly scene. Hopefully, NCIS would arrive soon and cordon off the room. If they didn't, then either his wife or one of his sons might find them first. For some reason he imagined Logan, his eldest, opening the door to find his father and his "uncle" dead. But Curtiss pushed the image away. It couldn't be helped now.

He picked up one of the Sigs, ejected the clip and inspected the rounds. Luger hollow points. A good choice.

He reinserted the clip and advanced the slide, putting a round in the chamber. Then he thumbed the safety off.

A sudden silence came over the room. It was as if the world had taken a long exhalation, and the night seemed to close in around the two men. After all that they had lived through, after all they had survived, this was how it was going to end.

"Nathan, it has been an honor serving with you."

Sawyer looked down at the pistol he was cradling in his hands. "Yes, it has, sir."

Curtiss heard a creak at the door.

"Daddy?"

Curtiss spun around. His eight-year-old son, River, stood in the doorway. His eyes were nearly closed, mere slits against the sudden light of the room. He held up a hand to shade them.

"River, you need to go back to bed right now."

His father's stern voice knocked away his drowsiness and for the first time he seemed to take in the scene. "Uncle Nathan?" Then his eyes fell on the pistols. "Dad?"

"Son, I need you to go upstairs right now."

The boy froze. He knew his father well enough to know that he had to obey, yet he stayed rooted to the spot. The strangeness of it, the odd supplication in his father's otherwise steely voice.

A tear escaped Curtiss's eye. "River, I need you to go. Please." Something in the night seemed to snap, and the boy rushed to his father and wrapped his arms around him.

"Don't send me away." A deep thud came from the front door, then the sound of wood splintering. Curtiss tried to push the boy away, but it was too late. Four NCIS officers, dressed in SWAT black, swept into the room.

"Drop the weapon! Hands in the air. Do it now!"

For a split second, Curtiss's eyes narrowed. He thought of shoving River away and pointing the gun at the men. *Suicide by cop.* But he rejected the idea. He didn't want one of these rent-a-cops accidentally shooting his son or the life-long case of PTSD it would give River.

"Do it now!"

He raised his free hand in supplication and set the sig gently on the desk. Then he embraced his boy as the four officers closed in. "I'm sorry," he whispered.

River clutched tightly to his father, but rough hands ripped them apart. Quickly the men handcuffed his father. "Admiral James Curtiss, you are under arrest for violating the Uniform Code of Military Justice, including one thousand four hundred and fifteen counts of falsifying official statements, one hundred and twelve counts of false imprisonment, one hundred and thirty-five counts of cruelty and maltreatment, eighty-five counts of maiming, and one count of murder."

Curtiss said nothing as the charges were read. River turned his head and saw his mother in the doorway, her hand over her mouth.

"Under Article 31 of the Uniform Code you may not be compelled to incriminate yourself or answer any questions the answer to which may tend to incriminate you . . ."

River then remembered Uncle Nathan. He turned but the man was gone.

One of the NCIS agents approached the open window, peered for a moment into the darkness, then turned away.

CHAPTER FIFTY-SIX

THE FIFTH TRIBE

December 17, 2026
Walter Reed Military Hospital, Bethesda, MD

"Dr. Singh says you are not being a very good patient," Jane said.

"I'm a very good patient," Eric countered. "I just don't need another test to find out something I already know."

"You had a major blow to your head, Eric, bad enough that you lost your sight. Don't you think it's worth getting an MRI?"

"No."

Jane shook her head.

At that moment Mei barged into the room, breathing hard. "Something's happened. Over at Curtiss's house. Police."

"What? Slow down."

Jane went to the girl, who almost collapsed into her arms. Jane guided her to the small sofa in the room.

A moment later Lili and Xiao-ping came in. "She won't talk to us," Lili said. "Said she could only tell you."

"Take a deep breath," Jane said to Mei and tucked some loose strands of hair behind the girl's ear.

The girl obeyed, breathing deliberately, her eyes trying to focus on Jane.

"It's Curtiss," she said, "he's been arrested."

"Arrested?" Jane said, "For what?"

"I don't know. I was upstairs in Logan's room. I didn't mean to stay, but I fell asleep. Suddenly there's a bang and shouting. The place was full of police. They took Curtiss away then they made us all come down to the kitchen.

"Mrs. Curtiss was furious, fighting them every inch of the way. She knows it's political and she doesn't believe it."

"Believe what?"

"About the children. They say that he kidnapped and tortured children."

Eric and Jane exchanged a skeptical glance.

"When did this happen?"

"I don't know. Forty minutes ago. I came as fast as I could."

Eric pulled out his iSheet. "It's already on the news." He opened the device to its biggest size. Dan Williams, the anchor for NBC news, sat behind his horseshoe desk: "This story is just breaking: reports of the torture and murder of children by US forces during the Syrian War. In a shocking report, Pentagon officials have confirmed that Admiral James Curtiss, a former Navy SEAL and war hero, led a rogue operation to kidnap, torture, and sometimes kill children related to the leaders of the warring factions in Syria.

"Joining us now is our Defense Correspondent, Josh Hewitt. Josh, what can you tell us?"

"Yes, Dan, a major scandal is rocking the Pentagon tonight: the abduction and torture of children at the hands of US soldiers. He's what we know so far: It appears that as many as a hundred and thirty-five children were kidnapped. Their ages ranged from fifteen to as young as six years old. All of the children have been linked to high-level officials involved in the Syrian conflict, including leaders of the Islamic Front, the Syrian Free Army, Al-Qaeda, ISIL, and the government of President Bashar al-Assad. It appears that Admiral Curtiss used US Special Forces including Navy SEALs to kidnap the children then blackmailed the various leaders into accepting the Zurich Peace Accord. Details are still coming in, but it appears that if the leaders resisted the admiral's demands, then the children were tortured on video. We have several reports claiming that many of the victims lost fingers, toes, and even hands. It is believed that the videos and amputated body parts were then sent to the Syrian leaders. The Pentagon says that one child was killed during the operation. It appears that about half the children were released after the peace accords were signed, but in order to ensure that certain leaders did not renege on the deal, many children were kept in a secret compound in Egypt for the past three years."

"Very disturbing, Josh. How did this story break and why are we just hearing about this now?"

"It appears that we owe a lot to General Chip Walden, Vice Chairman of the Joint Chiefs. He's emerging as the hero in this story. He just finished a press conference wherein he explained how he directed Air Force Intelligence to begin looking for the children after he became suspicious of the Syrian peace process. Thanks to his efforts, the children will now be reunited with their families. The Pentagon is stressing that this was an illegal operation and not condoned by the US government. Walden said that Admiral Curtiss and at least fifteen other naval servicemen and women are now in custody and will face court martial."

Jane turned off the iSheet. Mei immediately began crying. "It's not true. It can't be. It *can't*!"

"Of course it's not true," Jane said, wrapping an arm around the girl. "It's Walden trying to get control of the lab." Yet in her heart, Jane doubted her own words. The story was horrific and shocking in its magnitude, but it was quintessential Curtiss. In it she saw the same cruel logic that she had seen so many times before. The incarceration and mistreatment of 135 children (and the death of one) in exchange for what? Peace for millions. Stability in a war-torn part of the world. The lives of thousands of US soldiers who got to come home. *That's pure Curtiss*, she thought.

She brought Mei closer, tucking the girl's head under her chin. "Everything is going to be okay." But this, too, was a lie, and she knew it. A great purge was coming. Anyone who had ever touched Curtiss was now tainted—CNO Garrett, Bill Eastman, Jack Berhmann . . . even Eric's job and her own were now on the chopping block. Every decision that Curtiss had made could now be questioned, giving Walden and his allies carte blanche to restructure the NRL as they saw fit. Which, of course, included helping themselves to all their technology.

There were two taps on the door and to Jane's amazement, Bill Eastman and Jack Berhmann came in.

"We came as soon as we heard," Jack said. "If we are going to survive this, we're going to have to stick together."

Bill continued. "The thing that I have feared for so long is coming to pass. The technology we created is slipping out of our control. Worse, it is being handed to someone more interested in accumulating his own power than using it for the good of the country and mankind. I feel that it is now our duty, our obligation, to fight back."

"How can we do that?" Jane said.

"I honestly don't know," Bill replied. "All I know is that I've been irresponsible. Eric's story made me realize many things. Most importantly, how far I'd gone astray. When I was a boy, I learned important lessons about friendship and community and simplicity. But I forgot them as I tried to change the world. I see now that I am a lesser man for it.

"I've been on the sidelines for too long. I've watched idly as our society split into different factions, yet I refused to act, hoping that things would work themselves out.

"Now the time has come for me to pick a side . . . or perhaps it's up to us to make our own." He looked at them each in turn. "I cannot tell you what course we need to take, only that the path we have been on is wrong."

There was a moment of silence.

"I'm in," Eric said.

Bill came up to him and clasped his hand.

"Me, too," Lili said, and Xiao-ping nodded his approval.

Jane didn't answer right away, but turned to Mei. "How about you?"

The girl wiped her tears with the back of her hand. "Yeah, I'll do it."

"Okay," Jane said. "What do we do?"

An hour later, Bill and Jack said goodbye and left Eric's room. Bill knew they had a lot to do and little time to do it in. Foremost in his mind was the possibility that he might not have a job at the NRL much longer. *If they could fire Oppenheimer for political reasons*, he thought, *they can certainly fire me*. He would have to do his best to curry Walden's favor for as long as possible in order to maintain his access to the lab's technology.

He was about to ask for Jack's advice, when his eyes fell on the two bodyguards that had escorted them from the lab.

Over the past year and a half he had grown accustomed to bodyguards . . . who were all Curtiss's handpicked SEALs or Marines. He had befriended them and trusted them.

But these two men were new, picked by Walden, which meant they wouldn't hesitate to eavesdrop on Walden's behalf if they could. That's why Bill had insisted they wait near the nurses' station—outside of earshot from Eric's room.

As Bill saw them he gave a heavy sigh of annoyance. He didn't like either of them. One was an overweight MP who didn't look like he could pass a basic physical, much less a fitness test. The other was a heavily tattooed marine who clearly resented babysitting two scientists.

Irritated, Bill walked past them without a second glance, hoping to get into the elevator with Jack before they could catch up.

But the Marine scrambled to his feet and stuck his hand in the closing door at the last second. It slid open again.

Jack checked his watch as they waited for the fat one to catch up. "How did it go?" Fatty asked through panted breath.

"Fine," Jack said.

The man inclined his head for more information, but none was given.

In the parking lot, the four men walked up to the black Ford sedan.

Jack finally broke the silence.

"Eventually you'll have to tell them everything."

Bill knew that Jack was referring to Eric and Jane not the two bodyguards.

"I almost did, but I think it's better if we wait a little longer."

Bill heard a jingle as Fatty produced his keys, then the car alarm chirped.

At that moment Bill heard a strange *phhhissst* sound and felt a sudden movement of the air. The fat bodyguard's hand flew to his face reflexively, then he crumpled to the ground. Bill looked down at him, and in the low light of the parking lot lights, saw that his eye was a dark mass of blood. "Wha . . ." He looked across the roof of the car where Jack stood with the marine. The two old friends shared a puzzled look.

Phhhisssst.

The marine beside Jack collapsed without a sound.

Bill turned quickly to the right, then the left, trying to understand, but saw no one.

"Good evening, gentlemen."

Bill turned once more and saw a handsome man emerge from the shadows. He was wearing a naval officer's uniform, a black overcoat with the silver oak leaf of a commander on his shoulder. In his hand was a silver snub-nosed semiautomatic pistol with a suppressor that was dripping water.

"Who the hell are you?" Jack said, rising up to his full height.

"My name is Broc O'Lane," he said, "I'll be your driver this evening. My employer is very interested in meeting you."

CHAPTER FIFTY-SEVEN

LUCKY BREAK

General Chip Walden came awake slowly, the sound of the phone feeling like part of a dream. He reached for it and saw that it was Captain Kacey, his personal assistant.

"Yes?" he said.

Walden's face went slack with shock as Kacey told him the news of the abduction. *No*, he thought, *not now. Not when everything was going so well.* First the success of the Global Hologram and his open access to the president. Then the sacking of Curtiss. But now this. The two top scientists at the lab. Gone.

"Was it Finley?" he asked Kacey.

"We don't know, sir. But it's a definite possibility."

His first fear was that he would take the blame. After all, he had assigned the bodyguards himself. Yet he could spin that if he had to . . . blame it on someone else.

That's right, he thought. *The key was how to spin it. He had to turn this to his advantage.*

"It was her," he said emphatically, "I know it." He paused, the ideas suddenly connecting in his head. Yes, no matter whether it was her or not, he could use this to his advantage. In many ways the timing was perfect. His plan had been to use the Global Hologram to take control of most of America's existing surveillance programs. The more data the NSA, CIA, and the Pentagon fed into Eleven, the smarter it would become and, by extension, the more powerful and indispensable he would become.

"I'll be there in ten minutes," he told Kacey and hung up.

Riona Finley would clinch the deal for him.

His words to the president were already being dictated in his mind. He would call him first thing in the morning. The president would be shocked by the news, perhaps even angry. Walden would share his outrage but steer him to a solution.

Mr. President, we have to face the possibility that Finley could have a functional weapon within four or five months. She has already shown she has no reservations about killing large numbers of Americans to advance her radical agenda, and with access to the weapons that Eastman and Berhmann can make, the results could be catastrophic. He would pause to let that sink in. *But if you can fast-track our work on the Global Hologram, sir, I'm confident we can find her and recover Berhmann and Eastman.*

And that would be a big win for you, sir.

Walden knew that the president would have little choice: green-light the Global Hologram or risk looking weak on terrorism.

He smiled. It was all about how you spun it.

Thank you, Riona, he thought. *Thank you so very much.*

EPILOGUE

"Mom?"

Olivia Rosario's heart skipped a beat at the sound. She sat up in her bed, wondering if she had dreamed it. She kept perfectly still, listening in the darkness. It had been nine months since Emma had last uttered a sound. Olivia waited a minute, then two, listening with all her might. From outside she heard the distant siren of an ambulance.

"Mom!"

Olivia threw off the covers and ran to Emma's room. The voice was weak, but it was not a dream. Tears were running down the woman's cheek as she crossed the threshold. *Please be true. Please be true.* At the sight of her mother, the girl reached for her.

"Oh, my baby!" Olivia enveloped the girl in a tight embrace and, to her amazement, the girl hugged her back, albeit weakly.

"Oh my gosh, I don't believe it. My beautiful Emma."

"Mom, I've been so scared."

"It's okay, baby, Mommy is here. Mommy is here." Olivia's heart seemed to swell from emotion. She held the girl, swaying and crying. "Everything is going to be all right. I've got you and I'm never letting you go."

"Mom, I feel like I've been dreaming forever. There was a war and it seemed to go on and on."

"It's over now, sweetie. Don't you worry about a thing." Olivia was amazed. She had assumed that even if the gene therapy worked, Emma would need months of physical and speech therapy. But her voice . . . it was so clear. And different somehow, in a way she couldn't quite say, definitely deeper than she remembered. *Of course it's different*, she told herself, *she's almost a year older*.

"Where am I?"

"You're home, sweetie, in your bed. Don't you remember? We moved to Washington, DC."

"What's Washington, DC?"

"It's the capital, silly. Don't you remember?"

The girl shook her head. "I remember California. Horseback riding and playing soccer."

"We moved here for you. For your treatment. And it worked. Thank God, it's worked." She hugged her daughter again. "You are going to be okay. Everything is going to be all right now."

ACKNOWLEDGMENTS

First and foremost, my enormous thanks to my beta testers: Will James, James Bowie, Jennifer Otto, Randy Earle, Marcelo Alonso, Kathy Morrow, Erika Nelson, and Don Nelson. I know that reading a manuscript (sometimes more than once) and giving thoughtful feedback is not only time consuming but hard work. Know that your advice and encouragement were particularly helpful this time around.

For assistance on military matters and helping me connect with subject experts, I'm indebted to Guy Tchoumba and Sam Waltzer.

My thanks to Karen Hurst for helping me understand AI and quantum computing. For information on explosives and how bombs work, I'm indebted to Sabastian C. Also thanks to the excellent science writer Michio Kaku whose books sparked my imagination and helped me envision some of the motivations of the mysterious inventor.

In researching Sān culture I'm indebted to Laurens van der Post's seminal book *The Lost World of the Kalahari* and Craig and Damon Foster's excellent documentary *The Great Dance: A Hunter's Story*. Other documentaries that helped me visualize the culture and the hunting sequences were John Marshall's *The Hunters* and David Attenborough's *Life of Mammals*, among others. For general information on tracking, I'm indebted to the books of Tom Brown Jr.

There are numerous Sān societies with different rituals and customs. I decided not to depict a specific Sān culture; instead I created an amalgamation from the different groups I learned about. In this way, the group becomes a synecdoche of not just early African cultures, but all hunter-gathering societies that maintained a homeostasis with nature. Ultimately, however, this is a work of fiction, so there are certain things about my Sān tribe that are unique to them. For example, Sān women are not permitted to hunt, but I thought that they should be.

To Jill Marr and Andrea Cavallaro at the Sandra Dijkstra Literary Agency, who helped nudge this book along and were there with the crucial advice I needed each step of the way.

Generous thanks to the team at Blackstone Publishing, especially my editor Peggy Hageman for her wonderful guidance and support, Deirdre Curley for your thoughtful copyedit, and Sean Thomas for his excellent art and design work on the book cover.

I'm also indebted to the very talented artist Josh Newton who helped create some wonderful concept art that was morphed and fine-tuned into the final cover.

It was a pleasure working with all of you.

Last and most important, my enormous thanks to my

wife Natalia, who has always kept her faith in my aspirations to be a writer. Even when I was fresh out of grad school, unpublished, mowing grass to make ends meet, and—most dubious in the eyes of a young woman—(temporarily) living with my mother. We have come a long way since then. Thank you and I love you.